MORE DEEPLY
THAN LOVE

by

John Hohmann

Merlon Wolfe Press
merlonwolfe.com

To my parents, Robert and Joan

He alone who owns the youth gains the future.

- Adolph Hitler

Friendship marks a life even more deeply than love.

- Elie Wiesel

PROLOG - PROLOGUE

It is silent here, the deafening silence that surrounds you in a falling snow. The silence of the absence of life. The barracks, long gone, leave only their foundations as reminders, broken stumps of concrete teeth, gray and tortured, rising from the snow. After so many years, so much is gone, yet so much still remains. Little of the physical, but everywhere the unseen. The fear, the anguish, the deep hopelessness still hangs like strands of rusted barbed wire in the silent air.

An older woman, curled in a black wool coat, stands off at a distance, huddling against the old man at her side. She adjusts her collar against a rising wind, tendrils of snow embroidering her shoulders in delicate lace. A teenager pauses to snap a picture on her cell phone, sends it to some far off world with her thumbs, then continues on her way. From somewhere distant come the voices of children, bright as hope, faint as memory. They are there for but a moment then gone, stolen by the wind, devoured by the rising storm.

But I stand alone, to them, little more than vapor.

My name is Katerina. I have returned to the place where I ceased to be.

I face the entry gate, the winter wind now whispering against the sharp edges of words hammered out of wrought iron across the top:
ARBEIT MACHT FREI

Work brings freedom.

But not here. Not at KZ *Dachau*. *Konzentrationslager Dachau*. Concentration camp. Before the Great Darkness had ended, there would be over forty thousand concentration camps, slave labor camps, extermination camps, spread across the *Reich*. But *Dachau* was the first. The first to industrialize, mechanize, organize the extermination of a race of people from the face of the earth in the most efficient manner possible. An effort to erase them, six million or more, and all they stood for, as if they had never existed.

Beyond the gate, the sky is the color of parchment, the color of emaciated skin drawn tight against bone.

Follow me, my now near ghostly self, beneath the hammered iron words. Enter the gate through which untold thousands came but never left. Past the gas chambers. Past the crematoria, the smell of burning hair even now imbued in the very bricks. Past the *Bunker Hof* where punishment was meted out for crimes never committed. And the Parade Grounds, the site of executions, cobble stones still stained with the blood of martyrs. Do not look away. Do not be indifferent. That, of all crimes, is the greatest.

Walk with me now past the foundations of barracks in which I once stayed, huddled in lice infested rags against the cold, surrounded by shuffling skeletons of other women, alive if only barely. Near the barb wire fences, before the moat and empty eye sockets of guard towers, menacing still in their silence seven decades past.

And then there is the Canteen where the *Totenkopf*, the death's head soldiers, gathered. Where the Victrola played and the schnapps flowed, long gone now, no more than barren land.

Of all that was, now gone, and that which still remains, is the *Totenbuch*, the Book of the Dead. It lists the names of the tens of thousands that died in *KZ Dachau*. The names of those that came to *Dachau*, but never left. People for whom work did not bring freedom, only death. It contains the names of those who can no longer speak for themselves but plead with you; never forget.

The countless names.

And one of them is mine.

10

BUND DEUTSCHER MÄDEL

THE LEAGUE OF GERMAN GIRLS

EINS - ONE

Cleopatra and Nefertiti, our two *Milch* cows, lowed quietly behind me from the milking shed, their voices sad in the still emptiness of dawn. Not that cows ever have voices of mirth and humor, but somehow I could always sense a tinge of thanks as I'd leave the barn each morning, two pails of steaming milk escorting me out the door, the weight that once burdened their udders now burdening the carrying pole across my shoulders.

A filigree of frost still decorated the shadows as I clomped along a path of spring peas barely above my wooden shoes. Ahead, at the edge of our field, dawn's first glow began to tip the trees of our little woodlot forest, thick and ancient, as dark and tangled as the butcher's beard. I reached a small rise in the path, my "morning spot", and paused, readjusting the two milk pails dangling from the beam that crossed my shoulders. The sun had just reached the black iron weathercock on the top of our crooked white shed, bringing it to life. Far to the south, beyond the woodlot forest, beyond our Bavarian border, the Alps rose like an army of ogres set on ravaging our homes, their snow covered shoulders hunched against a cloudless sky.

I allowed my morning spot its customary pause, an early treat for having milked two Egyptian Queens, fed the pigs and freed a brood of hens from their coop in return for allowing me to rifle their nesting boxes for our morning breakfast. My right foot began to move forward, the pause having reached its allotted limit, when I made the conscious effort to return my wooden shoe to it's print. Not today. It was time to take my time. I forced my eyes open wide as if somehow this would allow more of the scene before me in, staring, not wanting to waste a moment with so much as a single blink. The sun continued up, painting the *Schwarzwald* in a slowly lowering curtain of liquid gold.

"Katerina!" the voice called, sweet and matronly, yet still able to call farmhands in for meals from the farthest fields. When there were farmhands. "Katerina! You must come, *mein Kind*, or you'll be late! Mr. Hochauser can't wait for you!"

I felt my face fall slightly. *Mein Kind*. My child. The words tight and constricting on me like wearing an old coat you had long outgrown. From far beyond the tree line, beyond the confines of our farm, a distant train whistle uncoiled a long, low, mournful moan into a plate of morning sky the color of corn flowers. A beckoning call, disappearing, fading as it traveled toward some far off unknown. The corner of my mouth hitched back up into a half smile at the thought of it.

"And please, *mein Kind*," she had to add, "try not to spill the milk!"

"Coming *Tantchen*!" I called to my Auntie and continued on up the path.

I clomped along another two minutes finally reaching our home, a small wooden corn crib converted to living quarters a century or two before the eight years I had come to live there. A packing crate of a structure with a simple peaked roof, comfortable in its tidy coat of brown.

Splashed around the outside walls, brightly colored hex signs were painted to protect us from the *Feldgeister und Korndämonen* that inhabited our land. Field Ghosts and Corn Demons and a Devil's litany of other evil creatures had stalked every generation of Bavarian peasant from the shadows, threatening their children, their farms, and their very lives. Evil entities, everywhere unseen but everywhere surrounding, their menace lurking in the rustling of corn on windless days or hay fields hoary in moon glow. Mostly, of course, they were simply the creation of parents wishing to scare their children into doing what they were told. But some still believed. I did not have the heart to tell *Tantchen* that my love of reading had long ago vanquished the supernatural in favor of natural explanations. But she still continued to believe in the perils of the netherworld and made sure we were protected.

One new hex sign had been added to the far corner of our home only two summers before in 1936 as a protection against, according to *Tantchen*, any further malevolent antics of the water spirit Nix. The worst spring storm of that year had washed the foundation and part of the footings away leaving a corner of our little *Hütte*, in danger of collapse. Money scarce but fieldstone plenty, *Tantchen* and I set to work and made the repairs ourselves. "Anything is possible if you believe you can do something and set your mind to it!" she had repeated to me over and over. And together we rebuilt the foundation, rising up from the bottom of the crater the storm had left us. One by one, layer by layer, stone by stone until the foundation was complete.

I set my milk pails gently inside the kitchen door, left my wooden shoes to the side of the granite stoop, and stepped inside. Before the miniature wood burning stove stood my *Tantchen*, as matronly in appearance as she was in voice, seemingly larger still in the cramped kitchen.

"Katerina, the pails."

I brought the milk pails over and set them on the wooden table in the small common room, and gently placed four eggs from the straw lined pockets of my battered barn coat alongside. *Tantchen* dipped her finger in one of the pails then tasted it. "Cleo." she said nodding with satisfaction. Wrapped tightly in a gingham scarf, her face resembled an apple left too long in the sun, crinkled, reddish and bruised in a few spots. Puppy dog eyes examined the other pail and she dipped her finger in. "And Nef," she said, crinkles sagging in a frown. She wiped her lips on her stained cotton apron. "You'll have to do better keeping our Nef out of the onion grass," she said, stopped, then corrected herself. "I mean . . . I'll have to . . ."

"It's only for a few months," I told her, "I'll be back in time for harvest."

"Yes," she said, quietly. "Yes," then she looked up and forced a small smile, puppy dog eyes bright for a moment, her four front teeth as long departed as her youth.

I returned the smile.

"Now hurry," she said. "Up you go! Get yourself ready for Mr. Hochauser. He'll be here shortly."

I climbed the narrow ladder to my sleeping loft where a small door at the top met the low roof in a crooked obedience. I opened the door and stepped inside. Hochauser would be here soon, but for now I was safely alone. Into my canvas rucksack I loaded my night shirt and a few other clothes then began the painful process of sorting my small shelf of wear-worn books.

"What friends shall I bring with me?" I thought, touching each in turn, the hint of moldy book binding always bringing me a sense of comfort.

My *Tantchen* had been able to keep the local *Schutzmann*, constable, at bay for nearly two years since the mandatory decree had gone out. Twice men from town had come to the door and twice *Tantchen* had sent them away explaining the first time that I was only thirteen and the second time pleading with them I was needed to help tend our small plot of vegetables. And after each visit, *Tantchen* had insisted that the hex signs had protected me from these *Hafermänner*, black hatted spirits in long coats that came to steal children. I could only smile politely and nod at her conviction.

But finally, less than a month ago, the third man came. He was handsome in his severe gray and black uniform, as handsome as any farm girl with limited male contact could ever hope to meet. *Tantchen* pled her best case for me to stay on our farm, and secretly summoned her best spells and hex signs, but to no avail. He would not take "no" for an answer. I was now fifteen he reminded me and my country needed me. And in some quiet, fertile corner of my heart, I knew he was right.

Rucksack packed, I took a deep breath, let it out slowly and began the final transformation. I stripped off my barn coat and tunic, freed my auburn curls from my scarf, then pulled on the pair of dark blue shorts and white tank top the man in the uniform had brought for me. They were second hand from who knows where as *Tantchen* and I could certainly not afford to purchase them new. But from the looks of the uniform, the previous owner seemed to have been a someone as, or even more so, clumsy than I. On the white top, just above my left breast, the ghost of some long past meal haunted my uniform. *Tantchen* had tried all of her best tricks, poultices and potions to exorcise the *Dämonen*, but to no avail. There it was, faded, yes, but still visible. I turned and looked at my reflection in the small bit of mirror hanging near the window. I squinted a bit and it seemed to fade.

"Maybe they will all be nearsighted," I said as my stomach sank a little lower.

The day would warm up soon enough, but a ride with Mr. Hochauser on a March morning would still be chilly. Best to wear a coat, I thought, and pulled my barn coat back on. I shouldered my rucksack, heavy with the weight of all of my "friends", then made my way to the door. I turned one last time to check the mirror, to see what sort of impression I was about to make on whoever it was I was supposed to make it on. I looked myself over. If I buttoned my barn coat coat over the small stain, no one would notice. First impressions would be made and all would move squarely on from there. But the knot in my stomach persisted. No, I would be fine, I thought and unbuttoned my coat. This is what I want them to see first, that I am a true patriot. This that binds us all together. Beneath my chin, on a field of the reddest of reds, the symbol of my country and the bright hope we all held for our future: the swastika.

#

Tantchen's words cut me off before I even reached the bottom of the ladder.

"And where might you be going, dressed like THAT?" she said, grinding her meaty fists firmly into the cresting folds of her hips.

"It's the uniform the man brought me!" I said coyly, knowing full well what she meant.

"The coat, Katerina, the coat. You can't show up wearing that. What would people think, hay poking from your pockets like some sort of . . . sort of . . . *Bauerntrampel*," bumpkin. "Please *Liebchen*, wear this instead."

She held out a lined chambray shirt that had once belonged to my father, a shirt that she had shortened and altered for me to make a serviceable light coat. It was one of the few things we had managed to recover from the house before it was confiscated.

"No, *Tantchen*. The barn coat will be . . ."

She shook the shirt-coat in front of me. "This!" she said. "This is what you shall wear. You must look *kleidsam!*" well dressed "for your new friends!"

Defeated, I took the coat from *Tantchen*, held it at arm's length for a moment then pulled it on. Immediately the smell of my father's turpentine bit into my nose wrenching hazy visions of paint cans, brushes and childhood before my eyes, then gone. *Tantchen* took me by the shoulders, looked me over and smiled. "*Kleidsam*," she said and nodded slowly. Then she cradled my face in her thick and calloused hands and stared into my eyes. From a dark corner of her belly I watched as some shadow of thought rose slowly up and caught in her throat. Not a sad thought though. Something worse. It tugged the corners of her mouth down as she struggled in vain to hold her smile, tears welling in her puppy dog eyes. "*Kleidsam*," she said again, her voice barely more than a whisper. But the word had nothing to do with the way I was dressed. It was merely a word to fill the empty void left by other words she could not tell me. Things she knew long before I ever did.

Then she hugged me. Tightly. "Please," she whispered in my ear as if the walls themselves could hear, "*Sei sehr vorsichtig.*" Be very careful.

"I'll be alright *Tantchen*," I said into the straps of her apron, "I'll be alright."

She held my face and looked into my eyes, the calloused pads of her thumbs rough against my cheeks, her apple face carved in worry. "Please. Promise. Very careful."

"I will," I said, "I promise. I'll be alright."

"I know," she said without conviction, "I know."

"I'll write to you!" I said, tears beginning to well in my own eyes.

She gave a little chuckle, "And who would read these letters to me? Huh? You are the reader in this family."

Her grip was only broken by the cackle of tin bells on Mr. Hochauser's horse Mad Ludwig jangling a bit more frantically than normal as he came up the rutted dirt lane.

"I'm late, Frau Mueller, very late! Be ready as I pass by!" he called ahead.

I crossed our dooryard in a dozen steps and met him at the edge of the lane with the two pails of milk as he arrived. I set the pails on the tail gate of his buckboard as he climbed down.

"*Guten Morgen* Herr Hochauser!" I said as brightly as anyone trying to hitch a free ride could hope to muster.

"*Morgen,*" he grumbled as he passed.

He dipped his finger in each pail and tasted. He, too, wrinkled his nose at the second pail. "Keep Nef out of the onion grass, Frau Mueller, or next time there'll be no payment!" He poured the two pails into a larger white enameled can before closing the lid with the heel of his hand. Grudgingly, he handed me some coins and I ran with them and our now empty pails back to the stoop where *Tantchen* stood. She hugged me tight to her stained apron, my nose buried in the earthy smells of wood smoke and raw potatoes. "Remember what I said, my Katerina," she whispered before kissing me on the forehead. Hochauser was already settling into his squeaky seat as Ludwig began to lumber down the lane, forcing me to race after him. I reached the tailgate and hopped on.

I kicked my dangling legs, naked and cold in my uniform shorts. Against the lining of my stomach, Excitement, and her darker twin Fear, danced a fluttery dance, each vying for my attention as our little *Hütte* began to recede behind the bend in the road. Adventure and uncertainty lay ahead in that which had become The Great Cause, and I was going to be a part of it! What could be more exciting for a simple farm girl!

Perhaps the handsome man in his handsome uniform had not been a *Hafermann* coming to steal me from home at all, but a good spirit. A releasing spirit. If it had not been for him, I might have stayed on the farm with *Tantchen* forever. Would that have been so bad? Perhaps not. The simple life has its merits. But nervous or not, something was calling me, something inside that demanded an answer. "The unexamined life is not worth living," Plato had said. *Tantchen* will survive without me for a few months.

But then there was the other matter, the one that had brought me to live at Tantchen's farm so many years ago. And with it the question that had haunted my nights ever since, demanding an answer: The question of my father.

Ahead of us the long cool shadows of morning striped the lane. Behind, *Tantchen* walked to the center of the rutted road and followed us for a short distance. When she could no longer keep up, she waved and smiled her toothless smile. A smile, that did little to hide the dark clouds of worry that shadowed her face.

It was the last time I ever saw her.

ZWEI - TWO

Ludwig clomped along in a steady rhythmic progression for well over an hour as we passed farm after field after farm. Villages came and villages went, some no more than a wide spot in the road welcoming a handful of houses then gone.

In time, the land beneath us began to gently rise, the rhythm of Mad Ludwig's hoofs beginning to slow. Hochauser laid the reins gently against his back, more in encouragement than demand and Ludwig continued to climb. At the top of the gentle rise, a white clapboard house, august and proud, secured an elevated post along the rutted dirt road, a newly painted picket fence around it containing not a single farm animal. A fence for keeping wanderers out, not animals in. Other houses of substance and posture rose around and beyond and behind, straddling *Hoch Strasse*, High Street, like royalty on a dais, the poorer houses spread out below like their unwashed subjects. This was the *Schicki Micki*. The *Hoity Toity*. Those who held themselves both physically and socially above the rest.

Ludwig reached the clapboard house at the crest of the hill and Hochauser tenderly patted his rump. Good job, Ludwig. Good job. As gently as the road rose, it began to descend, easing to the left, more clapboard and fences, one after the next, and not a chicken or Egyptian queen to be seen. To the left stood the train station, the grand dame of the town. The station's roof line swept gently, ornate scrollwork along

25

the edges like some great cuckoo clock helping to off-set the practical simplicity of the platform's concrete slab. At the end of the platform, a sign informed arriving passengers that they had reached the Bavarian village of *Ülmstadt*. A clock let them know that they were on time as should be expected, and the red, white, and black flag of the Third *Reich* told them everything else they needed to know about the town's inhabitants.

Surrounding the station were a dozen boxy warehouses, as plain as she was ornate, huddled around like bodyguards protecting her from the surge of clapboard. Plain roofs in neat rows radiated outward from the warehouses like ripples on a mill pond, held back from overflowing onto *Bundes Strasse*, Main Street, by a dam of shops just coming to life on either side.

Ludwig ambled through the center of town, the clacking of his tin bells keeping cadence to the rhythm of his hoofs on the short stretch of cobblestones. The baker was busy filling his shop windows with warm loaves while the blacksmith brought his forge to life. From the darkened windows of the dry goods store, the owner clattered over his hardboard sign from "Closed" to "Open" careful not to obscure the smaller sign beneath reading:

"Einlass für Juden und Hunde Verboten"
Entrance Forbidden to Jews and Dogs.

From both sides of *Bundes Strasse* the patter of people walking the sidewalks reverberated with a steady purpose. Things needed to be done and there was pride in their faces to have things to do. Gone were the days of not so long ago, when the bakery windows were empty, the blacksmith's forge was silent and a wheelbarrow was worth more than the pile of *Reichsmark* it could hold. No longer did you have to sleep in your henhouse to protect the eggs from others. Hungry people. Homeless people. There was a brightness to the air, a feeling that escaped your touch, but there all the same. Optimism was too simple a word. It was something much deeper, better. And everywhere, everywhere, the red and white and black flags snapped.

In front of his butcher shop Herr Traubweiss with his stained paper hat and thick black tangle of beard, poured another pail of water on the sidewalk and scrubbed. Passersby continued to walk where he worked but he pressed on, undaunted. He did not mind them walking where he washed. There were worse things that could be done to the butcher with the small yellow Star of David painted on his door.

We had all been taught from the cradle that the Jews did not belong among us. On the radio, in newspapers, in the songs we sang, even in the storybooks read to us as children, the Jews were the villains, sub-human, inferior. Even in the mathematical lessons we were taught in school: "If the greedy Jew demands ten *Reichsmark* from the war veteran's widow but she has only five, how many will she still owe the Jew?" Over and over, drummed into our heads, it was the Jews who were responsible for all the ills of our nation, for the dark times of not so long ago. They

27

had become the Field Ghosts and Corn Demons of this generation, for the educated and peasant alike. Their black hatted *Hafermänner* came to your door not to steal your children, but your bank accounts, farms, and businesses. And the red, white, and black flags had become the hex symbols that protected us from their evil ways.

So without complaint Herr Traubweiss continued to scrub the sidewalk in front of his shop, hopeful that a good cut of schnitzel still rose above all politics, until the storm had passed.

On the opposite side of the street, a boy of no more than seven skipped along the sidewalk, handing out flyers to each passersby. Post card perfect in a crisply ironed beige shirt, dark shorts and the ubiquitous red, white, and black arm band, he smiled at everyone who came within the beacon of his choir boy face and handed them a flyer. He stopped in front of a woman pushing a wicker baby carriage and beamed, handed her a flyer, took a step back and bowed. Then he leaned into the carriage, set a flyer inside, and continued to skip down the road. There must be something happening. Maybe today. Maybe a rally or a parade or some party official giving a speech. Or perhaps a book burning later at night, although those always left me a little unsettled. Even though the *Führer* had said it was important to purge the Jewish filth from our minds, there was something about burning books that seemed to go against reason. Shouldn't we try to learn as much as we can, then sort the wheat from the chaff? Don't diamonds come from coal? But if the *Führer* said it, then I believed it. He had done so much to steer us in the right direction, in the dark days following the war. He would continue to do so. Nonetheless, it would be wonderful to stay to see something. Anything.

Every once in a great while *Tantchen* had taken me into the village to purchase seed, sell a goat or have a tool mended by the blacksmith. If we had made a good sale, or had to wait for the forge to heat, we would spend our time near the stove at the general store, perhaps splurge on some penny candy or even a tin of peaches. Inside they had a radio, high on the shelf, and we were sometimes lucky enough to hear *den Führer* speak. And when he spoke, we would stay and we would listen, often long after our tools had been repaired or our goat had let out its last bleat. People would be called in from the sidewalk, and in the store they would gather around, closer to the radio than to the stove even on the coldest of days as if somehow it brought us closer together. And we would listen. And they would listen. Listen to him, his picture high on the wall behind the cash register. They would listen and smile and gently nod, eyes staring off in the distance to some future far brighter than their own. Far from a past not distant enough.

But there would be no rallies or parades today. Not for me, at any rate. Mr. Hochauser and I were parting ways. I hopped off the back of his wagon. *"Danke Schön!"* I said as I slung my rucksack over my back. Startled from his thoughts, Mr. Hochauser turned around. He smiled a sad toothless smile. *"Oh,*

Ja. Bitte.", he said and I continued down the road on foot.

DREI - THREE

I heard them before I saw them. The sound of marching. The Tramp-Tramp-Tramp of an army of feet acting as one, a drum keeping the beat. I continued to walk, suddenly realizing that I too was walking in their step. That I had been lured into their group without ever seeing them! A little hint of a smile caught my lips until I stumbled on the merest of ruts and the spell was broken.

Then came the voices, clear and high and crisp as alpine air. The bright voices of young women, loud and in unison, eager for all to hear:

Deutschland, Deutschland über alles!

Germany, Germany above all else!

Über alles in der Welt!

Above all in the World!

It wasn't just a song, it was a statement, a demand, sung loud so all the world would hear. Sung at the top of their lungs. Excitement ran her prickly fingers along the backs of my arms and the nape of my neck.

We were back.

#

A red brick building, church-like and pious, knelt in a stand of beech trees, their thick gray trunks spiraling up into hazy green crowns. Tight to one side several rows of tombstones stretched from the foundation like the sails of ships departing port on their final voyage home. Beyond, other buildings, white washed and clean, clustered and stood like acolytes in

31

attendance. I reached the sign out front, a small wooden structure with a shed roof to keep the letters sheltered and safe from the heavy Bavarian winter snows, a docile flag of red, white and black hanging alongside. The sign had been whitewashed with several coats of paint, but at its apex, a ghostly Star of David bled through. Below, it read in bold script letters:

Bund Deutscher Mädel
Division 687

BDM, The League of German Girls. They had come into existence some years prior, following the war, a sort of after school group where young women could meet and bond and hopefully learn new skills to make them more useful at home. But it took the wisdom of *des Führers* in his rise to power to see the true value and importance young women brought to the new *Reich*. In 1933 he disbanded all other youth organizations leaving only the *HitlerJugend* or Hitler Youth for boys and the BDM for girls. Enrollment for girls of ethnic purity had become mandatory two years ago in 1936. As much as I had desired to join and see what lay beyond the stone walls ringing our farm, Tantchen needed me and had managed to keep me at home. And that, as far as she was concerned, was that. Until of course the severe but undeniably handsome *Hafermann* arrived at our door.

The singing had stopped. The marching had stopped. There were three loud volleys of *"Sieg Heil!"*. I stepped into the circular drive.

Through the white washed buildings I worked my way until I stood on the edge of a large soccer field where groups of young women, perhaps two hundred or more in total, gathered around small flags noting D-687 and a *Gruppe* number. On the far side of the field other groups were practicing gymnastics while still others were on an archery range. It was without a doubt the largest group of women my age I had ever personally witnessed. All were dressed in the same white tops and dark shorts I now wore, spotless white tops, I assumed, their red flag and swastika proud and prominent.

I tried to move toward the group nearest to me, *Gruppe 6*, but my mutinous legs had other ideas. I took off my shirt-coat. Certainly now I looked like one of them and could blend in smoothly. A breath of wind wafted the pungent turpentine scent of both father and childhood to my nose catching me off guard, but I continued to push my traitorous legs forward. Forward for the *Reich*, forward for *den Führer*.

My legs shook without strength as I continued across the short grass toward Group 6. One girl turned and spotted me. She stared, nudged the girl next to her, but said nothing. Nothing needed to be said. The other girl too began to stare at this freakish apparition crossing THEIR field, toward THEM. I pressed forward, hoping the wind would clear the whisper of piney turpentine from my nose, clearing the brief visions of life before. It did not. Fifty meters from them they could certainly see the failure of my legs as more girls began to turn. I tried to smile but my lips began to twitch worse than my legs, my long past breakfast beginning to reassert itself in the empty hollow of my belly. Twenty five meters, all twenty or so girls were now facing me, staring as if a trundle cart of something foul and sticky was approaching them to be dumped on their pristine field. At their center was a woman somewhere shy of thirty in a perfectly fitted steel gray uniform with bits of stone black trim in precisely the right places. Narrow peaked gray side cap set on tightly bound blonde hair, she turned to spot me, her face unreadable. She checked her clipboard as I approached, then checked it again. I walked directly toward her, the dryness in my throat and mouth lodging my tongue in thickness. I opened my mouth to speak.

A sharp *"Achtung!"* came out, but it was not from me.

The cluster of girls snapped into a line perfectly bisected by the *Gruppen* flag, the *Gruppenführer*, Group Leader, in her fitted gray uniform carried her clipboard to the far end of the line. I dropped my shirt-coat and rucksack in the field and ran to the opposite end of the line praying with every ounce of my strength to God and *dem Führer* himself not to allow my rubber legs to fail me in the face of all. I safely reached the end of the line, brought heels together and wheeled my toes into the direction of all the rest. And waited.

Down the line she came, slowly, ever the inspection, words quietly spoken to a girl here or there. Trim the line, tuck in an errant element of blouse, a compliment or two. She stopped before me. I could feel rather than see the entire group to my right had suddenly become interested in the goings on at this end of the line.

"And you are?" she said, stoic.

"Kat. Katerina," I said. She waited, then coaxed me with her clipboard to continue. "Oh, um. Mueller, Kat, Katerina Mueller," she nodded slowly, flipping through the pages of her clipboard. She started over from the beginning, then began flipping through slower.

"You don't belong here," she said finally, an understatement if I had ever heard one. She looked to the shadow of a stain on my left shoulder then back to me. With a whiff of relief in her voice she said "You belong in . . ." slight smile. "*Gruppe Acht,*" she pointed across the field with the knife edge of her clipboard to the Group Eight flag, looked again at the stain on my shoulder then back to me. She gave a little smile, as humorless as a gravedigger's welcome. "*Gruppen-führer Kenstein* will take care of you," the line to my right began to giggle. *Gruppenführer* shot them a look then the gravedigger returned. "*Gruppe Acht. Auf Wiedersehen.*"

"*Auf Wiedersehen.*" I replied, and walked past her to pick up my rucksack and coat. As I walked behind her I heard her say loud enough that her girls could hear. " . . . *und viel Glück.*" which brought about a titter of laughter from the girls. "Good Luck," she said and I headed off across the field.

Gruppe Acht lay across the field, forcing me to walk past each other *Gruppe* in turn, always eliciting the same chain reaction of events. One girl spots me, then nudges the next, and she the next until eventually the whole group has turned, mumbling words amongst themselves like the buzzing of bottle flies on manure. It is then that their *Gruppenführer,* crisp in her gray and black, turns and shushes them to attention. Then I am on to the next. Ever the center of ill attention, I moved among them, a carnival curiosity children pay a pfennig to see. But soon I would reach Eight, my new home for the next few months, somewhere, hopefully, where I would fit in.

I approached my group, as always, all eyes upon me, nudges and giggles galore. Frau Kenstein's back was towards me, gray-black uniform, knee-length skirt, dark hair streaked with gray in a severe bun. I came up behind her.

"Frau Kenstein?" I said. The group of twenty five girls inhaled in unison then stopped breathing.

Frau Kenstein turned slowly. Very slowly. As she did, she brought her face down to my level, a hard face of hard angular edges, like rock broken with a hammer. More man than woman, severe black eyes, the tightness of her bun pulling them slightly out of round. Her broken rock of a nose came close to mine.

"What did you call me?" she whispered through her teeth, her breath a biting cloud of stale coffee and cigarettes. I tipped back on my heels.

"I called you . . . Frau Kenstein," I said, my tongue suddenly heavy and dry. "At *Gruppe Sechs . . .*"

I began to explain but was mowed down mid sentence by the sharpness of her voice and nose.

"I am *Gruppenführer* Kenstein and nothing else, *verstehen sie*?" This last part she said even slower than the rest, *verstehen sie*? Do you understand me? I started to nod quickly. Her nose slowly backed away from my face, her ice black eyes never leaving mine, I tried to look at her and away from her at the same time, from lapel to lapel, epaulets, swastika, skull head and lightening bolts.

When she reached full erect she said "*Achtung!*" but it was unnecessary, the girls behind her were already in line. An occasional giggle slipped out until *Gruppenführer* Kenstein turned. I slithered my way, once again to the end of the line. Oh God, I thought, please let this be the wrong group again.

But it was not to be.

Instead of turning her attention to the opposite end of the line as had *Gruppenführer Sechs*, Kenstein turned her attention first to me.

"*Wie heissen sie?*" What's your name? she said, I told her, never allowing my gaze to falter. She flipped through the papers on her clipboard, stopped, looked at me then at the clipboard then back to me. She made an erasure on one page, touched the tip of her pencil to the tip of her tongue and made a small check mark on the sheet.

"You are late," she said to me. I began to explain about the problems Herr Hochauser was having with Mad Ludwig when her ice eyes again cut me off at the knees.

"You are late TWO YEARS. The edict went out two years ago for you to report but you have ignored it. Why?" again I began to tell her about *Tantchen* and the farm but got no further than my first explanation. But none of that mattered either, she had become fixated on the faint ghost sitting on the shoulder of my uniform.

"*Was ist das*?" she said with an evil curiosity tapping the eraser of her pencil to the faint stain. What is this? For the third time I tried to explain but got no further than opening my mouth.

"*Halt die Klappe!*" she whispered beneath her breath. Shut up! I took an involuntary step backward as she leaned in, stale coffee and cigarette breath forcing me into a faulty step. I fell backwards and landed in the grass, square on my rump. *Gruppenführer* Kenstein stood at my feet, hands on the narrow, mannish hips of her skirt. "I have had enough of you already! You arrive late, soiled uniform, fail to address me as appropriate! You are a disgrace, a disgrace to everything you are supposed to stand for!" by now the girls of *Gruppe Acht* were standing behind her looking down on me as well in various states of admonition but perhaps more *Schadenfreude* than anything. It was someone else's turn to be devoured alive by *GF* Kenstein, a new target on the range, which would leave them free to live another day. "We shall have much to do, *Fräulein* Mueller. Much to do!" *GF* continued, her verbal assault hinting of darker things to come. She peered down her rock hard nose, black eyes boring into me. "But we shall succeed, shall we not?" again I began to nod my head vigorously, snot and tears making an appearance. I closed my eyes and gave up trying to remain composed and fell into a full-on blubber.

When I opened them again, they had all departed leaving me breathing in hitches. This was to be my gruppe, this was to be my home, my "friends" for the next however many months they decided I needed to learn my lessons, to show my value to the *Reich*. I closed my eyes and lay flat in the grass, hoping that the earth would swallow me up and be done with it.

But it didn't.

A bright March sun, warm as hope, shone down on me, offering its consolation.

Until a shadow crossed over my face.

I breathed in still more hitches and wallowed in a bit more blubbering hoping the dark cloud would pass and leave me alone in my misery.

But it didn't.

I creaked one eye open, still blurry through my tears. It was someone looking down on me, an upside down someone from how the world appeared to me. The sun haloed her head and a waterfall of curls descended from either side of her face almost reaching mine. But it was not a face of glee at my situation or *Schadenfreude,* or even consolation. Maybe a bit of curiosity, a dram of commiseration thrown in just because. She extended her hand.

"Kommen sie," she said. Come on, "Get up."

I began to blubber slightly again, my lower lip quivering. I shook my head, I did not want to get up again. Ever.

Still leaning over me, she put her hands on her hips and shook her head slowly, "I'll ask you again, just one more time. Get up."

"No." I croaked through quivering lips. Her upside down face, a face that could almost pass as my own, was directly above mine.

"I tried didn't I?" she said as if she had indeed tried everything. Her upside down lips went into an upside down frown. Then she pursed her frown, bright with red lipstick, as if she were about to deliver a huge, wet kiss. Between her lips a small white spot appeared, a spot of white bubbles. It began to grow, and grow, and grow.

"You wouldn't dare," I whispered to the up-side down stranger. But she did not answer as that would destroy the "present" she was about to deliver. I lay there horrified at the thought of it as a glob of spit began to slowly descend on me. I quickly rolled out of the way just before it landed in the grass where my head had been.

I jumped up dumbfounded. "What the . . . What's the big idea? Trying to spit on me? Is that what people do around here? *Arschloch*!" Asshole! I was furious, wiping the snot-tears-almost spit from my face with the back my hand. "What is wrong with you? You're . . .you're disgusting!"

She let out a machine gun rattle of a laugh. "I can be if I need to be!" her brown eyes bubbling with

40

mirth. "But it got you up didn't it?" A breath of breeze caught her golden brown hair and sent it back pennant-like over her shoulders. As if savoring the moment, she slowly closed her eyes and lolled her head from side to side like a proud lion displaying its mane. "And it stopped you from all of that stupid crying? Right?" She opened her eyes. "Now *Kommen sie!*" come on, she said again and began to walk away.

I looked at her, at this *verrückt,* this crazy person, and for some reason, against all my fury and anger and disappointment at my new found "friends" of the BDM only a moment before, something hooked the corner of my mouth into just the slightest of smiles. And I followed her.

#

Together we crossed the field, oblivious to the two hundred or so other girls in their various states of activity. Marching, archery, gymnastics. But the crazy one and I were headed toward the white washed buildings. We crossed into an old storage barn still flavored with the smell of cut grass and gardening tools that had been converted into the BDM barracks. Inside were tightly packed bunk beds neatly made in dark blue and white gingham spreads. Two near the wash station were still covered in only rough canvas fart sacks.

"Take your pick," said the crazy one. I tossed my jacket and rucksack on the top bunk nearest the window. "Follow," she said, and we walked past the wash station into a narrow corridor lined with lockers and wooden benches. In front of one close to the wash stations she stopped and opened the door. She eyed me over for a second. "We're about the same size, I suppose," she nodded to herself, then gave the command: "Hands up!" and I obeyed. In one fluid motion she yanked my blouse up over my head exposing my bare breasts momentarily until I got my hands back down to cover myself.

I stared at her in shock "You ARE *verrückt!*" crazy!

She smiled, "Yeah, crazy as a brew house rat so I've been told," she grabbed a crisp new BDM blouse with the miniature swastika on the front, as brilliant white as I had ever seen.

"Here, pull this on," *Verrückte* said.

"But where did you get these?" I said.

"They're mine. I've got more."

"I . . . I can't pay you for these."

Verrückte shrugged, "That's fine, I have more than enough. It's just *Kram,*" stuff. "That I've got plenty of."

I turned around to pull the blouse on, trying to cover my nakedness.

"No need to hide 'em," she said. "They're boobs. You've got 'em, I've got 'em." I turned around, my clean new blouse safely down. "What you do need though, which I don't have handy, is *der Sack,* a set of balls. I don't ever want to see that again from you," her face now serious.

"I'm sorry, I'll try very hard to keep my uniform clean."

She rolled her eyes, "I'm not talking about the stupid uniform. I'm talking about letting those hyenas get to you like that. Show a little spine, a little backbone, buckle on a pair of balls. *Verstanden?*"

My mouth hung open at an odd angle as I tried to adjust my ears to the crudity of her words, language I had normally heard only from the village gong farmer emptying an overly filled cesspit. She continued to stare at me.

"*Verstanden?*" she repeated.

I nodded, then croaked out, "I'll try."

"Don't try, do," she reached into her locker and gave me a few more new tank top blouses, shorts and other items, then she headed toward the door leaving me standing alone outside her locker. As she reached the door she turned back to me.

"Oh and another thing. *Gruppenführer* Kenstein? Never, EVER call her Frau Kenstein. She hates it."

I nodded a confused nod, "Oh, OK . . . But why?"

"Because that's what WE call her, behind her back. Frau Kenstein. Fraukenstein," she placed her arms out in front of her and did a pretty good stiff legged impersonation of the Boris Karloff monster in the movie posters I had seen of Frankenstein, "*Ich habs?*" she laughed. Got it? "Fraukenstein," she waved her hand in dismissal. "Don't worry," she continued to walk toward the door, "you will."

She was almost back out into the sunshine when I called out to her one last time, "By the way, who are you? What's your name?"

She continued walking without turning around.

"You don't want to know."

VIER - FOUR

A full two weeks passed without again speaking with the *Verrückten*. Occasionally I thought I caught sight of her from across the field, at the archery line or marching with one gruppe or the other. If the purpose of wearing a uniform is that we all begin to look and act alike for the greater good of the whole, it was working quite well. She had disappeared, if she was in fact still here at all.

I asked some of the other girls I met in the various lectures and cooking classes we attended, but no one seemed to know her, or even know of her. Yet almost without exception, I always ended up with the feeling that there was more they had to say. But didn't. Or wouldn't. At one point, a girl pulled me aside and in a low voice told me "Even if there was someone like that here at camp, I would be especially certain to avoid them," then quickly departed.

In the meantime, I had become out of necessity quite busy myself, ever under the icy gaze of Fraukenstein. No matter what she threw at me, I tried my best to hold up. Not to cry, or at least save it for the solitude of my upper bunk near the window. "Buckle on a pair!" the *Verruckt* had said and I did as best I could. But it wasn't easy. I had become Fraukenstein's Moby Dick. She was determined to see me sent home in disgrace. Pursue me across every "ocean" of the BDM camp from the gymnastics area to the marching field in order to try to bring me down. But just like Moby Dick, I would win in the end. I must win in the end. I could not bear to see the look on *Tantchen's* face if I had let her down and more importantly, let our country down.

Granted, I was my own worst enemy when it came to any physical activity that required even the slightest bit of coordination. When the gods assembled me, *Tantchen* always said, they included so much heart and soul and brain there was no room left for the brutish qualities of the physical. But in the BDM, certain skills were necessary.

How many times had I interrupted the march by coming out of step? How often had I fallen in gymnastics? And of course the whole incident which got me barred from the archery range! There was nowhere in the BDM I could succeed, or at the very least be comfortable in my own skills. Always the last to be picked for team sports, never invited to be a part of the dance recitals. I had become *persona non grata* to all team captains.

I did find some comfort in the kitchen skills and made it a point to spend as much time there as possible. Also the political classes where we learned about the organization of the Nazi Party commonly known as the NSDAP, the ever present filth of the Jews, and the life of our beloved leader, *der Führer*. I had made a few friends along the way, those that would allow me to sit with them during meals so I did not eat alone. But many meals I did. Sometimes I can be awkward that way.

Night became my solace, high atop my bunk in the back of the barracks near the window. From there

I was left alone, curled up with my books, reading by the light of the moon or my boxy BDM issued Daimon flashlight. It was there I could again walk the beaches of Troy with Achilles, survey the rooftops of Paris with Quasimodo at my side or weep for Cozi as she swept floors waiting for her mother. But then, I always wept for Cosette. Weren't we both the same? Hadn't she too lost her mother to the same illness as I had lost mine?

And hadn't her father abandoned her as well?

#

Near the beginning of the third week we had finished our breakfast of eggs and tea and had assembled on the marching track squarely between *Gruppe* Seven and Nine. The flag was raised and we pledged our allegiance to *dem Führer* and country, then settled into the business of the day. Today we would begin learning about forestry skills in the woods surrounding our field as we began to prepare for our nine month *Landdienst*, a group service to prove our value to the *Reich*. But before we left for the woods there was some administrative matters to attend to. Fraukenstein informed us that a new girl had joined our *Gruppe*. Well not completely new, she had been transferred over to *Gruppe Acht* as a result of some disciplinary action or another. The new girl was at the far end of the line as Fraukenstein made the introductions.

"*Gruppe Acht*, we have a girl joining our *Gruppe* today. Most of you, I am sure, already know her, but for those of you who do not, her name is . . ." without even consulting her clipboard she let out a little grunting noise then spat out the name, "Marta Koenigsberg. *Fräulein* Koenigsberg will be joining us on *Landdienst*. If you haven't already, please make your acquaintance," then added quickly, "during your leisure time."

With that, our morning formation ended. Together we all faced the flag and raised our right hands in salute, just as had been drilled into us. *"Sieg Heil!"* we shouted as one, a row of arms extended at the perfect forty five degree angle, palms down, hands extending like bayonets from the wrist. *"Sieg Heil!"* I turned slowly to stare down the line at the new unfortunate member of *Gruppe Acht*. But she was already staring at me. Smiling. With the final *"Sieg Heil!"* her hand was now no longer palm down in the proper salute, but waving at me! Her name was Marta Koenigsberg *die Verrückte,* and while I could not know it then, for the rest of my life, not a day would pass without my thinking of her with either the loftiest levels of my love or the bottomless depth of my hate.

And very little in between.

#

Like a German Shepherd, Fraukenstein began barking orders : *"Sie rechts ab, Marsch!"* the last word spit out. "To the right! March!" And we began to march toward the forest line. Luckily I was at the end of the line which meant that there was very little chance that I would trip up someone behind me.

Fraukenstein was alongside the flag bearer as we entered the woods on a narrow path, the air im-

48

mediately turning chill. Somewhere ahead was Marta. Sooner or later we would probably stop for a forestry lesson of some sort and hopefully then I could have a few words with her. The path wound up a slight grade and to the left, clusters of larch surrounded by skirts of blueberries to our right. I could now see the head of the line, Fraukenstein marching arrow straight, arms pinned to her sides, alongside the *Gruppe* flag bearer. I craned my neck but couldn't see Marta, couldn't catch sight of her long curly brown-blonde hair. I was now completely out of step and nearly tripped on the heel of the girl in front of me. Someone caught me by the upper arm and jerked me out of line.

It was Marta.

"Come on, follow me," she said and ducked under a blueberry bush alongside the path. I followed her in. When I stood up we were standing in a small "room" surrounded by brambles, the arms of a larch above forming the roof. Patches of blue, far above, were striped with long feathers of white.

"Enough of that nonsense!" Marta said. She reached into the crotch of the tree and pulled out a pack of cigarettes and a box of kitchen matches wrapped in a small square of oil cloth. She shook a cigarette into her mouth and smoothly lit the kitchen match off the seat of her shorts, the sulphur smell of Lucifer's breath suddenly surrounding us. She inhaled deeply and exhaled two dragon-like plumes of smoke from her nostrils, then shook the pack in my direction.

"Um, no thanks," I said.

"They're good for you, " she said. "Keeps you calm. Keeps the lungs open," she took another deep breath, then blew it out in a stream.

"No. But thanks," I said. "Isn't someone going to miss us?"

She shook her head, "No, probably not. Even if they do I have scouts up ahead."

"PROBABLY, not? Probably?! Look I'm in enough trouble with *Gruppenführer* Kenstein as it is."

"Who?" she said.

"*Gruppenführer* Kenstein."

"Who?"

"*Gruppenführer* . . . " I stopped and smiled. "Fraukenstein."

She smiled and nodded, "Correct. You can be taught. And as far as getting caught, getting in trouble, welcome to *Gruppe Acht.*"*Arg Acht*" The "Bad Eight" as we are known around the Six Eight Seven. They put all the rotten eggs in one basket. All the misfits and troublemakers. Thats where you landed *Küken.*" Young One.

"I'm not a rotten egg! They don't even know me! How did I end up in *Gruppe Acht*?"

"You showed up two years late," Marta nodded and took another drag. "That's pretty bad by their measure of things."

"I have my reasons."

Marta shrugged, "Reasoning is not something these people do well. At all."

"So how did you end up in this egg basket?"

50

"Choice."

"'Choice'? What do you mean 'choice'?"

Her cigarette was getting down to the butt so she pinched it between her fingers and stared at the dying ember at the end, "Choice. My choice. I got myself sent over here. Took a bit of doing I might add. The *Gruppenführer* normally don't want to deal with me. Not in a negative way anyway. Except for Fraukenstein. She doesn't care. She has a bit of stroke of her own."

"So why on earth would you want to get sent over here?"

She pointed to her eye, then pointed to me, "You."

"Me?"

She nodded, "You. I've been keeping an eye on you the past couple of weeks," she shook her head and crushed the cigarette out on the bottom of her shoe, "No offense, but, your abilities are . . . lacking."

I looked at her and waited.

"Your a *Klotz*," she clarified. "No *Koordinierung*." No coordination. "You're basically a hazard to everyone else out there. And if the *Reich* loves one thing, it's people acting together as one, you'll learn all about that in your political classes. They want everyone and I mean EVERYONE at the BDM to dress, look, act, think, eat, drink and squat to pee exactly the same." She reached for another cigarette and lit it, the gray smoke swirling about her like escaped wisdom. She sat on the knee of a tree root and I did the same across from her, our knees nearly touching, "No, you're not going to make it here *Küken* unless we can get you someplace where you are out of your own way," she held the cigarette lady-like between her index and middle fingers as she thought, "But where . . . "

A few more puffs, then she pointed the cigarette at me, "Can you sing?"

"Not a note."

She waved her hand as if wiping away all negativity from her plan.

"Doesn't matter, we'll get you in. You can't do much damage there. Fall off the risers maybe that's about it. I got myself in and I can't sing. Maybe the same trick will work twice." She took a big drag and blew it out of the corner of her mouth, a funnel of smoke from between her bright red lips, "I'll figure it out."

"What are you talking about?"

"Trying to get you out of some of this *gottverdammte* marching and shooting arrows nonsense. Ridiculousness."

"I like the lessons about our government and our country. They're OK."

Marta rolled her eyes, "*Politische Scheisse.*" political shit. "No, we need to get you out of trouble."

"Well thanks. That would certainly be helpful," I said, then had to add, "and I really mean it."

"Mean what?" Marta said.

"Thanks."

" For . . . ?"

"This. Helping me. People really don't seem to be ready to jump in and help someone around here."

She shrugged her shoulders, "Everybody needs a friend," she took another drag. "How old are you anyway?"

"Fifteen," I said.

She shook her head, "Too bad. You still have a couple of years before you move up to *Gruppen* leader. Seventeen. Then you get to tell other people what to do. Don't need to be in the bunkhouse with all the snoring and crying at night for their mama. *Guppe* hole up together in a smaller eight-man. I'll be there next year when I turn seventeen, hopefully. Unless I get myself pregnant in the meantime," she took another deep drag, squinting as she thought and blew it out. "But that seems to be more and more likely every day."

Once again, my mouth hung open at that odd angle as I stared at this puzzle of a person seated across from me. An awkward word began to tumble out of my mouth just as a disembodied face with freckles appeared from between the berry bushes.

"Fraukenstein is doing a head count, we've been covering for you but she's starting to wise up."

Marta crushed the cigarette out on her heel, "Thanks Wendi. We're coming. Our plan is made. Follow us *Küken*," and she disappeared through the bush.

#

And follow her I did, up the path and into to a small clearing in the woods. Before a seated semi-circle of girls stood a rotund male instructor who fit his name Herr Grossmann far better than he fit his Khaki uniform. In his white paper cap he spoke with intensity on the finer points of edible plants in the forest.

"We will be spending much of our *Landdienst* working in the forest," Herr Grossmann continued, eyeing a sprig of delicate leaves between his pudgy fingers, "and the forest can be a dangerous place for the ignorant. But it is the prudent *Fräulein* that is always prepared for the worst. Therefore, it is important you have survival skills in case you get separated from your *Gruppe*." Fraukenstein turned as the three of us arrived, the lightening bolts from her death's head *SS-Helferin* emblem, SS helper, now appearing to shoot from her own eyes.

"*Wo bist du gewesen?*" she said through her teeth. Where have you been?

Marta answered, "I was showing *Fräulein* Mueller how to make a latrine in the woods," she said, "very handy."

Fraukenstein brushed me aside with the back of her hand to come face to face with Marta. Marta never so much as flinched.

"I agreed to bring you to *Gruppe Acht* to see if we can bring you in line to our way of thinking *Fräulein* Koenigsberg," Fraukenstein leaned in closer. Marta stood like a statue, staring her eye-to-eye, allowing their noses to almost touch, "I know all about you," Fraukenstein continued, her voice getting lower, "you and your kind do not concern me in the least" she tapped the skull and lightening bolts above her left breast, then turned away and returned to the *Gruppe* where Herr Grossmann was in the process of demonstrating how to eat a mushroom he had found.

I let out a long breath thinking if cigarettes calmed you down, maybe I should have one next chance I get. I looked over at Marta. The hint of a smile cracked one corner of her mouth and she let her breath quietly whistle between her bright red lips.

We spent the remainder of the day in the forest under the hawkish gaze of Fraukenstein pacing behind us, not daring to talk, but passing glances back and forth across the group in response to things being said by Herr Grossmann. How each time he bent over to pick up a plant his butt crack gave us all a vertical smile eliciting sniggers of laughter. Adolescent behavior in its lowest form, but pure and innocent fun at its grandest. It was such a relief to not be alone in the *Gruppe*. To not be different, not be on the outside looking in. Herr Grossmann ate a small bug to which Marta made a face as if she were about to vomit. I pressed my hand over my mouth to keep from laughing out loud!

FÜNF - FIVE

The following morning we were back in formation, pledging our allegiance to *Führer* and flag. Fraukenstein was preparing to march the troops back into the forest when Marta grabbed me by the arm and dragged me over in front of her.

"*Gruppenführer*, Katerina here has a magnificent voice and she would like to try out for the chorus."

Fraukenstein looked from me to Marta then back to me again like a cat watching a mouse dash helplessly before it in a corner.

"A singer have we here, eh?" Fraukenstein said and for the first time I saw the hint of a smile, coffee stained teeth crammed together, buckled and beige, overlapping in the confines of her mouth.

"Yes," Marta jumped in, "quite an amazing voice!" she smiled. I nodded and smiled too, saying nothing, knowing that my best lie is one that is never spoken. Marta continued, "We understand there may be an opportunity to sing for Nazi Party leadership in Munich. It would be such an honor!"

"Wonderful," Fraukenstein said in a voice that saw nothing wonderful about it, other than the chance to catch two of her girls skylarking and get them elbow deep in some Extra Duty.

"Wonderful," she repeated. Then she moved directly in front of me, her buckled beige teeth forming the fractured corner of a smile mere centimeters from my own. I felt a trickle of sweat roll between my shoulder blades as I knew what was coming next.

"Why don't you sing something for me?"

"Now?" I croaked out, my mouth suddenly gone dry.

"Now," she said, and the buckled beige teeth disappeared from view.

I looked from left to right then back to her.

"Now," she repeated, her voice no longer a request but a command.

I began to open my mouth, unsure of what would come out next, a song, a squawk, an apology for lying immediately followed by volunteering for more Extra Duty but Marta was faster. She stepped in between us, "Oh no, *Gruppenführer*. She has her audition this morning and she needs to save her voice!"

Fraukenstein was ready, once again to press the issue when another member of *Arg Acht* came racing up. The young girl snapped a precision salute before Fraukenstein.

"*Heil* Hitler!" she said.

Fraukenstein gave a half hearted salute in return. "*Heil* Hitler," she said, her eyes never leaving the two mice she had cornered.

"*Gruppenführer*, Herr Grossmann is waiting for us at the *Wald* station."

"Tell Herr Grossmann we will all be along shortly," she turned her attention back to us as the smile returned. Only this time it was different, her black eyes now twinkling with sadistic delight. Somehow it appeared as if the death's head on her left breast was smiling too. She looked me squarely in the eyes. "Just a little song from this one."

Again I opened my mouth.

There was a crashing of undergrowth at the head of the trail and Herr Grossmann appeared. He of Khaki uniform now sporting dark rings under his arms, a stubbled balloon of flesh protruded beneath his chin. He was not at all happy,

"*Gruppenführer* Kenstein, I need to finish this session on tubers, then begin to prepare lunch!"

She made a move to silence him then thought better of it. Nothing is quite as dangerous as an angry cook.

"*Komm* Katerina," Marta said as she headed toward the old brick building and waved for me to join her. Fraukenstein gave me the slightest of nods, allowing me to go as Herr Grossmann again began to call her name.

#

It was cool as we stepped inside the brick structure, a former synagogue stripped of its purpose. The faint hint of incense still clung devotedly to the walls and pews, the lingering scent of religious rituals not even the Nazis could erase when they confiscated the building. An outline of the Star of David remained in bright paint at the front of the building peeking out defiantly between the flags and banners of BDM slogans. A group of a dozen or so girls were milling about a small organ watching a rather heavyset woman in pigtails adjusting the stops. She turned to face us as we entered, but then I realized she was reacting more to the sound of us than the sight of us. Her red and rosy face appeared to be permanently pressed up against a glass window, her puggish nose pointed toward the sky pulling her upper lip with it. Across the bridge of her nose sat two thick lenses, distorting each eye to twice their normal size.

"Is that you Marta?" she said as we came down the side aisle.

"Yes, it's me Frau Neidermeir," Marta said, "and I've brought a friend. She wants to sing for you." I pulled at Marta's arm but she continued to walk.

Frau Neidermeir smiled and adjusted her dirndl, "Well if she sings half as well as you do Marta, she will be more than welcome in the Division 687 Chorus!"

"I thought you said you didn't know how to sing?!" I whisper yelled to Marta.

"Shhhh," she said, "just play along."

"This is my friend Katerina. She is new here, " Marta announced to the group, "but she sings every bit as well as Amandine," Marta looked over toward Amandine, a thin girl with glasses and an angel's face. "Right Amandine?" Amandine smiled and nodded and made her way over to the risers facing the organ. But instead of standing on the risers, she walked around behind them, barely out of sight.

Marta turned to me and whispered, "Now you are going to audition for Blinky."

"Who?"

Marta motioned to Frau Neidermeir seated behind the organ leaning forward to see her music.

"Blinky," Marta repeated.

"Is she familiar with the Aria of Elisabeth, from Tannhäuser?" Blinky said.

I began to say no when Marta stepped on my foot, "Tannhäuser? Um . . ." Amandine gave a vigorous nod from beneath the risers. "Yes, certainly, I believe that is one of her favorites!"

I looked at Marta horrified and whisper yelled, "I have no idea what that is!"

Marta looked at me, "Now say that again, except don't let any words come out."

I shook my head, "What do you . . . ?"

"Just say what you said, only don't say it. Just mouth the words," I thought for a second about what I said and did it.

"Perfect!" Marta said. "Now when the music starts you watch me. I'll watch Amandine and tell you when to start, then just do what you're doing. And don't stop until I do. *Ich habs?*"

"Yes but . . ."

"Just trust me," she gave me a rather not-so-gentle pat on my fanny and I climbed to the center of the risers.

Blinky looked up from behind her organ music, two cartoonish owl eyes staring at me and said, "Are you ready?" I nodded. Then she repeated herself, "I said 'are you ready?'"

"Yes," I called out in a loud voice.

"Very well then!" she said, and with a great rhythmic ebb and flow of her mass, she began to pump the organ into the intro for the aria. I watched Marta for my cue. When she opened her mouth, I opened my mouth, and the most amazing voice I had ever heard came out! Of course it was provided by Amandine behind the risers, but as far as Blinky was concerned, it was all me. For a full five minutes I "sang" with a beauty I had only heard before on the radio at the dry goods store.

When she was finished, Blinky looked up at me and clapped her hands together once.

"Oh Katerina! You have the voice of an angel!" I gave Marta a slight nod and Amandine a wink as she stepped out of hiding.

"But we have much to do! The great *Führer's* birthday is only a week away and we have been truly blessed to perform in Munich at the celebration. So I need everyone's full attention and cooperation! Oh!" she hugged herself, "it will be *wunderbar!*"

#

And so it was that for the next week Marta and I were freed from the usual parade of marching, political speeches and excursions into the forest to prepare us for *Landdienst*. But more importantly, we were no longer mice scurrying beneath the hawkish beak of Fraukenstein. And a trip to Munich to top it all off!

Every day was now devoted to choir practice, beautiful voices rising and reverberating among the king posts supporting the old synagogue's roof. But not from Marta and I. The other fourteen girls lent their vibrant vibratos while we continued our false falsettos.

On the morning of April 20, the *Führer's* birthday, we rose early and were escorted by Blinky onto a bus decorated with alpine yodelers and flags of the *Reich* on each fender. From across the field I could see *Arg Acht* preparing for their own celebrations with the rest of Division 687, Fraukenstein pausing for a moment to watch us board the bus. But she could not stop us. Not today. Not when the residents of Munich so longingly awaited the voices of their cherished angels in the BDM singing the graces of *der Führer*.

#

The auto-bus motored through the rolling fields and plains of Bavaria for almost an hour. Along the way, every farmhouse, barn, tavern, and shop flew the red, white, and black flag of the *Reich*. The simple people of the hinterlands, proudly dressed in their very best gave the stiff arm salute to the crackling flags on our fenders as we drove by.

Progress slowed as we reached the outskirts of the city. Columns of soldiers in their hunter green uniforms, offset in belts, boots, and helmets of liquid black paraded past. Great convoys of machinery matched them stride for stride, trucks and tanks and cannons of every description, polished and proud, commanded the road. The might and muscle of Germany would be on display today. Woe to those hoping to repeat the desecration of our country not so many years ago. We were ready to defend ourselves.

Our yodeling bus navigated through the crowds as we reached the main thoroughfare of *der BundesStrasse*. Yes, I had seen pictures of Munich and Frankfurt and Berlin, but had never visited. Even painted postcards of the city *Platz* and *Hofbräu Haus* failed to live up to the magnificence before me. Government buildings, severe and autocratic, soared heavenward to the greatest of heights, sometimes six and seven stories above the cobbled pavers lined with people. Intermixed, like humble slaves, brick apartment buildings wandered off onto narrow side streets in all directions. Above all, the spires of churches and clock towers pointed their ornate crowns into the sky.

All polished, streets and stones and structures, gutters sparkling as if they expected silver to fall instead of rain. Individuals too, every person on the street dressed like collected dolls in a china cabinet. And everywhere the red, white, and black hung in flags; vertically, horizontally, from poles and crosses and street lamps. From the greatest buntings to simple flags pinned to a baby's carriage.

The auto-bus clunked to a halt with a hiss of brakes in a narrow alley alongside an obscure music hall on an obscure back city *Platz*. Shabby brick apartment houses crowded the square as if waiting for a free show to begin. From our seat on the bus we could see the leaders of the local NSDAP, business-like and dapper in dark suits and arm bands, climbing the wide front steps of the music hall, women in dresses and feathered hats draping their arms. On every step, young men, the oldest no more than eighteen, stood opposing each other, statue still, brown shirts, ties and creases in their dark trousers sharp enough to shave. If any were old enough to shave. Each held a spear supporting a banner of red, white, and black.

Marta nudged me, "HJs," she said and smiled a wicked smile, running the tip of her tongue across her top lip.

"HJs?" I said.

"HJs," she repeated, looking me in the eyes, her smile growing even wider. "*Hitler Jugend!*" Hitler Youth.

"Oh!" I said, understanding only slightly the importance of this nugget of information.

Marta looked at me again, "'Oh!' is right!" she said and we made our way to the front of the bus.

Once Blinky and the other fourteen girls had spilled out onto the sidewalk Marta and I stepped from the bus into a chill air thick with toasted chestnuts, diesel fumes and pride. Single file, we skirted the side of the wide stairs in preference for a nondescript side entrance, Marta and I bringing up the rear. Led by Blinky, the others continued to single file up a narrow flight of creaking back stage stairs. Just before the door, Marta grabbed my arm and pulled me back, her eyes quickly scanning the surrounding buildings as if searching for their secrets.

"Did you ever hear of Houdini?" Marta said.

"I . . . I think so. Magician or something, right?"

"A damn genius as far as I'm concerned," she said.

"Um . . . wasn't Houdini . . . Jewish?" I questioned.

Marta rolled her eyes in response, "more *Politische Scheisse.* Man's a damn genius, that's all there is to it," then we followed the choir up the stairs into a small side room of high ceilings, barren windows and a coat of paint twice my age. And there we waited.

Blinky studied her sheet music, looking up occasionally to make sure we kept our voices down. But speaking was unnecessary for Marta. Plans were being made and orders were being given around the room in a series of looks, nods and hand gestures. When it was done Marta gave a thumbs up sign, which was repeated around the room by several girls.

From down the hall speeches were being given on stage, long, loud, demanding speeches, filled with fury and thunder, fed to ever louder demands and fury by waves of applause. Speeches filled with pride and hope, always to the honor and glory of *zum Führer*, ever the call for the elimination of the Jews.

The speeches came to a stop, the voice drowned into silence by a tsunami of applause, rolling over it in a succession of waves.

There was the rap of knuckles on the door followed by a weasel's face appearing in the crack between door and jamb.

"*Frau Neidermeir? Es ist Zeit,*" it's time.

Blinky stood, looked around the room, not entirely sure that we were all there, then clapped her hands twice.

"*Komm Bitte,*" she said, and she led the way out the door and into a hallway, soft with darkness. She stopped just short of a slit in a pair of black stage curtains, brilliant yellow light spilling out in a series of tight, narrow "V"s across our shoes.

The announcer began to speak, a few stray voices still crossing each other in the darkness. Then he repeated himself slightly louder: "As our beloved *Führer* has said," the room becoming immediately silent "'it is the mission of the *Bund Deutscher Mädel* to make for him strong and brave women'. And so it is. And so they are. It is therefore my distinct honor to bring you the beautiful voices of our future, the *Fräuleins* of the *Bund Deutscher Mädel* District 687 to serenade us with music on our beloved *Führer's* birthday."

Then we stepped onto the stage.

The stage lights were blinding, allowing us to see no further than the front edge of the stage. Beyond, faces and shapes, dark suits alternating with colorful dresses muted by the darkness began to come into focus. Beginning her orchestration, Blinky faced forward and began to stomp her foot setting the rhythm as we marched to our places on the risers. Once the last girl had moved into position, we froze, perfect in our crisp white uniforms, statue dolls of glorious Nazi youth. Eyes frozen forward, each meticulously the same. Except of course for Marta.

And directly in front of her, Hildi. Marta, who's eyes had not stopped moving since she turned around on the risers, scanning the audience for her next adventure. And Hildi, only daughter of a doting father who never bothered to inventory the hard candies in his dry goods store. Pleasantly plump, filling her uniform to its full capacity, plus a little more. Blonde hair in pigtails pulled tight to the scalp forcing her face into a permanent, candy fattened smile.

Then Blinky began to play.

By the end of our first song Marta had zeroed in on her target. Two targets in fact. As our eyes became adjusted to the stage lights, figures lining the side aisles came into focus. Figures in Khaki shirts, black ties and razor sharp trouser creases. The HJs were standing guard, and Marta had made eye contact with one. She nudged me. The first song ended and applause crackled.

"Two O'clock, HJ tall blonde. Eyes on," she whispered from the corner of her mouth through the applause, face always forward. I tried to keep up, "on his right, little shorter, glasses, mini Himmler," I squinted and she continued, "That one's for you."

"What are you . . . ?" she continued to smile, as if to the crowd, eyes never leaving her blondie. "Get ready, middle of the second song."

"What are . . . ?" but Blinky was already pumping the pedals of the organ. Then the second song began. As one, we raised our voices, minus of course Marta and I, in an angelic rendition of *Deutschland Deutschland Über Alles*. Beautiful voices, the crowd in complete admiration. Marta discreetly tapped Hildi on the back. Imperceptibly Hildi nodded. The National Anthem was reaching its crescendo, voices raised on high. Marta reached out again and placed her hand squarely between Hildi's plump shoulder blades.

And gently pushed.

Forward Hildi went like a slow motion bowling ball hitting the "pins" in front of her. Down she went. Down they went. Dominoes all the way to the front row of girls. Blinky looked up from the music, her owl eyes aware that something was happening, but not sure what. The voices of pure angelic rapture had now become a string of "Ooofs" and "Ows" and curses, one after the rest like a locomotive going off a cliff pulling all the cars with it. Concert became confusion, became chaos. Several in the house stood and let out exclamations of *"Gott Im Himmel!"* God in Heaven! A woman screamed. Blinky was in full throttle panic, trying to continue the music as more girls fell. People from the audience were coming on stage in an effort to help. A woman in the front row fainted and the man next to her began to fan her face with his fedora.

Gradually the scene began to return to order. The BDM girls took inventory of themselves. All seemed there, at least that's what they told Blinky. All were present and accounted for.

Except for two.

SECHS - SIX

Before the third *"Gott im Himmel!"* was shouted from the audience, Marta and I and the two HJs had escaped down the back stairs and evaporated into the brick tenements packing the bowels of Munich. Marta led the way, as would be expected, pulling her latest diversion behind her by the hand. Himmler junior, weasley and spectacled, thrust his hand out to grab mine and I instinctively recoiled. He turned and looked at me, Marta and Blondie already halfway up the block running at full tilt. I looked into Himmler's spectacled eyes searching for even a flicker of something I could trust, Blondie's boots clattering farther up the ever narrowing street. Just a hint of trust, from this stranger, just perhaps? I held my breath. Tentatively I reached my hand out as if trying to touch a sleeping lion's tooth. I managed a half-step toward him when he grabbed my hand and jerked me forward.

"Komm!" he said, his voice an equal blend of excitement and annoyance pulling me down the street. I struggled to keep up, nearly losing my footing on the cobbles, his Himmler hand clammy fish cold. He squeezed tight. We ran faster, Marta and Blondie disappearing into a narrow alley in a cloud of loud giggles. Himmler and I followed them in, pulling up short of Blondie pressed tight to Marta's lips, Marta trying to press harder against his. Himmler and I skidded to a stop on the alley stones, Blondie's hands marching their way down Marta's

back. Just as they prepared to launch a full scale assault of her buttocks, Marta countered his attack pushing back against his shoulders. Blondie turned to look at us, Marta's red lipstick spattered like gunshot wounds around his lips, neck and beige uniform collar.

"Finally!" Marta said. "What kept you?"

Himmler looked from me to Blondie then back to me, my look letting him know in no uncertain terms his face and uniform were absolutely free from danger. He continued to hold my hand, cold and clammy, but showed no sign of an impending frontal assault.

"Hanzi and I," Marta continued as his hands began another march down her spine, "are heading off for a little while. We will meet you in the *Marienplatz* at eight PM. Don't be late!" she grabbed Hanzi by the hand and began to pull him back into the street, he more than willing to follow.

"But, but . . . how will we get back to camp?" I said, not the slightest interest in masking a mouthful of metallic tasting panic.

Marta called over her shoulder, "We'll figure it out!"

"And where in the *Platz*?"

Marta had already turned the corner when I heard one word ricochet off the bricks.

"*Glockenspiel!*"

#

Himmler, who's named turned out to be Norbert, continued to hang onto my clammy hand in awkward silence. But I had my defense! *Tantchen* and a lifetime of farm and animals had never prepared me for this! Alone in the back alleys of Munich with a boy! It was as if some god had dropped me in a rudderless little boat jam filled with everything I held close to me: safety, pride, emotional stability, and set adrift. Not to mention my virginity! Another precious item in my boat suddenly up for grabs! Certainly Norbert could feel the mental, physical, and emotional stability draining out of some hole in the bottom of my heel leaving me a shuddering block of cold, clammy wood.

I snuck a quick glance at him, fast enough to be certain no eye contact could ever be made. Head down, silent, he trudged along, like a boy left to tend the *Milch* cow while his friend was off to some sensual circus. He left not a single shred of doubt that Hanzi had gotten the better half of this duo.

Gottdverdammt Marta! Goddamn it! Abandoning me! Where are you? Is this some kind of bad prank? As we began to walk I searched the nooks and narrows of the endless walls of ever repeating brick and windows. Surely they were squirreled away in some embrace, doing what more confident girls do in such a situation. Surely she was close. But I could not find her.

Maybe there was still time to sneak back into the music hall. Blinky would never know. Slide back in amongst the others and leave traitorous Marta and the HJs and escape the neck deep broth of lukewarm awkwardness I now found myself swimming in. I caught Norbert in full stride and jerked him in the opposite direction. Caught by surprise he spun on the heel of his polished black jack boot and followed me, happy, at least I thought, that I had some speck of initiative in me to do something. I pulled him faster, back toward the music hall. It should just be around the next corner.

I began to slow, suddenly feeling the pull of an angel on the back of my uniform. An evil angel. The angel of Disobedient Adventure. To see the magnificence of Munich, to partake in the whirlwind celebrations surrounding *des Führer's* birthday and perhaps, the angel's strongest tugging at my blouse, a chance to see *den Führer* himself! I stopped as I reached the corner, not daring to peep my head around. Would it be worth it? The angel, as evil as I know it was, fluttered about, dressed in a sheer gown of excitement, trimmed in tassels and ribbons of bright red thrills. Below it, like a dampened moth hovered another angel. The angel of Reason. Her voice barely registering: "What will Fraukenstein say?"

I turned to Norbert. "Do you know where the parade will be?"

"Certainly! It will be . . . "

"And will *Mein Führer* be there?" I pressed him, a smile beginning to form.

"I don't know," his spectacled face began to fill out the other half of my smile, "but we can see!"

"Then come on!" I said and pulled him along, without the slightest regard for direction.

#

Alleys emptied into streets which emptied into the grand boulevards of Munich, great *Strassen* of pavement, their medians wide ribbons of grass overhung with trees. Norbert and I waded into the human current of the city and became swept up in a river of merriment and optimism now flowing inexorably toward the center of the city: *Marienplatz*.

And the streets were bustling! People, upon people, each dressed in their finest clothes, endless replicas repeating in their sameness. Men in their *Lederhosen* and feathered caps, women in crisp white dirndls, topped with white winged hats, each spotless in their attire, the perfection of the *Reich* ready for review, ready in case *der Führer* might happen to glance their way.

Norbert and I worked our way down the sidewalk, attention to my evil angel causing my awkwardness and wooden legs to ease ever so slightly. Confidence was still nowhere to be found, but I could feel the clamminess between our hands begin to dry and the nervous urge to run or vomit, or both, began to subside.

Farther along, we reached the point where cars, busses and other non-military vehicles were no longer allowed. Soldiers at checkpoints on every street were screening people as they passed, an effort to keep the riff-raff from spoiling the solemnity of the occasion. When we approached he saw our uniforms, our clenched hands and, with a poorly concealed smile, waved us through.

On the corner, a young boy half our age and size, spotted us and raced forward. He was wearing a brown shirt and black pants similar to those Norbert was wearing. Proudly he sported a red, white, and black arm band held on with a safety pin to keep it from sliding off his matchstick of an arm. When he stopped in front of us he reached into a small purse he fanatically guarded and gave us each a small coin, then dashed away.

"What's this for?" Norbert asked, curious, but not really wanting an answer.

"It's a present from *dem Führer* on his birthday of course!" the young boy replied as if the answer were certainly obvious.

We studied the circular bit of new found prosperity we each now held in our hands, the *Hakenkreuz*, the hooked cross of the *Reich*, spinning in its center. Together Norbert and I continued to walk, the sound of a band playing, a speech being given coming closer. Excitement too was walking every street, dressed in its own uniform of polished pride, busy handing out the even greater coins of hope and optimism. And from their faces you could tell, each and every citizen held them proudly in their hands.

More steps and I could tell we were approaching the *Platz*. Beautiful church steeples and stoic government buildings shouldered each other for a view and to be viewed by the soon to be passing parade. Light feathers of smoke rose from almost every corner, the smell of roasted chestnuts, popcorn and

Würstl like sirens drawing ravenous sailors by the nose to their rocky demise.

We stopped at a cart and feasted on two sausage-like *Würstl* each. When we went to pay the old man in his blue and white checkerboard paper hat, he proudly acknowledged our uniforms and waved the coins off. Instead, he raised three fingers to a buxom woman on the opposite street corner. She bent low on a barrel strapped to the back of a horse drawn wagon and came up with four *Masskrüge,* large glass drinking mugs, of amber beer and balanced her way across the raging torrent of humanity. She handed the old man in his paper hat a beer, then one to each of us. *"Die Zukunft!"* The Future! the old man said, then, *Masskrug* to lips, he tipped the other end to the sky.

"Die Zukunft!" we repeated in unison and followed suit, Norbert pulling at his mug like a newborn, me taking two swallows then spouting a mouthful of hopsy foam out into the street. Norbert, the buxom woman, and the old man laughed as a second evil angel gently settled at my side. And I continued to drink.

With the beer no longer outside my body, the effects were beginning to make themselves known. My rudderless boat was still floating freely, but I was becoming less and less concerned with direction or outcome and beginning to merely enjoy the ride, two evil angels now at my side. Somewhere out there a speech was rattling on, the applause like the crackle of static on the dry goods store radio. Whoever he was, he was ranting on about the Jews, *die Juden,* calling them *Schweine,* pigs, everything about them *Kot,* filth, excrement, their thoughts and literature *vergiften,* poison. But this was common knowledge about the Jews. Everyone knew it.

The Jews and all the evil they had come to represent had become as prevalent and normal as the blue that filled our skies. Everyone knew it. All the adults said it, so it must be true, correct? Granted, I had had little personal contact with *den Juden* outside of the occasional sale of a lamb or goat to the butcher. He had always smiled beneath his black tangle of beard and seemed quite pleasant, always making sure I had a stick of hard candy before I left and a pat on the head with his large fat hand. He had two twin daughters that worked with him since, as Jews, they were no longer allowed to attend school. Hadn't they always seemed envious of the candy I received? Certainly they wouldn't have been had it been poisoned. Or perhaps it was only certain Jews they were talking about. I could never really be sure, and trying to figure it out with the fizzy, fuzzy head the buxom woman had handed me was certainly not going to happen today.

Just as we reached the *Marienplatz* the speech came to an abrupt halt, not even the crackle of applause following. Everything became silent, only a murmur of voices and the shuffle of feet on cobblestones. What was going on? Why was it so quiet? Was I missing something? I listened harder, deeper. Deeeeeeper!

BONG! . . . BONG! . . . Directly overhead! Each BONG! as if the hammer were striking my head and not the great bronze bells above me. BONG! A short pause, then the music began to play, smaller and medium bells of every size and tone playing like the announcement of the Final Coming. I backed up into the crowd and followed their gaze to the clock tower at the southern end of the square where life-size iron figures circled and danced to welcome the new hour. It was the *Glockenspiel*. At least now I knew where to meet Marta, if in fact she ever did show up.

And if the *Glockenspiel* was to be believed, as I knew it most certainly should, the parade would be starting in exactly one hour. It was also equally true that unless we could find a higher perch to view the parade, we would be able to see nothing more than the back of dirndls and feathered alpine hats. I looked to Norbert who was already scanning for high ground. He found some before I did and grabbed my hand, pulling me through the crowd like a small boat towed through rising water. At the far corner of the *Platz* a fire escape had been let down to allow some children and a few small adults a vantage for the parade. Norbert pulled the ladder down a little more so I could reach it and we began to climb. Rusty rung over rusty rung we made our way up. The first platform was too crowded so we made our way further up. The same was on the next, so we continued to climb till we reached the fourth level. Once again our uniforms bought us a secure spot and we dangled our legs beneath the railing.

From our high perch we could see the dark mass of crowd spread out below us, packed together but careful not to touch the other, darker, motionless mass filling the center of the *Platz*. A mass that even through the fuzziness of my eyes I could see was a great dark pile of books. More books than I had ever seen before. More books than I could read in a dozen lifetimes. If I had a dozen lifetimes to read them. And if I was ALLOWED to touch them. But I wasn't of course. For there were not only books on the pile, but posters, paintings, banners written in the curlicue letters of Hebrew. No, I certainly would not be allowed to touch this pile of books and material, nor would anyone else. For it was the *Kot von Schweinen*, the *Vergiften der Juden*.

We could hear the parade before we ever saw it, coming down the main thoroughfare of the *Ludwigstrasse* to our left. The heavy drums setting the marching cadence followed soon after by the Oompa of horns and woodwinds, reverberating up the canyons of brick and stone, and, I hoped, beyond. To any outsider that would ever dare threaten us again.

Then the first column of soldiers appeared, carrying banners of the hooked cross above them. Row after row of banners. Row after row of shiny black helmets, the width of the *Ludwigstrasse*, each accompanied by the flash of a bayonet. On and on they came followed by horse mounted cavalry, trucks and tanks and mechanized machinery stretching far up the *Strasse*. Along the route, people applauded and whistled and threw flowers on the troops and trucks and equipment as if somehow a truck would appreciate a rose or daisy, only to have the tank behind it grind it into the pavement. .

On and on came the parade, different bands playing different songs and marches. Sometimes people in the *Platz* would join a song as the band passed while others were content to wave their flags. But when the marching band struck the opening brass chords of *Erika,* the entire crowd, from wide-eyed child to gray-beard adult joined in! How could anyone remain silent!? It was a joyous celebration. *Der Führer* would most certainly be pleased and proud of the people of Bavaria.

Then Norbert nudged me. He pointed to the left, where *Ludwigstrasse* emptied the parade into the *Marienplatz.* On either side of the parade route, two columns of men, dressed completely in black, flanked the road. Black helmets, black uniforms, shiny black belts and boots, machine guns hung across their chest. On their helmets were a shield containing the twin silver "SS" lightning bolts of the *Shutzstaffel.* The Protection Squadron; *des Führer's* personal soldiers, loyal only to him. They continued to the end of the *Platz,* then stopped. On a command they all turned and faced the crowd and the great pile of Jewish poison the people held captive. Men appeared from the crowd and surrounded the pile, as if somehow the pile would try to escape. But it couldn't. And it didn't. A man raced around the circumference of the pile with a lit torch lighting the torches of the other men who held the pile of poison captive. On another barked command, each man set his torch to the pile, which appeared to have been pre-dosed with something to get the fire quickly up to business. In less than a minute the flames had reached the height of our perch nearly four stories up, throwing off a heat that pushed the crowd even further back.

A line of long trumpets entered the Platz, stopped and blew a great fanfare, each trumpet draped in the red, white, and black. They continued on followed by a long convertible Mercedes-Benz. In the Mercedes, men in the closely cut gray and black uniform of officers, stood, their arms out straight, palms flat to the ground. Passing the burning heap of books and *Juden* lies, pages of ash and embers floated like non-repentant souls on the furnace of air.

Then Norbert grabbed my arm. He grabbed it so hard I could feel his fingernails digging into my flesh. He pulled my attention from the flames and toward the sound of more trumpets. Another Mercedes was approaching, this one larger and longer than the first, polished to the very depth of its chrome. It was surrounded by more men, only these did not did not wear helmets or carry machine guns, their only uniform long black leather coats. And as they walked, they watched the crowd, ever vigilant, ready, as of course we all were, to sacrifice their life at a moment's notice for the solitary man who stood in the Mercedes behind them. *Der Führer.* Our *Führer.* Adolph Hitler.

Der Führer too, held his arm out straight, palm down as he passed the mountain of flames. He could well have been a statue for all he moved, but that did not deter the crowd. Flowers began to be thrown in great volleys in front of the car, the men in their black trench coats even more vigilant for a flaming bottle of petrol or a "potato masher" grenade. But there were none. Not here. Not in Bavaria. And certainly not here in Munich, the birthplace of the Nazi Party. Only flowers, and more flowers and what seemed to be the endless roar of adulation from the crowd. On and on they went until long after *Der Führer* had left the *Platz* and continued on down *Ludwigstrasse* followed by the trench coats, the trucks, and the soldiers. Finally, those all in black, with the lightning bolts on their helmets, departed, leaving the crowd with nothing but the memory of his presence, and an optimism not even the darkening sky could contain. A sky. even now, being cleansed by the flames.

Norbert and I stood and stretched our legs. We both turned and passed each other a knowing smile that whatever punishment befell us tomorrow, it was worth it. Worth it by a dozen times. A thousand times. For we had personally witnessed *den Führer*. How many of the girls in the BDM could claim that? Had Marta seen it? Probably not. Probably too busy with her blonde companion for the evening to have taken the time to behold our perfect leader. The man who had saved us, and saved our country. The man to whom all men should aspire to become, but too many, most, never even try. But perhaps that is what the average man is about.

The fire escape had cleared out, but instead of climbing back down the way we came, Norbert took my hand and we stepped into the window of the apartment it serviced. It was dark and empty, a splendidly decorated room that the owners had left unattended to watch the parade. I made my way to the door. As I reached for the doorknob I felt Norbert's hand on top of mine. He gently pulled my hand away from the knob and pulled it slowly around his waist. The effects of the buxom maiden's brew were still with me, but I could feel their powers were beginning to wane. I stumbled a bit but Norbert held me up. Red and orange squares of light criss-crossed each other on the ceiling above us from the fire in the *Platz*, warm and comforting in some primeval way. He pulled me closer looking directly into my eyes, wide behind his rimless spectacles, our noses almost touching. Then he kissed me. Or should I say he pressed his lips against mine. Immediately the woodenness of me returned and I froze. Solid. My lips instinctively seemed to pull tight and in upon themselves as if defending against an intruder. He reached his arm around my back and pulled the statue I had become closer to himself, his lips still holding firm against their target. From below I could feel another unknown evil angel beginning to rise, this more powerful than the other two before it. More terrifying in its intensity, growing under the exploring touch of Norbert's hand on my back. It settled squarely in my loins and continued to burn. He slid his hand under the left side of my blouse, the pounding of blood in my ears deafening, blocking out all else. He pulled my head closer still as his bare hand moved up my naked side, the orange squares dancing merry above us, across his face and spectacles, mirroring the fire now consuming my entire being. Slowly the smoothness of his hand progressed up, my rudderless little boat now heading toward a great waterfall. And I letting it.

Further up still until it reached the lower hemisphere of my left breast.

I sucked in a deep breath and pushed Norbert away, staring him full in the eyes, my face, I'm sure, painted in fear, determination and the flames of the furnace raging below. He paused for a moment, awkward and barren air filling the gulf between us. Tears began to rim my eyes. He slowly shook his head, gave a little laugh and quietly slipped a dagger of words into my heart,

"*Du bist nur ein Kind,*" he whispered. You are only a child. He gave me one last look and left, leaving me alone in the empty apartment, his footsteps disappearing down the creaking floorboards of the hall.

I stood there in silence, unable to move, unable to even comprehend what had happened, but grateful for what didn't. The sound of the fire outside continued to crackle through the glass windows. I blew out a great long breath as the statue of myself began to thaw. Alone in this magnificent apartment, surrounded by ornate furniture and oriental carpets the blood began to return to my muscles. I stepped to the front windows to see if I could see Herr Himmler departing the building, never to return.

Outside, a starless April night had fallen across the shoulders of Munich. The heap had now burned down to half its former size, a black wavering lump criss-crossed with a spiderweb of flame. Most of the spectators had departed the *Platz*, but many still remained, enjoying the spectacle of the hate filled flames, singing, laughing, sloshing their *Masskrüge* on the cobblestones.

From the south end, a shadowy rabble of a half dozen men entered the *Platz*, bearing an object high above their heads like hunters returning with a trophy. The assembled crowd parted to let them through, their arrival heralding much applause, laughter and shouting. Trailing the rabble and their prize ran an older man in a flat black hat, stumbling across the cobbles in the life-or-death panic of someone fleeing a fire. Only he was running towards one.

The rabble stopped at the heap and raised their trophy high. It was only then that I could see it in the flicker of light. It was a block rectangle of bright purple cloth, embraced with golden letters in the Hebrew script, two polished wooden handles protruding from the base. From my school books and lessons of what to avoid of *den Juden*, I knew it to be a Torah, a book they read in their ceremonies, the first five books of the Bible. But hadn't *Tantchen* and I spent many a cold night near the stove reading these very books as well as the rest of the Bible? The stories of creation. Of Abraham, of Moses and Joseph with his colored coat. Certainly this was not poison. There must be some mistake here.

Two of the men grabbed the ends of the Torah and proceeded to swing it back and forth as *Tantchen* and I would swing a sack of grain into the barn to feed the pigs. Back and forth the two men swung it, building up momentum. Just as the man in the flat black hat reached them, he threw himself over the Torah and clutched it to him like a father embracing his child for the last time. The rabble began to laugh and shout and the rest of the crowd began to encircle the spectacle as it was unfolding. More laughter, more shouting as drunken men began to pry the black hat-ted man from their prize causing him to cling all the more tightly. Someone grabbed his black hat and spun it into the fire.

But he never let go.

Other men appeared and still he continued his death grip. Even from four floors up, through the glass of the windows, above the roar of the fire I could hear his unconsolable wail. Desperately he clung on, wailing, seemingly unaffected by the buffeting blows against his back until finally he was wrenched free. Fingers still extended, three men pulling him back, the two again began to swing the Torah. Then the crowd began to chant. *"Eins, Zwie, Drei . . . "* One, two, three . . . and on *"Drei"* the Torah was swung up onto the burning ribbons of flames. The old man let out a guttural wail to the delight of the crowd. He ran toward the fire, his toes reaching the embers before he was forced back. He stood and watched, surrounded by the crowd, by a hatred that filled the *Platz* from wall to wall and followed the flames into the sky. He continued to watch as the flames enveloped his Holy Word, devouring the wine colored cover, the golden script, peeling back the scroll layer by flaming layer. At last he let out a long howling wail and collapsed to the cobblestones in a sobbing heap. Their entertainment done for the evening, the drunken rabble shambled away into the shadows leaving the old man to sob for his lost "child". I stood and watched him, staring out the window for many minutes. He was unable to move, and neither could I.

This was no *Hafermann*.

I backed away from the windows of the apartment and made my way down the creaking hallway to the stairs. Out into the *Platz*, the dying flames painting the faces of the buildings, their tall windows like eyes wide in amazement. I made my way to the *Glockenspiel* to wait.

The life-size iron figures of the *Glockenspiel* danced their way though the hours as I stood alone. Seven, eight and then nine, but still no sign of Marta. It was half past nine when a familiar figure dressed in the blouse and skirt of the BDM appeared on *Ludwigstrasse*, walking amidst the crushed flowers and spilled beer. The fire was now a dark mass of embers when Marta came into view under the street lamp. She smiled the weak smile of someone contented but with all of their energies spent.

"*Jämmerlich*," she said. "Sorry for being my miserable late self, *Küken*."

I said nothing, allowing my fury to speak for itself.

"I know, I know," she went on, "I have let you down, I don't know how many times I can say I am sorry before you'll believe it, but I am."

I still said nothing.

"There is a laundry truck leaving here in an hour, headed back to *Ülmstadt*. I've managed to get us a lift. We'll only have to walk a few miles at most."

Silence was my answer.

She stood before me and stopped, wobbling back and forth on her heel, "I know, I know, again I'm sorry. Did you have a nice time with . . . "

"Norbert. His name was Norbert, and he had his hands all over me!"

She put her hand on her hip and cocked it out, a half smile on her lips, "Not necessarily a bad thing," she said.

"It was horrible! Where were you, why did you abandon me?"

"Abandon you? Hardly! I just left you two to, you know, get acquainted," her smile grew.

"He mauled me! Where were you?"

"Hanzi and I did a little tour of the town. We had fun," her smile began to curl into a frown, "I'm sorry you didn't."

"I can tell you had a good time. A VERY good time!" I said, this time almost yelling.

"You can?" she said looking at me confused.

"Yes, I can. For starters, your skirt is on inside out!"

She looked down, back to me, then back to her skirt. When her eyes met mine again, she burst into a rattling laugh that rivaled even the *Glockenspiel*.

SIEBEN - SEVEN

From three stalls down I could hear a song being sung, sad, mournful, reverberating among the tile walls of the boys latrine. Dramatic in its delivery, overly dramatic in fact, steadily chiseling away at the foundations of my anger.

The song continued:

"I'm sorry Katerina,

so sorry you see.

So please Katerina,

won't you forgive me?"

This followed by a chorus of the *SKRISH* - *SKRISH* - *SKRISH*ing of the concrete floor being scrubbed with a stiff brush.

"Oh please Katerina,

I screwed up,

you seeeeeee."

A deep breath is taken then the finale is belted out.

"My dear friend Katerina,

Entschuldigen Sieeee!" Excuse meeeee!

There was a CLUNK and a SPLASH as the scrub brush was dropped into a metal bucket of soapy water. Quick footsteps and Marta fell to her knees at the door of the stall I was busy scrubbing. She was wearing a long apron, her blonde hair coiled back in a checkered cloth, comically large orange gloves clenched before her in abject supplication. "Come on *Küken!* Come ON! You can't fight an apology song like THAT!" Marta said dramatically batting her over-ly large brown eyes.

And of course she was right. I couldn't fight it. Hard as I tried to remain angry I burst out in a laugh. She jumped over and gave me a huge hug, squeezing me between the wall of the stall and the toilet bowl. She whispered in my ear. "I really am sorry *Küken*. Your friend can be such an *Dummkopf* idiot some-times. Do you forgive me?" I gave a little nod and she hugged me a little harder. She backed away, but not before giving the slightest of kisses on my cheek, then sat down cross legged on the floor before me. I scooched myself out and rested my back against the front of the bowl. Marta looked at me, her eyes spoke nothing but compassion.

"What happened," she said, although some-how I was certain she had already figured it out. I started to talk but clammed up. "Come on," she pressed quietly. "I'm your friend aren't I? This is what friends do," she stared at the concrete floor as she waited for me to say more.

To say Fraukenstein was angry when she caught up with us was an understatement. After our rogue day in Munich, she was livid. At this morning's formation Marta and I were verbally flayed before the entire BDM for the wickedness of our break for free-dom and sentenced to spending the day cleaning the boys latrine. It was a filthy job. But it had the added benefit that we had avoided marching exercises and all of the other events that were going on that day. We were also left alone.

I told Marta what happened. Most of it, careful to leave my feelings out of it. No need to fill her in on the length and breadth and cargo of my little rudderless boat. Or the *Hafermann* in the flat black hat. Just stick to the facts. No sense leaving my heart out for someone else to stab. And who knows where that information would end up.

"And then he tried to kiss me," I said, concluding the facts.

"Tried?" she said, her voice still quiet in compassion. "Did he . . . succeed?"

I could feel my eyes beginning to well. No, no, NO! I screamed to myself, don't fall apart here! Be strong! God help me if Marta ever tells ANYONE I broke down over a boy trying to kiss me!! I'll be laughed out of the BDM! If Marta tells ANYONE, they will tell EVERYONE! I bit my lower lip on the inside trying to stem the flood. I said nothing.

Martha pressed quietly, "Was that your first kiss?" my traitorous head gave an imperceptible nod, my eyes beginning to well again. I bit my inner lip till I was certain I was drawing blood.

"And you didn't know what to do?" her brown eyes, never wavering in their compassion, drilled into me. Into my boat. Into my soul. Eyes never leaving hers, an immeasurable shake of my head.

She held my eyes, and returned the immeasurable shake of the head. She closed her eyes, and tipped her head back as if going into a trance. Then she slapped her two comical orange gloves together with a loose rubbery WHAP! and let out a great blow of ratcheting laughter!

I sprung from my spot against the bowl and launched myself on top of her like an injured animal. But she only continued to laugh. I tried to inflict some damage commensurate with the damage done to my pride but that would have certainly meant pummeling Marta to death. Or worse! She simply covered her face with her gloves as I punched her with mine. *"Küken! Küken!"* she said through the gloves and laughter. Even though she was almost precisely my size, she was still very strong and able to rebuke my large rubbery fists. *"Küken! Küken!"* I threw my gloves to the side and adjusted my position to deliver bare knuckle blows. But before I could Marta made a quick maneuver and in a blink I was flat on my back on the cold concrete floor and she was on top. It would appear that despite all my years of farm labor, I was no match for the wrestling moves of Marta Koenigsberg.

She calmly adjusted her hair as I tried in vain to wiggle out, "A little move an HJ taught me," she said and gave a little more of a chuckle. Then the smile disappeared from her face, "I'm not laughing at you. I'm remembering. Remembering THOSE days. Before I knew," she peeled her gloves off and tossed them aside, rubbing her nose with her forearm. She looked down on me.

"Why didn't you tell me?" she said. "Before. Why didn't you tell me before."

But my eyes once again spoke nothing but fury. I couldn't answer. She brought her nose down to mine, "Listen *mein Küken*, in another two weeks, we are heading off to *Landdienst*. For a couple of months. Back in the woods. And those woods, my dear *Küken* friend are crawling, and I mean CRAWLING, with HJs," she looked down at me, very serious. "And you and I, my friend, are going to get us a couple. Do you follow me?"

I looked up at her and tried to speak, but nothing came out.

"You are coming with me," she continued. "If you don't know what you're doing you've got two weeks to learn," she leaned back again and rubbed her forearm beneath her nose. A devious smile began to spread from her lips to her eyes as she finished, "and I'm going to teach you."

Marta hopped off of me and positioned her back against the wall. Her knees tight together pointing straight at me. She motioned me to the front of the "classroom" and stand before a long trough urinal, flecked with crusted yellow. I walked over and stood there, hands on hips,

"First things first," Marta began. "Rule number one: Men are *blöd, dumm*, stupid. Dumb as the dirt they stand on. Whenever you are wondering what is going on in their heads, remember rule number one. There is NOTHING going on in their heads! *Ich habs*? Look at that thing behind you," she pointed at the urinal. "They're not even smart enough to get their *Pisse* in that big damn thing! God help us if we ever get in another war the way they aim! A dog does better on a tree. And a dog has more brains, more feelings. Men will step on you and your feelings like a big *dummes* horse. They don't even know they are doing it!"

"Tell me something I don't know. I have not exactly had the best experiences with the men in my life."

Marta grabbed a cigarette and lit it, blowing the smoke at the factory light fixtures above. "*Gut!* Then we are on the same page. Don't ever stick your feelings out there for them. Ever. Keep them tight. In here," she tapped her chest with her thumb. "Himmler back there," she shook her head, "a piece of *Scheisse*. Shit. I'm so glad you DIDN'T kiss him. *Zecken!* Bloodsucker! He doesn't deserve you! We'll find someone good for you."

"I don't know Marta. Maybe I'm not . . . ready for this."

She pointed the cigarette at me, "Of course you are! Maybe you just don't know it yet. But you are. We'll find you someone, up in *Landdienst*. And if the first one doesn't pan out," she jerked her thumb over her shoulder, "*futsch! Raus!* Done! Busted! Out! We find another one! Like bowling pins, set 'em up, knock 'em down." by this time I was completely smiling again.

"Men," she took another long drag and blew it out, "they only want one thing," she said and separated her knees slightly.

"What?" I said.

Marta rolled her eyes and opened her legs up a little wider. My eyes went wide and I covered my mouth.

"*Ich habs?*" she said closing her legs and giving me a wink.

"*Die Scham?* I whispered through my fingers. The private parts?

Ich habs!" she said.

I nodded slowly in realization.

"That's not to say you don't give it to them. If they are good enough. If they are worth it. If they earn it. They just have to earn it. It's not free," she said. "and that's your decision, not his."

I nodded in understanding "'Too easily won makes the prize seem cheap.'" I said. She smiled in agreement. "Shakespeare said that," I finished.

"Smart guy. Yep. To any guy worth his *Schwanz* that's the *Volltreffer*, the bullseye. That's where they score the points. Your job is to catch their eye and lure them to it."

"No Marta. I don't. No, I don't know that I'm ready to . . . you know . . . just yet. I want it to be . . . right! The right man. I want things to be . . . special!"

She waved her hand in front of her face and rolled her eyes again, "*Gott im Himmel!! Jungfrauen!* God in heaven!! Virgins! That is what men are after. *Die Scham.* That is what they want. The trick is to get them close without actually giving it away. The way a fisherman dangles his worm on the end of hook. That keeps them interested, keeps them following you.

That's what you want. Create some . . . " she slowly blew a little smoke around her " . . . mystery."

I nodded slowly, "'The god of love lives in a state of need.'" I said quietly.

"Shakespeare again?" she said.

"Plato."

"You hang out with some pretty smart guys," she said hopping up, "time to start hanging out with some *Dummköpfen.*"

"*Ich habs,*" I agreed.

"We'll get you there cookie. Find you the right one. All you need is some practice. But, you must have all your tools ready and sharpened to catch the right one when he DOES come along! That's what I'm doing, just sharpening my tools. You must learn, *Küken,* experience! And practicing can be fun!" she gave me a sensuous look and ran the tip of her tongue across her upper lip. "You must practice! You must learn the ways of *die Zuckerstange,*" she said smiling. His "candy cane".

I must have been quite the sight standing there, staring at her, my lower jaw hanging loose. But as always Marta jumped in again and filled in the blanks.

"But before any of that you must FIRST, catch a man. And to do that the first thing you must catch is his attention. Now, "she said, again waving her ciga-retted hand, "show me what you've got!"

"What do you . . . ?"

"Walk. Walk back and forth. Right here," she laid out the track with her forefinger in the space before the urinal.

I walked back and forth a few times, then stopped and faced her. She had her hand over her face in complete embarrassment. She grunted softly.

"No?" I said.

"*Küken*, you are trying to attract a man, not lead a cow into the barn," she hopped up. "Here, you sit and watch."

I sat. I watched.

Marta walked back and forth in front of the urinal, her body undulating as she walked, like the pendulum of a clock. Head high, confident, the look of someone who knew what they were about. Back and forth she went. She flipped her long blonde brown hair casually over her shoulder, "Are you getting it Kat?" she said. She grabbed her rear with both hands as she walked, "*Die Kiste*, the butt, back and forth, back and forth, boom-bah-boom, boom-bah-boom. Up and down, up and down. Like *knallen*, screwing, only standing up. And these," she said, cupping her hands under her breasts, "*Die Möpse*, keep them up and out, show 'em what you got! *Ich habs*? Now you try it again."

She plopped herself back down against the wall and fiddled for a cigarette, her eyes never leaving me. I walked. *Die Möpse* up. Back and forth, forth and back. Marta called out commands as I walked and I continued to make adjustments until finally Marta said "*Sehr gut!*" Very good! I blew out my breath, tired from holding *die Möpse* up, and plopped myself down in front of her on the concrete floor.

"Sehr gut Küken, sehr gut," a cigarette bouncing on her lips as she lit it.

All through the morning Marta continued with her training, as tough and demanding as Fraukenstein could ever be. Continuing to polish my walk, teaching me how to look without being seen and how to speak with my eyes when I was. Body positions, how to sit, how to stand, how to turn on *die Lecker*, the yummy, as she would call it, when I needed it. By the time we heard the kangle of the mess hall triangle calling us to lunch, I was starting to feel more comfortable. More confident. I tried to practice some of my walk on the way over and Marta shot me a look. A serious look that said in no uncertain terms was I to show the others what she had shown me. Not to use my "secret weapons" unless the time was right. I stopped immediately and returned to my *Milch* cow stride.

We ate together by ourselves which seemed to delight all parties concerned. Us, because it gave Marta a chance to tell me what to talk about once I had a boy's ear. Them, because the odor of the boys latrine now hung over us like a septic cloud. As we departed heading back to the latrine, Marta took a slight detour toward the scullery. When she returned, she had something tucked up under her blouse. We continued to walk.

When we had reentered the latrine, she removed the pilfered article from under her uniform top. It was an empty clear glass bottle.

"What on earth do you plan on doing with that?" I said, nervous that our lessons had wandered dangerously into unknown territory.

"Kissing lessons," she said and handed me the bottle. "OK *Küken*, show me how you kiss," I looked at her perplexed. "The bottle," she continued, "kiss the bottle."

I did as she asked and gently gave the side of the bottle a peck. Once again, she rolled her eyes.

"No?" I said.

"No. Kiss the bottle. The opening of the bottle. Show me how you kiss the opening."

I turned the bottle around and, lips pursed tightly together, gave the open end of the bottle a peck. Then again and again. I looked over to Marta, but again, she had both hands over her face. She took the bottle away from me.

"Now pay attention, *Küken*," she held the bottle horizontal, the mouth gently to her lips. She opened her own mouth and closed it again against the glass, the tip of her tongue gently probing inside. I stood transfixed, unable to watch, unable to not watch. It was sensual and disgusting all at the same time. She pulled the bottle slowly away from her lips with a satisfied look on her face. She wiped the mouth of the bottle off with the hem of her blouse and handed it back to me. "Now try it again."

I did. It was a little better or so I felt, or at least it seemed to me. A little more movement, a little more flexibility, a little less keeping my lips like the beak of a bird. When I was finished again, I checked Marta's face for my score. She slowly shook her head.

"You've got to loosen up Kat! You've got to loosen EVERYTHING up! Loose, loose!" she rubbed my upper arms up and down quickly like someone trying to revive a person that had fallen through the ice of a frozen pond. She looked at me again, paused, grabbed the bottle and disappeared out the door. In a matter of minutes she returned with a few ounces of brown liquid in the glass bottle.

"Now try it," she said, handing the bottle back to me. I held it up and looked at the liquid swirling inside.

"What is this?" I said. I sniffed the mouth and flinched.

Marta took the bottle from me and sniffed it herself. Then she took a swig. She handed it back to me.

"It's OK, it's just a little *schnaps*. The groundskeeper Klaus keeps a bottle in his tool shed to keep things 'lubricated', if you know what I mean," again she winked at me.

I placed the bottle back up to my mouth. As it reached horizontal, a little sloshed against my lips. I jerked backward a bit, and lowered the bottle back down. The taste was sharp and bitter, a biting smell reminiscent of the turpentine my father used to clean his paint brushes.

"I don't know that I can do this Marta." I said wiping my lips. "The smell of it. It . . . It brings up some bad memories."

"Just try it. Once you've swallowed enough, you won't remember anything anyway!" She said with a smile.

I returned the bottle to my lips and pushed my father from my mind. I tipped it forward again and swallowed, just a bit, allowing Klaus's lubrication to hit the back of my throat. It burned on the way down, but warmed me inside in an odd sort of way, a familiar evil angel now fluttering beside me. The liquid amber of the *Masskrüge* on the Munich street once again began melting my inhibitions. I took another swallow. I began to kiss the mouth of the bottle like Marta, loose and sensual, at least in my mind. I kissed it as if I were kissing my very own *Prinz Wunderbar* for the very first time on the night of the ball. And he was kissing me back. Somewhere, far, far away, I could hear Marta Koenigsberg applauding.

ACHT - EIGHT

For the next two weeks Marta's lessons continued in earnest. The latrine project took a full three days for results to meet Fraukenstein's satisfaction, during which time Marta improved my walk, facial expressions, and bending over of all things! And almost every night, Marta would sneak over to my top bunk near the wall and together we would talk well past curfew, two solitary voices in the absoluteness of dark.

On one occasion, Marta showed up at my upper bunk, the *Adlerhorst* as she called it, the eagles nest, but instead of climbing up she reached for my hand. "Come on," she whispered, "class outing." I followed her quietly through the dark, threading the rows of bunk beds until we reached the exit door. A girl in a uniform with a heavy black flash light and red sash across her chest stood up as we approached the door.

"I can't let you go out, Marta," the girl said in a rather high voice. "Those are my Night Orders." She was barely thirteen.

"Sure you can Genevieve. It'll be Okay." Marta said.

"But what if there is a bed check?"

"You can cover for us, right?"

"No," Genevieve said timidly "I don't know if I . . ."

"Sure you can," Marta repeated, giving her a little pat on her shoulder and a look that made the girl wither a little bit more. "Sure you can," and we slipped quietly out the door.

We crossed the field in darkness, a quarter moon showing us the foot path we had walked so many times during the day that we could almost have done it blindfolded.

"The other girls are pretty good about helping you out with things like that. Like Genevieve watching the door back there," I said.

Marta was in front of me. I could see her shoulders shrug a bit in the dim light. "It's a gift I have. Mostly my charming personality," she said with a chuckle. Then she added with just a hint of darkness in her voice. "And they fear me," another chuckle, "just a bit."

"Why should they ever be afraid of you, for heaven sake?" I said.

She walked along the foot path for a moment in silence, carefully checking her steps on a path she knew too well. The flotilla of tombstones, pearl gray in the moonlight, rose from the grass before us. From this angle, the lines of Hebrew script across each were clear, cryptic runes fractured in moon shadow. Across the face of each stone, someone had painted a slap-dash swastika, the dark red paint purple in the moon-light, left to drip like blood from an open wound.

When she answered, a thin thread of serious-ness tempered her words.

"I know people," she said.

"People?" I asked

"People," she repeated as if somehow that would clarify things. When it was clear it didn't, she continued, "People who know people," she paused again, then finished. "Leave it at that."

But I couldn't. My face betrayed my concern.

She stopped and turned to face me, her face ghostly and pale in the alabaster light.

"Nothing to worry about Kat. Really. Nothing. You know why?"

I shook my head.

"Because of that," she said and raised the index and middle fingers of her right hand before my face. They were wrapped one around the other. "Do you know what that is?"

Again, I shook my head.

"That's how close you and I are. You and me. As close as any two things could ever be. *Verstehst du?*" Understand?

I nodded and gave a little smile which Marta returned. "Now to business!" she said.

Marta homed in on Klaus's shed and removed a key from a ledge under the deck. She opened the rusty padlock on the door and twisted the hasp with a loud groan crying out to anyone about its violation. But no one responded. A solitary bulb hung from the ceiling but Marta didn't touch it. I heard her rummaging in the dark on a top shelf, clunking about amongst some half-empty paint cans. She pulled a box down from the shelf and wrapped it in the painter's rag that had covered it then slipped back out, closing the door behind her.

But Marta's words continued at my heels like our following shadows as we approached the old synagogue. I turned them over in my head several times, rearranging pieces of thought, hoping for their edges to align in the form of a proper question. But they didn't. In the blue shadows of the old brick building my words simply tumbled out.

"Do you . . . think . . . these people you know . . . could help find someone? Someone . . . missing."

She stopped ahead of me and turned, her silhouette silent far too long, as if my words had crossed some invisible line.

"Maybe," she said, then added as only Marta could. "If it were done properly."

"Do you mean . . . ?"

Again her silhouette went uncomfortably silent.

I answered the question for her, "I know, 'Leave it at that'"

Silently she turned and continued to walk.

We entered through a side door and into a small room ornate with the Star of David and Menorahs carved into the polished cherry paneling. Marta put the pilfered package on a table and removed the painter's cloth with a magician's flourish revealing a paint spattered Telefunken radio instead of a rabbit. She plugged it in and it slowly came to life with a whistle and a crackle of static. Impatiently she turned the dial, voices and "old people's music" squirting out in bits and pieces between more whistles and static. Up and down the dial until one mesmerizing voice stopped her.

"*Das deutsche Volk hat noch nicht gelernt, welche Gefahren Adolf Hitler ihnen bringt.*" "The German people have yet to learn the dangers Adolph Hitler is leading them into."

Marta quickly twisted the dial hard, landing on a cloud of angry static. She let out a breath and looked around. Then she composed herself and continued to methodically work her way down the dial until she found what she was looking for. A trumpet was playing, soft and sweet, more magic than music.

Marta grabbed me by the shoulders, her nose almost touching mine. "Oh I love this one!" she whispered. Then a gravelly voiced man named Louis Armstrong began to sing and comically tone deaf Marta, joined in as well.

"Grab your coat and grab your hat, and leave your worries on the doorstep, just direct your feet, on the sunny side of the street."

When the song ended, the radio crackled contentedly while in some distant location someone put on a new record. What followed the crackle of static was loud! Very loud! A blast of horns, trumpets, trombones, several squealing at the end of their notes as if being asked to give beyond the limits of the musician's lungs. Then came the fast syncopated rattle of drums. Snare drums, base drums, thundering kettle drums. I stared in amazement at Marta. She yelled above the music.

"It's called Jazz!" she said, "do you like it?"

I was nodding quickly, unable to take my eyes off the radio as if somehow my eyes would help draw this magnificent music into my ears. Marta turned the volume down, afraid that the sounds of Benny Goodman would bring too much unwanted attention.

"Once we pick up some HJs we can get them to dance. Do you know how to dance?" Marta said.

I shook my head vigorously.

"Then it's time you learned!" she said, grabbed my arm and spun me around. And over the next two hours, rooted on by an audience of polished cherry carvings, Marta taught me, "Katerina *der Klotz*", to dance. And not just dance. Swing dance! Around the room we danced, my catching on quicker than I could have ever imagined under the tutelage of the most capable teacher. That and the unstoppable beat of Jazz music coursing through my veins like liquid lightning. Up and down, forward and back we spun and laughed, Marta spinning me around and flipping me over her back. Across the floor, bouncing me off her hip and shooting me through her legs, then showing me how to do the same to her.

It was just shy of two in the morning when the music finally stopped with a long screech of horns like an angry flock of geese and a crash of percussion. A commercial came on for some sort of soap.

"I need a smoke and a *Spritze*." Marta said. Squirt. She stepped out the door and disappeared amongst the tombstones. While she was gone, I fiddled with the dial for a few minutes, hoping to find some more music.

Then I heard the voice again.

"Er ist nicht der Anführer, an den Sie glauben. Die Gaskammer erwartet diejenigen, die ihre Stimme benutzen. Vorsicht, der Sturmwind ist angekommen."

"He is not the leader you believe him to be. The gas chamber awaits those that use their voice. Beware, the storm wind has arrived."

With those last few words, the ghost of a hand touched my head and was gone. Marta rushed through the door and turned the radio off with a ferocity that nearly spun the knob off in her fingers. Then she closed her eyes, collecting herself. Without opening them she whispered through her teeth.

"That's enough for tonight."

#

Silently we walked the path, the moon, now low in the western sky, trailing blue ghosts behind us past the ranks of desecrated tombstones. We reached the painter's shed, groaned the padlock open, and both slipped inside. Marta returned the radio back to its spot on the shelf beneath the painter's rag and left without a word. Turning in the darkness to follow her, I passed through a magician's fog of aromatic dreams, the piney-sweet scent of turpentine like Proust's madeleines immediately conjuring another childhood memory. It flashed across the mirror of my mind's eye like the hem of some specter's shadow passing behind me. Words my father had spoken every night as he tucked me in:

"Beschütze meine Tochter vor dem Sturmwind"
"Protect my daughter from the storm wind"

For several nights Marta did not visit the *Adlerhorst*, barely saying two words to me during the day. I tried to talk to her, but for one reason or another she had little time and when she did, her words were short and clipped. In the few short weeks that I had come to know Marta Koenigsberg I had also come to realize mercurial was just one of the many faces she wore. I thought it best to give her some space until whatever things that had appeared between us were sorted out and continued to make pleasantries with the other girls. It also became apparent that I needed to focus on the tasks ahead and getting some much needed sleep. I had a feeling that I would be needing it once we reached *Landdienst*.

But it was not peaceful sleep. The dream of the *Hühnerstall* had returned. It still had its effects on me, like certain words a close friend can say when they are angry. Pointed words that probe places no one knows you have. Painful places.

And then there was a new dream. A flat black hat thrown onto the fire, waves of heat carrying it up into the sky, into nothingness.

On the night before we were to depart to *Landdienst*, Marta reappeared at the *Adlerhorst*, and knocked on the slats of my bed as if she were knocking on a door.

"*Komm herein*," I said quietly. Come in.

Marta climbed up the end of the bed and settled herself crosslegged opposite me.

"Miss me?" she said.

"Of course!" I answered brightly. And I did.

For almost a minute, an awkward emptiness filled the darkness between us like a shapeless animal. Then I stabbed it in the heart.

"Thank you," I said.

"For?" she whispered.

"For teaching me. For teaching me EVERY-THING!" I said and squeaked out a little giggle.

I could sense Marta looking at me. "*Kein Problem.*" Not a problem. "I did the best I could," then she added, "you're a pretty horrible student."

"I know!" I agreed. Then we both started to giggle.

In the darkness she slid herself across my blanket until her knees touched mine then leaned over and hugged me. She kissed my cheek, soft and tender in the darkness.

"However did you learn so much about . . . things," I said.

She leaned back on her elbows. "Oh, I'm just an observer, I guess. And a bit of a mad scientist. You know, trial and error. See what works, what doesn't. What's working for some people and what isn't. Like Poppy and Mum, seeing how they treat each other. They are a pretty perfect couple in their own pretty perfect little world."

I settled back on my elbows allowing her the stage to continue.

"I don't know. It all just fits. They fit. Together. The way puzzle pieces lock together so you can't get them apart. That's the way they are. She's your classic lipstick Nazi, fingernails polished and perfect, eyebrows tweezed, wigs to match the dress and shoes. Everything just so. Loves to parade around the house telling the cook and the housekeeper what to do. Adjusting bedspreads and curtains. Fawning all over my brother."

"You have a brother?" I said.

"Yeah. Kurt," she said, the air going out of her voice. "He's pretty perfect too, I suppose. Eighteen. Tall, muscles, blonde hair, blue eyes, you know, like an Aryan youth poster stuck on the side of a bus. Dad loves to parade Kurt around at work. 'Look at my boy' he tells people. 'The face of the new Germany.' I hate him!" she said with a little laugh.

"He sounds pretty perfect to me," I said.

"Oh he is a tough one to have in the house let me tell you.'Why can't you be more like your brother?' Mum would always say to me, wondering why she could never get the 'wrinkles' out of me the way she could the bedspreads," Marta went silent. Someone in an adjoining bunk turned over causing their bed slats to squeak.

I changed the subject.

"And your . . . father? What does he do?"

"Do?" she said off guard. She looked into the darkness off to her left, "Oh, he's a bureaucrat . . . you know . . . *Politische Scheisse*. He's a *Bürohengst*, paper pusher."

I nodded unknowingly again.

"He sounds wonderful," I said. "They all sound wonderful. You are very lucky!"

114

"Yeah, they are all pretty wonderful, I suppose," she took a breath then silence.

"You're pretty wonderful yourself Marta!"

"Thanks. I'm glad you think so," she said. "Yeah, Poppy runs a pretty tight ship. Likes to keep everyone looking like the model family of the new *Reich*," she gave a sad little laugh. "We've been pretty fortunate. Good house, nice neighborhood. Lots of *Kram*, Lots of travel, vacations, Poppy up to Berlin every month or two on business. Skiing, *Innsbruck, Kitzbühel.*

"*Kram* is good," I nodded as if I could possibly have known.

"Very good," she agreed.

"They are pretty special Poppy and Mum. En-viable I guess. I mean really, what's not to envy? They have it all," then in a voice trailing off into its own darkness, "I want what they have," for a moment her chin dropped down onto her shoulder, and she was silent.

"I'm sure you will," I said.

"I know," she said wistfully, "I know."

She turned to me slowly as if waking from a dream, then settled back again on her elbows.

"Yep, I've learned a lot from Poppy and Mum. And a lot from Poppy's right hand drawer," she said with a laugh.

"His right hand drawer?"

"The lower right hand drawer of his desk, un-der the files. One day when I was a kid he was out. I was looking around for something, who knows what, and I looked in the drawer. I saw a bit of string in there and I pulled on it. Low and behold the bottom of the drawer came up. A false bottom to the drawer. And you know what was in there?"

I shook my head in the darkness.

"Postcards."

"Postcards?"

"Postcards. The naughty kind."

"Ohhhh . . . ," I said, not certain I wanted to hear more.

"Let me say this, you can learn a lot from some naughty postcards!" and we both giggled again. "I'm sure Mum wouldn't approve, if she ever found out. But she'd understand. Men are men. What can I say? They're all the same, no matter what age," she settled back down on her elbows. "How about your Poppy? Does he have a bottom right hand drawer?"

Once again the animal began to rise between us in the darkness, but now I couldn't find the knife.

"No. I don't think so," I said, hoping that would end the conversation. "We leave for *Landdienst* tomorrow. Is it a long way?"

"It's not too far," Marta said, "a couple hours of marching."

The animal continued to rise in the darkness, grow, as if feeding on the silence between us.

"Your Mum wouldn't mind?" Marta said gently, as if she already knew.

I shook my head, the dark silent air becoming heavy, difficult to inhale, catching in my throat. Marta set her hand gently on top of mine.

"Where's your mother?" she said quietly.

My eyes fell into my lap.

"Did something . . . happen to her?"

I nodded. She stroked my hand, "Want to . . . talk about it?"

I looked up at the ceiling, trying to keep the tears now piling up in my eyes from overflowing.

"Not really," I croaked through a melted smile.

"Might help. Might do you some good."

I nodded again then forced out four words.

"Tuberculosis. I was five."

Marta was quiet, " . . . and your father?"

I bit my lip, hoping that Marta could not see the tears now starting to roll down my cheeks. She leaned forward again and hugged me, tucking her chin over my right shoulder. "What happened?"

I began to snuffle, tears racing across my icy cheeks like salty rivers of pain, "I don't know. I don't . . . know."

More snuffling. More pain, "No, no NO!" reverberating in my brain.

Marta pressed, "What happened Kat?"

Again my inner voice clamored; "Keep it in, Kat, keep it in". No need to return to that morning. The morning of *dem Hühnerstall.* But something else was in opposition, something that needed the toxic mass inside me purged, removed, or at the very least exposed.

"I was seven," I began. Marta nuzzled her neck against mine, encouraging me to continue. "He left. My mother was dead and we were alone. Just him

117

and I," Marta pulled me closer as my tears fell freely, "and he left." Then just as quickly they began to subside, "He didn't return. He never did," my tears began to stop. My voice became stronger, "You're right, Marta. Men are shit."

#

The following morning we assembled as usual in the middle of the sports field to salute the flag and to offer allegiance to *dem Führer*. Only this time we were wearing our marching uniform: white blouse, calf length dark blue pants, black neckerchief. Our backpacks lay before us, ready for inspection. It was important that we provide a good representation of the *Reich* should anyone see us. A half dozen wagons were assembled in the turnaround, loaded with the supplies we would be needing to carry us through the next few months of *Landdienst*. Following the third *Sieg Heil!* we snapped to attention. Fraukenstein gave us one last review, gave the order and we slung our packs onto our backs. Then the leader of the entire BDM Division called out *"Kolonnen rechts, Marsch!"* Columns Right, March! As if as one, we turned right without so much as the single stray scuffle of feet. Flags held high and in the perfect precision our country deserved, we followed, *Gruppe* after *Gruppe*, from the sports field, up through the turnaround and out onto the road.

We marched along the roadside on that glorious May day as one, passersby in trucks and wagons waved and saluted and I was proud to be a part of something so magnificent. Fraukenstein followed our column, continually dressing our line, making sure the *Arg Acht* kept in cadence.

I saw Marta only twice all day, each time during a stop to rest beneath the trees. I could feel we were beginning to climb up slightly as we headed from the rolling grasslands of Bavaria to a higher tree covered elevation. The air became cooler and the weight of my pack seemed to diminish.

It was getting on toward three when we began to see flashes of white through the forest off to our left. With each passing step, white camp buildings came into view: a cook house-mess hall, an administrative building and a bunkhouse for the *Gruppen* leaders. There was certainly not enough room in any of these buildings to house the hundred or more girls that had arrived. The wagons were already there unloading supplies into the buildings and piling the rest on the ground before they departed. The pine scent of the air now held the slightest tinge of dampness and underworldy things. There would be rain by nightfall. Directly in front of us, beyond the camp buildings, flashes of light reflecting from a lake were visible through the trunks of the great pine trees.

Still in our *Gruppe*, we came to a halt in a clearing of short grass bedded with soft pine needles. Fraukenstein blew her whistle and began to read pairs of names off of her clipboard. Each of us had carried half of a two man camouflaged *Zeltbahn* tent on our backs and with the threat of rain on the horizon, it was time to set them up. Unfortunately, Marta and I had been involved in one punishment or another when we had received instruction onto just how to set up the tent, so I was completely at a loss. Hildi, however, had been thankfully paying attention, and as she was called as my tent mate, things would turn out just fine.

We pitched our tent along with all of the rest in perfect parallel lines facing away from the lake and by the time the dinner triangle sang its familiar kangle, our tent was secure.

Since the mess hall and galley had not been scrubbed and provisions secured, dinner would be cooked over open fires at several locations around our new "home" for the next few days. Marta joined me as we cooked our beans and a few bratwurst over the open fire. We found a place to sit, apart from the others on a patch of pine needled forest floor. Storm clouds were beginning to gather over the hills to the west, a freshening breeze ruffling the lake with catspaws. Directly across the lake from the BDM camp, at a distance of no more than a hundred meters, a large Nazi flag rose above the trees. Below the flag, activity could be heard. Oxen dragged tree trunks through the understory, a sawmill buzzed on, and everywhere, everywhere, could be heard the sound of voices. Young men's voices.

"What is that over there?" I asked Marta as she chased the last bit of beans around her tin plate.

She stopped and stared across the water, her eyes fixated on the sound of the voices. Then she answered in the most reverent of tones. *"Das Versprochene Land."* The Promised Land. "Are you with me?"

I could only nod.

LANDDIENST

NEUN - NINE

Far into our first night of *Landdienst*, rain hissed around our tent, the sound of bratwurst sizzling in a too hot pan. We had performed all of the appropriate trenching as required, according to Hildi, but I was sure she had forgotten to tell me one or two minor details. For Hildi was now fast asleep, the sound of her snoring loud enough, I was certain, to awaken the entire division. I, on the other hand, was having my difficulties. Not only with the diesel exhaust sound of a sleeping Hildi, but I was obviously on the downhill side of the tent, and water was leaking in from somewhere. My bed roll and its occupant, me, were now completely drenched.

The front flap of the tent flew open, revealing a gray sheet of rain and a ponchoed Marta.

"*Raus!*" Marta yelled, stirring Hildi to life with a series of snorts, snuffles and a single, loud, whistling fart. "*Raus!*" Marta yelled again. Out! she said, the three of us and the eye-watering aftermath of Hildi's fart now crammed painfully close in the two man *Zeltbahn* tent.

"*Raus* Hildi!"

"What do you mean?" Hildi grumbled back, rolling back over in her bedroll.

Marta leaned down and gave her a good sturdy shake, "Out. Out of this tent *Stinker*! " Stinkey! "Go take mine."

Hildi grumbled and snuffled a bit more but began to acquiesce. Marta's power over people was strong. Hildi began to work her chubby figure onto her knees in the low tent.

"Come on Marta! Wait till tomorrow," Hildi complained, all the while pulling on her shoes. She started to gather her bed roll.

"Leave the bed roll. Take mine," Marta said, working Hildi toward the flap.

"Which tent?" Hildi said.

Marta threw open the flap to a steel gray sheet of icy rain, "Four down, on the right, " she gave Hildi a shove out the flap and added, "Can't miss it. Light's still on. It's the one that doesn't smell like *ein Furz!*" A fart. Marta pulled the tent flap closed then opened it again and yelled out " . . . yet!" Then she collapsed on her butt on Hildi's former bed roll.

"*Gott verdammt* Hildi!" Marta said waving her hand in front of her nose. She pulled off her camouflage poncho and tossed it in a pile at the end of the bed. "One of Fraukenstein's punishments, I suppose, tenting you up with our own little Zeppelin," she let out a disgusted little laugh.

"Thanks Marta," I said sheepishly. "Yeah, she was a bit much for a tent mate," then I gave a bit of a shiver.

"*Was ist los?*" You OK? she said, true concern burbling up from somewhere. She reached out and touched my drenched night gown, "Ugh! Hildi! She can't even pitch a tent properly!" she shook her head woefully, "*Sie hat nicht alle Tassen im Schrank.*" She doesn't have all her cups in the cupboard. "Do you have another night gown?"

"Yes, one more," I pulled it on and slid my way to the narrow strip of dry in the center of the tent. Marta adjusted Hildi's bed roll and slid as far as she could to the tent wall. She patted the bedroll next to her.

I shook my head, "No, um. No that's OK Marta."

"What are you going to do, sit there on your little dry island in the middle of Lake Hildi all night? Come on, slide on over."

I started to shiver again. This time she didn't ask. Marta took me by the hand and gently, but firmly pulled me toward her. Shivering uncontrollably now, I slid into the space in front of her on the bedroll. She pulled the blanket over us and wrapped her arms around me. "Like spoons in the drawer," she said. Then she raised her two fingers before my face wrapping one around the other. "Like this we are," she adjusted herself in the bedroll pulling me in tight to her, setting off a crinkle-crinkle from beneath us. She rolled over and reached her hand under the bedroll and retrieved a handful of empty hard candy wrappers.

"*Hildi, du Hutziferkel!*" you dirty little pig! Then Marta said something else, but I was already falling asleep.

#

Over the next two days the girls of BDM's Division 687 set about unloading supplies and organizing the mess hall, administrative building and work shops. Marta and I got the tent she had commandeered reestablished and dry and what little personal items we had stored away.

All through the day, as we worked unloading the wagons and supplies, I would occasionally catch Marta staring off across the lake at the grand red flag with the black hooked cross circling its white center like a hurricane. When the wind was calm, voices of young men drifted across the water, smooth and sweet, like nectar to our ears. But we did not see them. Only at night, when two or three HJs in their crisp uniforms and rifles were sent over to patrol our camp. Ostensibly, they were there to protect us from wild animals that may come down from the woods, but the truth was obvious to any of us that tried to sneak out at night. The *Gruppen* leaders wanted to make sure boys and girls remained apart.

On the third morning, we assembled as usual and Fraukenstein began to pace with her ubiquitous clipboard. It was time to begin the true purpose of *Landdienst*, supporting the HJs in their work on the other side of the lake. Fraukenstein began to go down her list.

"I need four to work in the mess hall, two in the scullery, two in the workshop to mend uniforms and work clothes for our *Hitler Jugend* companions across the water," she said, "do I have volunteers?" A few hands sheepishly went up and they were immediately whisked out of line and sent to the dock.

Fraukenstein continued down her list of jobs, "I need two girls that have some familiarity with large domestic animals," my hand shot up. "*Fräulein*

Mueller? You have some knowledge of farm animals?"

"*Ja bitte Gruppenführer.* My *Tantchen* and I run a small farm. We work with cows and horses all of the time," she nodded and began to make a note on her clipboard. From farther down the line another hand shot up. Marta.

Fraukenstein looked at Marta dubiously, "*Fräulein* Koenigsberg?" one eyebrow went up nearly disappearing under her cap, "You know something of large animals, perhaps?"

"*Jawohl!*" Marta said snapping to attention.

"I see," Fraukenstein said, but clearly she did not. She pulled Marta out of line and turned her so she faced all of us. Fraukenstein leaned in closer, thought for a moment and squinted with one eye, "Tell me *Fräulein*, what is the difference between a cow and a heifer?"

Marta took a quick look over to me. I pantomimed miking a cow.

"We get *Milch* from a cow!" Marta said proudly.

"I see," Fraukenstein stroked her stony knob of chin as she nodded. "And tell me *Fräulein*, what is the difference between a bull and an ox?" with this, a brief moment of panic flashed across Marta's face. Again she caught my eye and I pantomimed scissors across my groin.

Marta proudly blurted out, "An ox has no penis!"

Fraukenstein recoiled quickly nearly tripping over backward. I slapped my forehead then placed my two fists at my groin.

"*Keinen Sack!*" she blurted out again smiling expansively. No balls!

Fraukenstein composed herself, tucking a renegade wisp of hair under her cap. "Very well, you and *Fräulein* Mueller report to the stables," Marta smiled brightly at Fraukenstein, snapped off a rather impressive "*Heil Hitler*" and together we marched down to the dock.

#

Many of the rowboats had already been taken so Marta and I grabbed a rather pathetic canoe that was pulled up on the shore. Ahead of us, the great red, white, and black flag rose above the trees. Along the shore on the opposite bank a line of HJs awaited our arrival to "help us from the boats". Even though I could not see her face I knew Marta was scanning the line-up, already making her selection.

I broke Marta's concentration for a moment as we paddled along quietly, "Will we need to travel across the lake every day?" I said.

"Yep," Marta said, "that's the way we've had to do it before."

"Seems a bit much. I'm guessing they don't trust us."

"That would be a pretty good guess *Küken*. Ever since two years ago, anyway."

"What was two years ago?"

"Remember that big Nazi rally in Nuremberg back in thirty six? The *Reichsparteitag?* Well, they let the BDM and HJs camp together and WhoooHooo! Big mistake! Like little bunnies they were, boys and girls getting together! Over nine hundred girls ended up *mit einem Braten im Ofen!* With a roast in the oven! The parents were furious! They called us the League of German Mattresses!" she broke into a loud laugh, "Ever since then, joint camping adventures between BDM and HJs are strictly *verboten!* But it was a wonderful time, *Küken,* I must say!"

From our position toward the back of the flotilla, Marta and I watched as the HJs now moved onto the dock, presumably to assist in unloading and inspecting supplies from the rowboats and canoes now arriving. It was obvious to all, however, that the young men were far more interested in unloading and inspecting the newly arriving members of the BDM. HJs muscled each other out of the way to offer the better looking girls more of a hand than the others. I watched with just a touch of sympathy as Hildi clambered out of the boat by herself and began to worry as to what sort of reception, if any, I would receive.

Marta and I were one of the last boats, announcing our arrival with a squeaking of our canoe against one of the dock's rubber fenders. Several boys offered Marta their hands to ease her out of the canoe, hands grabbing not only onto hers, but drifting down along her backside as well. Marta did not complain. I stood in the other end of the canoe, trying to steady myself, preparing to disembark. As Marta stepped from the canoe, the small boat suddenly became completely unstable and I began to gyrate uncontrollably trying to maintain my balance. It didn't work. In a split second the canoe was upside down and I was in the water. Immediately after, a half dozen HJs had jumped in trying to save me from drowning. Which I wasn't of course, but they all seemed to relish the opportunity to help a damsel in distress. To display their *Blut und Ehre*, Blood and Honor, the motto of the *Hitler Jugend*. Still on the dock, Marta stood there with a little smile for her student now surrounded by athletic young HJs. I could almost hear her say: "Bravo *Küken*, you have certainly grabbed their attention!"

#

After I had had a chance to dry off a bit, Marta and I were brought over to the stables, a ramshackle collection of barns, lean-tos and sheds, their exposed corners rubbed smooth by countless animals led into and out of the stalls over the years.

The HJ *Kommandant*, new according to Marta, had decided to personally give us instructions in maintaining the barns. It was obvious he had little interest in us or in the work that needed to be done other than that it needed to be done, and that he be kept upwind of the proceedings. But there was one thing in the barns he wanted to make certain we understood without mistake. He was crowding forty, tall and thin with a silver headed cane supporting a shallow limp.

"Keep it all clean," he said. "The stalls mucked out, then fresh hay brought down from the hay loft.

132

Silage distributed and water changed. Animals tended, harnesses cleaned and stowed at the end of each day." then he stopped and addressed us with the pointed end of his cane, "and whatever else you do or do not do, stay the fuck away from Vixen! *Verstanden*?" he said. Then without waiting for an answer he handed Marta a heavy steel rake, turned on the heel of his polished black boot and headed back to the administrative building.

Marta turned to me, "I've got a question," she said sarcastically, "who or what the fuck is Vixen?"

I turned to the *Kommandant* just barely out of earshot. "Shhhh, Marta! We'll figure it out."

Marta stared at the rake in disbelief, at the backside of the *Kommandant*, then back at the rake, "I don't know that I'm going to like this, *Küken*. Maybe we should be in the mess hall waiting tables or sewing buttons on somewhere. That's where I was last year. Wasn't so bad. Or maybe . . . " then our first customers appeared, emerging from the woods down a weather beaten rut of a trail

There were four total, two HJs and a team of two black oxen yoked together, pulling a log behind them. The two HJs were dressed in leather saw chaps, work gloves, wood chips, and sweat glistening muscles. Marta immediately decided that we may have a rather nice position here at the barns after all. The two HJs guided the ox and its log up to the entrance of the saw mill and unhitched the team. More HJs spilled from the mill like monkeys from an overturned circus truck and maneuvered the log onto the mill rails with their pikes.

Guiding their team of oxen between them, the two HJs stopped alongside a galvanized pail of water with a ladle and began to drink, sloshing more down the front of them than getting into their mouths. They finished off pouring one or two ladles over their heads then led the oxen to the water trough in front of the barn where Marta and I stood. Marta remained relaxed as always, turning on the skills she had tried so hard to teach me. As for me, I stood frozen, struggling to conceal my wonderment. As the pair of oxen snuffled and slurped, their heads chuffing deep in the water trough, the two HJs chatted between themselves. Marta and I held our position, allowing them to make the first move. At least I had remembered something. Then, on some unspoken signal, the HJs turned and began leading their ox team our way. I suddenly realized I had stopped breathing.

"*Guten Morgen,*" one said, tipping an imaginary hat. "I'm Detlef and this is my team mate Otto. Welcome to *dem Böser Wald,*" the wicked forest. He removed his leather glove and shook each of our hands, his grip firm and calloused. "You must be our stable hands for the next few months."

"That would be us!" Marta chimed in with a smile and did a terrible curtsey, "We are here to take care of your cows!"

"Oxen," Otto corrected without a smile. He spit a long brown jet of tobacco juice not far enough to the side to be polite.

"Correct," Marta said smoothly, *"keine Sacke!"*

Detlef let out a little laugh, while Otto said nothing and readjusted his wad of tobacco.

Detlef turned to me, "And you must be *unser kleiner Schwimmer,*" our little swimmer. "Yes," I stammered, feeling my face flush completely crimson.

"Be careful," he said, "or the alligators will get you!"

"Are there really . . . ?" I started but Detlef cut me off with a laugh.

"No, not really, just hippopotamus like my friend Otto here."

Otto punctuated the comment with a long jet of brown, finishing with a small stripe of tobacco juice clefting his chin.

With that the two oxen raised their heads to look around, signaling it was time to get back to work. Detlef and Otto turned, their leather logger chaps slapping against their legs as they walked away. Marta took a few steps toward Detlef and made one more stab at conversation.

"Say," Marta asked coyly, "just what are you doing up there anyway?"

Detlef guided the oxen's yoke back toward the trail, up into *den Böser Wald.* He called back over the animal's haunches, "Cutting trees for lumber," then answered the unasked question, "to build the new *Reich!*"

#

Marta and I went into the barn to dissect my first encounter with an HJ in post-mortem.

"Detlef was cute." I said, showing Marta the process of "mucking out" stalls. Marta tried to show some interest in the process, but clearly her mind was elsewhere. Most probably the potential cornucopia of copulation that our positions at the barns might bring.

"Not bad," she said nodding, "Not bad at all."

"I think he sort of liked you, Marta," I said with a little smile.

"Maybe," she said, "just maybe . . . Certainly something to think about. But that Otto! What was with him? Ugh, what an *Affe!*" Ape!

"Yes, I suppose," I said, lifting the soiled hay into a wheelbarrow with a pitchfork."More will come, my dear Katerina," Marta said. "I believe you have found us a good spot to meet some very fine specimens of *der Zukerstange*. Be patient *mein Küken*. Patient. The right ones will come."

And I was. For several more hours HJ loggers came and went, watering their animals, chatting occasionally and then continuing back up into *den Böser Wald* to fell more trees for *das Reich*.

As the day's heat grew, Marta disappeared into the cool blue of the barn more to avoid work than to seek it out, leaving me alone to meet more young men as they came and went. As the afternoon went on I began to speak more freely, and could feel myself becoming more relaxed, often quite the challenge in the presence of sweat slicked muscled young men.

It was of and from the ranks of such men of the forest that a new young HJ approached. He was stout and compact, more broad than tall, which served well

136

his commanding position atop an enormous wagon slung beneath with freshly felled logs. Four-in-hand, the young, broad, HJ teamster drove this *Gulliver Wagen*, the painted yellow wheels towering hub-high to a full grown man. Before and below the HJ, guided only by a whistle or word and a gentle flick of the reins were a team of four Belgian geldings, oversize *Last* horses inflated with musculature, majestic beasts that once carried armored knights into battle. The broad teamster eased his *Wagen* before the paddock. With a gentle tug on the reins the "wheelers", the two horses closest to the wagon and the brakes for the great wain, dug in and brought the cart to a halt. The broad HJ descended from his seat and approached me, removing his canvas gloves as he did.

"*Schönen Tag!*" He said. Good day! He shook my hand, "I am Werner but if you ask for Werner, no one will know who to look for."

"Then if I were to look for you, who should I ask for?" I said playing along.

"Ask for *Dachs*," Badger, he said and smiled a bright smile neatly bisecting a pointed nose and terminating on either corner with a mug handle for an ear. And indeed, beneath the stained and cocked M43 *Wehrmacht* Army field cap, Dachs's face looked every bit a badger's.

"And allow me to introduce my friends here," he pointed to the two rear wheeler Belgians "Anthony and John," then the two forward leader horses, "and Charles the Bold and Philip the Good. My Four Noblemen of Brabant!" he finished with a flourish.

137

I applauded, "From the opera Lohengrin, correct?"

"Ah, you know your Wagner."

"Well," I added a bit sheepishly, "I have read the libretto, but have never had the pleasure of hearing it performed."

"Then someday you must! Wagner is *des Führer's* favorite composer you know of course!"

I ran my hand along the barrel chest of Philip the Good, his head and face bobbing gently above me.

"Well, I can assure you The Four Noblemen of Brabant shall be well attended to by this humble stable attendant," I gave a little curtsey.

"And is this stable attendant too humble to have a name?" he said.

I smiled, "No, not too humble. Kat. Kat Mueller."

"Kat, eh?"

I nodded. Dachs again shook my hand, "It is my pleasure to meet you," he said. He remounted his seat on *Gulliver's Wagen* and with the flick of his reins was on his way to the mill.

#

It was getting on toward evening and Marta and I were filling the water trough in the oxen pen. Most of the teams had returned their beasts of burden to the barns, the surrounding forest, descending into a thousand shades of night, grew silent of falling trees. I could tell *der Böser Wald* would soon earn its name.

Marta nudged me. Four large shadows were emerging from the forest. Two fawn colored oxen in the middle, tinged blue in the fading light. On either side strode two tall HJs in heavy hobnailed boots, triangle shaped bodies rising from narrow hips to shoulders as broad as barn doors. One HJ was large. Auburn hair, wearing a formerly white t shirt now smeared every color of the forest. The other was larger, nearly a half a head taller than the first, blonde hair cut close on the sides but shaggy on top. Suspenders held up his chaps, his t shirt off and draped over his shoulders, a magnificent pair of polished granite curves. With one large hand he held the oxen's yoke, with the other a double headed ax.

Marta and I stood in the ox pen as they walked past us, just on the other side of the split rail fence. They were close enough to touch and I knew that even Marta, her desire to be *lässig*, cool, laid back, completely falling flat, wanted to reach out but didn't. We could only stare as they walked on by.

They never stopped. They never spoke. They never even acknowledged we were there.

ZEHN-TEN

By the time we reached our tent that night, Marta had already named them: The blonde *Perfekt Eins*, and his curly auburn companion *Perfekt Zwei*, Perfect One and Perfect Two. And Marta's wheels were already spinning.

"See Katerina! See! We were patient and the gods rewarded us! Rewarded us with two gods of our very own!" she said and fell back on her bedroll clutching her chest. "All we need to do is get them into our own yoke," she thought for a moment. "I'll take the blondie, just like before," she rolled over and looked at me, "if that's OK with you."

I waved my hand at her as if granting a thousand peasants their freedom, "Begone with him!" I said. "I guess that leaves me *Zwei*. He's cute. Hopefully he'll turn out better than the last one!" I began to make up my bedroll.

"No, Katerina, this will be different. *Zwei* is no Himmler. I can tell you that! He has class, integrity. And muscles on top of his muscles!" Marta said magnanimously. "That *grossartige Geschöpf*, magnificent creature, is all for you! He belongs to you. And you to he!" her voice was beginning to fade "And we WILL have them."

"They didn't even know we were there, Marta," I said.

She waved her hand dismissively in the air, "Details, *Küken*, details! We'll figure it out!" then she fell silent, her chest heaving slowly up and down as she thought, or dreamed. *"Das Leben ist kein funkelnder Ponyhof, Katerina,"* she said quietly. Then faded off to sleep.

And she, of course, was right. Life isn't a place for riding sparkle ponies. Everything takes work.

#

But it was more than just details. And of all the animals we tended to for the next three days, none were sparkle ponies. *Perfekte Eins und Zwei* continued to walk right past us, sometimes twice a day. Occasionally one would nod in our direction and we even got a *"Morgen"* one morning from Zwei. But little else. Marta threw all of her best tricks at them, coming just short of calling them by name and asking them to come over. Pretending to be trying to lift something heavy when they walked by. Nothing. Walking directly in front of their teamed oxen. Zero response.

Detlef and Otto had reappeared a few times and Detlef seemed to be enjoying our attention, especially from Marta. Even Otto seemed to be turning things around a bit, spitting his tobacco juice off to the side instead of directly between us, no longer creating some nicotine no-mans-land that no woman dared to cross. Dachs too stopped by on occasion, helping us groom the Brabant Dukes in their stalls after a hard days work. He was a fine fellow with a pleasant smile observing his world from so high a perch on *Der Gulliver Wagen*. But even so, *Eins und Zwei* were still at the top of our target list. Marta chided me not to even consider settling for less and promised me we would have them.

#

At the end of the fourth day Marta and I were again in the pen, moving hay and filling troughs with water when *Eins und Zwei* and their two yoked oxen appeared from *dem Wald*. Only this time something was different. One of the oxen was favoring its left front foot, limping slightly. When the oxen approached the barn, they refused to drink. *Eins und Zwei* brought the two oxen into the pen, still oblivious to the fact that we were even there. They unyoked the oxen in the pen adjoining ours and set the healthy ox free, so as to concentrate on the lame one. When they crouched down to examine the forward hoof, the ox pulled away and began to thrash his head about, nearly goring *Eins* with its horn. Again they would try to approach to examine the hoof and again the ox pulled away from them.

Eins und Zwei were standing together, puzzled and concerned over what to do next when I slipped through the rails of the fence between us and slowly approached the ox. I began to speak softly to the lame beast, looking it squarely in the eye, just as I had to do to with Cleopatra and Nefertiti occasionally when they had problems that needed to be dealt with. Slowly, ever so slowly, I approached the beast. When I reached him, I gently cradled his snout, velvet soft, in my hands, careful to avoid his horns. He exhaled a snort of bovine breath into my face and I recoiled a bit, wiping bits of spittle from my face with a smile. "Easy boy," I said quietly, "easy boy." His tail flicked peacefully. I slid my hands down his face, down his chest and down the troubled leg. I reached the hoof and began to examine it. Then I worked my way back up to the great ox's muzzle and leaned into the ox's ear. "You're going to be OK, boy. OK. *Alles ist gut ja?*" All is good, Yes? Then I kissed the ox on the nose and slowly backed away. I turned and walked toward *Eins und Zwei,* wiping my hands on my uniform apron.

"Your ox has hoof rot," I said to them in no uncertain terms. "Have you been working them in water or mud of some kind?"

Zwei answered, "Yes. We have. We have been hauling trees out of a swamp on the back side of *dem Wald.*"

I shook my head, "Can't do that all the time. They need time for their feet to dry. Now he has an infection."

"What should we do?" *Zwei* asked.

"Leave him here for a few days. I'll . . . " Marta had magically appeared at my side, "I mean we'll take care of him. Get some homemade remedies on his hoof, try to draw the infection out. Let it dry."

"Have you done this before?" *Zwei* asked, his voice deep with concern.

"Yes," I said

And Marta quickly added, "Yes, of course we have."

"Will he heal?" *Eins* said softly.

"We will try," Marta said and then looked at me.

I nodded, "Leave him a few days and we will do the best we can. Promise," I said and smiled at them both.

"Thank you," said *Eins* and the two HJs departed.

#

That night in the tent Marta could not let go of me. She hugged me and kissed me and raised her hands on high to whatever deities she knew were somewhere above the roof of our *Zeltbahn*.

"You see *Küken*, you see?! The merciful gods are shining down on us! *Eins und Zwei* have a problem and the gods provide the answer: You!" she hugged me then hugged herself and fell backward onto her bed roll.

"Yes, well, let's get their ox healed first. That may take a bit of doing. We'll need to scavenge up some supplies," I said.

That night we both slept. From the smile on Marta's face, dreams of *Zuckerstange* were most probably dancing in her head. But for me, it was the flat black hat again, floating above the fire, buoyed by the column of heat, only different. This time the hat was surrounded by a rising cloud of cryptic Hebrew letters, spinning, reversing themselves, rising from the burning scroll.

#

By the time we had reached the pen the following morning, *Eins und Zwei* had already headed off to *dem Wäld* with their one remaining ox. When I approached our lame ox, he turned, revealing a small

145

paper sign hung around his neck. The sign read: *"Ich heisse Jupiter."* My name is Jupiter.

"Jupiter it is!" I said gently embracing the animals snout. "Let's see what we can do for you," I turned to Marta, "We are going to need some supplies."

Our end of the barn was noticeably barren of any sort of veterinarian supplies where beasts of burden, seemingly, were considered disposable. At the other end of the great structure, however, things began to take on a much grander appearance. The dirt center causeway turned to cobblestone, the stalls were painted a pristine white and iron hooks and hanging hardware were replaced with polished brass. This end of the barn even had its own private opening, where an HJ stood guard.

"This looks promising," Marta whispered.

Marta and I worked our way silently along the stables of this more pampered end of the barn. We peeped in each carefully manicured stall, finally stopping at one with a closed double door, the nicker of a contented horse slipping through the cracks. In the mirrored finish of the polished brass plaque on the door I could see Marta's devilish grin. The plaque had one word on it:

"Vixen".

We slipped the latch and went inside.

Before us surely stood the animal for which Shakespeare had said "When I bestride him I soar, I am a hawk: he trots on air". Here was the *Kommandant's* Vixen, a pure black stallion, lithe yet muscular, a solitary white diamond between his eyes. Mounted to the wall above the horse's head were multiple flags and ribbons denoting the many victories Vixen had secured for its owner. On the wall nearby we found a white tin cabinet with a painted green cross. Marta used a thin wafer of metal to slide the locking mechanism back without a key and the cabinet opened up without so much as a squeak. Inside were a number of liniments and dressings and bandages for wrapping the stallion's legs.

I pulled a couple of bottles down from the cabinet and tucked them under my shirt, then Marta reclosed the lock. "This should get us started," I whispered.

We worked our way undetected back to our side of the barn where I gave Marta a short list of other materials I needed to make a homemade poultice for the ox's leg. Once she had returned and the poultice was in place, Marta and I got about the business of tending to the other animals in the barn.

The sun was now heading for the lake and darker shades of blue were beginning to stripe *dem Böser Wald* when *Eins und Zwei* appeared at the head of the trail, their single ox now between them. When they saw Jupiter, slowly moving around the pen without a limp they both smiled.

"You have both done remarkably well with our Jupiter here. Soon Mars will no longer have to work alone," *Zwei* said.

"Just keep them both out of the mud for a while. Give their hooves a chance to dry," I admonished him.

"Whatever the doctor says!" he said, and smiled broadly.

"A few more days and Jupiter should be as good as new," I said.

"Thank you again," said *Zwei*. "By the way, my sincere apologies, where are my manners. We never formally introduced ourselves. I am Rolf and my friend here is Dannar."

Dannar quietly reached over the fence rail, his hand engulfing mine "Dannar Bremm."

Rolf took my hand as well, holding onto it a little bit longer before he let it go. I began to feel myself drowning in his eyes, dark and blue, the color of the deepest portion of the lake. Marta caught me before I went under.

"And I am Marta," she said, reaching over the fence, "and this is Katerina. Kat." followed by still more shaking of hands, each a bit longer than the last.

"Yes, well," I said, looking down to hide the hot red flush rising in my cheeks, "a few more days and Jupiter will be all well. In the meantime we must get about our business," then I turned and headed back toward the barns. Marta made a few small comments to Dannar and Rolf then trotted after me. She caught up to me just as I entered the barn's sliding door and grabbed me by the shoulder.

"Where are you going? We had them! Talking. Laughing. Eating out of our hands like feeding grass to a pony!" Marta said.

"I just needed to . . . " I stammered, something uncomfortable crossing me, the way the shadow of a solitary cloud sometimes crosses a sunny field. Then I turned and disappeared into the cool darkness of the barn.

"We don't want to lose them!" Marta whisper yelled into the darkness after me. But when she turned and saw Rolf and Dannar still standing there, and the expressions on their faces, she knew we hadn't lost them in the least.

#

In the darkness of the *Zeltbahn* I bolted awake with a start, a half moon grinning like a cheshire cat through the brown and green mottle of *Waffen* camouflage surrounding me. But I had nothing to smile about. It was *der Hühnerstall* again.

The chicken coop dream. It had been many months since I had had it last, but here it was again, slipping its poison into my ear, into my brain as I slept, just as Claudius poisoned Hamlet's father the King.

I tried to combat the angst with rationalization. All nightmares by their very definition frighten us, I thought. Some nightmares frighten us with potential visions of the future, for what they portend, fears for what may be. Ghosts of Christmas Yet to Be. But some nightmares are terrifying in the dark memories they revisit, actual traumas of your past reappearing, now

149

re-spun, tipped and twisted, warped out of square. *Der Hühnerstall,* my nightmare, was of the latter. Something had triggered it back from the nothingness where dark dreams lurk. Two handsome young men in a paddock perhaps, spawning a solitary cloud.

From the present darkness I heard a voice, "Are you OK?" asked Marta quietly.

I just nodded, trying to find my throat before I spoke, hoping I didn't sound like a child that had wet their bed, *"Ich habs,"* I said, my voice still breaking slightly.

"Böser Traum?" she said, a new depth to her compassion. Bad dream?

I continued to nod, tears beginning to well in my eyes.

"Tell me," she said.

I shook my head.

"I have bad dreams too, sometimes," she continued, consoling me.

Again I shook my head.

"Yeah, I know. I understand. I don't like to talk about mine either. Makes them a little too real when you tell them to someone else, when you hear them out loud," she made a funny gagging noise with her mouth as she gave an exaggerated shiver.

She rolled over on her back and stared into the mottle overhead, thinking for a bit, then went on. Her voice now serious.

"In fact, I have a nightmare that I have never told anyone."

"Really?" I said. Her silhouette nodded.

"Never," the silhouette said in a grave tone. "Ever."

"What's yours about?" I said.

The silhouette shook again, "Nope. Sorry. Only if you go first."

Maybe it was the compassion, this something new in her voice, that let me know it was safe to drain the poison from my ear, at least a little. Slowly, painful and foul, the words began to flow giving a certain feeling of relief, like a lanced abscess.

It was in the depths of the depression, I began, and everyone was starving. Everyone. We had a small farm but no animals. Only chickens. Neighbors and homeless wanderers were always stealing our eggs, sometimes the chickens themselves. My father was a sign painter and of course there was no work. Who needed signs when there was no food and what money we had was worthless. All we had to survive were our chickens and the eggs they left for us in *dem Hühnerstall*. The chicken coop. My father had me sleep in there at night with a gun. Imagine me, seven years old, with a gun! But they were difficult times and people did whatever it took to survive one more day. He stayed in the house, protecting what little we had there. He would go out sometimes at night, doing odd jobs, trying to find food or fuel. One night we were in the house. He kissed me good night and told me how much he loved me, as he always did, and I went out to sleep in *dem Hühnerstall*.

"In the dream, I wake up in the chicken coop, peering through the chicken wire surrounding me. I creak open the low door and head down the ramp toward the rear door of the house. The screen door is cracked open a bit as I approach. It is very large and the steps approaching it are very tall, almost too tall to climb. When I walk inside, it is our small cooking area, the small kitchen table with yellow legs and white metal top. Papa is sitting there smoking his pipe, surrounded by a veil of smoke. I see his face, but his face is unclear. Somehow I can't remember what he looks like. But I know it is him. He turns to me as I enter, 'Hello my Katerina! Did you have a good sleep?' he says, his voice metallic and wobbly as if coming from the bottom of the well. I try to answer, but for some reason I don't know the words. I try to nod, but I am frozen. I try to reach out to him but I am paralyzed. He cradles his pipe in the corner of his mouth and inhales. When he exhales the room becomes filled with a thick smoke, almost a fog. When it clears, he is gone."

A long empty moment passed. Something skittered in the grass and leaves outside of our tent, a dark and rattling noise.

"Go on," said Marta quietly.

"That's it. That's how the dream always ends. In reality when I went to look for him that morning, he was gone. Just gone. I looked for him everywhere, as best a seven year old could. I stayed in the house for over two weeks fending for myself, living on eggs, hoping he would return. But he never did. Eventually I went out to look for him. I started to walk toward town, even though I really wasn't sure how to get there. Finally a woman picked me up, my *Tantchen*. She brought me to her house. Gave me her last name. And I have been there ever since."

"What do you think happened to him?" Marta said.

I could barely get the words out, "I don't know. Maybe he couldn't handle it. Taking care of me. Trying to feed another mouth other than his own. I guess those things can happen."

"Maybe," Marta said, then remained quiet.

I lay in my bed roll, silently staring into the camouflage, hoping to see some semblance of reason in the mottled patterns interlocking above me. But there was none. No answers. Only that my father had abandoned me. Left me at seven years old in the deepest chasms of the depression. Was I not worth it for him to stay?

Marta remained silent for a very long time. From the lake, a bullfrog let out a long, low, ominous note like a Bass violin. Then I heard Marta throw back her bed roll. She climbed across the tent and slid in behind me, pulling the covers over both of us. She wrapped her arm around me and pulled me close. When she finally spoke her voice was quiet, "*Es tut mir Leid, Küken.*" I'm sorry.

I nodded and snuffled a little trying to pull myself together. It felt good to be so close to Marta. She nuzzled against my neck.

We lay that way for a while until I had composed myself a bit. I broke the silence.

"Your turn."

"What?"

"Your turn. Your *böser Traum.*"

"Um, no," she said, "I've changed my mind."

I rolled over quickly coming face to face with her, "No. Sorry. Not a chance. It doesn't work that way. I told you, now you tell me."

"I don't think I can now."

"Yes!" I demanded, "We had a deal! A promise! Now you tell me. And not just any old nightmare. I want the one you have told to no one else."

"You won't like it."

"Of course I won't like it! It's a nightmare! What's to like? Now out with it."

She looked me in the eyes and frowned a petulant frown.

"OK," she said finally, "but only if you turn around."

"Why?"

"I have my reasons," she said.

I grumbled a bit more, then turned over again allowing Marta to rest her chin on my shoulder as she spoke.

"Yeah, I have bad dreams too, sometimes," she whispered. "Different people, different places, different . . . situations. But always ending with the same feeling. When it's all done, always the same."

"What feeling?" I said.

"Emptiness," she said, her voice barely a whisper in my ear, "like there is nothing inside. Like I'm a hollow statue. Trying to fill it up with fun, *Kram,*

154

drink, boys . . . but it never fills up. Never. Like a bucket that has no bottom."

She pulled me even closer still.

"At one point, the feeling got so bad, so empty, so . . . nothing I . . . tried . . . to . . . "

"Tried to what . . . ," I whispered.

She was silent as if she were holding her breath, knowing it would carry words beyond her lips that she could never retrieve.

"I was in the kitchen. My parents were away. The servants off for the day. I stood on a stool under the rack. The rack that holds the pots and pans. I tied one end of a rope around the rack. Good and tight so it wouldn't slip. I remember making it good and tight. Then . . . then I put the other end around my neck. It would have been so easy then. So easy. To make the emptiness . . . go away. To make it disappear for good. But then . . . then I imagined my parents, my Poppy and Mum, my *wunderbar*, happy, Poppy and Mum, coming home, to find me, to find me there dangling from the pots and pans rack. Having my Mummy say 'Oh Poppy, did you purchase a new pot while we were gone?'" Marta took in a deep breath, then she began to laugh and cry at the same time until finally the crying was all there was.

I turned to face her and cradled her in my arms, "Oh Marta," I said, "I'm so sorry. I'm so sorry I made you tell that. That's a horrible nightmare. But it's OK, it was only a nightmare," she stared at me, deep into my eyes and slightly shook her head.

"Only it wasn't."

I held her face in my hands, trying to think of the right words to say to her, words that would help. But all I could think of was my own anger.

"*Gottverdammt* Marta," I whispered, "how can you even think to do such a thing to yourself? You are so lucky! So fortunate! So . . . blessed! The whole world on a string like a kite! You have everything! Good parents, money, stuff! Any boy you want at the tips of your fingers. Things I can only dream of and here you are on top of a stool ready to throw it all away! *Um Gottes Willen!* For Christ's Sake!"

She pushed me away. "You don't know! *Du hast keine Ahnung!*" she spat out; you don't have a fucking clue! "You have no idea what it is to be left alone by everyone, to not have a single friend, to always, always be empty . . . inside," she put her hands over her face and filled them with unconsolable tears.

I let her cry for a moment watching her grief spill out between her fingers before me. From some distant ether *Jane Eyre's* voice hitched quietly in my ear: "If others don't love me I would rather die than live — I cannot bear to be solitary."

Then I reached out for her. Even as she tried to fend me off I gently pulled her back toward me until I could fully reach both arms around her. I pulled her in close and whispered in her ear.

"*Das ist Blödsinn,*" that's bullshit.

She shook her head as she tried to pull away from me but I held her tight.

"Complete bullshit. I'm your friend. And you are mine," I pushed her away so I could face her at arms length, "like it or not! Right?" she gave the smallest hint of a nod and the tears, began to subside.

"Well," she eked out with just a touch of the old Marta, "if there is something farmer Katerina knows about, it's bullshit."

"Absolutely!" I said. "And here is some more bullshit! I don't believe for a second you always, AL-WAYS feel empty inside."

"I am afraid you are wrong on that," she said sadly, lowering her face.

I tipped her face back up to meet mine, "When you handed me all of those new blouses you still felt empty? When you saved my ass from Fraukenstein and got me into the choir you still felt empty? When you marched me back and forth in front of the boy's *Piss* pot, showing me bah-boom, bah-boom and how to dangle the yummy?" a smile began to creep across her face. "You who rescued me from Lake Hildi and the fart tent! You still felt empty? With all you did for me, you . . . still . . . felt . . . empty?"

She lowered her head again as she thought. Thought and remembered, "No," she said quietly, "maybe not. Maybe not always."

"Over and over and over again, every time I got in trouble . . . "

"Because of me usually."

"Usually," I agreed. "But whenever I got in trouble, who comes to the rescue?"

"Me?" she said sheepishly.

"You. Always. To my rescue. And how does that make you feel?"

Reluctantly she admitted, "Good."

"And how do you feel now? Here with me? Your friend? Kat Mueller?"

"Good," she said, her lips curling into a funny sort of smile, runlets of tears draining her eyes.

"People that only think about themselves, THEY are the ones that are always empty," I looked deeply into her eyes, "and that is not you. That is not my friend Marta. My best friend Marta Koenigsberg."

#

By the third day, Jupiter was orbiting the pen in smooth fashion. Rolf and Dannar came down at the end of the day as always, covered in sweat and wood chips, hob nail boots stiff and heavy with each step. When they entered the pen, Jupiter circled one last time then came up to them. Rolf stroked his nose. *"Mein Freund."* he whispered to the great animal.

"He is much better now," I said, entering the pen with two pails of silage slung over my shoulders. Rolf moved forward to take the pails from me, walked them to the trough and dumped them in. Marta followed me with a bag of grain to dump into the manger. Dannar met her and removed the burden from her shoulder with one hand and followed her to its destination. He dumped it in then they both followed us to the fence rail.

"By tomorrow he should be fine to go. Just take it easy on him for the first few days and stay out of the mud," I said.

Rolf smiled, "Of course! You are like a magician!" then laughed. When the laughter fell off to either side of the fence, a new seriousness settled in squarely between the four of us. "You have saved our teammate. Jupiter is more than just a simple animal, he is a friend."

Then Dannar turned to me. I could feel a hot red flush rising in my face as he looked at me, his eyes a soft blue gray. "What can we ever do to repay you?" he said, his eyes burrowing into my soul.

My face was now full on red, my cheeks as hot as a winter's stove. Words began to fight each other in my mouth and throat until a pathetic few started to find their way out.

"Oh there's no need to . . . "

But Marta cut me off, "Join us for a picnic on Sunday!"

160

ELF - ELEVEN

And of course Rolf and Dannar agreed. How could they deny us? Hadn't I just saved Jupiter's life with some homemade remedies and pilfered liniments? But now what to do?

"Leave that to me!" Marta said as we paddled our canoe across the water back to our camp, "I know just the spot! We shall bring new meaning to the term *Waldeinsamkeit!*"

And that would be doing something. There was truly something wonderful, magical even to the feeling of *Waldeinsamkeit.* The feeling of being alone in the woods. The peace. The silence. Only the sound of wind in the tree tops, speaking to you as a man with white whiskers, whispering to you to empty your heart of all that is ill. All that is heavy. To become one with the forest. This is the feeling of *Waldeinsamkeit.*

But I'm sure Marta had a different definition.

"We need to perform a little caper tonight," she said.

#

Clouds scudded the three quarter moon like a slow moving freight train passing a celestial station. Once again I had let Marta talk me into something that seemed headed down its own set of tracks, most certainly terminating in another filthy latrine.

"You need it Kat, for the picnic. I'm telling you. This is for your own good! Stick with me!"

The HJ that was patrolling our camp was down by the docks as we moved low and steady behind the column of camouflaged tents. We crossed an open space beneath the trees and pulled up short alongside the administration building where Fraukenstein kept her office along with a few other lower level paper pushers. It also held something Marta definitely wanted.

We slid silently up the back stairs, dark silhouettes painted on the bright broadside of the building, visible to anyone who cared to look. But at two AM, who would be looking.

Marta took a skeleton key from her pocket, "A little souvenir from one of last years HJ guards," she said, slid it into the lock, and we were inside.

The hall was short, the smell of wax and wood polish hanging in the air from end to end. From front to back the hallway ran with three offices on either side, large windows masquerading as walls from the chair rail up allowing any and all a clear view of what was going on inside each room. We stopped in front of one of the doors.

"I suppose you have a key to this one too," I whispered.

"Wouldn't that be nice," Marta said. "Come on, boost me."

I laced my fingers together and Marta stepped into them. A hand on my shoulder the other on the transom above the door and she pulled herself up. She swung the transom open and dropped down on the other side, turned the bolt and I was in.

Moonlight streamed through the windows painting the wooden floor in cold blue squares, like the ghosts of summer days past. On top of a small cabinet, sat a wooden box shaped like two hands in prayer. The front of the box contained an ornate grille and three knobs. A cathedral radio. Beyond the radio, beyond the window I could see the HJ's flashlight slowly sweeping the path as he walked. Marta settled herself in front of the cabinet.

"Something tells me this will not end well," I whispered to Marta.

"*Alles hat ein Ende, . . .* " she said, using her slim metal wafer methodically against the cabinet latch. Everything has an end. There was a quiet pop and the cabinet opened, " . . . *nur die Wurst hat zwei,*" she smiled. But the sausage has two.

She pulled out a bottle of clear schnapps and emptied the contents into her canteen then handed me the empty bottle.

"Fill it back up at the water cooler," she said. The gravel below the window crunched as the HJ came up the path. I began to fill the bottle from the water bubbler standing near the corner. "Gotta move faster," Marta said. Marta jumped to the office door and threw the bolt. I gave her the schnapps bottle now filled with water, and she slid it back into position in the cabinet.

A key turned in the lock of the outside door. Simultaneously Marta and I dove under the desk just as the door opened.

The HJ entered, the sound of his security keys jingling as he walked the short hall, the beam of his flashlight sweeping the contents of the room back and forth like a drunken lighthouse. Marta and I sat beneath the desk with both hands over ours mouths.

Then he stopped. Our eyes went wide as we stared at each other and held our breath. Silence filled the hallway, a peaceful prelude to what came next. The glass corridor reverberated with the freight train rumble of a long, loud belch!

"Und das ist der heutige Farmbericht, die Sau sprach selbst!" the HJ said. And that's tonight's farm report, the sow spoke herself! He chuckled to himself, started to whistle softly and left the building.

#

The following night it was time for a much needed rest, and a little alone time. A little time to visit with the friends I had brought from home. I lay in my bedroll, my flashlight tucked between my neck and shoulder. I felt peaceful and serene in the silence.

Then the flap flew back and Marta entered. She opened her coat and an assortment of wursts and jams spilled out onto her bed roll.

"What's that all about?" I said.

"Oh just some little somethings for the picnic. Donated by Herr Grossmann. From his pantry."

"Donated? Does he know that he 'donated' them?"

Marta let out a little laugh, "Of course not silly! What fun would that be?" she bit into one of the little sausages and rolled her head back in delight, "Mm-mmmm. Nothing quite so tasty as a pilfered wurst," she pointed the bitten end at me. "Some?"

I looked up, "No, but thank you," then returned to my book.

She put the wurst back in her mouth like a cigar and continued to chew.

"Whatcha reading?" she said.

"Oh, just a book."

"Which one," she said. "Maybe I've read it."

I held the cover up where she could see, "A Tale of Two Cities".

She scooched herself next to me and examined the cover, "Nope, never read it. Is it good?"

"Yeah, I like it. I've read it a few times," not looking up.

"What's it about?" she said continuing to chew.

I closed the book, "Well, let's see. It's about these two guys Charles Darnay and Sydney Carton who . . ."

"No, no, no," she waved me off. "What's it about? What's it ABOUT? What does it all mean?"

"Um, well, let's see. I guess you might say it's about the sort of things people need to do in the face of evil to, you know, to keep the world moving forward. How people need to do things to protect humanity."

"What kind of things?" Marta said wrinkling her nose.

"Selfless things," I said. "You know, noble things."

She rolled on her back and stared into the top of the tent, still munching on her wurst. "They don't sound like fun things to me! Not at all!"

\#

Sunday came too soon for me but not soon enough for Marta. Sunday was our one true day of rest and a chance to associate more on a social level with each other, but more importantly, with the HJs. Despite the events of Nuremberg and the multitude of "roasts in the oven", there was a consensus of most in the Nazi party that it was good business for the girls of the BDM and HJs to mingle on a social level. If the *Reich* were to last a thousand years, someone would have to do the heavy lifting of propagating the party and bringing new members into the world. Just do it on someone else's watch.

Sunday morning brought a joint formation between the girls of the BDM and the HJs on their side of the lake, beneath the slow languid flap of their red, white, and black flag. Marta had left our picnic basket filled with leftovers and items she had pilfered from Herr Grossmann's stores in the barn, but blatantly, almost daring to be caught, she carried the canteen with her as part of her uniform to the formation. All together we raised our voices as well as our right arms in salute of our great nation. Before we were dismissed, Fraukenstein walked our line, letting each and every member of the *Arg Acht* know that they were to behave. Each was to remain in full uniform throughout the day and no one was to travel beyond the limits of the central camp. In short, no one was to get out of her sight, or out of line.

"And just to make sure you have no idle time to fill with mischief, I want you each to compose for me a thank you letter to our beloved *Führer* for all of the wonderful things he has given to us."

A quiet moan rippled through the *Arg Acht* which earned us all Fraukenstein's sadistic smile.

Once we were dismissed, Marta and I made a circuitous path back to the barns. The sun was just cresting the tops of the trees and it was promising to be a lovely Sunday. We stepped into the cool of the barn where we met Rolf and Dannar. Without hesitation or discussion, Marta handed her makeshift picnic basket to Dannar and grabbed his other hand. Rolf made a motion to take my hand, but I conveniently looked the other way as he did and he returned his hand to his side. So, single file, Rolf and I followed Dannar and Marta out a side door and up into the stillness and heady pine scents of *Dem Böser Wald.*

We continued along a dappled path edging the lake, ever so slowly climbing a gentle rise. Birds sang and woodland creatures scurried like a page out of the Brothers Grimm.

On a small knoll, in the shade of a gnarled oak's arms, we spread our blanket far from prying eyes. Excitement raced like battery acid through my veins and I struggled to keep my face from going flush at the slightest "accidental" touch of Rolf's hand. But I held myself together. It felt good to be a part of a group, my mentor ready at my side, and, not like Munich, left alone in my little boat of emotions, cast into a maelstrom of testosterone.

Under the spreading oak we ate and laughed and told stories of BDM and HJ adventures of the past. Dannar and I mainly listened and laughed while Marta held the throne to Rolf's court jester. Marta passed the canteen around and we each took a bit as she regaled the group with the adventure she and I undertook to secure these spirits. She, of course embellished things quite a bit, but still it was a wonderful tale. The canteen passed around again, and I could feel the evil angels beginning to rise around and within me.

The first, Disobedient Adventure, having led me up a path with my *verrückten* friend and two handsome soldiers in training. The second, Alcohol, had now made its entrance on the stage, stealing the spotlight. And for what reason? Laying the groundwork for the third evil angel? Passion? Not if I can keep my wits about me, I thought.

Marta clapped her hands together grabbing all of our attention. "Alright!" she said, standing, "First things first! Katerina and I have an assignment from Herr Fraukenstein that we need to get out of the way, before we can get on to other things," she smiled wickedly. "A thank you letter to our beloved *Führer* for all that he has done for us. Would you two like to help?" she said and continued without waiting for an answer. "Wonderful! So, let me see . . . ," she tapped her finger to her lips, comfortably assuming the role of teacher at the head of the class. "Rolf, would you like to go first?"

Rolf remained stretched out on the grass and waved his hand at her. "You're already standing. You go first."

Marta continued to tap her lip, looking over her imaginary spectacles and said, "Very well, students, I will go first," she dramatically cleared her throat and began, writing on an imaginary piece of paper, *"Mein Lieber Geliebter Führer"* My Dear Beloved *Führer*, "Thank you for all of the wonderful things you have given to me. A beautiful house, two wonderful, happy parents, a shiny new Benz," with this she leaned forward to clarify, "well it is not new, but Poppy says as he climbs the ranks in the party someday it will be a new one," she continued writing. "And for the petrol for the Benz, and food and drink," she motioned to our picnic, "and of course a chance to have an outing with two wonderful, strong, handsome members of your *HitlerJugend!*" we applauded Marta as she took a bow. Then she motioned to Rolf to take the stage and sat down.

Rolf stood and stepped before us and he too cleared his throat, *"Mein Führer!"* he said, coming to full attention and automatically snapping a raised arm salute as if the man were standing before him, "I thank you for all you have done for us," he barked, "for our great nation, for our new *Reich*. You have done great things for us. You have defeated our enemies both outside of our country, and within. You have raised our military from the ashes, in defiance of those who said we must never rise again, but you have done so anyway. No longer shall we ask for what we want, for what is rightfully ours. Never again shall we face the humiliation of that abominable railroad carriage in France where we were forced to surrender. And why did we surrender?" he posed the question to us all. "Not because of their great leaders, but because of our weak ones! But that shall never happen again! We are prepared to follow you wherever you may lead us, ever ready to defend you with our blood and honor!"

Marta stood up and gave Rolf a vigorous applause, and he finished with a flourish and a bow, "Magnificent Rolf!" Marta said. "Exactly what I had said!" she applauded some more then took a deep breath, the teacher having returned, "Now, let's see, how about you Dannar?"

Dannar lay stretched languidly in the soft grass, his fingers laced behind his head.

"The same as what my teammate said. That's what I say. Honor yes, but as for the blood, I'd rather keep that inside my body, where it belongs," Marta gave that an applause too, more for Dannar than for the content.

Marta turned to me, "And now, my dear sweet *Küken.*"

I could feel my face already beginning to flush as a heavy weight settled into my stomach. I gave Marta a look of "Must I?" and she returned one of "You must!". I struggled to my feet, suddenly feeling the effects of the schnapps and stood before the "class". I looked at each of their faces as they waited in anticipation, then closed my eyes and began, my voice barely above a whisper.

"*Mein Lieber Führer,*" I began. "I thank you first of all for the peace. For the peace and for the quiet.

That we have food again on our tables. That people can afford to buy milk again. For the smell of soup on the stove and not having to wait in bread lines, hoping there will be something left when it came your turn. That we are safe in our beds and we have the freedom to become as great a nation as we could ever hope to be. I thank you for showing us, for setting the example for us all, of how to be a great leader, a great *Führer* and how to be great man." Then my face broke into a hint of a smile, "And I thank you for my friends." When I opened my eyes, Rolf was already applauding as was Marta who gave me just the slightest shake of her head at my naïveté. When I turned to look at Dannar, he was staring at me, clapping his hands together in slow motion and finished with the slightest of nods.

I returned to my seat as Rolf made a move for more of the cold wurst Marta had pilfered and he conveniently ending up alongside of me. He nibbled at the wurst and took another swig from the canteen then offered some to me. As I sipped again, rewarding myself for my bravery to stand before the others, I felt his left arm slide behind my back. Evil Angel two whispered in my ear and I took another swig of the canteen. The brief flurry of panic subsided.

"You know Kat," Marta began, the schnapps beginning to speak for her, "if you follow that trail down aways, there is a little bench overlooking the horseshoe dam. It's a lovely spot for you and Rolf to . . . observe nature," she gave me an exaggerated wink and Dannar let out a knowing little laugh.

Rolf stood, "What a splendid idea!" he said and pulled me with him. I got to my feet on wobbly knees now needing Rolf's arm around me just to stand, suddenly realizing that the schnapps I had taken had now taken me. Together, slowly, each with an arm around the other's waist, we began to walk down the trail.

#

To our right, the lake was visible through the trees, the deep blue color of Rolf's eyes, the afternoon sun splashing flashes of brilliance across its surface. Rolf kept his open hand around my waist as we walked, keeping me tight to him, much needed support against the schnapps accentuating every rise and dimple in the trail. I kept my arm around his waist, my hand a fist balled up against the small of his back.

Ahead of us I could see the path curve gently down and to the left. A small bench on a clearing offered an unobstructed view of the end of the lake where a horseshoe shaped dam held back the dappled water, a neatly scribed curve on the random canvas of nature. On the far side of the dam was a small, fairy-tale cottage, grass and moss comfortably at home on its slate roof. From the central point of the dam, a rickety wooden causeway stretched back into the lake for twenty five meters, ending on a large circular platform of rusted grating. Below the grating, water disappeared down a hole in a whirlpool. On top of the grating, an HJ stood, statue still, dressed in full combat uniform from helmet to jackboots, a large red, white, and black flag at his side.

"What is he doing down there?" I said in amazement.

"He is guarding *Das Höllenloch.*" The Hell Hole. "There is a small power station at the base of the dam. It provides electricity to our camp and the saw mill. That hole is where the water goes down to run the power station."

"Why does he have to guard it?" I said, trying to keep the HJ as soldier in focus.

Rolf tipped back his head and laughed, "He doesn't! It's punishment for doing something wrong. One of the *Kommandant's* favorite forms of 're-educating a wayward HJ,'" he laughed again, "An hour on that rusted grating with that great sucking of water beneath you gives you plenty to think about, but mostly just worrying you will fall through and disappear down the tube forever!" his eyes were bright as he told the story.

"Have you ever ended up guarding *Das Höllenloch?*"

He shook his head, "No, and I hope never to!" he said.

We continued to walk in an awkward silence, which I finally found the courage to break.

"And who lives down there? In the little cottage."

"*Der Muttertierhalter.*" The dam keeper.

"Well at least someone is there should anyone fall into *Das Höllenloch.*"

"Not much he would be able to do at that point even if he did see someone fall in, and I doubt he would even see anything unless it was through the bottom of a beer stein!" he made the universal motion of someone tipping back a beer mug to his lips, "He spends most of his time in town guarding a stool at the *Wirtshaus*." The tavern.

We continued to walk down toward the overlook, the schnapps suggesting I leave the conversation to Rolf.

"The lake is magnificent!" he said

I nodded and mumbled an incoherent "Uh-huh" my voice discordant in the rhapsody of *dem Wald*. I dared to look up, taking my eyes off my feet for a moment. Up, craning my neck slightly. Up and into his eyes. I was rewarded. He was looking back at me, and smiling.

I looked back down again, focusing on the trail, the splash of forest birdsong obliterated by the hammering in my ears. He held me in closer still. I looked to the right, at the lake and trees playing hide and seek with the sun. The schnapps was in full stride, my limbs and spirit warm and loose. The second evil angel of Alcohol began to relinquish its spot to the third, Passion. From somewhere distant I heard Marta's voice *"Du hast es!"*. You've got it!

I nodded slowly to myself, *"Ich Habs."*

I turned slowly back toward Rolf, craning my neck slightly, turning my face toward his. My eyes toward his. And his turned to mine. I tipped my head fractionally back, ever so slightly. We stopped walking. I watched his face as it slowly grew larger, filling the sky as it descended toward mine. His eyes open, clear, brilliant flashes of light racing across them. *Ich bin KEIN Kind.* I thought to myself, slowly closing my eyes. I am NOT a child. His lips lightly touched mine, firm and moist. Everything Marta had taught me now coming back smoothly in the confidence of the schnapps. His open lips became the bottle mouth, now animated and warm. Slowly, I progressed as my lessons unfolded. The fist I had balled up into the small of his back now opened, fingers spreading wide then digging into the material of his shirt.

Ich bin kein Kind again raced through my mind.

We never reached the lookout.

#

I don't know how much time passed, time now being an enemy in this new world I had entered. My boatload of emotions was steady and smooth, the waters calm beneath it as we walked back up the path. I clutched his shirt from behind, occasionally nuzzling my nose into his chest, inhaling the warmth of his scent.

When we reached the clearing, Marta and Dannar were laying side by side, Marta's head against his triangular chest, several sprigs of grass trapped in her tousled hair. Her eyes were closed and she was at peace. Dannar nudged her awake.

"Welcome back!" Marta said. "Did you find the overlook alright?"

"No," I said, smiling a mischievous yet bashful smile.

Marta looked at me, her lower jaw hanging open on a loose hinge. She bit her lower lip to pull her mouth back closed then gave me a knowing little nod that said in no uncertain terms "Good job Kat, good job!"

#

On the canoe ride back to our side of the lake, Marta and I passed the remnants of the canteen back and forth, laughing and giggling and struggling to keep on a steady course. I gave Marta every intimate, intense detail of my afternoon with Rolf, from the moment Rolf and I left to our return. Rolf and I had kissed, and kissed as if in the final hour of Judgement Day. But only kissed. I'm certain it was little more than an appetizer compared to the buffet of delights I assumed Marta and Dannar had indulged in, but I was content. Beyond content! I had been in a wonderland of sensual kissing with a tender caring boy. And it was magnificent!

Our canoe reached the other side, squeaking against the fenders at the BDM dock. I tipped my head back, canteen to lips, waiting for the last drop to land on my tongue. Trying hard not to dump ourselves in the lake, Marta sloppily threw her arm around me as we both laughed and giggled our way out of a canoe not nearly as tipsy as we were. It was an effort, but somehow we both managed to reach the safety of the dock. Still laughing and falling we decided it was best to stay on hands and knees until we were a little more stable. We crawled a few meters up the dock.

Until we came face to face with a pair of highly polished boots.

Fraukenstein's boots.

I suddenly felt the uncontrollable urge to vomit.

ZWÖLF - TWELVE

Fraukenstein had many skills and talents that enamored her to the higher ups at the BDM and handing out punishments was one of her best. As a result of our afternoon of drunken debauchery, not to mention my desecrating her boots, the following morning we found ourselves on kitchen duty at the BDM camp mess hall.

"I want this place to shine, shine, shine!" *Gruppen Frau* had said, a twinkle in her eye of pure sadism. But it wasn't too, too bad. Splitting headache aside, it was another rainy day so not much could be done that would be of any enjoyment around the camp. Rolf and Dannar were unavailable to visit, now that they too were under the thumb of their own leaders. We were all busy doing our own penance for an afternoon well spent.

And I was with Marta. She would keep *die Strafe,* our punishment, lively and fun through the day.

With hair tied back and each of us sporting our heavy orange rubber gloves once again, we split up duties, Marta tackling the stoves and griddles while I waded into a collection of over-sized steel pots and pans encrusted with the remnants of last night's dinner. The rain slapped the leaves outside and sizzled around the cook house with the sound of applause at our antics. It droned on outside the screened-in windows and drummed the tin roof like Fraukenstein's fingers on her desk during our explanations. Occa-

179

sional explosions of lightning and thunder burst overhead like aerial bombardments, each time causing Marta and I to link eyes in frozen, terrified stares, then burst into hysterical laughter. Marta pulled on an apron and put one of Herr Grossmann's paper hats on her head and waddled around the work table doing a barely passable but none-the-less hysterical impersonation of the large man's zeppelin-like movements.

On and on we went, making more progress with entertaining ourselves than with the job at hand, but making the passage of the day fly by.

Then Marta pulled the racks from one of the large baking ovens and climbed inside. She tried to pull the door closed on herself but her knees wouldn't allow.

"Kat, look!!"

I laughed.

"Who am I?" she said.

"Hmmm, let me see, the witch in Hansel and Gretel? A really big Turkey? A lopsided cake?"

Marta shook her head, "No, no, no! One more try!"

I looked at her and shrugged my shoulders, "I'm out of 'try's."

Marta looked at me disappointed and again shook her head, "I'm a Jew!" she blurted out, "Yes? Do you think so?" she laughed.

I laughed too, but my face let on I truly wasn't sure why.

"A Jew in the oven!" she said again as if somehow that would suddenly make it all crystal clear.

My laughter fell away to nothing and the corners of my smile began to sag.

"I know they try to keep it quiet, but certainly you have heard of this?" Marta said in her way that always made me feel just a little inferior. She clambered out of the oven and school was suddenly in session.

"Jews in the oven? The relocation camps? You have heard of them of course?" I nodded my head slowly, my stare never losing hers.

I had learned of the relocation camps in our political classes at the BDM. They were camps where the "non-pure" of our country were sent to ultimately be moved to other areas, other countries. Away from *dem Vaterland*.

"Why, silly, they're not relocation camps at all! Not some merry place where the Jews and misfits and other troublemakers of the Party are sent to start their lives anew and clear the decks for us and the HJs to populate the world. They're work camps, slave camps, and the troublemakers end up in the ovens! Up the stacks! Poof!" she sat down close to me, her knees almost touching mine, "Late at night, when they think I am asleep, I've heard Poppy and the other members talking about the camps, *Dachau* and what goes on up there."

I could only stare at her, my mouth slightly open, unable to close.

She put her finger under my chin and gently closed my mouth.

"My little ostrich," she said, "time to get your head out of the sand!"

"I don't believe you," I stammered.

"Don't!" she said. "Believe what you want, but I am telling you the truth. Things are not all sunshine and birthday cakes, *Küken*. We are forging ahead to a wonderful, great society, but before that can be done, there are . . . elements . . . that need to be dealt with. Like the nasty burned business in the bottom of Herr Grossmann's pans, you clean them out and we are ready to start fresh and new."

I continued to stare at her as she turned away and began to whistle.

"You're making it all up. We don't do such things," I said, barely above a whisper.

"Oh don't we?" she continued to whistle as she closed the door to the oven. "Then don't believe me. But I suggest you continue cleaning the scum from the bottom of your pans, and allow the Party to do the same."

#

That night the black hat flew into the air, rising on a column of smoke and flames, Hebrew letters as bits of ash, like the pillar of fire that stood between the Israelites and the Egyptians of so long ago. The man watched as his hat disappeared into the sky, the letters evaporating into nothingness. Then the burning mass rose up like some beast, its blackness riven with rivers of flame. High over the man's head the fire rose, above and around it gathered. Until it engulfed him.

#

Yet another week had entered and exited the *Böser Wald*. Rolf and Dannar, their punishment performed to the *Kommandant's* satisfaction, began once again to stop at the end of each day to visit before we headed back to our side of the camp. Most days Marta and Dannar would disappear up the ladder into the hayloft while Rolf and I would content ourselves below with simple, but sensual, kissing and caressing. We had now progressed to exploring each others bodies, above the waist, like blind adventurers. His hands were warm and gentle, not the rushed fumblings of Herr Himmler. Granted it was probably pretty tame compared to what Marta and Dannar were doing, but I was comfortable with the speed of things. At times, Rolf's hands would begin to drift south, and I would need to separate ourselves just a bit to allow the situation to cool. He seemed to be alright with it for now, but I knew sooner or later he would want things to progress further.

#

Laying on the bedroll I listened to the ebullient spring of Marta bubble on about Dannar. How wonderful he was, how different from the rest, a true *Prinz Wunderbar*. A true gentleman. "*Blut und Ehre*" was the motto of the HJs, Blood and Honor, well, Dannar Bremm certainly had the honor. Then, Marta added with just the quietest sigh of chagrin, "but perhaps just a bit too much."

"Not such a bad thing," I said.

"Hmmmm . . . " Marta acknowledged, neither in favor nor opposition to my thought, then continued on, "Either way, Poppy will be very pleased with me when I bring my grand, magnificent Aryan man home for the first time," she nodded and smiled a little smile, staring into a happy place in the future. " . . . very pleased."

She stopped and propped herself up on one elbow.

"And how is Rolf?"

I turned to face her. "Well, if you must know . . . " I said, hoping for some guidance on Rolf's desires to "march his forces south".

Marta listened attentively, rolled onto her back and began tapping her finger against her lip.

When I had finished, the tapping stopped and she began to stroke her lip with her finger.

"*Ja*," she began, "I can see that. Rolf's definitely the 'handsy' type. But I guess most men are, once you get their motors running a bit. Not all, but most. Some take a little petrol to get their fire going I'm finding out. But sooner or later, they all come around. But not our Rolf. His motor is always running. Doesn't take much at all to get him revved up and trousers down. He is your straight down the line, dozen-to-a-box, cookie cutter of a man. And what do men want *Küken*?"

I let out a sigh, "*Die Scham*".

"*Die Scham* is right. Not enough to have *die mopse*, they want more. More! Everything! Men. No patience. Always *scharf*," horny. "What to do?" she turned back to me.

"What to do is right!"

"Well," she said, "was what he did . . . *Spass?*" Fun?

I shrugged a bit. Then gave a little bit of a smile, "I suppose!"

"Perfect!" she shouted. "Progress! So, remember, you don't want to give the store away, but it's OK for the customer to . . . you know . . . handle the merchandise a little. Nothing wrong with that *Küken*. Yes, it takes a while for things to feel right, give that part a chance. Sometimes it never feels right," she let out a laugh, "not that that's stopped me before!"

"Ugh! Marta! Look, let's face it. Yes you've taught me, trained me, for which I thank you from the bottom of my heart! But I don't know what I'm doing Marta. I'm a lamb in the lion's den when it comes to men. This is all so new to me! If only Rolf would understand and be patient, maybe then . . . "

She rolled onto her back again. "Just relax, see what happens, boys are handsy, sad but true. And you're right about the feelings part. I didn't really believe that. Thought it was all *klatschen*, clap trap. Until I met up with Dannar of course," she stared into the camouflage for a long moment as if waiting for the blotchy bits of brown, green and tan to reveal some secret, "He has taught me some things I did not know," then she opened her mouth in a slow yawn. "give it a chance, go slow, see what happens. Don't need to give him the store. Sometimes it's better if you don't. Keeps them . . . "

I looked over and her eyes were closed. I waited a bit, hoping there would be more, but I already knew the rest. I rolled over and closed my eyes hoping that my *Prinz Wunderbar* would visit me in my dreams. Whoever it might be.

Like someone flicking their finger against the canvas of our tent, slow at first, then over and over, the first drops of rain began to fall.

#

And fall, and fall, for two straight days, turning all the trails around the camp to running rivulets of muddy brown.

Most of the HJs were now undercover making repairs to equipment, wagons and tools. Several teams were still moving logs trying to keep the mill fed with felled trees for the greater glory of the *Reich*.

Marta had disappeared with Detlef on some project or another giving me a chance to savor some solitary time in the barns, just myself and the animals, alone. Rolf was spending the day at the blacksmith's forge mending a broken two-man buck saw.

From the north end of the camp, Dachs' *Gulliver Wagen* crested the ridge, loaded down with one massive trunk, his four Belgians parting a curtain of gray-white rain. Brilliant lightning crackled and broke on all sides of the forest, each followed by cannonades of rolling thunder. The Belgians, noble warhorses of old, glistened in the rain, their chestnut coats and blonde manes plastered against their necks. All were doing their duty, drawing the massive load through the swollen ruts of the washed out road under Dachs' commands. All of the animals, except for one.

Standing in the shelter of the open barn doors, I spotted the Belgian closest to me, Philip the Good, favoring his outside forward leg. I pulled on my poncho and ran into the driving rain waving my arms at Dachs.

"Kat!" Dachs yelled through the rain. "What are you doing?"

"Philip is hurt! He needs attention!"

"Let me get this load to the mill then we'll have a look," he shouted back.

I stepped to the side, observing Philip's faltering gait as he passed. Dachs angled his team to the staging area outside of the mill's wide doors and a group of HJs in ponchos and steel helmets began to muscle and pike the log onto the rails, bound for the humming saw.

Dachs was down studying the Belgian's fore leg in the yellow light of his hurricane lantern when I reached him, "Couldn't you tell Dachs? Couldn't you tell something was wrong?"

"They were all pulling fine. And we needed to get this load to the mill to make quota."

"Philip is hurt Dachs. You should have stopped," I said running my hand down the lower portion of the Belgian's forward leg, the diameter of a small tree trunk itself.

"It was slippery and dark. Philip lost his footing and slid off the road," beneath the hood I could see the worry in Dach's eyes.

When I slid my hand along the fetlock, where the lower bone joins the dinner plate-sized hoof, the Belgian pulled back its leg.

Dachs looked at me from beneath the cowl of his rain hood and whispered *"Gebrochen?"* Busted? The rain continuing to hammer down around us.

"Maybe," I said. "I can't be sure. It may just be a sprain. I know someone who'd know though, and if it is just a sprain, she'll be able to help."

"Who?" Dachs said.

"My *Tantchen*. She'll know what to do. You get Philip unhitched and I'll see if I can arrange some transportation."

Through the rain roiled puddles I ran to the blacksmith shop. Rolf, dressed in blacksmith leathers, worked the forge with the ringing of hammer on anvil. Showers of sparks surrounded him like Faust in Hell when I burst through the door.

"Philip the Good is injured. We need some transportation to get him back to town so my *Tantchen* can have a look at him. If anyone can save him, she can."

Rolf set his hammer on the anvil, "I will talk to the *Kommandant* to see if we can borrow a truck."

"Thank you Rolf!" I said beaming. "Where is Dannar?"

"He is on the other side of the camp mending the yoke."

"OK, I'm sure we can handle this ourselves," Rolf headed off into the rain to the *Kommandant's* cabin while I returned to the mill. Dachs had already unhitched Philip when I approached.

"Take care of the other horses," I said to Dachs. "Rolf should be returning shortly with a truck."

"I want to go with you," Dachs protested.

I shook my head, "Stay here. It will be OK."

"But I really should . . . "

I patted him on the shoulder of his poncho, "Wait here Dachs, we'll take care of Philip."

"*Versprochen?*" he said, the howl of rain beginning to pick up. Promise?

"You have my word, Dachs." Dachs went into the barn and returned with a bridle for Philip. Instinctively the horse brought his head down and Dachs slipped the bridle over his head. Then he pressed his nose against the horses face. From around the barns, headlights swung and bounced cutting twin cones of light through the fusillade of rain. Rolf backed the covered Bussing-nag stake-bodied truck in front of Philip and immediately the massive Belgian began to rear up, flashes of lightning painting the scene in brilliant light. Dachs pulled on the rein trying to get the giant horse under control but to no avail.

"*Alles ist gut Philip! Alles ist gut!*" I said moving toward Philip.

"Careful Kat," Dachs said evenly, trying not to cause Philip any further alarm. I gave him a nod.

"*Ruhig sein,*" I continued. Be calm. Slowly Philip began to settle down, finally coming back to all fours. I began to stroke the Belgian's side. *"Alles ist gut,* Philip. *Alles ist gut."*

I led the lame war horse slowly up the ramp into the back of the truck, the truck's suspension groaning in protest under the weight.

Rolf closed the back of the truck, secured the tailgate, then clambered behind the wheel. He eased the Bussing-nag into gear, allowing the truck to slowly roll forward, jostling and splashing through puddles like a boat on a storm tossed sea. Nearing the front gate of the HJ Camp, we passed the *Kommandant's* cabin, his tall frame silhouetted by the porch light beneath the overhang. Rolf stopped the truck and jumped from the running board, crossed to the front of the *Kommandant's* cabin and met the tall man. The two exchanged words then a raised arm salute and Rolf dashed back to the idling truck. When he had slammed the door I banged my hand on the rear of the cab and Rolf slid back the small rear window.

"Is everything alright?" I asked.

"Yes, yes," Rolf said, "everything is alright." And the Bussing-nag swung its headlights toward the front gate.

"Do you know where we are going?" I said.

"Ülmstadt," He answered.

"Yes," I said. "Get us to *Ülmstadt* and I will give you directions from there."

"Jawohl!" Rolf replied and slid the rear window closed.

DREIZEHN - THIRTEEN

We jostled the back roads for less than an hour while I stroked Philip's coat and whispered reassuring words. Rain rattled the canvas top as lightning continued its siege of the Bavarian country side. The Bussing-nag rumbled along a short while longer passing farm houses in the distance, their windows warmly lit by hearth fires. Finally the jostling settled into the low rumbling hiss of rain slick cobblestones. Then the truck shuddered to a halt, the engine humming in a low idle, ghosts of exhaust appearing then disappearing from the tailpipe. I looked out between the slats of the truck's stake body, the small yellow star on the door of the butcher shop clearly visible in the glow of the head lights. I banged on the rear of the cab and the window slid open.

"Why are we stopping here?" I said to Rolf.

"Sorry, Kat," Rolf said, "end of the line. *Kommandant's* orders."

"No, no, NO!" I screamed through the window, "No Rolf! There must be some mistake! My *Tantchen* can save him. Please Rolf, we need to try!" I ran to the back of the truck and began to rattle the back of the gate.

Rolf came around and opened the rear gate.

"Sorry Kat," Rolf said compassionately. "I tried to talk to the *Kommandant*, but he insisted. Ordered in fact. The horse needs to be destroyed."

"He's not just a horse, he's Philip and he can be saved!" I snapped angrily.

Rolf shook his head. "Orders are orders."

"Maybe there is a way . . . "

"No, sorry," he climbed into the back of the truck, grabbed Philip's rein and began to lead him down the ramp.

I grabbed the rein and began to pull back, "We could bring Philip to my *Tantchen*. If she heals him, great! She keeps him. If she can't heal him, she can bring Philip to the butcher," I smiled at Rolf "No one will be the wiser. Either way Philip doesn't come back!"

Rolf jerked the rein out of my hand, "Absolutely not! That would be deceitful, a betrayal of the *Kommandant* and of the very *Reich* itself!"

Rolf led the horse to the door with the small yellow star and banged on the window. He waited for a moment then banged again even harder, almost breaking the glass, "Open up! Open up *Gottverdammt!*"

The butcher, clad in a white apron and a paper white hat appeared in the door. Behind him, two blonde twin girls, watched from the shadows.

Rolf forced himself directly into the butcher's face, "How dare you Jew! Filthy Jew! How dare you keep a good German citizen waiting in the rain!" Rolf handed the reins to me and stepped forward, slamming his hand against the center of the Jew's apron, pushing him backward into the shop. The Jew was a big man with broad shoulders and forearms to rival a grown man's leg. In a fair situation he could have certainly held his ground against Rolf. But this was not a fair situation. Rolf had the full weight of a nation behind him.

Rolf shoved him again and again the Jew went back, further into the shop leaving me standing beneath the rain soaked eaves, the storm rattling shop signs up and down the *BundesStrasse*. Rolf flailed his arms as he spoke, his words lost in the storm. Before him the Jew stood, nodding, acquiescent, his meaty hands knotted and twisting against his apron. When the conversation was done, Rolf placed his hands on his hips and the Jew traced the path from his front door to the back in the air with his finger. Rolf stepped back outside, turned into the alley adjacent to the shop and motioned for me to follow.

"Rolf, please!" I begged one last time, but Rolf would hear none of it.

"I"m sorry Kat," he said, "orders are orders."

He took the reins from my hand and led Philip down the alley, the slow clip-clop of his hooves on cobbles reverberating in the narrow confines like the drumbeat for a fallen king.

At the rear of the shop the Jew waited, standing in the frame of a large sliding door. Philip stopped and would go no further. Rolf pulled on the rein but Philip refused to enter, the room heavy with the smell of animals, blood and death.

Rolf looked at me, "Tell him Kat," I shook my head, "Please, Kat. Tell him. Tell Philip." I looked to the Jew, a man who knew what battles not to fight. Rain came off the corrugated roof in sheets. There was nothing more to be done.

I took a deep breath, let it out slowly and gave a singular reluctant nod.

I stepped before Philip, his great and noble chestnut face high above my own, and my eyes began to fill with tears. He cocked his head to better see me, his honey colored eye soft and gentle, in its depths a millennia of lineage to whatever knight or Chevalier held his rein. An eye filled with gentle wisdom. And trust. I tipped my head back to speak to him and the rain purged the saltiness of my tears away. I opened my mouth and struggled out the lie.

"*Alles ist gut*, Philip. *Alles ist gut.*"

Then Philip lowered his head and entered the space.

Rolf led the injured war horse into a narrow pen of steel pipe and closed the low door behind him, then grabbed the Jew by the arm and forced him into the front room. With his large hands the Jew motioned his daughters into the safety of his shadow. Through the crack in the door I watched as the Jew took a small metal box from under the counter and unlocked it with a key from around his neck. He reached into the box and took some bills and handed them to Rolf. Rolf counted them and shook his head and shoved the Jew against the counter. Rolf stuck his hand into the box grabbed the remaining bills and stuffed them into his pocket.

Rolf stuck his head inside the back room.

"Time to go," he said and left the shop, headed for the truck.

But I could not leave Philip's side. I continued to gently stroke the side of his nose through the steel bars, his gaze tranquil at my touch.

A shadow fell across the room's sloped concrete floor as the Jew reappeared in the door to the slaughter house. Above the black tangle of beard, his eyes were filled with deep compassion as he took my pain on as his own. I tried to say something, my heart unable to find the words. But they were not necessary.

"Your friend will be a great blessing," the Jew began, "to those up in the relocation camp. His death is not a loss. He will provided much needed food for so many. And there is nothing more noble than when one gives their life for another."

I covered my face with my hand as I turned to leave the slaughter house. Passing the Jew, I stopped and buried my face in his apron and began to cry.

"Thank you," I whispered, "thank you . . . Herr Traubweiss."

He said nothing, but patted my head in the comforting way that he always did. I snuffled, gave the best bit of a nod I could muster and followed Rolf out the door.

From the slaughterhouse I could hear Herr Traubweiss speaking quietly as he sharpened his knife.

"Gepriesen sei dir, der Herr, unser Gott, der König der Welt, der uns mit seinen Geboten geheiligt hat und befahl uns bei diesem das opfern . . . "

"Blessed be thee, the Lord our God, King of the world, who has sanctified us with His commandments, and commanded us on this sacrifice. . . "

#

For nearly a week I avoided Rolf, unable to look him in the eyes. He made attempts, but I made excuses. Anything to avoid conversation.

I spent my time at the barns with Marta and with Dachs, helping him, as best I could, find and train a new replacement for Philip. It was a time to console each other, to help clear the shadows in our loss.

It was also a time for me to begin to pay my private penance. For betraying my promise to Dachs to protect Philip and for the poisoned trust I gave to Philip himself at the very end. *Alles ist gut* I had told him, then sent him to his death.

Time heals all wounds supposedly, but is there ever enough time in one's life or a dozen lifetimes to heal the wounds you inflict when you betray your loved ones? I don't know that I will ever live long enough to find out.

It was toward the end of that week that the poultice of time first began to work its balm upon my heart. The rain no longer soaked the Bavarian plains, Dachs had once again found his infectious smile, at least on occasion, and a new Belgian settled into position at the head of the *Gulliver Wagen*. Life was returning to normal, the ship returning to an even keel. But for all the good humor and companionship Dachs could provide, something of him was missing for me, some necessary ingredient in the elusive elixir that bound a woman to a man.

I still wanted to see Rolf, or at least talk to him. To understand why it was so important to blindly follow the *Kommandant's* orders, even in the face of reason. Perhaps there are just things that I will never understand. The fire that I had felt in his embrace along the footpath was now little more than a single ember, the flames we shared having been quenched in the deluge that night surrounding the butcher's shop. But an ember remained nonetheless. And embers, properly attended, can grow into a comfortable warmth.

#

It was on the eighth day since the butcher shop that Rolf, once again, made an effort to return the gray between us to black and white. He and Dannar returned from the hill and, as usual, giggly Marta lured Dannar up into the hayloft above the stalls. I continued to work, moving pails of silage into the paddock. Unwilling to give up, Rolf approached me.

"Need a hand?" he said. Inside me I felt the log jam of my emotions creak and groan, begin to free. I looked at him and this time, for the first time since then, gave just the slightest of nods.

"Sure."

He gave his best old Rolf smile, grabbed both pails from my hands and followed me.

"How are you?" he said in an awkward attempt at matter-of-factness as he dumped the pails into the trough.

"Good," I said, allowing the word to dangle alone in the awkward breeze.

He nodded, "Good . . . Very good . . . Nice to hear." then he continued to nod, trying desperately to maintain his composure.

Until he couldn't any longer.

"I'm sorry Kat," he said, his facade of matter-of-factness suddenly crumbling before my eyes, "I'm very sorry Kat."

"I'm sorry too," I said, sorry for the dark vein of poison that had risen between us. Hoping the words might somehow stanch the flow. I fumbled around with my thoughts then continued with what was really on my heart, "I . . . I saw a . . . different side of you."

"I'm sorry," he said again, as if those two words in that precise order might serve to lubricate the machinery of forgiveness.

"Why?" I said, finally letting it out. "Why did you . . . ? You wouldn't even let me try to save Philip."

"It was the *Kommandant's* orders. He . . . He insisted. He would not take well to us, me, not following his orders."

"Why was it so important to him. Philip. Being sold to the . . . "

Rolf did not answer.

But suddenly it all became clear. Sickeningly clear. "It was the money, wasn't it? Strictly the money."

He hung his head, examining the weathered tops of his boots, then ever so slightly nodded. From deep inside of me a guttural sound emerged and I shoved him hard against the trough.

"How could you?" I screamed at him. "How could you!?" I shoved him again as hard as I could. He reached out and grabbed me by the shoulders. He brought his face down to mine and stared into my eyes.

"Yes. I did it. I followed the orders given to me. That is what I did. That is what I do. That is what we all need to do. Leave the thinking, the emotions, the 'my way would be better' out of it. Leave it to the leaders to do their job and lead. And we, the followers, do OUR job and follow. That is how we have gotten out of the mess our parents have made of things. That is how we will return to the greatness that is truly ours. But we must stand ready to do whatever it takes. Whatever it takes."

"Does that include robbing Herr Traubweiss?" I spat out.

"The Jew? I robbed the Jew?" he threw back his head and laughed. "I robbed the Jew and you are upset with me for that? I find that . . . incomprehensible! Why should I NOT rob the Jew when I have the chance? For years they have been robbing our country of everything that is important. I had a chance to even the ledgers, just a little, and I took it. And you are upset with me for it? My dear Katerina. My dear little farm girl. You have so much to learn about the way the world works."

I stared at him, snuffling back my fury. But as I searched his eyes, I began to stare even harder inside myself. In a world of deeper and darker shades of gray, maybe, just maybe, he was right.

"*Du bist nur ein Kind*," the words continued to haunt me. You are only a child.

Maybe I am too naive to know the workings of the world. Maybe a steady, firm hand on the tiller of things was necessary to keep the country on course. In all my books, things always seem to favor the right, the positive so that good prevails over evil. But this is not some story book. This is the real world. Who gets to define what is good and what is evil here? Isn't the good of one soldier standing in a trench the evil of the soldier in the opposing trench? Can good and evil be simply a matter of what trench you happen to be standing in? Or born into?

Rolf cradled my face in his hands and looked tenderly into my eyes.

"It's OK, Kat," he said. "I'll help you. I'll help you to understand things. Or, who knows, maybe you can you can help ME understand things. OK?"

His eyes were compassionate and soft and my fears and worries slowly dissolved into them.

"OK," I said quietly.

"OK," he answered.

Then he kissed me.

#

The criss-cross confusion of camouflage above me was replicated in my heart and my heart would not lay still. To see the man who had stirred my passions not so long ago send Philip to his death then rob a man, all for . . . what? Money. All on the orders of his *Kommandant?* His leader. The man he is supposed to follow blindly, without question.

Long into the night, good and evil wore each other's mask and battled in my heart for domination of my soul without solution. Morpheus could not find me, nor I him.

I sat up in bed, careful not to rustle the covers of my bedroll or ruffle the top of the tent. I slid my way to the foot of our *Schlafsäcke,* sleeping bags, where Marta kept her rucksack. I looked over at her, her breathing slow and rhythmic, the hint of a smile on her face, surely honorable Dannar Bremm was with her, wherever she was. I turned back to her rucksack and began to carefully rummage through. When I found what I was looking for, I stuck it in my pocket, pulled on my clothes and slipped out of the tent.

It was nearing a new moon, with barely a sliver of white in the sky to light my way, a blessing for concealment, a curse for navigation. Careful to avoid tripping on the ropes holding tents in place, I moved my way to the administration building. Before I approached the back door I scanned the camp for any HJs that should be on patrol, but there were none to be seen. No sweeping flashlights, no unbridled burps. I took Marta's key from my pocket and slid it into the lock. A smooth turn to the right and I was in.

I walked down the hall, glossy and smooth, the smell of wood polish in my nose. I stood before Fraukenstein's office door, but with no one to boost me I couldn't reach the transom. There was a small table in the hall for mail which I slid over in front of her door. I clambered up on top, flopped the transom open and was in, then opened the door and slid the mail table back into position. No one would be the wiser.

Once inside, I took the cathedral radio down from the table and carried it under the desk. There was an outlet there for the light which I unplugged and plugged in the radio. Sitting under the desk I began to dial around, intermittent to the bursts of static were music, farm reports and of course, the ever present speeches. Back and forth I dialed, keeping the volume down as low as I could, searching the airwaves. Searching for answers. Maybe the one who had spoken of the *Sturmwind* knew. Perhaps, just maybe, it was the same *Sturmwind* my father would speak of each night in the *Hühnerstall* when he would tuck me in. When he'd lay his hand upon my head and whisper:

"Gott schütze mein Kind vor dem kommenden Sturmwind".

"God protect my child from the coming Storm Wind."

It was growing late and approaching the time to abandon my quest. Ever so gently Morpheus began to stroke my eyelids. I dialed the tuner to the far end of its range and the static stopped. Something was there. I turned the volume up slightly and a man's voice came alive. THE voice.

"Die Trommeln des Krieges haben begonnen. Steh auf, steh auf…."

"The drums of war have begun to beat. Rise up, rise up…"

Curled up beneath Fraukenstein's desk, I continued to listen.

#

It was the darkest edge of morning when I finally returned to the tent. Even the sliver of moon had abandoned its work for the night and gone to bed leaving the camp in total darkness. Only an HJ flashlight was sweeping the area around the dock when I quietly slipped open the flap, crawled inside and slipped into my bed roll. I turned my face to the outside wall of the tent and closed my eyes, hoping for even a few hours of blessed sleep before returning to work.

"Kat."

It was Marta, her voice quiet, but different. Serious. Void of the bubbly humor that made Marta Marta.

She continued.

"You're my friend, right?"

"Absolutely!" I said, my voice breaking with a sticky dryness that had suddenly filled my throat. A long silence followed from her side of the tent, every second piling another dark heavy stone on our conversation.

"Then why did you steal from me?"

A lead cannon ball the size of my fist appeared in the lower portion of my stomach, threatening to pass through my side and into the ground beneath us. The dryness in my mouth nearly sealing it shut. A dozen lies and excuses flashed quickly across my mind, but this was Marta.

"I'm sorry," I croaked. "I . . . I didn't want to disturb you."

"You wouldn't disturb me," she said, not buying my efforts to soften the crime. "Where did you go?"

The cannon ball moved slightly against the inner lining of my stomach, offering me the chance to make it lighter, or much heavier. I hesitated. Then chose the former, I told her where I went.

Her side of the tent again went silent, so I continued.

"You told me things about us, about our country. I don't believe you. I can't believe you," then I too fell silent for a long heavy moment, "but I need to know."

Silence filled the void between us, this time not only filled with darkness, but danger.

"Be careful," she said, "I can't help you if you get caught."

VIERZEHN - FOURTEEN

Following dinner in our mess hall the following day, Marta and I took our canoe back to the HJ's side of the lake, Marta met Dannar at the dock and I exchanged places with him in the canoe. Together Dannar and Marta moved smoothly away and headed off toward the far end of the lake, toward the horseshoe dam. Marta sat in front and Dannar in the rear, paddling together in smooth union, Marta talking nearly non-stop, Dannar quietly nodding from the rear.

I walked up the dock towards the barns. Rolf was busy on an HJ project for one of the leaders so I had the evening to myself, a chance for some *Waldein-samkeit,* a chance for some peaceful time in the woods. Only this time I would not be alone, I was bringing a companion with me.

Word had spread to the *Kommandant* of my good work with Jupiter. The *Kommandant's* own leg had been acting up so he was unable to ride and I had been commanded to exercise Vixen around the paddock for a few minutes each day. But today, I had made up my mind, would be a little different. When it came to things you really wanted, Marta had always advised, better to beg forgiveness than ask permission. Besides, my heart was clamoring, even if only in some small way, to betray the *Kommandant.*

I walked into the barn, the snort and trammel of hooves in stalls on either side of me. I crossed over into the officer's portion of the barn, opened Vixen's door and stepped inside. Ever so gently I walked along, stroking my hand across Vixen's glossy black flanks. I ran my hand along the barrel of his chest, his muscles tight beneath the short coarse hair. Working my way to his nose, I stroked it gently, and kissed him lightly on the muzzle.

"Want to go for a ride boy?" I said. "A real ride?" I placed my face against his nose and closed my eyes, "*Ich habs*?" I said, "Then let's go!"

I threw a blanket over Vixen's back and pulled the *Kommandant's* saddle from its rest. I slung the saddle onto Vixen's back and snugged up the girth, opened the gate and swung myself into the saddle. Gently I stroked his withers and instinctively Vixen turned his nose out the gate, the sound of his hooves on the cobbles like blocks of hard, dry wood knocked together in a gentle rhythm. We exited the barn. Together we circled the paddock several times as I casually canvassed the area to be sure there were no telling eyes. None to be seen, Vixen and I slipped from the paddock and headed up the trail into *den Böser Wald*.

The air was starting to cool from the heat of the summer's day and we began to climb high onto the trail at a gentle walk. Behind us I could still catch glimpses of the HJ camp, the barns we had just left, the sawmill, the administration building, the rows of camouflaged tents lined up like piles of man-made nature. Far in the distance, the lake was peeking out among the trees, spread out below and beyond like a sheet of rippled blue glass. Somewhere down there were Marta and Dannar, perhaps tucked into some tranquil cove, chatting quietly, or perhaps, knowing Marta, wondering how she could get closer to Dannar without tipping the canoe.

But none of that mattered, Vixen and I were headed up the trail, alone together. We crested a small rise in the trail and began to descend slightly down, the sights and the sounds of the HJ camp disappearing behind us.

And we were alone with the forest.

I put my heels slightly to Vixen's barrel chest and he began to move forward at a trot. He wanted to go, but had enough discipline to wait for my command. So I gave it to him. With a loud "HA!" I gave him my heels and we were off! Bestride him I soar, I am a hawk!

Down the path we raced, rider and mount one, my neck pressed against his as we moved through the forest, the smell of pine and fresh air filling both our nostrils. It was wonderful, exhilarating as I clung to his chest with my knees and thighs. Down trails, up the other side Vixen thundered, the sound of his hooves against the trail Ca-dah-CRUMP! Ca-dah-CRUMP! Who needs men, I thought when I am me! For in that moment, in the synchronicity of rider and mount, how in control I felt, comfortable in my own skin. Me, oh happily me!

For a full half hour we raced through the forest, always my eye on the sun until it tiredly began to settle below the ridge. The forest began to turn a faint shade of blue and it was time to return to the barns. I turned Vixen around and allowed him to cool down as slowly we began to retrace our steps on the trail.

I dismounted from Vixen in the paddock and walked him back into the barn, returned the saddle and groomed him before settling in for the night. Alone I walked back through the barn, from the cobblestoned center and brightly painted stables to our little, dingy corner of the world.

When I reached the stable where Marta and I had spent so many weeks, where Marta often led Dannar into their own little *Adlerhorst* in the hay loft, I saw Rolf standing there, calmly leaning against the ladder. I walked up to him and put my arms around his waist. He smelled good, a manliness about him as I inhaled the scent of his clean white cotton shirt. I tilted my face up and he leaned down and gently kissed me. Me, oh happily me, I thought again. When his lips broke from mine, his eyes remained fully locked and loaded. I burrowed into those eyes, my soul now completely open and exposed, vulnerable, but willing in what I knew lay next. Then he took my hand and led me up the ladder into the hayloft.

A lantern hung from a wooden peg jutting from a timber, the wick trimmed down low, casting only the dimmest of yellow warm lights in a tiny pool. Within the pool of light, a horse blanket was laid out on top of a pile of hay, bales surrounding it creating a small, intimate enclave. This was where Dannar and Marta had spent so many hours while Rolf and I contented ourselves below with kissing and cuddling.

At least I had been contented with just that. Until now.

I felt myself freeze as I approached the blanket, Rolf leading me by the hand. He lay down on the blanket and gently pulled me beside him. I went. I lay there looking in his eyes and he eased his face closer to mine, his hand gently stroked my arm, which only caused me to tighten up more. Perhaps if the canteen had been there, things would go more smoothly, provide the lubrication of love's machinery, but there was no schnapps in sight. Ever so gently he pulled my neck toward him and we began to kiss as Marta had instructed, tenderly, passionately my mind focused solely on his lips pressing, exploring against mine. His left hand slid up my side and under my uniform. My heart was racing, enjoying the familiar exploration of his hand. He pulled the tail of my shirt from my shorts and began to ease it over my head. I did not resist. This is what they want, Marta had told me, let them have a little. I raised my hands above my head and he pulled my uniform top off, leaving my bare skin available from the waist up. I settled into his strong arms as his hands continued to explore, his kisses deep, probing. The third Evil Angel of Passion was here in all her glory, hovering, tantalizing, encouraging. His hands were calloused but strong, working their way down, farther, farther. My breath began to take on a new pace, as did his. Faster, heavier, a locomotive approaching a grade. Lower still went his hands. I arched my back, only the sound of his breath and the cheering of my Evil Angel in my ear.

From deep within my stomach I felt as if a small hole was being torn in my integrity, my soul. A wrongness about things that began to leak, spread from its center outward, engulfing my belly, traveling up my arms until I could no longer bear the weight.

My eyes flew open wide and I began to hyperventilate as he forced himself on me. I pressed my hands into the hollows of his shoulders and began to push as he rolled the full of his weight on top of me. I responded with a full throated scream. He clamped his hand over my mouth and I began to fight, punch, kick. His hand slid down from my mouth and engulfed my throat. I struggled in another breath and opened my mouth to scream but there was no sound, only the flat crack of his hand across the side of my face.

The burning in my cheek and ringing in my ears was nothing to the shock of the blow. I managed one hand up and into the fleshy underside of his chin forcing his head back, Rolf's once passioned blue eyes now bearing down on me with the thin, red-rimmed glaze of insanity.

I pushed harder into his chin, hoping to force even a little of his weight off of me. I locked my elbow and with all my effort gave a mighty shove and, as if by some miracle, he began to float upwards. Only then did I see the massive fingers of one Dannar Bremm around his neck.

Dannar tightened his grip and continued to squeeze, Rolf's red face now spouting curses as a series of grunts and squawks. With the speed of a striking snake, Rolf was around and started swinging. Dannar returned fire. Instantly the two were engaged in mortal combat in the hayloft. Punches thrown, some missing, some connecting, body slams and wrestling grips, choke holds set and broken. I lay curled up still struggling to breathe as the two battled on, their voices screaming, yelling, shaking the beams and rafters of the barn with each thrown punch or body slam to the floor boards. Rolf managed to get Dannar in a wrestling hold, Dannar's head now held under his arm, forearm collapsing Dannar's windpipe. Rolf growled at Dannar in a low rumble of voice. "I'll take what I want, where I want," he heaved up, tightening his forearm on Dannar's windpipe even more, "whenever I want. Understand Bremm?" Dannar let out a grunt, and a wheeze, a seeming capitulation to the death grip his partner had him in. Dannar's face had now turned crimson as Rolf heaved his forearm even tighter still into Dannar's wind pipe. *"Verstanden?"* The look on Rolf's face was smug, satisfied at his vanquished partner. A face of pure triumph.

Until it wasn't.

Rolf's eyes flew open wide as he realized his feet were coming off the ground, his toes struggling to remain in contact with the floorboards of the loft. He was now up on tip toes as Dannar began to straighten up, carrying Rolf with him, the veins in Dannar's arms and hands standing out in stark relief against his straining muscles. Dannar let out a great grunt and extricated his head from Rolf's arm, lifted him a little higher and pushed Rolf out of the hayloft and onto the dirt floor below with a dusty crump.

Dannar said nothing as he watched Rolf drag himself out of the barn door, then he turned back to me. He wrapped me in his work shirt, cradled me in his arms, and a deluge of tears surged down my scalded cheek.

Another face appeared alongside Dannar's then gently muscled him away until I was face to face with the brilliant brown eyes of Marta, cradled in a rim of tears. "This is all my fault," she whispered, "all my fault," she wiped her nose on the back of her hand, "I should never have told you to . . . "

I shook my head ever so slightly, "No, it . . . was . . . all . . . me," then tried to smile. She hugged me and held me close. Then she stood up and wiped her eyes.

"Take care of her till I get back," she said to Dannar.

"The *Kommandant* will take care of him, I will see to it," Dannar said as Marta began to descend the ladder from the hayloft.

"There will be nothing left of Rolf to take care of," Marta whispered through her teeth and disappeared down the ladder.

#

Marta was true to her word. Rolf never returned to camp and it was rumored Marta had left him with only one serviceable eye.

#

What followed was a week of healing, both the physical bruise on the side of my face and the emotional damage in the crater of my self esteem. Little was said by anyone in authority. I'm sure I wasn't the first, nor would I be the last to experience an HJ, fueled with testosterone and driven by the belief that they should be able to take what they want. There was a sense of that that filled the air at the logging camp. And in the country. The power to do whatever they wanted, all beneath the red, white, and black. All blessed by the gods of the broken cross.

I continued to work the barns, quietly tending the animals.They would do me no harm. I kept my eyes down, unwilling to risk the sniggering looks of others. Everyone knew, word spreads quickly among the hens of the BDM *Hühnerstall.*

But Marta was not one of them. She was there to comfort me, to help me heal, crossing her fingers before my eyes when my shadows were especially dark.

At night, when the others were all safely asleep, Marta would pull me from my bedroll. Her arm draped around me, we would walk down to the lake, down along the path that shadowed the stony shore, the dark tranquil water our silent escort. It was only here that the first signs of normal life began to reappear like scintillating speckles of moonlight fanning out across the darkness of the lake.

As we walked, Marta shared her wisdom. Set out before me along the path she placed breadcrumbs of thoughts for me to digest, or ignore. Little by little, bit by bit, I began to take them, the way I would lure ducks from the pond on our farm with small crumbs of bread and large volumes of patience. And eventually they would come. Soon they would understand I meant them no harm. Only good. Patience is ever the handmaiden of love. Thus ever was Marta.

"Things will be OK, Kat," Marta said quietly, her words discordant in the silence of the path. "OK?" she put her arm around my waist and pulled me closer, "I told you, this happened to me before, right?" again I nodded. She had told me many stories of aggressive boys that had made the mistake of crossing Marta Koenigsberg.

Her voice began to ratchet up. "One guy tried that, tried putting his hand over my mouth and forcing himself on me!" she had told me before, but I never pressed the issue further. I didn't want to even think about it. But something inside me felt different, like a window cracked open in a fetid room.

"What did you do?" I asked for the first time.

Marta looked at me and smiled as if I had just risen from the dead. She threw her arms around me and gave me a great hug. Then, almost nose to nose, she answered in a near yell.

"Why, I bit his hand of course!" then she let out a laugh. A laugh that bounded from one side of the lake to the other, echoing back to us across the cold flat calm. The flickering scintillations of moonlight began to multiply and divide. And dance. I smiled at Marta.

Then she laughed even louder, "That *Scheiss-Kopf!*" shit head! Then she mimicked how she did it, pretending to bite out a chunk of his hand and spit it off to the side, "They're ALL *Arschlöcher!*" she said, and I smiled again. I nodded in agreement. She was right. Men, ALL men, were Assholes!

Shakespeare was right "What wound did ever heal but by degrees?" I could feel myself slowly growing stronger. Coming to grips. Spitting out the evil that Rolf had performed on me the way Marta mimicked spitting out the piece of the hand that had tried to keep her quiet. Bit by bit. Piece by poisonous, treacherous piece.

On occasion Dannar would stop by and make sure I was OK. He was gentle and did not press things, his sentences short, leaving his presence alone to convey the message: "I am here if you need me." But I didn't. I said nothing to him. Marta spoke less and less of him, perhaps in her efforts to keep me from seeing her happily fulfilled in her relationship while I had slipped so far in the other direction. Or maybe it was something else, I couldn't be sure. My sense of things had been so damaged.

Detlef too even appeared one evening, offering to help, but I felt as if he were more interested in talking to Marta than to me. He even asked with some great concern how she was doing with things. Eventually she shooed him away, which was fine with me.

And as the days passed, Marta's lessons on life continued, culminating each night asleep in the security of each others arms.

#

Like bandits that lie in wait for you along dark stretches of road, nightmares seem to prowl your subconscious when you have other troubles on your mind.

The pile of flames began to circle, gather themselves upwards, into a funnel, a tornado of fiery destruction engulfing everything it touched.

I woke with a start, sitting straight up in my bedroll, sweat gleamed against my arms and chest, my nightgown plastered to my back in dampness.

"You OK?" Marta asked. I could see her silhouette propped up on one elbow, a black cut out against the illuminated fabric of camouflage.

"Yes," I whispered, as if the nightmare could hear.

"The chicken coop again?"

"Yes," I lied, hiding the truth in the darkness.

The silhouette lay back down again. I could see the outline of her face and nose against the pattern of the tent. A full minute passed before she spoke again. An owl who-hooted in the darkness.

"Maybe we can find some answers for you," she said tapping her finger against her lip. "But we are going to need some transportation."

"Transportation?"

Her silhouette nodded.
And left it at that.

FUNFZEHN - FIFTEEN

But of course Marta had already figured out the transportation problem. It just took me a little while to catch up with the devious workings of her mind.

I patted Vixen along the barrel of his chest then slung the *Kommandant's* saddle on. He snorted a blast of warm breath and spittle from his nose, and Marta reflexed backward.

"Ew!" she said. I shushed her, reminding her that this side of the lake was crawling with HJs and if we were to pull this off we were going to have to operate in the purest of silence. I cinched his saddle snugly against his girth and opened the gate. Marta and I led Vixen out through our end of the barn.

Vixen was quiet, as if knowing he was complicit and not just a victim in what we were about to do as we led him to the trail. Lights were on about the camp and HJs milled about in the distance as we moved silently along, our work cloaked in the invisibility of a black horse on a dark trail. Above, a starry sky draped the treetops, brilliant in the absence of a moon yet to rise. I walked Vixen up to the ridge before mounting him and then pulled Marta aboard behind me. She wrapped her arms tightly around me and buried her cheek against my back, her touch setting off comforting warmth in my belly. I put my heels gently to the barrel of Vixen's chest and we were off.

Through the woods we went, following the miles of trails that Vixen and I had explored before and soon we had reached the main road, a band of darkness unspooling beneath a panoply of stars. Marta gave directions over my shoulder as we followed the road, galloping through the night. It was marvelous and exhilarating, racing through the emptiness, my neck against Vixen, Marta arms wrapped tightly around my waist.

We followed the road for over an hour, retracing the thirty kilometers we had marched out to begin our *Landdienst* almost three months past. Ahead of us, the lights of *Ülmstadt* began to appear like fireflies among the trees, winking on and off as we approached. Vixen began to slow as we climbed the low rise toward town, the very hill Mad Ludwig had climbed with Herr Hochauser's wagon a seeming infinity ago.

Marta pulled against my belly and spoke into my ear.

"A little farther then into the woods."

I followed her instructions, crossed a small swale alongside the road and guided Vixen up into the forest. We dismounted and began to walk along, the backs of the grande dame houses along *Hoch Strasse* on parade through the trees.

Marta put up her hand in a signal to stop then turned to me and dragged her finger across her lips. She tied Vixen's rein to a tree branch and stealthily we began to move forward.

The back of the house before us was a large dark Victorian, commanding and foreboding, a turreted structure dominating the ridge overlooking the smattering of lights in the town below. All was dark and quiet, a solitary window lit on the second floor. Marta rummaged through her rucksack and pulled out a small paper wrapped bundle. She pressed her finger against her lips and motioned me forward.

Down along the foundation wall we crept, trying to blend with the shrubbery and plantings as we moved to the front of the house. Through the darkness we found our way around another large planting until we met with a turned iron newel post. From the newel post a cast iron railing wound alongside a grand set of stairs leading up to two tall entry doors.

Inside, a dog began to bark.

"*Verdammt* Gretchen!" Marta whisper yelled and ran up the steps, I right behind. Fumbling through the paper package she pulled out a bratwurst and quickly stuck it through the mail slot. The barking stopped immediately. From inside we heard the approaching clatter of toe nails on a hardwood floor stopping just beneath the mail slot. Marta flipped open the mail door and whispered "Good girl, Gretchen. Good girl!" A snuffling of nose against the floor was her response.

Marta backtracked halfway down the wide entry stairs to a series of flower pots along the railing. She stuck her hand in the third one and pulled out a skeleton key, went up to the grand double doors and unlocked them. Inside Gretchen continued to snuffle in the darkness at the floor below the mail slot, the bratwurst long gone. Marta took another bratwurst from the paper and squatted on the floor directly facing the enormous German Shepherd and put the end of it in her mouth. Gretchen came forward and gently plucked the sausage from Marta's lips.

"Hows my little watchdog doing?" Marta said and patted her head. She stood and we continued past a curved set of stairs leading to the second floor, a light on somewhere dimly illuminating the upper landing. We tiptoed down the front entry hall, at the far end a smaller second set of servant's stairs rose near the entry to the kitchen. To the right, another door, heavy and tall.

"Give me a boost!" she whispered and, re-membering our efforts at Fraukenstein's office door, I laced my fingers together and boosted Marta up. From the ledge above the office door Marta retrieved a key. "*Sicherheit mein Arsch*," Marta whispered. Secu-rity my ass. She inserted the key, turned the ornate glass knob and pushed the door open.

Stray light from the homes below filtered up the hillside and found its way through the three tall windows along the outside wall. What little light there was was enough to pick out elements of the room. A large desk, oversized chairs, dormant fire-place, file cabinets, and bookshelves floor to ceiling, interrupted occasionally by photographs, broadswords, and a painting of a knight on horse-back. I inhaled deeply at the warmth and all envelop-ing comfort of the room: leather, tobacco, and the smell so deep and dear to me: books.

Marta clicked on a small, boxy Daimon flash-light, splashing the room with indirect light. She began opening drawers and thumbing through manila folders.

"What are you doing?" I whispered.

She placed her finger to her lips, "Just keep listening at the door. Let me know if you hear anything," she continued flipping through files, careful to keep the Daimon close to her work, "Ok, now, who am I looking for?"

"My Father, remember?" I said in an incredulous whisper.

She looked at me with an expression that said beyond question "You are a *Dummkopf!*".

"Oh," I said, "you mean his name," she nodded slowly, *"DUMMKOPF!"* still spelled in capital letters across her expression, *"Holländer,"* I said, "that's his name, our name."

"Perfect," she said and dug back into the files mumbling under her breath.

I looked closely around the room, now more detailed in the half-glow of the Daimon. A Nazi flag stood guard on the dormant fireplace, a raised swastika in the iron fire back. Plaques and photographs covered a section of the wall. Above two crossed broadswords was a large framed photograph and a framed certificate beneath. The certificate read:

Rudolph Koenigsberg
Geheime Staatspolizei

The hair stood up on the back of my neck.

The photograph showed an airfield. In front of one of the planes stood a distinguished man in a long black leather trench coat, tall and rugged, short dark hair meeting a hint of gray at the temple. In the black and white photograph he is smiling and shaking hands with another man who is smiling as well. The other man is Adolf Hitler.

"Your father is . . . Gestapo?" I whispered hoarsely. The floor above us creaked with footsteps as someone walked across the room.

Flashlight in her mouth Marta froze, her eyes rolled toward the ceiling. The footsteps crossed again upstairs then we heard the creak of a bed, "Uh-Huh," Marta nodded, still holding the flashlight in her mouth. She let it fall into her hand as she continued to the next drawer of folders, "If anyone around here knows where your Poppy went, it would be my Poppy," she popped the flashlight back in her mouth and continued rifling.

"Can't you just ask him?" I said.

She popped the flashlight out again, "Not hardly. Everything is 'State Secret' around here. Poppy thinks it best if I just don't know things," she went to his desk, slid the top drawer open and rifled around inside. She pulled out a small key on a fob, "One last cabinet," she said and opened a drawer labeled "N & N".

She began to rifle through folders, still holding the Daimon in her mouth, stopped, pulled out a folder toward the end of the row and spread it out on top of the others. She flipped through some of the neatly typed pages, pausing to read through sections. She pulled two small photographs from the folder and studied them, then she looked up at me.

"Do you have something?" I said starting to walk over.

"Um . . . no," she said. "Stay there. Hold your post on that door," she stuffed the folder back in the drawer and switched off the Daimon.

"Nothing?" I said.

"No, sorry, nothing," I couldn't read her face in the darkness. "Time to go."

We slipped out of the house and back to Vixen. We retraced our path back to the camp, the sky in the East just beginning to lighten as we returned Vixen to his stable. In all that time, Marta barely said a word.

#

Over the next two days Marta seemed to make less of an effort to interact with me and at times even seemed to disappear altogether. But someone she HAD found time for was Detlef. At one point I watched unseen from a distance as she led him into one of the horse stalls then pulled the gate behind them.

At the end of the third day, Marta reappeared from the other end of the HJ camp. She offered no explanation and I was not in a position to press for one, our lives for the moment seeming to be unyoked. So together, in silence, we began to paddle back to our own side of the lake, carving soft "V"s in the placid water. Toward the middle of the lake, she stopped paddling and turned over her shoulder to stare at the neat rows of camouflaged HJ tents. She smiled, gave a little shrug, reached into her pocket and pulled out a small cigarette case. Pulling out a cigarette, she tapped it on the case, then lit it from a kitchen match. She inhaled deeply and let a long, slow plume of smoke drift from her lips.

"*Das Leben ist eine Schachtel voller Überraschungen*," she said and inhaled again. Life is a box of surprises.

Then she let out a short puff of smoke and began to blow smoke rings, "But I'm up here smoking and you're back there doing all the work. No surprise there!" she said, then burst into a machine gun laugh so hard she slipped from her seat and landed in a puddle in the bottom of the canoe. Then she turned to look at me and burst out into another rattle of laughter. And I knew my friend Marta had returned.

SIXTEEN - SECHSZEHN

In the stifling heat of August's dying days, Marta and I finished our business at the barns for the evening and paddled back to our side of the lake. As the sun settled gently into the tree tops, the small patch of water began its own business of releasing a cooling balm back over the forest. Marta and I walked along the path, familiar now even in the approaching darkness. But tonight we were not alone. An uncomfortable silence had joined us, cool and clammy, like storm clouds straining to hold their rain.

The first drops began to fall.

"So . . . " Marta started, "how have you been feeling?"

I nodded, "Better. I'm getting there."

"It's a bit like trying to put a smashed teacup back together," Marta said, lighting a cigarette. I nodded again as she continued, "sometimes you gotta look under the sofa to find all the pieces."

"But it never does go fully back together, does it?" I said, a thread of depression still woven through the fabric of my thoughts.

"Yeah, sure it does!" she blew a long stream of smoke at the lake. "Sure it does. And it is better than before, because now you're smarter!" she waved away the smoke in front of her face as she walked. "You're doing fine *Küken!* Making progress! You've got this!"

The tone of her voice let me know. I did have this. And if I didn't have it, well, it was all up to me from now on. For a while anyway.

I bit my lip, but the words tumbled out on their own, "You're leaving me aren't you?"

Marta continued to walk, her eyes fixed on the path in the dimming light. She inhaled on her cigarette. As the smoke drifted from her open mouth she slowly began to nod.

"When?" I said, "For how long?"

Again she waved her hand in front of her face, "Not long. Not too long. A few weeks."

"A few weeks?!" I began to sputter. I looked around trying to imagine the forest, the camp, the path where the tattered sails of my life were being mended, without Marta. "What's . . . What's going on?"

"Oh, it's Poppy. Wants us to have a little family vacation. Up in Berlin. A little family time. All must be fun and merry in the Koenigsberg household," she continued to look at the ground as she walked puffing on her cigarette. And then she went quiet. An un-Marta-like quiet. I noticed she was no longer staring at the trail as she walked, but at her belly. She ran her hand over her stomach and pulled at the cigarette again.

"Just family time?" I said, pressing ever so slightly against Marta's veneer.

She turned to face me. The veneer dented slightly, then rebounded, "And to take care of some things," she said, her hand never leaving her belly. She laughed a little laugh, her brown eyes glossy and

228

wet, dropped the cigarette to the ground and crushed it.

#

Three days later, Marta was collecting her things in the *Zeltbahn*. She rolled up her bedroll and stashed it in the corner, collected her clothes and stuffed them into her rucksack. She sat crosslegged on the ground cloth our knees touching and stared at me.

"OK," she said, "this is it. I'm leaving you to hold the fort here. *Verstanden?*"

I gave her a salute, pathetic at best.

"You are going to be fine. You are well on your way, clearing those rain clouds . . . ," she tapped my skull, " . . . in here. Blue skies ahead and all of that. Am I right?"

I nodded sadly, "You are always right Marta."

"Good. I'm glad we have that straight. Now loosen up a little. Relax. I need you to relax a little," she slid to my side, threw her arm across my shoulder and began to sing in her so terrible yet so hilarious voice, "Grab your coat and get your hat, leave your worries on the door step," she nudged me to join her but I couldn't find the breath to sing, so she just plowed on. "just direct your feet, to the sunny side of the street!" she kneaded her fingers into the muscles at the base of my neck.

"Yeah, I'm not expecting to do much relaxing."

"You gotta! Crucial. You can do it if you try!" she pulled out a cigarette and lit it, filling the inside of the tent with smoke like a magic trick gone wrong, she peeled back the flap slightly allowing some to escape. She reached into her rucksack and rummaged around, pulling out her fist.

"Hold out your hand," she said, holding the cigarette in her lips as she spoke.

I held my hand out, palm up.

"Now you have to promise me. Promise me on . . . on . . . " she rolled her eyes in thought, "on . . . the *Führer's* mustache, that you will only and I mean ONLY listen to music. None of that crazy *Scheisse* you dial in on. Christ Kat, you don't know how much trouble you can get into listening to that!"

"I don't . . . I'm not sure what you're talking about."

Marta rolled her eyes, "Just promise. That's all I need. Just promise. I just need to know you are not going to get yourself into any kind of trouble that I can't get you out of."

"Well you certainly are good at getting me INTO trouble!"

"But I get you out of it don't I?"

"Hardly ever!" I said smiling.

"Well just promise anyway."

"OK, Marta, whatever you want. I promise."

And with that she opened her fist and a solitary key and a flake of metal fell from her hand. I stared at them. She picked the key out of my hand and held it up before my eyes, "Key to the administration building," she picked up the shiv of metal. "Key to the liquor cabinet. Go in, keep the lights off, listen to a little music, drink a little schnapps, *sich er-*

holen." Relax. She again tapped my skull, "Get this back to where it needs to be. *Verstanden?"*

She pulled back the flap and gave a sideways glance out into the glaring sun. *"Verdammt,* they're already here," she turned back toward me. "Should only be gone a few weeks. A month tops. OK *Küken?"*

I nodded, trying my best to force a smile. She leaned over and kissed me. She wrapped her arms around me and squeezed tight, "You'll be fine," she whispered in my ear, "you are getting stronger every day. I can see it," then she peeled back from me and stared me in the eyes. "And who knows, maybe some new someone will appear in your life!"

I pushed her away, "Hardly! I am so done with men! *Arschlöcher,* the whole lot of them!"

"Well don't be so quick to write them all off. When you find the right one, it makes a difference!"

And with that she got to her knees, blew me a kiss and exited the tent. I sat there for a moment, watching Marta through the gap in the tent's flap. She walked straight and confident, the rucksack slung over one shoulder. Directly ahead of her was a large Mercedes, a soldier holding the back door open, a serious man in a serious suit standing next to him. I closed my eyes as a new heaviness settled on me like a cold, dirty stone, a different sort of loneliness I had not felt since my very first day at the BDM. I opened my eyes and stared into my hands at the key and the metal shiv, then stuck them into the outer pocket of my rucksack. As soon as I turned back, the tent flap was thrown open and Marta burst in. She grabbed my face in both of her hands and kissed me. I wrapped my arms around her, pulling her close, and returned the kiss.

Slowly she pulled away from me, her brown eyes never leaving mine. She gave me a curious smile, kissed me again quickly, crossed her fingers before my eyes and disappeared through the flap.

I watched her back as she walked away, across the grass and up to the gravel turnaround. She slowed as she approached the large black car, the soldier staring off in the middle distance, the serious man focused intently on her. The man I saw shaking hands with *dem Führer*. When she reached him, she stopped, her fingers laced together behind her back. The man's face went from serious to stern to furious. He began to stab his index finger at her, over and over, Marta reacting as if his finger had been a trench knife, drawing blood with every thrust. But Marta stood there, head down, acquiescent, nodding slowly with each verbal assault. When he was finished he made one last stab of his trench knife finger at the rear door of the car. The soldier went to open the rear door, but the stern man waved him off. Marta opened the car door herself to get inside.

As she turned, I could see she was crying.

SIEBZEHN - SEVENTEEN

Despite the brilliant August sun, a dark melancholy had settled over *Landdienst,* leaving things sad and cold. Not for everyone, I suppose, but for me. No one had yet been sent to the barns to replace Marta, not that anyone could. A simple laborer perhaps, but no one, simply no one could match the solace Marta Koenigsberg could provide. I crossed to the ox pen troughs with two pails of silage on a beam across my shoulders. It seemed a half dozen lifetimes ago that I was doing this very thing with milk from Cleo and Nefertiti. But that was a different Kat. An innocent Kat. Innocent of so many things. A Kat long gone. I dumped my pails in the trough and returned inside. Overhead, clouds of stable flies danced in and out of a beam of sunlight cutting the cool shadows of the barn. Marta would have made a joke or a song about the flies, but she too was gone. The flies droned on.

Mars and Jupiter, as obedient in their movements as their heavenly counterparts, appeared from the trailhead flanked by Dannar and an HJ I did not recognize. Neither man spoke, their sweat stained clothes spattered with wood chips speaking volumes. The heat of the day had taken its toll on both man and beast. I stayed in the shadows as the new HJ unyoked the twin planets and Dannar headed for the water barrel. He raised the enameled dipper to his face and gulped it dry. As the ladle came down, he caught sight of me watching him from the shadows. I

233

immediately turned and headed further into the bowels of the building.

Behind me came the heavy steps of hob nailed boots and the slow, rhythmic flap of leather chaps. I picked up my pace and headed down the center aisle of the barn, the steps behind matching mine. I tried to go faster, just short of a run but the steps behind persisted.

"Wait Kat," came Dannar's voice behind me. I ignored it and kept going. The steps behind me broke into a trot and I tried to do the same, but Dannar's long stride soon overtook mine. He appeared in front of me forcing me to stop.

He looked at me, his face frozen in the realization that he should have thought of what he would say when he had reached me. I took the lead in our awkward dance.

"I have work to do," I said, keeping my voice as flat and cold as a frozen lake.

"I know. I'm sorry," he said as I tried to walk around him. He moved slightly to block me again. I tried to step the other way and again he parried. I finally stopped in front of him and crossed my arms, my face a rising storm. "I'm sorry," he said once again, his entire being seemingly trapped under the spell of two words.

"You've already said that," my voice remained flat, dry of emotion, "twice."

"I know," his words stumbling out over his teeth. "But, I am sorry." The words continued to tumble out of his mouth like the chain of a ship's anchor as it plummeted to the bottom. "I'm sorry . . . you don't . . . want to . . . " I crossed my arms even tighter and glared at him, my eyes hard as flint. The anchor hit bottom " . . . talk to me anymore."

I could feel something inside me change, like a knot beginning to slip, my arms no longer gripping quite so tightly across my chest. I let out a soft breath through my nose, feeling my eyes soften.

As if on their own, my arms dropped to my side. I studied his shoes, "No . . . I don't." He waited for more but I had no more to give. I turned and walked away. He did not follow.

#

More days passed and September was upon us painting the sky a perfect shade of blue, not a single cloud to mar its canvas, the temperature as comfortable as heaven.

But it mattered little to me. My body and mind were busy in their bunker, working together to shelter my soul. The bruise on the side of my face was now nearly gone, physically, but not emotionally. I kept to myself, ate meals by myself, moving through the regimental machinations of *Landdienst* with the mechanical precision so admired by the Nazi machine I was now coming to despise.

Yet I was never truly alone. Marta was never far from my mind, her friendship, her love, a healing balm over all. In the evening I followed our old routine, walking the path along the lake. But without Marta, it was now up to me to repair and rebuild my damaged past and as time progressed, I came to realize, there was no one better to perform the task.

The sun was beginning to set as I made my way back toward camp, its fiery brow beginning to extinguish itself in the tree tops. I rounded a high clump of brambles nudging me onto a narrow strip of packed earth skirting the water's edge. I hitched up to a stop at the form directly in front of me, a triangular chest pointing into narrow hips mounted on twin legs of pure muscle. Atop all, a close cropped blonde head and steel gray eyes belonged solely to one person: Dannar Bremm. He was standing athwart the path, arms crossed powerfully yet casually across his chest, his forearms knitted together like the twisted cables supporting a great bridge. For anyone else, it would have been threatening, the sort of sight to stop one in their tracks and reconsider the long way home. I did not. I continued to walk straight toward him, around him if he chose not to move, over him if he tried to stop me. I returned my eyes to the path.

"Kat, wait," he said, "I want to talk to you."

I continued toward him, eyes still concentrating on the packed earth trail, still holding my course, and course of action.

"Kat," he said again as I drew within a few meters. "Please."

I looked up from the trail, the hard flint of my eye meeting his gray steel, setting off the slightest spark. I slowed to a halt directly in front of him, my course of action delayed, if only for a moment.

"What?" I said, unable to remove the flatness from my voice, my body and brain on guard for the protection of my soul. "What do you want?"

"Kat, I . . . I want to . . . talk to you," he said, drawing a jittery breath. "Need to talk to you."

"About?"

He looked at me. Somehow that had not been the answer he had heard in his obviously prepared speech. Perhaps he had only rehearsed his answer to a simple "OK", but that was not to be.

"About?"   he said, verbally taking a step backward.

"Yes, you said you NEED to talk to me," I cocked my head defiantly to the side. "What do you NEED to talk to me about?

"Its not that I NEED to talk to you about any-thing, only that I . . . need . . . to talk . . . to you," he began to become flustered at the way his words were failing him. He closed his eyes and opened his heart, hoping the right words would float to the surface, "To be ABLE to talk to you. Still," his voice was soft, bare-ly audible. A voice I could not imagine calling out to beware of a falling tree. Or barking his allegiance to *dem Führer*. But he did both, " I don't like the fact that I see you every day and yet I can't talk to you, you won't let me talk to you. You . . . you are my friend. Aren't you?"

"I have enough friends already. All the friends I need in fact," I said and began to push past him.

He stepped in front of me again, his hands out-stretched both as a barrier, and in supplication, "Look,

Kat, what Rolf did was horrible. Beyond horrible. You don't know how it sickens me. He was wrong for what he did," but I couldn't bear to hear the words, their weight dropping on me, draping me like piles of rusted chain. I tried to slip under his outstretched arm but he gently turned my shoulder to face him. Then he finished, "but he isn't me. And I'm not him. WE, men, we are not all the same."

I looked into his eyes, the spark extinguished and a single tear tracing down my cheek. I did not give him the satisfaction of wiping it away. I whispered through my teeth, "You ARE all the same. You all stand there every morning and face the flag. You pledge your allegiance to *dem Führer*, but what you are really doing is giving yourself permission to take whatever you want. For years everyone has taken from us, I know, but that gives you no right to now take from everyone else. Especially from me. And then you laugh about it with your friends when you do. You don't care about me or anyone else, only yourselves. Blood and honor? Blood yes, honor? You have none."

He tried to speak, teeth and stupor blocking all. He looked around, fearful that my voice carried across the lake. He whispered, "Kat, you must be careful. Careful of what you say."

"And what does that tell you that I must be careful of what I say? You are all the same. All of you," he stared at me. His words dry in his throat. I pushed past him and continued down the path. Once again, no footsteps dared to follow.

#

As always, Marta was right. Not only that men were *Arschlöcher,* but that music and a little of Fraukenstein's schnapps could ease the soul. I curled myself under the desk into a comfortable position draping my arm over the cathedral radio and took another sip, the clear liquid giving a comfortable burn as it headed for my stomach. I adjusted the knob in the center of the radio trying to lessen the static violating one of Mozart's piano sonatas. I closed my eyes allowing both schnapps and sonata to seep into my soul and let out a sigh. Peaceful and perfect, mind and soul beginning to lose the sharp edges, thoughts becoming fuzzy and soft.

The sonata ended. I began to massage the station selector up and down the dial, easing though the peaks and valleys of static and whistles, distant music, hard voices, a far off marching band. I moved farther down the end of the dial, pretending to myself that I did not know what I was doing. Just searching for music, not answers. What if I didn't hear music? What if I accidentally stumbled onto . . . him. I wouldn't completely be breaking my promise to Marta. Not if it was an accident. Not if I didn't mean to . . .

"Frage nicht. Gehorchen Sie einfach. Diejenigen, die nicht in der Nacht und im Nebel verschwinden"

"Do not question. Simply obey. Those who do not disappear into the Night and Fog."

I turned the volume up a little louder to clear the static. I closed my eyes and continued to listen. Words fitting like pieces of puzzle. Razor sharp

239

shards of china from some unknown shattered object coming together to form a whole. Confusion giving way to sense. A terrible purpose.

My eyes snapped open. Did I just hear a floor-board creak in the hall? I silenced the radio, nearly snapping the bakelite on-off-volume dial loose in my hand. Another footstep. Definitely a footstep. *Gottverdammt!* Why did I have to turn it up so loud? Another step, then the grind of a sole turning on the hardwood floor. A flashlight clicked on and began to play along the outside of the office. Slow and steady the beam traced the far wall, pausing at the empty spot where the radio normally stood. Back across the far wall, now moving to the floor, the oblong pool of light slowly sweeping the area before the desk. It stopped. Centered in its interrogating pool, an errant loop of cord from the radio escaping from under the desk. The jangle of keys on a ring followed by the hard metal-on-metal sounds of a key entering a lock. "Clunk" went the bolt as it retracted into the door. The door creaked open on a tired hinge and a footfall entered the room. I pressed myself tight against the underside of the desk, my pounding heart drowning out my inner voice rapidly sorting through pathetic excuses for being under Fraukenstein's desk with her schnapps and radio. Slowly the footsteps entered the room, the sound of a hard soled boot on hardwood floor. I scrunched myself up tight under the desk. A right boot appeared, shiny and black. Then a left one beside it, the light beam focused on the looping cord. The beam of light began to move, toward the underside of the desk, booted knees beginning to bend as it did. I forced myself even tighter, smaller, a badger cornered under a porch. The beam shone directly in my eyes obscuring the face behind it. I began to blather something, but the voice on the other end of the light beat me to it.

"Kat?"

I found a slippery handle on the voice, "Dannar?"

He switched off the light and scrunched down lower, filling the opening of the desk. "What are you doing in here?" his voice an odd blend of concern, surprise and amusement. " . . . under there?"

Again I began to stammer, "I was . . . I was . . . Marta showed me . . . "

He began to laugh, "Such things always come back to Marta!"

"She thought . . . she thought it would be a good idea if I had a chance to . . . to listen to some music. Help me relax a little. After . . . "

He was now on his knees before me, the illumination of his flashlight filling the confines beneath the desk, "Hmmmm. And that too? To help you relax?" he took my glass and sniffed at its contents. He set it back on the floor, "Is it working?" he said, his voice quiet with concern.

"Yes, sort of."

He sat down on the floor, "*Gut*," he said nodding, "I'm glad it's working. You need something, to . . . relax you."

"I know," I said, "I know. It's still all so very . . . real. Painful. It doesn't want to go away," I pulled my knees up tight under my chin and stared down at my feet.

"I'm sorry," he said, his voice soft and true, "so very sorry."

I gave an imperceptible nod and closed my eyes. He reached over and patted my arm. His hands hardened by long days wielding an axe handle yet gentle on my skin.

"I am glad the music is working for you," he held up the glass. "And a little of this as well," I laughed and snuffled a little at the same time, "But I didn't hear music when I came in." he said. "What were you listening to?" I looked up at him, my eyes making poor work of hiding my crime.

"Nothing," I lied. "Just a man . . . talking."

"I see," he said. "And what was he talking about? Science? A cooking show perhaps? The weather in Frankfurt?" he smiled. He took his hand off of my arm and reached for the on-off-volume knob on the radio. I reached the knob first and his hand surrounded mine.

"Come on Kat, let's see what you find so amusing," I stared into his steel gray eyes and switched on the radio.

"Menschen in Deutschland erwacht, Ihr weidet in die Zerstörung geführt"

"Awaken people of Germany, you are being led to destruction."

In the half light beneath the desk, Dannar's eyes opened wide.

"Kat!" he whispered. "You . . . you cannot listen to this! It's . . . It's illegal! It's against everything we stand for!" he lowered his voice and locked his eyes on mine, "I have heard people have been put to death just for listening to this!"

"And what does that tell you?" I whispered back. "What does it tell you when there is something, someone out there that to listen to their words alone can bring you death? Is their message that bad and we are being protected from it?"

"This is poison, Kat. Pure poison. Being poured into our ears from . . . from a traitor."

"If you listen to him, you will know, he is a German, a TRUE German, and he is a patriot! He knows what goes on inside the upper levels. The sickness and corruption. The Party is not all it appears to be Dannar."

"No, I can't listen," he switched off the radio. "This man is poison. He is an infection in the Party. The Gestapo hunts him but they have not caught him. Not yet anyway."

"Who is he?" I said, eager for more information.

"I shouldn't tell you."

"Please Dannar" I said, reaching out to touch his arm.

He let out a defeated sigh, his eyes searching mine.

"He goes by the name of Gustav Siegfried Eins. But everyone thinks that is code for GS-1"

"What does GS-1 mean?"

Dannar shrugged his shoulders, "No one knows. He gives out numbers and coordinates during his broadcasts, but no one has been able to quite figure out what they mean. Or how to catch him. His nickname is '*Der Chef*, The Chief." then as if coming back to life. "But you are not allowed to listen to him Kat! It is illegal!"

"If it were all just lies, what difference would it make? Why would they care?" With this I could see synapses starting to fire behind his eyes. "But what if maybe, just maybe, some of what he says is true? What if it is true? What if *der Führer* and all his group are not patriots? What if they have a sinister purpose in mind," Dannar began to look around. "What if he is right?"

"We are still not supposed to listen. Maybe it is better if we don't know."

I shook my head, "It is never better to be an ostrich. But OK, maybe I am wrong, maybe they are all lies, what he says. Maybe the great and glorious *Reich* is all it claims to be. Don't you want to know? Don't you want to get your head out of the sack?"

"No, Kat, it is better, better to not . . . "

"What? To not know?" I shook my head. "The truth. The truth is important."

"Important enough to die for?"

From somewhere deep inside me, the answer rose from a place I did not know to exist. "Yes," I said quietly, my eyes meeting his gray steel. "Yes, it's that important."

He looked at me, unable to answer. Words forming and reforming behind his teeth but unable to come out. I continued.

"Please, Dannar. Listen with me. Just for a few moments."

He began to get up, backing away, shaking his head. His eyes never left me, "No Kat . . . " he continued to shake his head. "No, I . . . "

I reached out and took his hand in mine, calloused and strong. I squeezed his hand, "Please Dannar, just for a moment."

Gently he returned the squeeze and slowly lowered back down, "Alright," he said, "just for a moment. Just long enough for me to show you the error in your ways." I smiled at him and guided him back down to the floor. He slid as best he could into the space beneath the desk his body in full contact with my side, holding the radio on his lap. His feet stuck out into the middle of Fraukenstein's office. He looked at me with worried eyes. I switched the radio on and the voice of Gustave Siegfried Eins crackled over the radio.

"*Böse sind diejenigen, die unter unserer heiligen Flagge stehen.*"

"They are evil those that stand beneath our sacred flag."

Minutes became an hour as we listened, our bodies close, our minds becoming closer. He began to nod as we listened.

We both froze.
A key was turning in the outside lock.

ACHTZEHN - EIGHTEEN

Like a silent explosion, Dannar burst from beneath the desk, the radio tucked under his arm. With three great steps he crossed the office, simultaneously jerking the plug from the outlet. He plopped the radio into its spot pushed the chair back under the desk pinning me to the back wall with a muffled "OOF!". He stood in the middle of the room and flicked on his flashlight just as the front door opened. From the hallway I heard the flapping of leather as someone unholstered their pistol.

"Halt!" Fraukenstein snapped.

Dannar raised his hands, the light now reflecting off the ceiling, bathing the room in flat shades of gray, "It's Dannar Bremm," he said, "I . . . I have the duty tonight."

"I saw lights in here. What are you doing in my office?" Fraukenstein said, her voice even and cool in the thrill of the capture.

"I . . . heard an animal in here," the silence that followed told him she was not convinced.

"How do you know?" she said finally. "Have you seen it?"

"No, I haven't. But I hear it every once in a while. Scratching," he said punctuating the last word.

"Why am I not believing you?" she said from the hall.

"No, I swear. I heard a . . . " With the small bit of metal for the liquor cabinet I scratched the side of the desk twice. Fraukenstein chambered a round into her Lugar and entered the room forcing Dannar to back up. I heard her begin to slowly make her way around the room peeking into corners with her flashlight. I watched her legs pass the liquor cabinet with the radio neatly back in place. Her polished boots became visible between the legs of the chair as she approached the desk. She began to bend down, her light falling inches from my curled up leg, the barrel of her Lugar pistol coming into view.

"Be careful!" Dannar said. "You don't want to surprise it."

"What do you mean?" she said.

"You don't want to surprise it. I think it is a skunk. If you surprise it, it will be bad for us. You. And I. . . . and your office."

Fraukenstein paused, straightened up and with more flapping of leather returned the pistol to its holster.

"Please, help me look," Dannar said pretending to look behind the cabinets on the opposite wall.

"No! If there is a skunk, YOU will find it and YOU will have it removed from my office immediately! *SCHNELL!* I do not want that in my office! *Verstanden?*"

"*Jawohl!*" Dannar snapped, raising his hand in salute. "I shall not let it get away *Gruppenführer!*"

Dannar waited while Fraukenstein returned the salute.

"When I find it," Dannar continued "I will kill it like *den Schädling,* the vermin, it is and bring it to you to show you my success!" Fraukenstein took another step toward the door. "That will not be necessary." she said and closed the door behind her.

Dannar stood motionless in the darkness filling the center of the room, his arm still raised at a perfect forty-five degree angle. Slowly he lowered his arm. When it returned to his side he let out a muffled laugh, pulled the chair out from under the desk and I popped out laughing. In the darkness I took one step forward, wrapped my arms around him, and continued to giggle as I buried my face in his chest. Gently I felt his arms cross behind me pulling me in closer, my giggles beginning to fade as I inhaled his musky scent. I let out a long sigh and felt all of the tension of the brush with disaster evaporate from my muscles allowing my knees to buckle slightly, Dannar's twisted cables of arms supporting me. He gave me a gentle squeeze, the soft pressure releasing a butterfly from its cocoon inside the steel box of my inner self. It began to flutter its wings against the lining of my stomach. Until a shock hit me like stray electricity. I pushed Dannar away but he continued to hold me at arms length in the darkness.

"Thank you," I sputtered, staring up, but unable to see the expression of his face in the darkness, "you saved me."

But he said nothing, only continued holding my arms.

#

Over the next few days, Dannar and I began to talk briefly every time he returned from the trail. His new partner, whose name I learned was Klaus, would take the oxen to the pen allowing Dannar and I a chance to talk. On several nights we agreed to meet back in Fraukenstein's office, careful to keep the lights off and the volume low. We were almost caught again by a rather industrious HJ on patrol, but Dannar managed to redirect him away from our hiding place. None-the-less it was becoming obvious that we needed another, safer place to conduct our "sedition".

An unusually hot September sun was racing toward the horizon like Phaethon's renegade chariot when Dannar asked me to follow him up the ladder into the *Adlerhorst*. I looked up the ladder and back at him, then again up the ladder. I had not been back up there since that day, had no intention of ever going back, and here was Dannar asking me to join him.

Up there.

I shook my head, "No. I'm sorry. I . . . I just can't."

Dannar raised his hands in defense, "No, wait! No, don't . . . That's not what I had in mind!"

I gave him a half smile, "I know . . . It's just . . . I can't. Too painful."

He raised a finger, then held his hands up in front of me, "OK, wait. Stop. Wait right here." he clambered up the ladder, his footfalls fast and unusually hard on the narrow treads of the loft ladder.

I waited below, hearing Dannar rummaging around above me, bits of hay and dust floating down from the cracks between the floorboards overhead. There was a moment of silence, then a click. From above me music began to play. It was Mozart, and it was beautiful. An aria *Voi Che Sapete*. Whatever fear was in me, whatever apprehension for what lay above began to slowly dissipate in the balm of that music. In a trance, I walked toward the ladder. I placed my foot on the lowest rung and then the second, not even requiring my hands to climb. At the top of the stairs, a few steps back, Dannar was waiting, the spot no longer there. Hay had been moved, blankets, saddle pads, all gone. It could just as easily have never existed. But it had. Dannar motioned me with his hand to a small new enclave further down the hay bales, but I did not need his direction. I simply followed the sound of the glorious music, still ensconced in Mozart's trance. When I reached the source of the sound, it was a small bunker of hay bales with a tiny radio sitting just beyond. Inside there were blankets on bales like chairs in a room.

I stood staring, unsure of the meaning, but somehow Mozart made it all right. Dannar came behind me.

"Sooner or later we were going to get caught in Fraukenstein's office, and that would not be good."

"Not at all," I said, still in my trance.

"For now, I have the radio on top of the bales. But when the radio is inside this little space . . . " he set the radio down into the little hay bunker and the music went silent. Dannar continued, "The hay blocks the sound from going any further. It's perfect if you would like to come up here and listen to music . . . or other things." he said.

"Or other things," I repeated.

"Yes," he said, "we'll continue to talk about that. I'm still not sure you are right."

I looked at the small box radio, "Where did you get this?" I said.

"From one of the other HJs," he said. "I have to pull some extra duty for him but it is OK. It will be worth it if it helps. Helps you."

I continued to stare. A flutter of a whisper, barely audible drifted from my lips, "You did all of this for . . . me?" I looked at him.

His steel gray eyes crinkled to slits as he smiled, "Of course I did! I told you before. I'm your friend."

#

The new *Adlerhorst* became my refuge in a world that had become so different, so dark, in the months since I had joined the BDM. Life on the farm with *Tantchen* had been poor, but simple. The world had been allowed to spin on without us, past us. We were no more than specks in what was going on, ants on an elephant's back. We left them alone, not interfering in their business and they did the same in return. And we were just fine with that.

But now my eyes had been opened. And once your eyes have been opened to things, you are never able to un-see them. I watched every morning as we saluted the flag and pledged our honor and our lives to *Dem Führer*. He had taken us from the depths of the depression, the doormat of the world, and led us back. And the skies of Bavaria had somehow become more blue. The air more fresh, drawn in deep breaths by heads held high. That had become our truth: the flag, *der Führer*, the great and powerful speeches. The parades of endless shiny black helmets each accompanied by a flash of bayonet in the sun. This had become our truth and we were all so very proud of it. But in those short months since the ride on the tailgate of Herr Hochauser's buckboard I had come to realize: "Our" truth can sometimes be very different from "The" truth.

The fire in *Marienplatz*, the man with the hat, Herr Traubweiss, GS-1 on the radio. The more I knew of the third truth, the "Other" truth, the more I began to see the black *Hakenkreuz* swastika as something different. Sinister. An evil black spider, spinning a web from which there was no escape. And the more I learned of the Other truth, the more I needed to know. Especially one very important piece.

I began to visit the new *Adlerhorst* almost every night, slipping from my tent after hours and paddling our canoe down the lake shore, heading across only when out of sight of the camps and patrolling HJs. Often I would meet Dannar there, and together we would sit among the hay bales listening to GS-1, the other side of the truth we had been taught to believe. And we would discuss it all. Compare it to what we saw, what we heard in our civic classes, what we knew from our limited view of the world. A view limited by leaders that chose to keep blinders on their people, the way we put blinders on the oxen so they were not distracted by what was going on around them.

And then there was Marta. How much of this did she know? Certainly her father was aware of *der Nacht und Nebel*, the Night and Fog GS-1 alluded to over and over. As much as I wanted to believe Marta knew nothing of this, somehow I could never convince myself of that. Marta was too smart, too street smart. The Jew in the oven. How did she know? She heard her father talking to the others. Who were the others? Were they the ones GS-1 talked about? The ones beyond our blinders. "Go about your work people, there is nothing to see here" they would tell us without actually saying so. "Leave the country to us. Leave the leaders to lead and the followers to follow. We will tell you the truth you need to know." And if you dared to look beyond their truth, peek beyond the blinders? You disappear into the Night and the Fog. Forever.

There was so much I didn't know. So many questions I needed answered. I would have to ask Marta when she returned. But would she tell me? Could she tell me? Would that be crossing some line that I was not allowed to cross? I would have to think about that.

One night I told Dannar about how Marta and I went to her father's office searching for information about my father.

"And what did you find?" Dannar asked, stretched out on a horse blanket, his face bathed in the dim yellow light of the radio dial.

I just shook my head, "Nothing really. We both looked through files, but didn't find anything." I rolled onto my back and stared into the lattice of beams crossing the barn's ceiling. Birds nests sprouted from nooks and corners in several spots like tufts of hair. Moments passed.

"What?" Dannar said finally.

""Hmmm?" I said, still staring at the triangles of roof frames, tufts and twigs.

"What are you thinking about?"

"About that night. When we went through her father's office."

"What about it?"

"Right before we left. We were going through files. Marta said it was the last cabinet we would check. She needed a key to open it. Which of course Marta had," I smiled.

"Of course," Dannar said, not returning the smile.

"Anyway, she unlocked this file cabinet and started going through folders in the top drawer. Pulling them out, looking at them, putting them back. Then she found one, pulled it out and looked at it. She looked at it for a long time before she put it back. After that she told me we had to go." I continued to stare at the birds nests in the beams, but my mind was still leaning on the great mahogany desk with the green marble top in her father's office.

"And . . ." he said, knowing there was more to the story, even if I wasn't quite sure what.

"And, I don't know, I just think it was kinda funny."

"What? What was funny?" he said.

"I don't know. Just funny that after she looked at that file, that one from the top drawer . . . she never bothered looking though the rest of the file cabinet. Another three of four drawers she never even bothered to look in. No reason we couldn't have finished."

"Do you think she may have found something?" Dannar said rolling toward me on his elbow.

I stared silently into the rafters knowing fully, there was only one way to find out.

#

The following night, Vixen and I raced beneath a starless sky, the warmth of the dirt road caressing us with every step, the wind of our rapid progress pasting my hair across my back.

Evening was turning over her watch to night as we reached *Hoch Strasse*, the lights of the village below twinkling on and off in the heat waves escaping from the patchwork of dark roofs. I tied Vixen to the same tree as Marta and I had before, careful to follow Marta's ritual of stealth.

I worked my way through the backyard and along the bushes to the front of the house, wrapped my hand around the iron pillar at the base of the wide front steps and began to move up. First step, second step. At the third step I dipped my hand into the flower pot just as Marta had done and found the key buried in the soft grit of the potting soil. On the fourth step, a tread groaned and almost simultaneously I heard Gretchen explode into a staccato of loud barks. I covered the last few steps in two strides pulling my rucksack from my back as I went. I dropped a bratwurst through the mail slot and the barking immediately turned into a series of snuffles and slurps at the base of the door.

I peeked through the mail slot and saw no lights coming on, stuck the key into the lock and turned it, the bolt withdrawing with a simple "click". I returned the key to the flower pot and slipped inside, locking the door behind me with the thumb knob. With a pat on Gretchen's head, I tiptoed down the hallway past the dark polished curves of the main front staircase, twin newel posts guarding the risers like life-size chess pieces. Past the parlor to the right and dining room to the left, then straight ahead to the kitchen and the narrow servant's stair winding up to the second floor. On the right, at the back of the house was the door to Marta's father's office. I turned the handle. Locked. From the kitchen I pulled a chair and checked the ledge above the door just as Marta had, but the key was now gone. Gingerly, I stepped off the chair and returned it to the kitchen. In the bleed of half light from the village below I saw the hammered iron pots and pans rack next to the work table, the ice cold fingers of suicide suddenly circling my neck. I shook it off and returned to the office door, the ornate glass knob glistening in the dimly lit hallway. I slipped Marta's brain inside my own skull, trying to figure out what she would do in this situation. She always had, if often devious, a solution to things. Rubbing the metal chip in the bottom of my pocket I could hear her whisper *"Du hast es!"*. The metal shim slid into the crack in the door and I began to wiggle the bolt back. Blessed German efficacy, I thought, the well lubricated bolt slid smoothly back into the door and I was in. I closed the door behind me and locked it.

In the stillness of the room, Marta's Poppy's top desk drawer seemed loud as it slid out on its waxed rails. With my hand, I rummaged around under the papers, thinking for a moment about the "naughty" postcards her Poppy kept hidden in the bottom drawer, giving me a bit of a giggle. Then I looked up to see the picture of Poppy shaking hands with *dem Führer* on some unnamed airport tarmac and my giggling stopped immediately. I located the key to the wooden file cabinet. I switched on my flashlight, and keeping the beam close to the palm of my hand, I examined the front of the sturdy, four drawer cabinet. The key slid into the lock at the upper right hand corner of the cabinet, the circled swastika fob swinging gently as I turned the key. More bolts unlocked, I reached for the upper drawer as my light fell on the small brass frame holding the drawer's label. I froze.

N&N

I slid the drawer open, unusually heavy with the amount of manila folders inside, each a few millimeters thick of typed pages and photographs. Everything was neatly organized, each folder containing a tab typed in capitals: last name, first name followed by a six digit number. Alphabetical order. Holding the flashlight in my mouth I began to rifle through the folders. Nothing jumped out at me. What had Marta found? Had she found anything, or was this just a wild goose chase? With Marta I could never be sure. I stopped. Footsteps crossed the upstairs room. I was not alone in the house. Didn't Marta say she was taking a family vacation? Wouldn't that mean everyone? I began to look less thoroughly, more rapidly through the files. The footsteps stopped. Whoever it was had reached wherever they were going. For now.

"Come on, Marta," I thought quietly out loud. "What did you see?" I reached the end of the top drawer files. Nothing. No one named *Holländer*. But she had had a folder out, looked at it for a long time, then decided it was time to leave. "Think Kat," I whispered to myself, "what am I missing?" I went back to the first folder, this time looking at each more closely. While they were all different, papers, typed descriptions of things, newspaper clippings, single and group photographs, each had towards the end a carbon copy form titled *"EINTRAGSFORMULAR"* "Entry Form" and a small photograph clipped to the upper right hand corner. In every photograph attached to this form, the individual, regardless of their being a man or a woman, had had their head shaved, giving them all a rather similar appearance. I continued to look.

Near the end of the files a name caught my attention.

Van Posen, Franz

My father's name was Franz but I was quite certain our last name was *Holländer*. That's what everyone called him. I stopped and scratched my head, trying to reach some nagging spot deep beneath my hair. *Holländer* means "Dutchman". Maybe that was just a nickname, because his name was Dutch? I pulled the file from the drawer and dropped it on the green marble top of Poppy's desk. I flipped the cover open and began looking for pictures, starting from the rear of the folder with the one on the entry form. It was hard to tell if this was the father I remembered. His full head of hair had been shaved to the skull. He was not wearing glasses as my father had, and the face . . . I felt something sink inside of me. The face was puffy and bruised, one eye swollen shut so badly he could no longer see. This was the face of a man who had been beaten, and beaten mercilessly. I quickly turned the page, going back to the beginning of the folder, burying the image beneath several typed pages. There were no other photographs. I began to skim the typed pages.

Herr Franz Van Posen had figured out early on the depth and latitude of the evil going on within the upper levels of the *Reich*. Things that I was only beginning to learn through GS-1. He felt it was his duty to warn the others, make sure that people knew the truth. While his work against the *Reich* had become known to the members of the Party from the pamphlets and other seditious material he created and helped distribute, the Gestapo had never been able to identify who was doing it, and thus he had eluded them. Ultimately he had been betrayed by a woman who ran the printing press when it was discovered in a hidden portion of her shed. In exchange for her life she divulged the names and locations of all the pamphleteers involved in the sedition. She was later sent to *KZ Dachau* where she was executed.

I again went to the back page to look at the picture of the man so badly beaten. Could this in fact be my father, his hair shaved off, glasses gone, the face I always remember as being so warm and smiling now beaten and swollen. The man who had prayed over me every night in the *Hühnerstall* to protect me from the coming *Sturmwind*. I flipped to the second page of the form where physical and personal characteristics were listed:

Height: 190 cm
Weight: 73 K
Eye Color: Brown
Hair Color: Brown
Physical Scars or Characteristics: None
Occupation: Sign Painter
Nationality: German
Religion: Jewish
Spouse: Deceased
Children: Daughter Katerina, approximate age 7, whereabouts unknown.

I sucked in a deep breath and reread the form trying but unable to absorb every word. I could feel my eyes staring, bulging out, afraid to blink. But I couldn't stop reading, the word "Jewish" stopping me frozen every time. I read more inside the folder finally stopping when Gretchen began barking. Barking and scratching at the office door.

I stabbed the folder back into the file cabinet and slammed the drawer tossing the swastika key into the top drawer. Above the sound of the barking dog I heard the rumble of footsteps coming down the polished main stairs. I threw open the window then dashed back to the door, just as I heard a key stabbed into the lock. I pressed myself against the door frame as the door flew open and a man burst inside, sweeping the room with a heavy flashlight and the glint of a pistol. When he saw the open window he ran past without seeing me. But I saw him, I saw Marta's Poppy. As he hung his head out the window, I slipped out of the office and dashed toward the servant's stairs. Passing Gretchen, I quickly patted her head, wishing I had brought another bratwurst. But I hadn't. She watched me until I had reached the first stair, then started to bark furiously. I bolted up the servant's stairs three at a time.

I entered the first room at the top of the stairs, closed the door as quietly as I could and locked it. The room was a woman's room, with a vanity, dress manikin and a half dozen wigs lining the wall. A wig for every dress as Marta had said of her mother. I reached the opposite wall and threw open the window as I heard the door knob begin to rattle furiously. I stepped out of the window onto the roof and pulled the window closed behind me, muffling the sound of a shoulder slamming against the door. Down the drain pipe I slid and dropped to the ground just as I heard the door burst off its hinges. I was halfway to the tree line when I heard the window thrown open, and shots began to ring out. But I never looked back. Never slowed down, not even after Vixen and I had reached the open road.

NEUNZEHN - NINETEEN

I lay in bed that night with tears streaming from my eyes, welling in my ears, my stomach a sick knot of thoughts and realizations twisted and racing through my head and heart. It was as if I had unearthed some heavy metal chest, clotted with dirt and surrounded in lengths of rusting chain. A chest I could not let go of, struggling link by link, lock by lock until I had finally opened the last grit clogged hasp to discover its secrets.

Then wishing I had not. Like opening a buried casket to find not only the rotted corpse inside, but all the secrets it had sought to carry with it to the grave.

I rolled onto my side and squeezed myself into a fetal position. As hard as I had shaken my head all the way back atop Vixen's fury I could not dislodge the photograph of the beaten man from my mind. From my soul. The photograph of the man I was now convinced was my father.

The photograph. What he must have endured. The fear he must have carried with him every day and every night when I was a child, fighting against the insurmountable tide of darkness flooding our landscape, the coming *Sturmwind*. The darkness GS-1 speaks of over and over. That was why he had me sleep in the chicken coop. To protect me. From the inevitable knock on the door. He was a patriot, fighting for the Germany we loved, not this new Germany of parades and flags and thundering speeches. More tears began to flow. Should I . . . should I say "was"?

"Was a patriot" ? It has been many years since I had heard anything of him. The pain he obviously endured before . . .before what.? What had happened to him? What was the *EINTRAGSFORMULAR* "Entry Form"? Entry to what?

Was he still alive? Alive and being held somewhere? Somewhere where people are taken in the Night and Fog? The ache in my belly turned to nausea as I thought of my selfishness. How I had told Marta my father had abandoned me. Left me to wander the streets of *Ülmstadt* hungry and alone. And how, for years, I had hated him for it. The nausea rose up inside of me like a wave. I struggled over my bedroll, barely making it outside of my tent when I began to vomit, over and over, my body trying to expel the disgust and hatred I felt for myself and my own selfish feelings. I wretched myself dry until, bathed in sweat, I backed my body into my tent on shaking hands and knees and collapsed onto my bedroll.

#

In my fevered sleep I was surrounded by flames, a sprinkling of stars dotting a night sky just beyond the tongues of fire. From among the stars a black circle floated down. A flat black hat. It landed at my feet.

#

At formation the following morning I stood and faced the flag. The drums played their machine gun roll, calling our attention to the red, white, and black, and all it stood for. I had not even bothered to try to eat breakfast, my stomach still churning, trying to digest the evil contents of last night's discoveries.

"*Sieg Heil!*" the girls chanted from their bright smiling faces, arms held at perfect 45 degree angles. The words would not appear in my mouth. I struggled to raise my arm, unable to find neither the strength in my muscles nor the treason in my conscience to salute. Another "*Sieg Heil!*" but I still remained silent. Fraukenstein was nearing the opposite end of the formation, but soon she would turn. I struggled my arm up, knowing not to do so would risk the wrath of Fraukenstein and worse yet, discovery. Discovery of who I truly am. I raised my arm and loudly joined in on the last "*Sieg Heil!*" as Fraukenstein passed by.

Following formation I headed for the barns, unable to focus on anything other than the previous night. Dannar and the other HJs yoked their animals in the pen and began to set out for the forest. But before he did so, Dannar made a sweep of the inside of the barn, looking for me, I'm sure. I hid in one of the stalls until I heard the clump of his hob nailed boots come, turn and go. From a crack in the gate I watched him disappear up the trailhead into the forest.

#

For much of the day, I went through the motions of tending to the animals, filling water troughs and hay mangers, but always my mind was on the events of the previous night. What to do next? Could I tell anyone? Certainly Marta knew. Marta knew everything, as always. Would she say something? Tell someone? Tell someone of the new Jew in their midst, the ethnically un-pure member of the BDM who, by the way, had a father caught handing out flyers against the *Reich*? Surely that would end in my own disappearance to who-knows-where. Pacing the cool September shadows of the barn, I closed my eyes and pressed the tips of my index fingers to my temples. I shook my head.

"No," I said firmly, "Marta will say nothing. If she had wanted to say something, she would have already. She had known everything for days. It would have been easy for her to go to Fraukenstein and point me out. Point out the Jew girl with the seditious father. But she hadn't. Hadn't she always told me we were friends? True friends that could tell each other anything? And in my heart of hearts, I knew Marta Koenigsberg and I were more than mere friends. I studied my index and second finger on my right hand, crossed without a second thought. Marta told me things she claimed to have told no one else. About the boys and the key to the administration office. And about her emptiness. Her attempts to fill that bottom-less void with sex, alcohol, adventures and who knows what else. And how, when all else failed, how she had tried to end it all in the kitchen of the fine home on *Hoch Strasse*. And how she said knowing me, having a true friend, had brought some meaning to her existence. No. Marta Koenigsberg would never betray me.

But I needed more time to think. To plan. Should I try to escape? What threat is a fifteen year old girl to the line of tanks and shiny helmets parading down *Ludwigstrasse*? And if I did escape, to where? This is my home and I am ready to die to defend it. As perhaps my father already had.

Afternoon had arrived and very soon teams of HJs and oxen would be returning to the barn. I dropped my rake and picked up a bucket, carrying it up the trail into the forest. Once beyond sight of the camp I dropped my bucket along side the trail and continued. Up the path, past the spreading oak tree under which we all sat, discussing politics, pledging our blood and honor to the greater glory of a nation that it now appeared counted us as nothing more than sheep, creatures to be fed into whatever maw they required to fulfill their evil dreams. I continued on past the spot where I had received my first true kiss from a boy, the personification of their evil, who took me just as I now knew they planned to take everyone else.

I stopped. Marta might be true and protect my secret, but what about Dannar? How many nights had we listened to GS-1? Hadn't he agreed that things were not what they seem? Could he be trusted with my secret? I could certainly use an ally until Marta returns.

Again I shook my head. "No." Not Dannar. Perhaps someday. Perhaps never. Dear God, how would he feel about being involved with a Jew girl, *Der Kot von Schweinen*, the filth of pigs!? It was completely against everything he stood for, everything he had been taught from the cradle. And not just a Jew girl, but one whose father had plotted against his glorious leader? No, not Dannar Bremm. For all he is, this was beyond even his ability to accept.

But hadn't we both listened to GS-1? Wasn't he equally at risk if we were caught in the *Adlerhorst* listening? All someone else had to do was hear us and we would both be in trouble. No. As much as I wanted to believe his moral compass no longer pointed to the *Reich*, he too was just as vulnerable to disappear into *die Nacht und Nebel*, the Night and Fog. I could not tell Dannar. If he became suspect, all he need do is point to me, the Jew girl with the traitorous father and he would be left alone.

I reached the overlook and sat down allowing myself time to sort through things, weigh options and wonder what lay next for me.

#

Hours passed and the sun disappeared into the grove of larch on the opposite side of the lake. The pale blue sky gave way to a counterpane of twilight and inky stars slowly being drawn over the coolness of evening from east to west. I could feel myself beginning to calm down slightly as I sorted problems into boxes, dealing with the ones I could, leaving the others like unknown pieces of a puzzle to the side until a solution begins to present itself.

"You found something, didn't you?" the voice was low and quiet, but soothingly familiar. Dannar's silhouette straddled the trail. I looked at him and again, something inside me fluttered, moved. It would be so easy to have just said no and be done with it, shut him out, pull the castle doors closed behind me and be safe. That had been the plan. Stick to the plan, you know how dangerous those feelings are. But somehow this feeling seemed different. Genuine. But still I was afraid.

"No," I said, the word feeling sharp, like bile emerging from my throat.

He walked toward me. He had cleaned himself up and changed his clothes before he came looking for me. He sat down next to me on the bench, his form filling the twilight beside me, his smell heady and warm. His muscular arm rubbed against mine on the narrow bench.

"OK," he said. I could feel his head nodding next to me in the near darkness. Crickets chirped around us and a coolness rose from the bottomless black pane of glass spread out at our feet, "I believe you," he said, then paused, my ears straining for more. Then he continued, "I understand if you don't want to tell me," he said, then he reached over and the calloused mass of his sinewed hand swallowed my own. "But I also want you to understand this: You are my friend, but more than just my friend. So much more . . ." I could hear the words beginning to fumble and tumble in his throat, his first hand holding tight, the second now stroking my forearm. He paused again finally settled and secure in the proper words, "I just want you to know that I am your friend. More than a friend. That I would . . . take a bullet for you. To protect you. That you can tell me anything, and your secret will be forever safe with me." In the darkness he let out a long sigh and let go of my hand, confident that, yes, he had said what he had to say.

Silence filled the narrow darkness between us. Then I took a deep breath.

"I . . . I found out who my father is," I began then paused, allowing my mind and soul to decide if I had said too much already or if I should continue. If I could ever trust a man again.

"Can you tell me about it" he said, "what you found?" His voice was low, knowing what may come next, and fearing the surrounding trees of treason. For in this world I had now come to know, even the trees could be traitorous. I remembered the Bible passage from Ecclesiastes "Curse not the king, no not in thy thought; for a bird of the air shall carry the voice, and that which hath wings shall tell the matter."

I shook my head in the darkness. Very slowly, he nodded his.

"I understand," then again he fell silent. But it wasn't an awkward silence. There was a warmth to it somehow. The silence of someone thinking, and not just random thoughts, but thinking with you, placing their mind in conjunction with yours, the way Jupiter and Mars yoked together could pull with far more than the strength of just two oxen. Dannar was thinking with me, to help me find an answer, and there was a great comfort in it. He leaned forward, staring at the ground, his forearms braced against the tops of his knees, "Then perhaps I can tell you a bit about my father instead."

He sat there silently for a moment as if collecting his own thoughts from different corners of his mind. Corners he rarely if ever chose to visit, at least not on his own, "My earliest memories were lying in bed at night in the loft of my family's house, a small, ramshackle structure in the warehouse section of our village. A house, if you could call it such a thing, more down than up! *Gestürzt!* Tumbledown! Not a straight angle in the place!" he said, the faintest thread of a laugh weaving through the fabric of his voice as the memory played out in his mind's eye. "To look at me now, you never would have guessed, but as a child I slept in an old drawer my mother had laid out on the floor, up in that loft. The tiny mattress in it stuffed with straw, something she made from a couple of old pillow cases she had sewn together end to end. It was meant to be my quiet spot, my safe spot. But it was there, lying in my little drawer of a bed, no more than five, that I learned what it meant to be a man. Or perhaps, how not to be.

"My father was a *Bremser*, a brakeman, working on the freight lines from Munich to Frankfurt, Hamburg, Berlin then back home. A one-week circuit, back every Saturday afternoon with his pay in his hand. Then off to *Klucks*, a little tavern down the street, near the rail yards. And there he would spend the day, and all of his pay with it, returning late at night, stumbling, falling over what little furniture we had, empty handed. I would lay awake at night, in my little drawer, my fists clenched in fear as I heard the knob on the front door turn. On the door hung a

273

small bell from the *Appenzell*, the type the cows would wear. When you heard the clucking rattle of that tin bell on Saturday night, it was him. We would all be in bed by then, my two younger sisters each in their own drawer nearby, and when the bell would chuckle, we would all become paralyzed with fear. The bell would chuckle, and the furniture would rumble and my father's voice would fill the house, loud and angry. Bemoaning his life and the loss of it and the uselessness of wife and children. And then . . . then I would hear my mother. My mother's voice over and over again. "No . . . please . . . don't . . ." and the beating would begin, sometimes far into the night. Until one of them collapsed and could go no further.

"Sunday he would sleep as my mother would shepherd the three of us to church, careful to tie her scarf in such a way to hide the bruises. But the neighbors knew. They knew and would do nothing. They would simply look away.

"By Monday morning my father was back on the train to once again begin the cycle. For five and a half days we had peace. We had love. We had our mother. We had few books in the house, Grimm's tales, Bulfinch's Mythology, the Bible and my treasure. My salvation. A book of knights and their valors. That was my favorite. How I would beg my mother to read to me about chivalry and honor and the quests they would pursue. To be something greater than you are, in here," I felt him next to me, tapping the solid pane of his chest. "At the age of five I vowed . . ." again he paused, thinking,   "that I would become

274

a . . . knight," he sat back on the bench and allowed himself the tired laugh of every adult that had outgrown their dreams, "Oh I'm sure I'm not the first five year old who dreamt of chivalry, riding his steed into battle. Banners snapping in the breeze ready to offer his life to some greater cause. It has been many years Katerina, but you know, deep inside, I still believe that to be true. And that is what brought me here, to this," he said, waving his arm in the direction of the camp, "and this," he tapped the swastika above the pocket of his shirt, "*Hitler Jugend*! Blood and Honor! To protect and, if necessary, die for the Fatherland, " he stopped, the threads of his story tailing off, "or at least it did".

I reached over and took his massive hand in both of mine and cradled it gently in my lap. I clumsily stroked his calloused thumb, "What ever happened to your father?" I said, my voice little more than a whisper.

"I grew up, that's what happened to him. I grew up and grew stronger. When the bell would chuckle, I would meet him at the door. I would try to calm him down, but that would never work. I cannot count the number of Saturday nights I was thrown to the floor. I became the one walking bruised to church on Sunday. But I did not hide them. They were my badges of honor. My knight's pennant flying triumphant! I let my bruises show, shamed the neighbors that would not help. And as Sunday's went by, the bruises became less. Still I stood my ground and still I was thrown to the floor, but it was less and less.

And it became more of an effort for him each time. Until one night he tried . . . but he couldn't. Couldn't throw me to the ground. Eventually he stopped coming. And we haven't seen him since."

With that he again went silent, and I continued to stroke his calloused thumb. I wanted so much to tell him, tell him everything. Everything that I had found, good bad and all. I opened my mouth to speak, but the words did not come forth, as if they knew better than I. "Remain in place." they whispered amongst themselves in the safety of my heart. Trust not. Remember Rolf.

"I'm so sorry Kat. So sorry. So many lies we have been told. About everything. So many lies," I leaned into him. "I want so much to believe in my country. To be a patriot. But now . . . I don't know anymore."

"No, I'm sorry," I said, but could go no further.

He placed his arm around me and, with little resistance, pulled me closer. I began to sob softly. I rested my face beneath the craggy overhang of his chin. "It's OK, Kat it's all OK," from behind, delicate as a soft breeze, he stroked my long auburn hair, his fingers gentle, as with each stroke, he returned to my forehead. He brushed my tears away with his thumb, "It's all OK. Whatever your problems, we will talk. We'll figure things out. We will find answers. Don't worry though," he placed his lips tenderly against my forehead, "it's all going to be OK."

I looked up at him but he was already looking down at me, his face noble, reassuring in the blue tinge of starlight. He wiped my tears away again with the pads of his thumbs. Then he lowered his face and kissed me tenderly. I closed my eyes and allowed the softness of his lips to rest gently against mine, frozen in a perfect moment. I raised my head to bring my lips more in contact with his, then slowly and ever so gently his lips began to explore mine. I climbed into his lap and his massive arms engulfed me, cradled me in a security I have never felt before. Whatever feelings of fear and pain and remorse I had faded momentarily in the flood of emotions surging from my stomach to my loins. How long the moment lasted I cannot say. If I had opened my eyes and it was dawn I would not have been surprised. When I did open them again, the canopy of stars still surrounded the face of Dannar Bremm, his gray eyes inseparably locked into mine.

Then I pushed him back and sucked in a deep breath. *"Scheisse!"* I said.

"What? What's the matter?" he said.

"Marta!" I said. "That's what's the matter!" I shook my head. *"Gott I'm Himmel* what is the matter with me." I slid off of his lap and stood up, brushing myself off, straightening my clothes, trying to look anywhere but at him, at his eyes, thankful the dark night hid what must have been my brilliant red face. "I'm so sorry. I shouldn't have done that. Sorry. I mean, what would Marta say?"

"Marta?" he said. "What about Marta?"

"Well," I said, "I don't know, that you and Marta are, you know. . . together." Even in the starlight my face must have been brilliantly red, *"Mein Gott!* Please don't mention this to her."

"OK," he said, still seated comfortably on the bench, "but I don't think that would be a problem."

"I'm guessing it would be a problem. A pretty big problem!" I said. "You don't know how she talks of you. Like you are some sort of . . . well . . . knight in shining armor! *Prinz Wunderbar* she calls you! No. Please don't tell her about . . . what we just did . . . please. She would be very upset." I buried my face in my hands *"Mein Gott!* What have I done?!" And in the darkest shadows of my soul I thought: and what if she decided to tell her father of the Jew girl that stole her man.

"I don't know," he said leaning back, ". . . maybe not as upset as you might think."

"What do you mean?"

"Well, let's just say we had a bit of a falling out. "

"Those things happen, I suppose. But I'm sure she will be back. I'm sure things can get patched up. I just . . . don't . . . Marta is my friend. My dearest friend. I couldn't dream of . . ."

"She wanted more. More than I was willing to give her," he said, his voice tailing off. "She found it with another guy."

I stared at him in shock. My mouth hanging open in uncertainty. He nodded his head and continued, "That's why she had to leave. Her parents wanted her away from things for a while. Try to get her under control," he motioned sadly to his belly, "and get her roast taken care of."

I continued, my voice barely able to find itself, "You were . . . her everything—"

"Maybe not," he said. "I'm not like Marta that way." he tapped his heart " . . .here. I know that sounds old fashioned and all, but that is just the person I am. It needs to be right," suddenly I began to feel cold, a dampness settling in from somewhere across my neck and shoulders. Dannar stood up, and took off the light coat he was wearing and wrapped it around me. He faced me, I tipped my face up to meet his.

"Tomorrow night," he said, "in the *Adlerhorst, we* will talk some more. Yes?"

I looked into his gray eyes, surrounded with a crinkled smile. I nodded.

Then he reached out and took my hand in his and together, bathed only in the purest of starlight, we headed back to my canoe.

ZWANZIG - TWENTY

Crossing the lake beneath a canopy of stars, each dip of my paddle into the black glass water seemed loud and discordant, a fracturing of the night's peaceful silence that surely would wake up every mortal soul in either camp. But I knew I was the only one that heard it. On either side of the lake, nothing stirred. I was alone in my canoe, suspended in space between the stars above and their reflections filling the water below. It was a moment of pure and tranquil peace in a world that no longer had a place for such things.

But my mind was not at peace. My heart ached with all I knew and all I did not know, throbbing with secrets eager to be free, secrets I now knew *Tantchen* had carried with her for so very long but could not tell me for my own safety. So many thoughts racing through my mind, elements once secure in the compartments of my heart now upside down and shaken, spilled out and jumbled together. But one thing I now knew to be certain, and that was this: Marta was my friend and so much more. As perfect as a relationship with Dannar might be or might someday become, I could never violate what Marta and I had become. Even if they were no longer together, I could never be with him. And thus I knew, that in this world of ever increasing uncertainty, one thing had become absolute: tomorrow night I would go to Dannar and tell him that I must never be with him again.

By the time the prow of my canoe ground into the opposite shore, I had developed a plan. To the west, a storm cloud was steadily devouring the stars, leaving the sky empty and dark. By tomorrow there would be rain.

For the next few hours, fitful sleep filled my night, my mind drifting in the twilight state from semi-awake to a dark kaleidoscope of dreams. As the first stray drabs of gray dawn broached the entrance to my tent, rain began to patter around the outside.

Once again, I hid my cowardly self should Dannar come looking for me. But he didn't. With the heavy rain, the HJs would most probably be in the shops and Dannar would be in one or the other. I made it a point to conduct my chores as best I could, but remain out of sight.

At the end of the day when he would normally make his rounds to secure Jupiter and Mars for the night, and come visit me, he was still nowhere to be seen. I continued to remain out of sight, hiding in the stalls when I heard foot falls coming through the barn, but it was never him. As relieved as I was that I did not have to face him just yet, there was also a certain sadness that he was not there. A sadness that I was coming to realize, must now become the norm of my every day, and would be far more difficult than I could have ever imagined. I shook my head. But it still must be done.

The rain had let up long enough to allow me to paddle back to the BDM side of the lake where I ate alone in the mess hall, then returned to my tent to wait for darkness to shield my movements. When it neared our time to rendezvous in the *Adlerhorst* I slipped from my tent and headed down to the lake's edge. Rain was once again beginning to pour and I thought for just a moment that my conversation with Dannar could wait until tomorrow. But it couldn't. No longer could I bear the torment of knowing that something so wonderful was still alive, but needed to be end, and I was to be its executioner. Once the deed was done, I could move on to other decisions that needed to be made, but for now I must start with this one. With my poncho wrapped around me, I pushed the canoe off from the shore and began to paddle for the HJs camp. In my mind I again repeated the speech I had rehearsed to let Dannar know, in no uncertain terms, we could proceed no further.

When I reached the barn it was quiet inside, only the gentle lowing of the animals and the occa-sional stomp of a hoof or nicker from some unknown stall. I hung my poncho on a peg and headed for the ladder to the *Adlerhorst*. When I reached the top I walked down the rows of hay bales, cursing my heart for pounding so hard, anticipating the sheer joy of staring into his soft gray eyes. I shook it off, "No!" I said quietly to myself, there was important work that needed to be performed. There would be no GS-1 tonight. I would meet Dannar and say what I had to say, exactly as I had rehearsed. I reached our private enclave and turned inside to meet Dannar face to face for the last time.

But he was not there.

I stood there waiting, knowing that at any minute he would round the corner of the hay bales, his face bright and smiling, gray eyes surrounded by the crinkle of his smile. "Hello Kat!" he would say, and perhaps press forward to kiss me. Would I let him? As much as my heart raced at the thought of it, no. No, I would not let him kiss me. Not again. Not ever. With that thought a trap door in my emotions fell open revealing a whole new, deeper, darker depth that I had never realized existed. Like the bottomless shaft of a long abandoned mine. Never kiss me again. The trap door hung open wide, creaking on its hinges, a gaping maw of dark nothingness below. I shook my head and steeled myself for his approach. I must tell him. This must be the end of it.

But he did not arrive. I waited for another half hour, listening to GS-1 speaking in a low whisper of a voice:

"Die Nazimaschine versucht, den Juden aus seiner Mitte zu entfernen."

"The Nazi machine seeks to remove the Jew from its midst."

The words hit like daggers through my heart. Evil was closing in. As if Perun, the thunder god of mythology, wished to accentuate the point, a peal of thunder-like cannon fire rumbled across the roof, shaking dust from the repeating triangles of the rafters. A deluge of rain followed, sounding like handfuls of gravel being flung at the barn's slate roof by Perun's minions

And still there was no Dannar. I had to find him. It was time to end this, before it ever takes hold. I turned off the radio and climbed down the ladder.

I made a quick tour through the stables, hoping to find him, but without any luck. I checked the shops and the mill wondering if he had been detained by some project or another, but again he was not there. The rain had now become a gray curtain of icy cold, undulating in the wind, sizzling in puddles as I moved around the HJ's camp. My poncho tightly around me, I headed for Dannar's tent. Even the normal HJ guards that patrolled the camp had abandoned their posts and found shelter out of the weather, knowing that no one would come looking for them. When I reached Dannar and Klaus's tent, I peeled back the flap and ducked inside.

Pulling back the hood of my poncho I blurted out, "Where have you—?" but Dannar's bedroll was empty. Klaus stared at me evenly from behind his HJ manual.

"He's not here," he said without lowering his book, his normally pleasant disposition as cold and damp as the rain soaked fabric of the tent.

"I can see that," I said doing a poor job of hiding my annoyance.

"And you really shouldn't be over here. If someone catches you—"

"I know," I said, my annoyance beginning to fade, "but I had to talk to him. It's . . . It's important."

"I guess so," he said.

"Do you know when he'll be back?" I said.

Klaus returned his attention to his book, "Not until morning."

"Where did he go?" I said, looking around the tent as if I might possibly find him there.

"He's not here," he repeated.

"But where did he go?" I said again, as if he hadn't heard me the first time.

He lowered the book slowly, his blue eyes, knowing eyes, cold as marble, "He's standing *am Höllenloch*," The Hell Hole.

"Wha . . .?" I whispered. "Why?"

He closed the book and stared at me, his eyes like the twin barrels of a shotgun, "Why? Because the *Kommandant* found out someone had taken Vixen for a joyride the other night," his stare grew icy. "He said he did it."

"But he didn't—"

"He took the blame. *Der Kommandant* was so upset he sentenced Dannar to take the point for the entire night," he watched the rain ripple the fabric of the tent, "tonight of all nights."

"I . . . I . . . " I began to back out of the tent.

I stood in the rain, the grass surrounding the neat rows of HJ tents now more water than land, then took a step in the direction of the path. And then another and another until I began to run, past the spreading oak tree, never stopping until I reached the overlook.

Far below, barely visible through the gray curtains of rain, a silhouette soldier stood at attention,

286

statue straight against the buffeting rain, the flag raised at his side.

I stared at him from my secluded perch high above, the waters of the lake surrounding his outpost hissing and gray like something alive. He stood facing the causeway that led out to his post, a rickety finger of wood linking the sucking whirlpool *vom Höllenloch* to the horseshoe dam. He never moved, never flinched, even when daggers of lightening stabbed at the forest surrounding him or thunder barreled through the valley like the arrival of his father's train, he stood motionless. Defender of his post. Defender of me.

I turned my face away. I could look no more. I turned and began to walk up the trail, and began to cry, my only consolation knowing that the rain hid my tears and the thunder my heavy sobs.

I crossed the hissing lake, returned to my tent and climbed inside, shivering and soaked to the skin. I stripped out of my wet clothes and wrapped myself in my warm dry bedroll, but found no comfort in it. How could I be comfortable, warm and dry when he was not? And he was not because of me. I continued to cry. I rolled my face into my pillow hoping that I may somehow be blessed with sleep, turning this way and that, twisting the bedroll into a chaos of covers. But my heart granted me no mercy, no relief, for I deserved none.

Slipping my dripping night shirt on, I wrapped my poncho around me and stepped back out into the onslaught of icy rain. But I deserved no comfort. I took off my poncho and tossed it back into the tent and began to run down the trail, the occasional fusillade of lightning showing the path as its brilliant fingers drew scratch marks down the blackness of the heavens. Through the driving rain, never stopping until I reached the dam at the far end of the lake.

I could see him, still standing there, as if made of stone. True to his determination to do penance for a wrong, regardless of who had committed it. Rain buffeted his face, dripping off the lip of his helmet. With neither rain gear nor poncho he stood, the flag of the broken cross planted at his side. I ran across the crest of the dam and didn't stop running until I reached the causeway. There I stopped and stood, facing Dannar on the opposite end, the rain pasting my hair to my head, my nightshirt to my naked body.

I began to walk toward him. Slowly at first, unsure, going against all of the plans and speeches and rehearsed lines to sever the ties that I now came to understand bound our hearts as one. Against the voice, loud and pleading, of the angels that knew the danger I faced, I began to walk faster, no longer fearing the retribution of Marta, nor the penalties of her father. Ready to tell him who I am, all that I am, and face the consequences of my words, for there can be no room for other than the truth. For the first time I saw his face move, his eyes brightened beneath the brim of his helmet as I picked up the pace, my shoes heavy against the decking of the causeway. But there was no sound, only the hiss of the rain around us and the growing, sucking roar of water spiraling into *das*

Höllenloch. Then my tears began to come, full and unstoppable, no match for the rain itself or the roar of the spillway beneath us. I began to run, unable to stop until I reached him, knowing that no force on earth or in heaven could now hold me back. As I neared him, he let the flag fall and opened his arms wide until I was between them, enveloped by them, wrapped in their great sinewy cables, knowing that that was precisely where I needed to be. In fact the only place I ever wanted to be. He placed his hands gently on either side of my face and held me, staring into my eyes with a look that meant only one thing "Are you sure?"

I answered him by gently pressing my lips against his, the fortress of his arms encircling me, pulling me close. Together we kissed, oblivious to the torrential rain and the crumbling world surrounding us, the water disappearing below our feet in a black *Hakenkreuz* spiral. I pressed my face against his chest, his uniform soaked through. I could feel him shivering.

"We have to get you warm. You're freezing to death."

At the far end of the dam was the small cottage of *dem Muttertierhalter*. I led Dannar by the hand across the causeway and the grating of the spillway to the door of the small cottage. He leaned his weight against it and the door gave way. Inside was a small table and chair, a bed, a small stove and a series of levers on one wall for raising and lowering the weir. I found some wood and stick matches and in short order had a small fire burning in the stove. Dannar stood by the fire but continued to shiver. I began to undress him from his soaked uniform, gently peeling the sodden wool from his shoulders, his eyes never leaving mine, nor mine his. I let his uniform blouse fall to the floor. I reached my fingers under the hem of his undershirt, soaked and translucent as it clung to the contours of his chest and pulled it over his head. From the bed I pulled the blue and white gingham bedspread and wrapped it around his broad shoulders. I knelt and helped him out of his boots, removing each with a sucking sound, followed by his stockings. Slowly I stood, running my hands along the outside of his trembling legs to steady myself. Half way up I felt his gentle hands reach under my arms and lift me to a standing position. Again our eyes met. He leaned down and kissed me, his lips physically cold, yet soft and probing, my lips responding as if somehow I could transfer my warmth to him though their touch. Heat from the stove was now filling the space between us, rising along the contours of his chest, pausing beneath the gingham for a moment then wafting past the craggy overhang of his chin.

I rested my head against the solid flesh panes of his chest and he pulled me closer. I tipped my eyes up and he poured his into me. I bit the corner of my lower lip, lost in his steel gray eyes. Then he gave me the slightest nod. I unbuckled his pants and allowed them to fall about his ankles, pulling the rest of his clothes with them. He stepped back, sliding the jumble of wet clothes to the side, our eyes inexorably locked together, the primeval flicker of flames and crackle of wood playing across the angles of his naked form. Whatever before had been my life had brought me to this point, this place, this single, insuperable moment in time. Whatever came before was about to change forever, disappear, without any chance of ever going back. But there was no going back. And there was no doubt. The sum total of all my yesterdays could never tip the scales against the man who stood before me. The rain rattled the slate shingles of the roof. Barely perceptible, I gently gave him a nod.

One by one, he slowly unbuttoned the top three buttons of my nightshirt. With gentle fingers he eased my collar back over my shoulders where it hung for a moment, then dropped to the floor. He wrapped his hands around my shoulders pulling me against and into the hollow of his chest, enveloping us both in the fire warmed gingham, the naked curves of our flesh filling the empty spaces in our bodies and in our hearts. I pressed my ear against his chest, his heartbeat racing, filling my ears with the pace and intensity of Vixen's galloping hooves. He brought his hooked index finger under my chin and tipped my face up, away from his heart, if only physically. Again he kissed me, his lips now warm, soft, his shivering stopped, and together he poured himself into me and I into him. How long I stood there, eyes closed, his lips gently exploring mine, could not be measured in the earthly scale of minutes and seconds. But when it reached its apex, on a signal known only to our hearts, we turned together and walked to the bed.

#

It was far into the unseen hours of night that I finally fell asleep, wrapped in the cables of his arms. But before we did, we talked, and I told him. Everything. Who I was. Who my father was. I told him without the slightest attempt to mollify my words, how I now felt toward the country I once so loved. I told him if he hated me now or never wished to see me again because of who I am, or what I believed, then I would have to live with that. There could be no other choice. There could be no other way. For the most important foundation of love is truth. And it was in that very moment that the gray veil of doubt surrounding all my unanswered questions fell away leaving only one clear, concise, coalescence of reality. I had to leave the country. When I had finished, he never even paused before he next spoke.

"I'm coming with you."

EINUNDZWANZIG - TWENTY ON

A thin gray thread of dawn parted the curtains of *vom Muttertierhalter's* only window, bisecting the now empty bed beside me. Outside, Dannar once again stood *am Höllenloch*. A new day was upon us, clear and bright, my soul purged of the great dark mass I had been carrying alone. The words of Plato whispered in my ear "He whom love touches not, walks in darkness."

We had become something, together. Something that transcended mere mortal bonds. I had shared every secret with him, cleared every shadowed corner of my heart and he had accepted it as his own. And together we had made our plan.

In eight days would be the new moon. The trails would be dark but Vixen knew the way. In the week plus one before us, we would gather our supplies each night, forage, pilfer, whatever was required to assemble the pieces we would need. With all in order, we would mount Vixen by the dark of the moon and follow the trails south and west, up over the mountains and into Switzerland. It would take two days, possibly three avoiding the roads, but we could do it. And after that? I stood at the window peering at the gray stone statue of a man that had taken my heart and joined it to his. After that I would be with Dannar, and that was all I needed to know.

And thus began our planning. I worked through the camp at night, opening doors with Marta's special key, pilfering canned goods here, a flashlight there. I stashed oats for Vixen in a saddle bag and hid it among his tack gear. Dannar found a tent and additional food as well as maps, a compass and an old rifle and ammunition, just in case. And every night, following our evening roll call, we would rendezvous in the *Adlerhorst* to discuss our progress, listen to GS-1 and talk excitedly about our plans for the future. Our future. And before falling asleep each night, wrapped in the cables of his arms, we made love.

Then came the night.

I gathered my belongings and bedroll from the tent Marta and I had shared for so many months. Where she taught me and I learned the things that had transported me from a simple Bavarian milkmaid to a love infused soul preparing to depart from one world to the next. From a world where I had been deceived into believing was my country in a new and more perfect form. But it was all a lie. A dark, sinister lie. What new world lay ahead, I did not know. Only that with open eyes, and Dannar at my side, we would succeed.

By the dark of the moon I paddled straight across the lake, carefully dipping the paddle with each stroke to avoid making a sound. When I reached the barn, I stashed my bedroll in Vixen's stall. He seemed agitated and stomped his hoof as if he knew there would be danger tonight, but I stroked him softly and whispered in his ear. *"Alles ist gut. Alles ist gut."*

Moving quietly through the dark barn I reached the ladder ascending to the *Adlerhorst*. My heart began to pound with excitement as I climbed and headed toward the entrance of our secluded hideaway. I rounded the last hay bale, almost breathless and giddy with anticipation.

But Dannar was not there.

I stared at the hay bales arranged around the small radio. Perhaps he was late. But he wouldn't be late. Not tonight. Every minute of darkness is a minute farther up the trail. It won't be long past morning formation that they will come looking for us, and the farther away we are the —

Directly behind me I heard the scratch of a stick match and the sound of it flaring into life, the sulphur smell of Lucifer's breath biting my nostrils. Marta cupped her hands around the burning match as she lit her cigarette, her face alight in a demonic glow. She blew the match out with a casual puff and dropped it to the floor of the loft. The space between us immediately thick with caustic silence. We stared at each other, eye to devouring eye.

"You were expecting someone else, I presume?" she said, her eyes crinkled in her best devious smile. But she wasn't smiling. She took a long drag on her cigarette and blew it to the side. My mouth was dry, a knot of barbed wire in my belly, my body solid ice.

She inhaled again and exhaled gently, allowing the smoke to waft from her nostrils, "I asked you a question," her eyes locked on me. She motioned toward me, with her hand in a gesture of faux courtesy, "Your turn to talk."

I tried to speak, but the ice cold fingers of panic were firmly clamped around my windpipe. And squeezing.

"OK, then I'll talk," she said, a touch of the merry Marta in her tone, like a poisoned sugar cube. "But not too much. No need to. We both know the story." Inhale. Slow, deliberate exhale, her eyes rolled to rafters as she thought, "Dannar Bremm and I, we have a . . . *Irgendwas.* A . . . something. Something . . . special. Remember those late nights, in our tent. How I would tell you about him, swoon about him!" she gave herself a big hug. "*Mein Schatz*! My treasure! *Kapitän Wunderbar*! Don't you remember?" her eyes returned from the rafters and became hard again. Her voice barely a whisper, a hint of a musical lilt to it. The voice of a mind becoming unmoored from reality, "Surely you remember, Kat," she took a step forward, "Me. Marta. Your friend. How many times I helped you, cared for you. Loved you." another step, "and this . . . this is how you repay me?"

I shook my head, the icy fingers pried loose long enough to utter a single dry word.

"No."

She cocked her head slightly, her eyes narrowing to slits, the cigarette dangling from the corner of her mouth, "You had your chance to talk, *Küken*," she spat the last word out of her mouth.

"No," I said again, tapping some well of strength against Marta's approach, "No. He said it was over. Over between you two."

She took another step forward, "Nothing is ever over until I say it's over," she hissed. Then her smile returned. Her full Marta smile, "He has just been away from me too long. We just need to spend a little more time together. A little . . . alone time," she pointed at me with the glowing tip of her cigarette, "And you are going to give it to us," then she made a comical nod of her head, never losing eye contact with me.

"He . . . He won't go with you," I croaked out.

"Oh, I don't know," she said, once again finding something very interesting and amusing in the rafters, "He might, . . . if you weren't around."

"No, he won't. I'll tell him. He'll be here any minute," I said looking past her at the opening to the *Adlerhorst*. A shadow moved behind her, causing my heart to soar, but only for an instant. Fraukenstein filled the entrance and crossed her arms.

"I told you," Marta said, dropping the cigarette to the floor and crushing it underfoot. "He's not coming. Didn't you notice how quiet the camp was. Not even the guards were moving. The *Kommandant* got word someone might be trying to steal his horse again so *Gruppenführer* Kenstein convinced him to confine everyone to their tents for the night. Not one step out of their tents. Not even for a squirt. So consequently, Dannar Bremm will not be leaving," she took another step closer, backing me up against the hay bales, "but you will be," another step. "In the morning. When everything is returned to normal, the HJs will all emerge from their tents and you . . . will . . . be . . . gone. For good. And when Dannar says 'What happened to Kat?' I'll explain the whole sad truth to him: you realized you two were never really right for each other after all, he being a tall, brave, handsome young Nazi and you being a Jew girl and all, so you decided to leave . . . on your own. Poof! Gone."

"He'll never believe you." I hissed into Marta's face slowly approaching my own.

Marta backed up slightly and gave a little shrug, "Maybe. Maybe not. But we will have plenty of time to discuss it. Just he and I. And if he does have a broken heart over you abandoning him, well, I'll be there to help pick up the pieces of his broken little teacup," she smiled, "that's what friends are for, right? Helping each other? Loving each other?" then she let out a machine gun laugh and turned her back on me.

"No, Marta. You're wrong. I'm not going anywhere," pushing myself back from the hay bales.

"Sorry, Jew girl," Marta said turning around, "I'm afraid you are," and then she lunged at me.

Bracing myself against the assault, I avoided her first thrust and returned one on my own, throwing her against the hay bales. Fraukenstein made a move forward but Marta waved her off, pushed herself to her feet and again attacked. Again I defended myself, each of us now in a savage battle for certain life or death. But Marta Koenigsberg was unstoppable. Street fighter, wild, enraged animal, all the lessons she had learned from the HJs far superior to my many years of physical labor on the farm. In a twisting wrestling move, Marta pinned me on my back, descending on me, landing a staccato of punches to my face, the salty metallic taste of blood leaking from the corner of my mouth, running freely from each nostril. Then she stood, stepped back and landed a kick to my unprotected stomach, driving the breath from my body. She kicked me again, this time in the head, causing me to momentarily lose consciousness. Lacing her fingers into a hank of my hair, she lifted my head off of the floor boards, my eyes already beginning to swell shut. Above me she stood and looked squarely into my eyes, studying me, the corner of her mouth hitched into a slightly amused and satisfied smile. Blurry and gray, her face hovered above me, fading in and out as I began again to lose consciousness.

She shook me, "No you don't. You don't want to miss this part. But in case you do . . . I'll leave a few souvenirs of the time you crossed Marta Koenigsberg. A little reminder every time you look into a mirror," she spread her fingers like the claws of a cat, her finger nails descending slowly onto my face and eyes. I could feel them dig into my skin along my temple. I tried to shield my face, but I was completely at her mercy.

Then she stopped, intently studying my face. My nose, my eyes, my cheek bones. Carefully she removed her nails from my skin and gently lowered me to the floor. I could feel tears rolling across my cheeks. Through my closing slits of eyes, I could see her standing over me, her face an upside down image of my own. At least how it once was. She hovered above me, studying me still. Then she spit on my face and whispered one word:

"*Verräter.*"

Traitor.

I lay there unable to breathe, fading in and out of consciousness as the loft began to spin and pitch violently from side to side. Marta moved past me and, with the assistance of Fraukenstein wrapped my limp body in a dusty tarp. Together they worked, dragging me from the loft, down the ladder and out into the near perfect darkness of the night. Whispers of fog rolled out of the forest and down to the lake, pale gray specters drifting among the dark tree trunks. They lay my body in the puddle of water in the bottom of the canoe and we set out across the lake. On the opposite bank we were met by two large men who carried me to a black Mercedes parked in the turn-about. They heaved me onto the floor in the back where I landed with a hollow thud, still wrapped in the dusty canvas, still struggling to breathe. Gravel crunches of footsteps approached the car door which then creaked open. The flap was pulled back from my face and a flashlight blinded my blurry eyes. When the flashlight went out I was face to face with Marta's father standing over me. He smiled slightly.

"So *Fräulein* Van Posen, we meet again," he said, then threw the tarp back over me. From beneath the filthy canvas I heard his voice again.

"You have done very well Marta. Very well."

"Thank you," responded a familiar voice now happy, swelled with pride.

Then the door slammed and the Mercedes rumbled to life. The gravel beneath its tires began to crunch, and my world went black.

#

Painted concrete, cold and damp pressed against my face and swollen eye. I coughed dry blood from my mouth and struggled a shallow breath into my lungs. More coughing, shallow breaths. I creaked one eye open. All was still blurry, twisted, the room a harsh shade of dark green, across the floor and half-way up the wall. And I was not alone. An elderly man with a banker's face and trembling fingers slipped his hands into my arm pits and began to gently lift.

"*Du stehst besser auf. Lass mich dir helfen.*" "You better get up," he whispered. "Let me help you."

Every nerve and bone and sinew began to cry out in pain as he helped me to my feet. I struggled to gain my balance and set my weight against the concrete wall. It was a small room without furniture, several people stood nervously around, a young girl of no more than seven sobbed softly as she clung to her mother in a corner. A man tried to console her.

"*Alles ist gut. Alles ist gut,*" he said giving a poor imitation of a smile. The words sent an involuntary shiver through my bones. She buried her face in her mother's dress. Her father removed her gold rimmed glasses and wiped her eyes with his handkerchief. He smiled at her reassuringly. *"Alles ist gut, ja?"* the girl forced a feeble smile and nodded once.

"*Ja, Papa.*"

I struggled my way to the only door, slumping against the rusted metal screen covering a small window. I peeped through the screen into the outer room, an office filled with file cabinets and a worn metal desk. Two men milled about in black uniforms, shiny leather belts, and holstered pistols. On their lapels were twin silver lightning bolts. On their hats a silver skull and cross bones.

"Who are they?" I asked the banker.

" *Schutzstaffel,*" he whispered. "The SS. Secret Police. They are of the *Totenkopfverbände,* Death's Head Units," he shook his head slowly. Behind the desk sat Marta's father, organizing papers and studying information in manila folders. A commanding portrait of Hitler glared down from the wall behind him, a large Nazi flag securing the corner.

"Do you know him?" the banker said.

I nodded ever so slightly, my stomach filled with ice water as I said the word, "*Gestapo.*"

Inside the office, the level of activity began to increase as a stake bodied Bussing-nag truck backed to the door. Soldiers pulled on ponchos as a driving rain pelted through the now open door. The truck squeaked to a halt but left the engine idling.

One of the soldiers approached the metal door of our holding area. "*Alle Raus!*" he said, banging his

baton several times against the door. "Everyone Out!"
The group of us, six total, moved to the door under
the soldier's watchful eye and knowing smirk. Some
carried small satchels or suitcases. The child clutched
her mother even closer as she buried her face in her
dress. As she went through the door, the soldier beat
the door louder still with his baton, causing the child
to disappear even further against her mother's side.
"Schnell! Schnell! Mach Schnell!" Faster, he said and
we all picked up the pace, crowding closer together
and toward the front door.

Rain fell in cackling sheets as we stepped from
the building. On either side, warehouses disappeared
into the mist as we left the basement of the local police headquarters, the church tower of Ülmstadt visible in silhouette through the squall. We clambered up
into the back of the battered Bussing-nag, a canvas
tarp pulled over the top to provide us some shelter
from the rain. Once we were all inside, the truck gate
was closed behind us and the driver clamped a padlock on the handle. He climbed into the cab and the
two soldiers joined him, the back of their helmeted
heads visible through the oval rear window.

Up we drove the cobbled streets, bumping
across two sets of train tracks, passing the cuckoo
clock station on our right. One of the soldiers com-
mented on the driver's poor skills at handling the
truck and the driver responded with a curse causing
the soldiers to laugh. Up and out of the warehouse
section of town we drove, water running between us
down the cobbled gutters like miniature rivers. We

turned onto Main Street as the driver missed a gear causing the engine to grind and the soldiers to again laugh spouting a river of curses from the driver. Down Main Street and on our way out of town, we passed Herr Traubweiss' butcher shop. But now the shop was empty, the windows broken, the shattered glass and head frame above the window dark with soot. In yellow paint, words and symbols were slap-dashed on the door and remnants of front window. A haphazard Star of David and the word *"Juden!"* Jew!

"What happened?" I whispered to the banker.

"A few nights ago. *Kristallnacht*," he said, fingers trembling more. The Night of Broken Glass. "The Nazi Party attacked Jewish businesses and synagogs all over the country."

"What happened to the . . . people?" I said.

"They were rounded up. Taken away."

The truck rumbled out of town, the tires hissing on the road as it picked up speed. Occasional peals of thunder forced the young girl closer to her mother, her father trying to shield them both in the corner with a strong back but worried eyes. None of us spoke as we watched the Bavarian countryside, now finding its first dabs of autumn colors, slip past us. After a half hour or so, the truck ground to a halt, rain beginning to slow, popping like popcorn as it struck the tarp above us. The driver began to beep the horn in long annoyed bleats, but the flock of sheep and the attending shepherds seemed oblivious to the driver's impatience. Awkwardly the sheep ambled up and out of one field, crossed the road and slipped and tumbled down the other side.

From the tall grass along the truck three shepherd children, no older then the spectacled girl enveloped in her mother's dress, pointed at the truck and in unison began a sing-song rhyme:

Lieber Gott,
Mach mich fromm,
Dass ich nicht,
Nach Dachau komm!

Dear God make me,
Good I pray,
Let me not go,
Dachau way!

DACHAU

ZWEIUNDZWANZIG - TWENTY TWO

Another twenty minutes or so down the road, the landscape began to change, fair and flaxen fields giving way to bleak and barren peat bogs, made doubly so in the driving rain. I supported myself as best I could, digging my fingers into the body stakes that made up the back of the truck. Every portion of my body without exception yammered for attention with aches and sores and bruises and what I suspected was at least one cracked rib. But of all the body parts clamoring for my attention, all paled in comparison to the sickening, sour, debilitating poison of fear that coursed through every vein of my body. A fear that filled the silence and permeated the soul of every individual confined to the hay and manure strewn truck.

The Büssing-nag slowed as it reached a fork in the road, the arms of a typical Bavarian sign pointing destinations decorated with carved figures. A group of comical marching soldiers paraded across the top of the arm pointing to the left, the label *Shutzhaftlager* beneath. "Protective Custody" Camp. To the right, a party of strolling musicians crossed the top of the arm of a blank sign. The truck turned to the right.

After a few more minutes down the road the rectangular dark block of a guard tower appeared from the mist alongside of us, anchoring the ends of a barbed wire fence five meters high that marched off into each gray distance. Inside the confines of the fence, rows of nondescript buildings the color of ashes faded into a scrim of rain. Rising from the center, a slender brick chimney spouted fiery embers, demon's eyes cloaked in an oily black smudge of smoke .

The truck creaked to a stop before a series of two tall wire gates, a sentry post to its right. The driver again beeped his horn in an annoyed bleat. One of the soldiers called from the cab of the truck and a grumbling guard emerged from the sentry post, scurrying through the rain and pushed the two gates open. When the truck was inside, both gates closed and a cross bar set with a sickening clang. The Bussing-nag bumped over more railroad tracks, stopped, then backed up to a low concrete platform.

The elderly banker turned to me, "How old are you?"

"Fifteen," I said. "Why."

"Tell them you are eighteen."

"But . . . ?"

"Don't ask questions, just do it."

The two soldiers stepped from the cab of the truck and walked to the back, banging the side of the truck with their batons. "*Aus! Aus!*" They said: Out, Out! The driver came around and fumbled with the padlock in the pelting rain. With a clack and a rattle it was opened, and he returned to the cab of the truck, his delivery complete, his work done. He diverted his eyes from the goings on around the camp, staring only at the gates ahead of him, waiting for them to open.

"*Schnell, Schnell!!*" Faster! The half dozen of us pressed our way out of the back door of the truck as the soldier again beat his baton against the side of the truck. The elderly banker lost his footing and stumbled on the way out earning him a rap across the back of his naked skull with the baton sending him to the ground. The attention drawn away from me for the moment, I slowly slipped from the back of the truck holding my ribs and squeaking for breath. Struggling to his knees, a dazed stare fixed the bankers eyes, his trembling fingers reaching for some unseen object before him. The young girl and her parents followed.

The truck, now empty of its contents, wasted no time in departing the camp, back through the double gates. I watched it leave from the corner of my eye as it turned left and disappeared in the mist, leaving a ghost of blue smoke in its wake. I felt the crack of the baton across my arm and I struggled to keep from going to the ground.

"Something of interest *Frauline*? They will not be coming back for you any time soon if that is what you are thinking. Keep your eyes forward and line up! *Alles von Dir*! All of you! *Schnell! Mach Schnell!*"

We moved quickly across the puddled concrete platform as a group and lined up facing the railroad tracks before us, tracks which traveled through double gates and disappeared beyond the camp in either direction. From our left, a large, heavy, dark mass of rhythmically clanking machinery moved towards us straddling the tracks. The headlight of a locomotive cut through the rain, a slow clanging bell warning of its approach. "*VOOOOOT! VOOOOOOOOT!*" The steam whistle blew, plumes of white vomiting from

311

beneath the front wheels and more soldiers appeared to open the gates for the arriving train. Once inside the camp, the double gates were closed behind it and the locomotive, shiny and black in the downpour, slowed to a stop alongside the platform with a chunking sound and the hiss of steam. Six cattle cars in various degrees of disrepair followed the locomotive.

More soldiers, all bearing the twin lightning bolts and silver skull scurried from the buildings and opened the doors to the cattle cars. Men, women, and children fell from the open doors landing on the platform, many turning to the skies to try and catch some of the blessed rain on their tongues. Those caught doing so were greeted by the crack of whips from the soldiers herding them onto the platform. From the *Jourhaus*, a castle-like brick building, a tall man with a steely, pockmarked face emerged, trailing a shorter man in a blue and gray striped coat and trousers bearing an umbrella over the first. The tall man was dressed in a crisp black uniform, his black officer's visor cap brandishing the skull and cross bones. He crossed to the platform and stepped up onto a small wooden stage built for only one, raising him still further above the rest. The man in striped garb strained to keep the umbrella above him.

The forest and bogs surrounding the camp were fast disappearing into the darkness furthering our sense of isolation as night began to fall. Large spotlights began to sweep the concrete platform from the watch towers and various points. Soldiers with machine guns surrounded the occupants of the cattle cars as they spilled out onto the loading dock. In the background, a well rehearsed crew of blue and gray striped skeletons entered each car and began dragging out dead and near dead bodies which they piled onto a rusted steel trundle cart. With an obvious joy in their work, the SS guards moved forward brandishing clubs and whips and beat the survivors into a line before the tall man. In quick fashion, the tall man, whistling quietly to himself, began to sort the new arrivals: able bodied men and women sent off to his left, children, the elderly and disabled off to his right.

Now to his feet, the still dazed banker began to wander away from the group on the right. Without a moment's hesitation, one of the soldier's unhitched the German shepherd already straining at its leash and the dog tore after the elderly man. In an attempt to protect himself, he weakly threw up his arm which the dog immediately locked onto. "*Hilfe! Hilfe!*" the banker began to scream in bloody howls. Help! Help! But the only response was laughter from the death head guards as the snarling dog continued its attack. Another dog was set on banker and then another, the soldiers standing by, laughing and chatting among themselves, watching the attack until the dogs lolled the old man's lifeless body around in the rain like a broken doll.

When my turn in line came, the pock marked man eyed me over and began to motion with his riding crop to the right. He stopped.

"How old are you?" he said.

"Eighteen," I answered in the remnants of my strongest voice.

He cocked his head and looked at me suspiciously. He allowed his eyes to slowly wander my body "Perhaps someone may find some use for you," he said with an oily smile, then motioned me to the left.

Near the end of the line, I heard a commotion, the young girl was screaming as a machine gun wielding SS guard, chunky and fat in an ill-fitting uniform, tried to pull her from her mother's side. The father quickly stepped in and pushed the guard who brought his baton down squarely on the man's skull sending him limp to the concrete. The chunky guard, belly straining against the buttons of his uniform, then casually cocked his machine gun and leveled it at the inert man.

"*Nein! Nein!*" Shouted the pockmarked man in annoyance. "Not workers! Not workers!" The chunky guard, frowned, turned to the woman and vented his fury at her instead, pulling the child from her arms and pushing the woman, whimpering and pleading, to the ground.

It was only then that I noticed the first car behind the locomotive had not yet had its doors opened. Until now. On the inside, bodies were strewn about in the hay, laying in various states. And there they stayed, no effort being made to remove them from the boxcar and add them on the already overburdened trundle cart. More shuffling skeletons in blue and gray stripes, a seemingly endless supply, arrived from somewhere to begin the slow motion process of pulling and shoving the equally weak group assembled on the right side of the platform into the first boxcar behind the locomotive.

The chunky guard, his hand locked around the screaming child's wrist, dragged her down the platform, her mother, limping badly, struggling to keep up with her. When the guard reached the door of the car, he turned to the child, the mother now crawling across the concrete on bloody hands and knees, her face in torment, her moans guttural. Gently the guard reached down and removed the child's glasses and examined them in the glare of the spotlight. He bit one of the arms of the glasses and reexamined them, then turned to the mother with a crooked smile. *"Jüdisches Gold, ja?"* Jewish gold, yes? Then he tucked the glasses into his pocket and patted it, pushed the child into the boxcar and closed the door. Her arm outstretched, her face contorted in impossible pain, the mother collapsed onto the platform as the locomotive began to hiss and chunk, great iron wheels slipping momentarily on the wet steel tracks, easing its shiny, black, hulking mass forward. All cars were empty now, except for the first, several small arms reaching through its slats, their voices like the bleating of lambs, weak calls of "Ma-ma! Ma-ma!"

"Schnell! Schnell!" The guards yelled, the delight in their voices sickening and bright, like the cloying smell of flowers at a funeral. They herded the healthy and strong through a metal gate in the *Jourhaus*, above the gate a hammered metal sign:

"ARBEIT MACHT FREI " Work Brings Freedom. From there into the building to begin a process known as *Aufnahme*. Reception. Behind us, a group of blue and gray striped skeletons pushed and pulled the overflowing trundle cart, its metal wheels void of rubber tires, clattering on the cobblestones, disappearing in the direction of the smokestack.

Always in a line, always subject to a crack of the baton across the back of the legs or arms, we lined up in the *Jourhaus* in the first of many instances of poisoned justice. The line inched forward, and as each new prisoner approached the large gunmetal desk, a man known as the *Rapportführer*, asked each individual one bored question:

"Warum wurdest du verhaftet?" Why have you been arrested? A cloud of blue cigarette smoke wreathed his greasy comb-over as he waited for a response.

If the person answered that they did not know, they were summarily beaten about the head and shoulders by the guards until they came up with a reason, any reason, to prevent a further thrashing. Papers were completed and stamped, a number was assigned to each person and a bald headed scribe in striped blue and gray clattered away at a typewriter inserting sheets in the prisoners new file. As he inserted another blank form I saw the name written across the top in block letters: *EINTRAGSFORMU-LAR*, Entry Form.

Some, however were accompanied by their own folders, which seemed to bring some small sense of accomplishment to the *Rapportführer,* as if perhaps there were some actual crimes that had been committed among them. I reached the table, and the SS guard who had been riding in the truck, dropped my folder on the table before the *Rapportführer.* He leafed through the papers, letting them drop from his nicotine stained fingers one by one and took a long pull on his cigarette. He looked up at me, boredom filling his watery eyes. "And so *Fräulein* Van Pousen, *Warum wurdest du verhaftet?*" Another long pull.

"Because I am a Jew," I answered, trying to keep my trembling fear from reaching my voice.

He nodded slowly, "*Ja.* But so much more." He closed the folder and made a slight motion with his head to the left. Trying my best to hold my head high and moving forward on wobbly legs I followed the rest out the door.

I entered the next room and stopped short. Several "barbers", bald themselves in the gray and blue, stood behind new prisoners seated in straight back wooden chairs, each chair surrounded by knee deep piles of hair in every length and color imaginable. The barbers wielded hand held clippers, the sort I had used on the farm to shear sheep in the spring. But their clippers were rusted and old, many heads from their last sharpening. My turn came and I sat in the chair, my first chance to sit since I could remember last of little consolation as the barber, a woman I believe, began her work. I tried to remain still as the dull, rusty clippers crossed my head over and back several times, my long auburn hair falling past me to join the ever growing pile around the base of the chair. When she was finished, wordlessly I stood, and followed the rest of the prisoners, now more like them than not.

From the barber, another room, an antechamber, where we stripped naked under the leering eyes of the death head guards, accompanied by their vulgar comments, then deposited our clothes on a table, where more gray and blues, whisked them away. From the antechamber and into the showers for alternating scalding and freezing blasts of water. Once on the other side, we were sprayed with disinfecting chemicals that burned my still swollen eyes and the cuts and bruises I bore from my assault the night before.

In the last room the SS guards again began their cries of "*Los! Los!*" And more beatings to keep us moving at a fast pace. Another gray and blue draped skeleton handed me a pile that I took from them with trembling hands. It was my own gray and blue striped uniform, coat, pants and cap, a pair of ill-fitting clogs, a bowl and spoon. When I pulled my uniform on, the coarse material rough against my skin, a wave of fear and finality rose inside me like nausea. Surrounded by the others, all once different, now, all of us, the same, I had made the transformation from Katerina Van Pousen to *Zugang*, KZ inmate.

Once in uniform, we made one more line before three chairs. I waited my turn and finally sat down, a gray and blue handing me a chalk board with a long number written on it. My number. The number by which I would always be known in *KZ Dachau.*

D33416

They pressed the side of my head against a nail hammered into the wall to keep my head still while they took a photograph. Then I turned my puffy beaten face toward the camera. I pressed the back of my head against the nail, wondering if this was the very nail my father had pressed his head against, when they took the photograph I found in the *Nacht und Nebel* cabinet in Marta's father's office.

Marta, I thought. Then shook the poisoned thought away.

Out the back door and into the rain soaked night, the women were separated from the men with more shouts of *"Schnell! Schnell!"* and accompanying blows. The women were then double timed to a barrack near the end of the camp known as *Block Zweiundzwanzig* Block Twenty Two, where we were met at the door.

There were fourteen of us women that arrived that night in Block Twenty Two, the woman who had lost her child had been left on the concrete platform and we did not see her again. The other thirteen women were of various ages and ethnicities, I being the youngest. As I entered the Block, it momentarily reminded me of the BDM barracks I had once slept in, in what now seemed an eternity ago. Row after row of bunks, crowded closely together, three high, two women to each single bed. Rows of skull-like faces staring from the darkness at the new arrivals. The room was dark, the light from the compound and *Blockstrasse,* the central "street" connecting all of the Blocks, wept into the sleeping area from various angles.

A woman in her gray and blue striped uniform, appeared from around the corner of one bunk holding a leather riding crop and slapping it threateningly against her thigh. Her name was *Frau Grunberg* and she was the *Blockführer,* the woman in charge of the Block. While her head was not completely shaved as were all of the other inmates of *KZ Dachau,* her hair was still short and she was not as much a skeleton as the others. She was the woman in power in Block Twenty Two and it was obvious that she ate her fill before the rest .

She slapped the riding crop against her thigh as she approached. "Well?" she said. "Why are we standing here? Find a bunk my latest *Schachteln ficken!*" Fuck boxes. "Morning roll call is Oh Six Hundred, have your patches on by then or you'll have your turn in the *Bunker* yard." she said. She turned my way, stopped and walked toward me. She stabbed the leather handle of her riding crop into the soft underside of my chin and studied my black and blue face. "Looks like you haven't been following all the rules. I'll keep my eye on you to make sure you do. Oh Six Hundred. And you best not be late," I stared into her eyes and never flinched. She dropped the riding crop back to her thigh, "Grab a bunk, *Jetzt!*" Now!

I scanned the dark room quickly, looking for an open space, knowing full well that if someone had a bunk to themselves they were in no hurry to share it with a stranger. On the far left wall about half way down, a sliver of light from the *Blockstrasse* caught a pair of crystal blue eyes staring at me from the shadows of a top bunk. Below those eyes, I saw her hand, slowly motioning me to come. I moved as quickly as I could to her bunk, tucked my shoes under the bed and climbed the rough narrow ladder to the top. There I was met by a beautiful pair of crystal blue eyes, set in a face little more than a skull. She shook her head.

"Bring your shoes up," she said, "use them as your pillow. A person that loses their shoes here is as good as dead," I retreated back down the ladder and retrieved my wooden clogs, then climbed into the narrow bed onto a thin straw mattress next to the blue eyed woman. I could not guess her age, but assumed her to be less than fifty. Her weight, however was probably little more than half of my own.

She slid her hand across, her fingers, thin and skeletal, trembled ever so slightly. "What's your name, child?"

I took her hand and held it, her slender fingers like a small bundle of sticks disappearing into mine. "Kat," I said, my name sounding broken and foreign in the back of my throat, "Katerina."

She squeezed my hand slightly, "Mira. I am Mira. Did you bring your patches?" she said, "We will need to get them sewn on now. I have a needle and some thread that I have hidden away."

I pulled out the patches they gave me and laid them out in the narrow space on the mattress between us. A white rectangle with a five digit number on it, D33416, and a yellow Star of David, an orange triangle at its base, pointing down.

She saw the orange triangle and took an involuntary breath, a slight clucking sound from her mouth gone suddenly dry. She passed her hand slowly, cautiously, over the orange triangle, careful not to touch the coarse material.

"What does it mean?" I said.

She passed the needle and thread to me in slow motion, her head nodding in the acceptance of someone far too accustomed to the unstoppable forces of fate. I tried to sew the symbol on my tunic with a trembling hand. The Star of David was obvious, the orange triangle was not. I asked her again, my voice now beginning to tremble as well.

"What does it mean?" I whispered.

She placed her hand over mine to help stop the shaking.

"It means you are a Jewish political prisoner," she said with a slight frown.

"Political prisoner?" I said, "I'm not a —" then remembered my father's activities and nodded slowly, my eyes beginning to water at the finality of it all, as if a dozen steel doors had just closed and locked behind me. She too had a yellow Star of David on the breast of her tunic, but in addition, an orange circle with an orange dot in the center. She noticed me staring and drew a bony finger across it.

"In time, I will tell you of mine. And other things."

Ever so slightly I nodded my head.

"But for now, remember only this: here in *KZ Dachau*, your rights, all of them, are gone. Anyone who wears the death head, you must submit to. Completely. They are not to be challenged. Keep your eyes down and do as you are told."

I nodded again then watched her face wrinkle into the sincerest sympathy as once again tears began to well in my still swollen eyes. She placed her hand upon my head and recited what I knew to be the 91st Psalm:

"Er wird er dich mit Seinen Flügeln bedecken und unter Seinen Flügeln wirst du Zuflucht finden"

"He will cover you with His wings and under His wings, you will find refuge."

She looked at me again, "Now sleep. As best you can. And remember, even here, there is hope."

DREIUNDZWANZIG - TWENTY THREE

All that night, wind and rain howled through the cracks in our Block's barrack walls, like the whispers and wails of tormented souls. I could not sleep, not in the sense of the word. All I could manage were fitful images of locomotives and fences, dogs and eyeglasses, twisting on the twilight edge of my consciousness.

It was still the blackest corner of night when a klaxon began, jarring and urgent, stirring the bodies surrounding me into movement. But not all of them. Frau Grunberg, still wrapped in her blue and white checked blanket approached a middle bunk with her flashlight. She rolled back the body of a skeletal woman beneath a threadbare blanket. Grunberg flashed the light in the woman's eyes, now dry, fixed, and vacant, staring off in the middle distance, her toothless mouth hung open and frozen at an awkward angle. Grunberg grabbed one of the women climbing down from the upper bunk.

"*Nimm die Ratte. Zwölf Mitte,*" Grunberg grumbled. Get the Rat. Twelve Middle. And pushed the woman towards the door. "The rest of you, *oben, oben*!!" Up, up!

Mira and I helped each other out of our top rack, bringing our shoes with us. I tried to support Mira as we worked our way toward the latrine, but she gently pushed me away. "No," she whispered, "thank you, but no. We must not show that we are weak or unable to work. If you are unable to work,

325

you are useless to them and something to be eliminated."

She continued under her own power, into the latrine. The smell was intense, sewage and vomit. Two rows of boards stretched the length of the room, spaced holes, mostly occupied, were open to the sewage pit below. I found my way to one.

Back in the barracks, two gray and blue runners delivered a large metal container on the double from the cook house. Everything in *KZ Dachau* was done on the double to the *Totenkopf* shouts of *"Schnell, Schnell!!"*. Everyone lined up at the metal container with their bowls, nervously fidgeting, time being of the essence. A black liquid was measured into each woman's bowl and a crust of stale bread. Some had a privileged spot at the front of the line and received a slightly larger portion of bread. Mira would later tell me these were the ones that had cooperated with the death head's in some way, and therefore had earned an extra measure of the three "Good Bs" at *Dachau*: *Brot, Bett, Bad.* Bread, Bed, Bath. This bread was our "breakfast", the liquid our "coffee". It was little, but at the very least the coffee was warm in the chilly, fetid dampness of the Block.

Behind me, a small weasel of a man known as *die Ratte,* the Rat, was examining the body in rack *zwölf Mitte.* With a little curl of a smile showing his yellow buck teeth, he checked the number on the dead woman's tunic and wrote it on his clipboard with a pencil. Then he disappeared out the door. Mira whispered in my ear, "It is for the *Totenbuch,* the Book of the Dead. It is the record of all who have died in the camp." Mira took the end of the line, receiving a smaller portion of bread than anyone else. She ate it slowly, savoring the taste. I ate my crust in three bites, drank the coffee from my bowl and followed the rest, double time, out the door to the parade ground. In the distance I could hear the clatter of irregular metal wheels on the cobblestone as the trundle cart went from Block to Block to collect the last night's losses.

We assembled on the parade ground, a cobbled square ringed by double rows of Blocks, separated by a *Blockstrasse,* Block Street. To the east, the tops of trees that surrounded the concentration camp at a far distance, were beginning to appear in the twilight. It was the time I was so accustomed to milking Cleo and Nef. The peaceful time of the morning when all of the birds began to sign at once. But there was no birdsong this morning. Only the clatter of wooden shoes on the cobbled pavement.

"Ausrichten! Ausrichten!" several of the *Totenköpfe* began to yell. "Line up! Line up!" the rest, many with large dogs straining at their leashes, moved among the assembling skeletal ranks spilling from the Blocks, thousands of them, all in absolute silence, all in their gray and blue striped uniforms, their clogs rattling the cobblestones. *"Ausrichten!"* A baton to the back of the knees, a poke to the stomach. Sometimes to get them into line. Other times for what seemed to be the simple amusement of the SS guards.

One of the Block Seniors, in our case one of the women privileged to be at the front of the line for the morning "meal", appeared before each assembled group and gave the command. *"Mützen . . . ab!"* Caps . . . off! On the word *Mützen* every prisoner reached up and grabbed their cap with their right hand. On the command *ab!* Caps were removed in unison and held firmly against the right thigh. Two rows ahead I could see Mira do the same. The senior then reported to each *Blockführer* the morning tally. The Block senior for our Block, *Block Zweiundzwanzig,* yelled her report to *Blockführer* Grunberg in a husky voice, puffs of vapor popping from her mouth with every syllable in the cold morning air.

"Block Zweiundzwanzig, angetreten mit Belegschaft von 385 Häftlingen, 14 in Revier, 6 in Arbeit, einer tot, zum Appell angetreten 364 Häftlinge!" Block Twenty Two on parade with compliment of 385 prisoners, 14 are in sick block, 6 at work, one dead. On parade for roll-call 364 prisoners. Then she handed her notebook to Grunberg.

Then came roll call. Alive or dead, everyone in *KZ Dachau* was considered *Stück,* an object that had to be counted, and counted daily, numerous times a day. Numbers instead of names were shouted by the Block Senior to which each individual called raised their left hand in response and shouted. *"Hier!"* And woe to anyone whose number went unanswered. That privilege belonged only to those who rode the trundle cart.

I checked my number three times, reciting it in my head D33416. D33416. D33416. When the Block Senior called out my number, I thrust my left hand up and yelled *"Hier!"* Roll call continued until all were accounted for and the tally presented to the SS guard standing nearby. He then took his own head count, often tapping heads lightly, or not so lightly, with his baton as he counted. When he was satisfied, the command was given by the Block Senior "*Mützen . . . auf!*" Caps . . . on!

The Block Senior checked a second sheet on her clipboard and yelled "New Arrival *Juden* D33416 *Melde dich beim Muhldorf Kommando.*" Report to Muhldorf work party.

A voice, loud and in the distance, called out to the entire assembled mass. "*Arbeitskommandos formieren!*" Assemble into your work parties. I began to look around quickly, trying to determine where Muhldorf work party was assembling. There was the crack of a baton across my back and I went down to the cobblestones, losing a wooden clog in the process. I turned to look at the source of the assault. A jack-booted SS guard, barely beyond his teens, was pointing his baton straight at my face. He then pointed at an assembly of men and women heading to the loading docks.

"Muhldorf Kommando." He said, spitting involuntarily with the hard "f" in "Muhldorf" from his snaggletoothed overbite.

I scrabbled to my feet before him, the star on my tunic with its orange triangle catching the attention of the SS guard accompanying him as I rose. He was barely older than myself, a bullfrog of a face, and a body to match, his uniform flatulent with the smell of cabbage. A crooked smile settled across his bullfrog lips like a rope of melting lard. I straightened before him and in response he drove the end of his baton into my belly driving the breath from me in a "WOOOF!". I doubled up and again went down to the cobbles.

"Learn to stay down, Jew, where you belong," the bullfrog said in an oddly girlish voice.

Snaggletooth smiled in agreement, his overbite jutting out like a locomotive's cowcatcher. Lying on the ground, their jackboots filled my vision, the left toe of one bearing a cheap black patch. As it reared back, I covered my face with my arms, catching the blow full with my forearms. Work done for the morning, they turned in unison, the bullfrog chatting in his girlish voice about their upcoming breakfast, and disappeared across the parade ground.

I lay there, a heap of blue and gray crumpled on the cold, wet cobblestones uselessly trying to suck in splintered shards of air. From the corner of my eye I could see the Muhldorf crew headed for the trucks. I pulled myself together, grabbed my shoe and stumbled after them.

The sun had still not made its appearance when the *Muhldorf Kommando*, a work party of nearly three hundred, moved to the various trucks and vehicles assembled at the loading dock. Fellow gray and blues shepherded us into the vehicles, ever under the watchful eyes of the SS guards. Ever to the calls of *"Schnell, Schnell, Mach Schnell!!"* and the brutal beating of the skeletons who could no longer keep up.

Locked in the back of another cattle truck, packed shoulder to shoulder with perhaps thirty other men and women, we passed through the double gates and out to the right. We jostled and bounced on the rough dirt road, slowing occasionally for sections that had been washed out during the previous night's rain. Several SS guards with rifles at the ready, supervised another *Kommando* of a hundred or so *Dachau* prisoners repairing the road by hand, few digging with shovels, most on their hands and knees, digging the dirt with their dinner bowls.

After a half hour or so, the Muhldorf factory came into view, a sprawling dark structure with a sawtooth roof, several smoke stacks rising above the tree line. The truck rolled into a barbwire enclosure alongside a dozen or more other vehicles. *Totenkopf* unlocked the back of the truck with more calls of *"Raus, Raus!"* and into the factory doors. As quickly as.we entered, another group left, filling the trucks we had just vacated and headed back to the camp.

Once through the doors of the factory, I could not help but stare in awe. And in fear. Awe at the sheer scope of the operation, fear in the realization that my country, my homeland, was no longer simply interested in defending themselves. Spread out below me, on a factory floor covering tens of thousands of square meters were row after row after row of military vehicles of every shape and description, each attended by a swarm of gray and blue clad skeletons. Another crushing blow to the backs of my legs and I went to my knees in pain. *"Weitergehen!"* The

Totenkopf said and again raised his baton. "Get going!" I struggled to my feet and followed the rest of my *Kommando*.

On the factory floor a group of men and women were climbing on and over a large piece of machinery with tracks and a gun. One of the men kept referring to it as a half-track. It was a beastly and lethal looking thing, a purveyor of death. Overhead, large pieces of metal, plates, wheels, and engines, moved around on tracks, pulled by teams of skeletons. Occasionally one fell down, only to replaced by another.

There was a foreman who was neither SS nor prisoner. He wore coveralls and a fedora and smoked a pipe blessing the area with aromatic cherry smoke. It was the scent of my father and the kitchen of our home and I felt the blood wrung from my insides by a demon's hands at the thought of it.

"This is your assignment," he said to me and gave he a hand cart. "Bring the parts from that storage area," he said pointing down a long lane toward the outside of the building. I nodded and dragged the cart over to a square place loaded with wheels and tracks and other things that I could only guess at their function. The cart alone was heavy and the wheels did not run freely, but I managed to drag it to the storage area. There, four men picked up a part and placed it on my cart and I pulled the heavy load down the assembly line to the place where it was needed. My first trip with the cart was excruciating. In each lane, other prisoners were doing it as fast as they could and I made it a point to keep up with their pace. I already knew how this situation worked.

The perimeter of the work area was surrounded by SS guards. Some were stationed on raised platforms above and around the work floor where they could monitor the operation of the prisoners. And make sure there were no escape attempts.

We had already worked for what must have been five hours when a bell was rung and some gray and blue "runners" brought large metal containers of soup and bread. We lined up quickly in the orderly fashion guards demanded, but this time the privileged prisoners, went to the back of the line. As I reached the soup kettle, I handed them my bowl and the soup was ladled off of the top giving me only broth for my lunch. Those towards the end of the line, the privileged, the cooperators, were given the bottom of the soup pot, where vegetables, potatoes and even some bits of meat made it into their bowl. Horse meat I later found out and in my heart I blessed noble Philip for his sacrifice as Herr Traubweiss had done before.

Following our meager lunch, I went back to pulling my laden hand cart up and down the factory floor. To my left, an older man was pulling the cart as well, just as I was doing, but he was obviously beginning to slow, each time struggling to pull one of the half-track's wheels on his cart. I continued my work, but watched him from the corner of my eye. *"Schnell!* One of the *Totenköpfe* yelled in the man's direction. *"Mach Schnell!"*. The old man made a valiant effort to pull the cart faster and deliver his wheel. He turned around and pulled the empty hand cart back to the staging area. There, four men lifted together to place another wheel on the man's cart and he started to pull it away.

"*Nein!*" yelled the guard. The man stopped. The guard walked slowly over, the smile on his face growing with every step. He motioned to the four men in the staging area. "*Einer noch,*" he said to the men. One more. The four men looked at each other, then at the old man and placed an additional wheel on the old man's cart. The old man looked at his cart, now loaded with two heavy wheels, then back to the guard. "*Bewege es,*" the guard said quietly. Move it. The old man removed his cap quickly and snapped his heels to attention addressing the *Totenköpfe* in a loud voice. "Prisoner E64157 will be pleased to comply with *meinem Hauptscharfuhrer's* request to . . ."

"*BEWEGE ES!!*" the guard yelled.

The old man looked at the cart, summoned all of his strength and pulled at the cart's handle, but it did not budge. The guard looked at him and took another step forward. Then another step and another, forcing the man, trying to maintain his mandatory three meter distance from the guard, to back up against a crate. The guard did not stop coming forward until he was yelling directly into the old man's face at the top of his lungs. "*BEWEGE ES!!*" the old man grabbed the cart handle and with every ounce of his strength pulled at the cart until the veins stuck out like cords on his neck, his face crimson.

But again the cart did not budge. The guard looked at him and a smile crept over the guard's face. A crafty, sinister smile that left the old man bathed in the purest of terror.

The guard straightened up and calmly adjusted his own uniform. *"Mützen . . . ab."* the guard said quietly. Instinctively the man took off his cap and held it pressed against his right thigh. The guard stood before him and held out his hand. "Now . . . Give me your cap." The guard said, his voice quiet and deadly. The man began to tremble and gave the guard his cap in a hand barely under control. The guard took the cap, wadded it into a ball and threw it over the head of one of the perimeter guards standing near an exit door.

"Now," said the smiling guard, "go get your cap." The old man looked at his cap, then at the guard, then back to his cap and began to tremble, " *JETZT!"* the guard yelled. The old man looked again at his cap and at the guard who was now beginning to unholster his pistol. The old man moved quickly through the staging area and stopped short of the guard standing near the exit door. He made a step toward the door and stopped. The guard near the door was now smiling too, enjoying the little game the first guard was playing, knowing ultimately how it would end. The guard on the factory floor, had now unholstered his pistol and was bringing it up, level on the old man, *"JETZT!"* the guard yelled. The old man raced through the staging area and past the guard near the exit door. He grabbed his cap and in one smooth move, turned to race back to the manufacturing floor. As he passed the guard near the door, a great toothless smile broke out on his face. Then there was a "POP" from somewhere above. Backward the old man collapsed in a heap, his cap still firmly clutched in his right hand. The silence that followed was broken only by the "CLACK-CLACK" of the guard on one of the towers ejecting the shell from his bolt action rifle and the "Ting-Ting" of the spent casing hitting the floor. Then the guards broke out in laughter followed by the first guard yelling to all nearby. *"Alle anderen alten Schildkröten heute?"* Any other old turtles here today? "Or maybe just a little time in the *Bunker* yard is all it will take? Perhaps?"

No one reacted. No one could. We all went silently back to our work, each knowing their turn could be next. The old man, still clutching his hat, was left to twitch uncontrollably near the exit door in an ever widening puddle of blood until eventually the twitching stopped.

After another six hours of work a whistle blew and we reassembled into lines along the war machines. The doors of the factory were opened and the next shift came in and we departed, back into the cattle trucks, back to *Dachau*. As we passed several areas where *Kommandos* had been busy repairing the road early that morning, waning daylight had now forced them to abandon their work. Occasionally, adjacent to the repair areas, a gray and blue bundle lay lifeless in a drainage ditch.

It was past 9 PM when we finally returned, the burnt hair smell of the crematoria greeting us through the barbed wire with its portentous fingers, stroking our faces, settling in the phlegm at the back of our throats. Beyond the spot lights, night, suffocating night, had blanketed the camp and enveloped the moors, the claustrophobic darkness inside the hangman's hood.

It was then the morning routine reversed. Unloading from the trucks and reassembling on the parade ground, we re-formed into our Blocks, "*Mützen . . . ab!*" Caps off, roll call was made and "*Mützen . . . auf!*" Caps back on. As we were not destined to report as a work party following evening roll call, the *Totenköpfe* now took as much time as they chose before releasing us to our beds. Tonight, my first night, their mood was better than most, the signal sounded and we were released to Blocks by 10 PM. Within twenty minutes I was back in my wooden box alongside of Mira and the signal was given for lights out, with a severe punishment for any movement in the camp afterwards.

In the darkness I bit my lip and stared into the framework of the Block's roof as twisted ropes of inky depression cinched around me, binding me to my bed, soaking into my bones like poison without antidote. Not only am I hopelessly here, but Dannar is gone, and he thinks I abandoned him.

And this, all of this, because of Marta. Repeatedly I had forced her from my mind, every thought of her a sickening gut punch more devastating than any physical blow her fists could ever deliver.

#

In the weeks that followed, Autumn began to take the first slow, cold steps toward winter. Every evening, one additional moment of daylight lost to the darkness. And with each now shortened day, each new longer night begged the question: what would tomorrow bring? Less food than the day before? Another beating? Would tomorrow be my day to ride the trundle cart to the crematorium? And each new night I went to sleep, the answer was no. Not today. But here in *Dachau*, every tomorrow is uncertain, every life, in danger.

And every day I scanned the faces of my fellow prisoners, looking for any semblance of the one that had tucked me into the *Hünnerstall* and bid God to protect me from the storm wind I now found raging around me. But with each passing day, my hopes sank further still, little more than the flame of a guttering candle that eventually went out.

#

And so it continued, every day, the same repeated struggle, laborious and without end. The morning formations, the cattle-like ride to Muhldorf in the pre-dawn darkness, forced labor assembling the machines of war, returning in a night near full. And every night, the hope of a few hours of sleep and blessed oblivion.

It was a damp, cold night in winter's dooryard when we began unloading from the trucks returning from Muhldorf. As I stepped onto the tailgate, one of the last to leave the truck, the odious stench of *Dachau* was tinged with the gaseous smell of cooked cabbage. A snaggletoothed smile and bullfrog face blocked my way. They allowed the others off, then stepped up onto the tailgate, forcing me back into the truck.

"We have found again the little political Jew," snaggletooth said. The bullfrog's rope lard lips creased into a smile. I continued to step backward till I came to the rear, pressing my back against the window of the cab.

"*Mein Hauptscharführer,* prisoner D33416 seeks permission to pass to attend formation with . . . " I blurted out, but never finished. Bullfrog caught me full in the face with a meaty haymaker and I went down to the foot-worn floorboards of the truck.

"You should learn to listen, *Fräulein,*" snaggletooth said, spraying spittle with the sarcastic "f". "I told you to stay down, now it is our job to keep you there."

"Perhaps we can arrange some time in the *Bunker* yard if you wish," the bullfrog said in a voice too high for his large body.

I covered my head and curled into a ball as the kicks and blows began to shower down on me. Then a voice broke out, the gray and blue truck driver.

"*Mein Hauptscharführer,* please," he said, "I need to get this truck reloaded and back to Muhldorf for the evening shift. The *Kommando* will be waiting impatiently so we don't slow production."

Snaggletooth and bullfrog landed a few more blows, took a moment to slick back their well oiled hair, and departed. The gray and blue truck driver looked at me, pitiable and bloodied, wincing with every attempted breath. His eyes met mine, bloodshot and jaundiced. I gave him the slightest nod of thanks then he walked back to the cab.

#

Tenderly Mira ran her fingers across the cuts and bruises on my face, a new welt rising above my eyebrow.

From the Block shadows surrounding us came the nightly dirge of quiet moans and whispers. The rattle of infected lungs, labored breath and calls for comfort from fellow prisoners long committed to the *Totenbücher*.

"What they do to you," Mira whispered, slowly shaking her head.

I began to cry quietly as she gently rubbed my shoulder. I had told Mira how I had ended up in *KZ Dachau*, of Marta and, of course, Dannar, and she listened compassionately.

"I know it is difficult, but you must be strong. You must have hope."

Gently, but firmly, I pushed her fragile hand away from my face and locked my eyes into hers. I shook my head.

"There is nothing to hope for here."

"You must not be discouraged," she lowered her voice still further, "that is what they want."

"That is easy for you to say! You are not a political prisoner! I am the lowest of the low here. No better than the vermin that scurry across our floors. I am beaten almost daily for no reason."

She nodded slightly "You are right. I am not a political prisoner. You have it very difficult here, I know. But still, you and I, we travel much the same road," she began to stroke the cloth circle within a circle on her breast, "There is a reason this looks so much like a target."

My eyes, defused of some of their fire, drifted from the passion on her face to the "target" on her breast and back again.

"It means I am under a 'Special Surveillance'."

The fire was now gone from my eyes, from my voice, replaced with quiet worry.

"What . . . what does that mean."

She gave a hint of a mischievous smile. "It means they want to get rid of me. But I have something they need."

"What could they need?"

"I am a Botanist. University trained," she nodded, a whisper of pride still in her voice, "Here I help them manage their greenhouses. They are interested in increasing food productivity, to feed their growing *Reich*."

Again I slowly shook my head unable to find sense in anything at all.

"But also, I cause them a bit of . . . trouble," she smiled.

"Trouble? How?"

"I bring something to the other prisoners that the *Totenkopf* absolutely detest, what the *Totenköpfe* fear the most."

"I can't imagine they fear much of anything,"

"Ah, but they do. They fear the most powerful weapon anyone in a place like this can ever carry."

I could only stare at her in response.

She lowered her voice a little more.

"Hope."

"Hope?"

"People who hope for something, who believe that something better is possible, no matter how remote the chance, these are dangerous people. They are difficult to control. Hope is the heart. When you remove a person's heart, they become nothing more than a machine, something to be used up, then disposed of."

"Is this why they . . . they . . . keep you at the end of the line . . . for food?"

"To them I am a troublemaker, filling the others with evil thoughts of hope. I know they would just as soon send me to the gas chamber, but perhaps it is in their sadistic ways. Better to starve her then gas her. Takes longer. More painful. So every day I wake again. And I keep on breathing. And in each breath, I win again," her eyes crinkled into a smile.

"But how can you have hope . . . here?"

"Look for it, and you will find it. Even in the darkest of places, there is hope. Every day you see the sun rise again, you have won another victory. And every new day is the possibility of change. Something different. Something better."

"I don't know . . . that I believe that," I said looking away.

"I know you don't believe that. I saw that in your eyes the moment you entered the Block." a little smile, "and that's why I motioned to you. To come."

#

With the arrival of December, just as Mira had promised, enough sunrises had passed and the grinding repetition of *Dachau* changed. Work had been continuing seven days a week at the Muhldorf factory, helping to assemble machines of war, day after day, week after week. Winter had arrived leaving the moors now frozen in black patches of ice, blown clean of snow by the steady rawness of a southwest wind. I was pulling a particularly heavy item on my cart, straining with ever weakening muscles when I hit a patch of ice. In a flash my legs went out from under me, tearing a gash along my calf from some rusted point of metal. Now bleeding profusely, I wrapped a rag around my leg and struggled to my feet against the cart only to collapse back down again. Seeing me sitting against the cart, a guard came over ratcheting back the bolt on his MP-40 machine gun as he approached me. I waved my hands at him not to shoot and showed him my trouser leg was bloodied. Another guard approached the first and the two had a brief conversation at the end of which, a pair of gray and blues were summoned and I was assisted off of the floor.

The gash was wide and a row of rough stitches and some safety pins were used to keep me from bleeding to death. When we returned to camp I was sent to the *Revier*, the sick Block, where prisoners with the potential to be able to return to work were treated, as much as necessary.

#

Upon arrival at the *Revier* one of the gray and blue "nurses" was assigned to me. An SS Doctor came in and gave me a brief exam and concluded that I was indeed worth saving and over the course of the next few hours, a more significant effort was made to mend my leg. When the leg was bandaged, the Doctor returned to examine the work the nurses had performed to make sure it was to his satisfaction. He nodded his approval and allowed me two days time in the *Revier* to mend. After that, he said Dr. Schneiderman would continue to monitor my condition.

"The condition of my leg?" I asked.

"No, your condition. Aren't you aware? *Du bist schwanger.*"

I stared at him in disbelief.

You are pregnant.

VIERUNDZWANZIG - TWENTY FOUR

"Dr. Schneiderman," Mira said and pressed her lips together.

"I'm not stupid," I said, "I've seen what happens to people that aren't of any use to them. I've seen too many children taken to the moor train and never return. What will happen to me?" Unconsciously I touched my belly, "Us."

She closed her eyes as if looking for words that didn't exist.

"You'll be taken out of Muhldorf . . . " she said finally, "and receive a new *Kommando*. Something a little less stressful. Better food when it is available. You'll be given a blue square to wear on your tunic. That is what happened to the Bungartz woman. She is in bunk Forty Seven. She too is pregnant and under Dr. Schneiderman's . . ." she paused " . . . care. She is a few months ahead of you."

"What it is the blue square for?"

"It lets the others know, you are not to be bothered. Not to be harmed. It will be a blessing for you."

But I was less worried about blessings for me. "And what will happen, when—?"

"Take every day as it comes."

"But what about—"

"Be patient and see how things unfold."

During the following morning roll call, I was separated from the Block and told to report to the *Revier* which I did, as best I could with a leg still on the mend, on the double. In the *Revier,* two gray and blues removed my own striped tunic and placed me in a cotton examination gown. I was trembling, but the clean gown felt nothing short of magnificent against my skin now covered with bite marks from bed bugs and lice. They helped me onto the table, the white enameled surface sending cold chills through my legs.

The door opened. Dr. Schneiderman entered, set his hat on the side table and cleared the room of the other prisoners. He was a small man, quiet and gentle of face with gold pince-nez glasses.

"And how are you feeling today?" he said.

"*Herr Doktor*, prisoner D33416 is doing well to-day, *Danke dir!*" I shouted, but he waved me off.

"That is unnecessary here. You are of a delicate condition. Now I need to examine you."

He pulled on his rubber gloves and began, stopping to jot notes on a piece of paper. He took my temperature and listened to my heart, again making notations on his sheet.

"*Gut!*" Peeling off the gloves he slid the paper into a manila folder bearing my neatly printed num-ber across the top, "Your new *Kommando* will be at the *Schutzstaffel* Camp next door. One of the attendants will bring you over," with that he stood and retrieved his hat from the table and held it in his hand. I knew there would be consequences for my outburst but the fear of uncertainty inside me was far worse than any beating I knew would follow. I blurted out:

"*Herr Doktor*," I said. He turned, surprised and inquisitive at my bold outburst. I stammered, trying to jam the words back into my mouth, but my fears would not stay put, "*Herr Doktor*. Please, I must know, what is to become . . . of my baby?"

He approached me, his face gentle and kind, "Why, your child will be what all children should be, a blessing to *das Vaterland*," he said, then he placed his hat on his head, the *Totenkopf* on his hatband staring down at me with its crooked smile, and exited the room.

When he had left, I was returned to my uniform and a camp runner was sent to escort me from the *Revier* to the adjacent SS Camp. I had been given strict orders by Dr. Schneiderman not to perform arduous work, and the blue square, as Mira predicted, was sewn to my tunic. I now had permission to walk, or limp in my case, across the camp, even as the runner escorting me was forced to run in place beside me. We reached the gate bearing the now backward hammered words *Arbeit Macht Frei* and passed from the concentration camp directly into the adjoining SS Training Camp.

#

The Training Camp was a sprawling complex of creme colored buildings that extended far beyond the gate. It was here new members of the SS learned the principles of the *Schutzstaffel* and the power of the *Totenkopf*. Where feelings of pity for enemies of the state had no place. Where they learned to live by the motto: *Nur eines ist wichtig, den Befehl gegeben*. Only one thing matters, the command given. And, if the command were given, they would, without hesitation, murder their closest relatives.

The camp itself was clean, and unlike the concentration camp, had some trees and areas of grass, although these were now covered in a thin blanket of snow. My runner escorted me to a larger wooden building, taller than the others, bearing a black and white sign *"KANTINE"*. The entry door had stained glass windows with Bavarian beer steins, each one topped with a frothy head. We went inside.

It was an ample room of scrubbed wooden floors, dark wood panel walls and a hammer beam ceiling. A scratchy Victrola wobbled out music from one corner. It smelled of floor wax and stale beer. And schnitzel! The most magnificent schnitzel! My mouth began to water uncontrollably. The room was comfortable both in size and welcome, with amenities that I had not seen in a very long time. Cushioned chairs and curtained windows, tables with real linen table cloths. Twenty or so soldiers in their black uniforms and polished jack boots occupied some of the chairs, drinking glass steins of beer and eating food. Real and blessed food. I would have gladly rooted through their trash for a few bites of their waste! It was as if I had landed miraculously in some magnificent place, so close to a world I once knew, yet now so distantly far. At one end was a stage, a brooding portrait of *dem Führer* commanding the room. On the stage beneath his fixed and frozen gaze, some gray and blues were opening boxes labeled *"Weihnachtsdekorationen"* Christmas Decorations.

To the right there was a kitchen with two swinging doors and a scullery window for returning plates. At the opposite end from the stage was a long bar, beer steins and glasses lining the wall. Above them, mirrors and wooden shelves held knick-knacks, gnomes and multicolored bottles of *Schnaps,* stained glass lamps illuminating all. Near the light switch for the lamps was a locked door at the end of the bar where the additional liquor was kept.

A woman in a dirndl dress came out of the kitchen wiping her hands with a towel moving across the floor in my direction. She was not smiling. She nodded to the soldiers as they ate and gave them a wooden smile which vanished immediately as our eyes met.

I tried to smile at her, but it was not returned. *"Nutzlose Scheisse! Nutzlose jüdische Scheisse!"* Useless shit! Useless Jewish shit! She said trying to keep her voice low, "Standing around, useless." I began to stammer apologetically, standing at attention, spouting my number, and not knowing at all how to address her, *"Frau . . . Kantinenleiter."* Canteen Leader.

She made a face like she had eaten something sour, then pointed at the kitchen doors, "I am *Frau Dunkleboch* and I am responsible for all of this," she said waving her hand around the Canteen, "now get in there and start cleaning!"

So I did.

#

That night, Mira and I huddled under our single blanket, trying to share our warmth, ferns of hoarfrost fanning from the corners of the Block windows.

I told her of the *Kantien* and that at least I wasn't moving heavy parts in a cold factory for a while. She nodded and gave a weak smile.

"But still, I . . . I can't stop worrying about my baby, what will become of my baby," I said. Our baby. This magnificent union of Dannar and I.

Mira tried to change the subject.

Dannar and Marta continued to be the oft repeated subject of our nightly whispers and Mira did her best to sooth the bottomless pain in my heart. Most often she just listened, always ready to console me when I had said too much for my own heart to bear. But tonight she asked if I regretted the choice I had made, about Dannar. It was a question I had asked myself many times since my arrival at Dachau.

"No," I told her finally, "I don't regret it." But my words betrayed their weakness. In my heart, with every day that passed in the shadow of the guard towers, I still had my doubts. How could anyone not have doubts about the decision that ended here? Only in the perfection of my dreams, when Dannar again holds me in the cables of his arms, am I certain.

Mira gave a simple nod. Her eyes brightened in a face becoming more and more like the skull on the SS guards hat. What remained of her body seeming to grow weaker with every setting sun but she struggled her thoughts forward. "Promise me. Never give up. For you, for your baby, for the man you love.

Never. There is always hope. No one can ever take your hope away from you. Not even the *Totenkopf*. Only you can give it over to them. Never give it up. Remember what I said: hope is the most dangerous weapon we have here against them."

I began to cry, the silent crying I had taught myself over the weeks to keep from being dragged from my bunk and beaten, "Yes," I said, "I promise." I tried to return her smile, as much of a smile as I could muster, but her eyes had already closed, and she was fast asleep.

#

It was during the second week of December, my first week at the canteen, that I saw an opportunity to help Mira who was growing thinner and even weaker with each passing day. She had always been left to the end of the food line, and more and more she received very little or nothing at all to eat. It was on this day that I had scavenged half of a sausage and hid it in my uniform to bring to her. Up in our bunk, I was very excited to give my little early Christmas present to her, but when I unwrapped it from a bit of paper, she began to panic and begged me not to do it again.

"Stealing food is a very serious offense. If we were found out, it would mean a visit to the *Bunker Hof* for both us."

"What it is the '*Bunker Hof*'? No one will tell me." I said. I had heard it threatened many times, but when I would ask my fellow prisoners about it, people would move away from me in fear. Mira looked at me, purposely pressing her thin white lips a little tighter together. Then she said in the lowest of whispers. "It is forbidden to talk of the *Bunker Hof*, what goes on there, that is why," she thought and then continued, "so please don't ask me again".

I tried for several days to let it go, but I could not. Again I asked others, and they too remained silent.

It was now only ten days before Christmas and every day, as Mira had taught me, I clung to hope. And sometimes at night, on special occasions, my quest for hope was rewarded, and Dannar would visit me in my dreams.

I stayed in the scullery of the Canteen, scrubbing pots and pans as my leg healed. It reminded me of working with Marta in the kitchen of the BDM camp as punishment. And what she had said about Jews in the oven.

Marta.

All of this, the true earthly hell that was now my life, was because of her. Every time she appeared in my head, I shook her out. There was no more room for ugliness and hate in my heart. It was already overflowing.

With my leg healing, more and more I was going out on the floor. When it got busy and the room was filled with SS, I was reassigned to the bar by *Kantinenleiter*.

On the third day of my new assignment taking drink orders for guards, I approached from behind a table with two SS soldiers facing the stage. I had not yet reached their table when I was hit with the earthy odors of stale cabbage and frozen to my spot. Collecting my thoughts, I took a deep breath, exhaled through my nose and pressed forward.

Snaggletooth and bullfrog, seated in the half light of Christmas decorations surrounding the stage, recognized me immediately. Bullfrog lumbered to his feet, his belly thrusting his uniform blouse out of the top of his trousers as he did so. He reached out and buried his pudgy fingers into the material of my tunic and pulled me toward him, preparing to launch me backward. When his face came close to mine he said in a girlish voice "Won't you ever learn to stay down Jew Bitch?" I suppose I didn't deliver the expression of fear he was hoping for which only made him pull me closer. When he did he noticed the blue cloth square on my tunic near the gray and blue material wadded in his fist. His fingers immediately released their grip as if he had suddenly realized he had been holding a poisonous snake. I took a step back, smoothing my tunic as I did. Deflated, he eased his frogish mass back into the chair.

Without ever looking at me he said, "*Zwei Bier,*"

When I turned to head back to the bar I had all I could do to stifle my victorious smile.

With the holidays approaching, more and more SS began to fill the Canteen so *Kantinenleiter* kept me carrying drinks to the guards. It seemed, if their rude and vulgar comments could be believed, that they would rather be served by a fifteen year old girl than the crusty *Kantinenleiter*. It was not as strenuous working the tables and resupplying the bar from the locked cabinet, and the taunts of *Jüdische Schlampe*, Jew Slut and the like, were pale in comparison to what the others in the *Kommandos* within and outside the camp experienced every day. And as an added bonus, I was allowed to wash my uniform on a regular basis, a request by the drunken soldiers who repeatedly pulled me into their lap.

It was from the vantage point of the bar that I watched gray and blues assemble a small set of steps on the stage. It appears there would be some sort of entertainment for the SS and their families around the holidays beyond the Christmas Carols wobbling from the Victrola. I could only stare in disbelief at the irony of shuffling gray and blue skeletons preparing holiday celebrations for the very people that ruled their hell beyond the gate.

#

For the next two days, a steady snow blanketed the camp and *Kommandos* set about to clear the damp white drifts using only dinner bowls and raw labor.

It was our evening formation. The weather continued foul early in the afternoon, and by nightfall sleet was coming down in wavering gray curtains. The signal was given and we marched in groups of ten on the orders of the Block Seniors to the *Appellplatz* where we fell into our formation. "*Mützen . . . ab!*" Caps off. Reports were given on the returning workers and roll call was taken, the naked heads of the prisoners glistening in the glare of the search lights trained on us. Some were already beginning to shiver as we waited in silence. Mira, as always, two rows ahead, stood standing bare headed in the rain, tilted, shivering.

And something was wrong.

Block Seniors conferred with guards and guards rechecked tallies. Roll call was taken again, our uniforms now becoming drenched in the freezing, pelting rain. Then it became obvious. Someone had escaped.

For the next two hours the entire prison population stood in the driving sleet, silently shivering, the hiss of falling ice occasionally broken by the sound of a body collapsing in the accumulating layer of slush, never to move again. The camp *Kommandant* arrived with his umbrella bearing gray and blue trotting behind him. A *Totenkopf* approached him, saluted and the two exchanged words, unheard against the hissing of the sleet. But when the conversation was finished, the *Kommandant* smiled. Almost simultaneously, from the corner of my eye I saw lights coming up the road, twin white cones carving through the falling sheets of ice. There was a commotion at the gate and two men were dragged from a truck onto the parade ground, one a fellow prisoner drenched to the skin, his uniform blotted in mud, the other a simple peasant in a drenched night shirt, both men already showing signs of beating. Both with eyes wide with terror. The Block *Führer* paraded them both before us, the prisoner wearing a sign around his neck which read *"Ich bin wieder da!"* I am back again! The peasant in his night shirt wore a sign as well *"Verräter des Vaterlandes"*. Traitor to the Fatherland. They were forced to kneel side by side with their backs towards us.

The *Kommandant* approached and stood before them, the searchlights harsh against his chiseled, pockmarked face. He raised his voice, projecting through the hiss of a thousand snakes. "We have here before us two men who have betrayed the Fatherland. One of our fellow workers here who no longer wished to contribute to the great and glorious work before us, and this swine of a man, who gave him refuge from the night. Here at *Dachau* we believe in rewarding good and honest labor with a hearty meal and a warm bed. But there is only one recourse for those who deal in sloth and treachery," With a gloved hand, he fumbled with the flap on his holster and retrieved his Lugar pistol. "Bear witness, all of you! The rewards for hard labor here at Dachau are great! The punishment for sloth and treachery, swift," and with that he placed the Lugar inches from each man's forehead and fired, sending them back into a heap like a discarded rag doll.

The *Kommandant* re-holstered his pistol turned to the *Totenkopf* and said something, gesturing with his arm across the population as he did so. Then he departed, the umbrella wielding gray and blue trotting along behind.

"To allow you time to consider the consequences," the *Totenkopf* began "of your misguided, traitorous comrade and the man who helped him escape, both who here now lay before you, the *Komman-*

356

dant has recommended you remain here, at attention, for another four hours." With that two more individuals in our ranks collapsed immediately face first into the slush. I shifted in my wooden shoes, now filled with ice water. The silhouette of *die Ratte,* moved to the prisoner lying in the slush, a neat bullet hole in his forehead, wrote the man's number on his clipboard, and disappeared behind the search lights.

Through the gate came a small man moving quickly, he was wearing a house coat which he was busy tying around his waist. Behind him a pair of gray and blues carried an umbrella and a flash light.

"*Nein! Nein!*" The man was shouting in an agitated voice as he crossed the parade ground. "*Nein!*" I caught a flash of light off of his Pince-nez glasses as he approached one of the *Totenköpfe*. It was Dr. Schneiderman. He was making angry gesticulations toward us with his index finger and the guard was clearly interested in making him happy. The guard checked his clipboard then pointed toward our assembled block. Dr. Schneiderman came quickly to our formation and began checking numbers and faces with a flashlight as he went up and down each row. When he reached me he stopped. Checked my number, checked my face and checked my number again. Then he placed his hand against my belly as a final check. He gave a little hint of a smile, pointed at me then pointed at the *Revier* and two *Totenköpfe* whisked me away to the warmth of the sick room.

#

357

Just as Mira had promised, every new sunrise holds the possibility of hope, of change. Something different. And today would be different.

December 23, 1938 rose bright and crisp from the nights proceedings. Of the thousands assembled on the parade ground, thirty eight prisoners, in addition to the two executions, had died of exposure in the freezing rain before they were allowed to replace their caps and return to their Block for a few hours of sleep. *die Ratte* and the trundle would be having a busy morning. The sleet had frozen a solid glaze over the entire camp.

When I arrived in the kitchen of the Canteen, the crusty *Kantinenleiter* was in a particularly foul and panicked mood. Food had not arrived, some of the new table linens were stained and the SS guard who was to play St. Nick for the children could not find his beard. I remembered a time not so long ago when such problems might have been important to me as well, but the world had shown me what true problems really looked like and the rest were not to be troubled over. But *Kantinenleiter* did, and there was no escaping her.

Evening arrived as did the food and the beard and the Canteen began to fill with SS guards and their families dressed in their holiday finery. Children in expensive coats and hats, girls, not much younger than myself, wore velveteen coats trimmed in embroidery, their hands tucked into rabbit fur mufflers. Guards that I had witnessed kill a woman for going back for an extra crust of bread now shepherded their young ones to St. Nick's side. The prisoner orchestra played Christmas Carols, filling the hall from the hammer beams to the table tops and every corner with the purest of music. Gentle and soft, the music flowed. *"Leise rieselt der Schnee"* – "Softly Falls the Snow" hung in the air as the *Kommandant* and his family entered. Greeted by other officers, they clicked their heels and saluted, and smiles were everywhere. Others continued to flow in, filling the tables in the center of the room.

Night had now fallen and the room had reached its capacity in both guards, their family and holiday cheer. St. Nick wandered from table to table handing out presents to children from his sack, beautifully carved wooden animals, toy trucks, and wagons, all, I knew, carved by hand by the prisoners in the wood shop. If the children knew what blood had been shed for their toys, would it have made a difference? Or were they too far under the spell of the monster that glared at them from above the stage to care.

The *Kommandant* left his bubbling wife and two small blonde daughters to take the stage, waving people and orchestra into silence. It had been less than twenty four hours since he had murdered two men in the driving sleet on the parade ground, no more than one hundred meters from where he now stood. One for the crime of trying to escape the hell that had become his and our lives, the other for helping a fellow human being out of the storm. He smiled brilliantly, his pockmarks washed clean in the stage lights, his black and silver uniform crisp and sharp. The audience grew silent.

"*Offiziere und Soldaten, Frauen und Kinder von unserem herrlichen Reich!*" Officers and soldiers, women and children of our glorious Reich! "*Herzlich willkommen!*" Welcome! "The holiday season is here, and it is our chance to join together, beneath the eyes of our beloved *Führer* and celebrate all of the greatness and bounty he has bestowed upon us!" I tried to fade agains the opposite wall as he continued, trying to separate myself from the madness as it began to spill across the room. "St. Nick has brought presents for all of the good children, the meal is about to be passed and soon the entertainment will begin. So please, one and all, it is time now to savor and enjoy the fruits of our labors, the bounty that is our Fatherland," then he turned to the orchestra leader, gave him a grand gesture, and once again the music began to flow.

With everyone seated and the orchestra filling the hall with joyous *Weihnachtslieder* Christmas Carols, I worked the floor, bringing food and clearing plates. I was sickened by the wasted food, knowing how many people in the camp beyond the gate could be kept alive with the scraps of this one night. But that was not to be. That is not the plan. We are not there to be fed, but to be worked until we ride the trundle cart. I scraped the food into the trash.

Dinner and desert had been served followed by coffee and schnapps, chatter and merriment blending with the sound of cups on saucers and forks on

360

china. Then the lights in the canteen went out in banks, leaving only the small oil lamps on the tables to brighten the faces surrounding each. The stage lights came up and St. Nick came out, acting as the leader of the festivities and began to sing to the children in a low, rumbling voice. He was followed by other groups and individual singers, Bavarian Carolers, children in traditional dress singing songs in honor of *den Führer*. I continued to stand my post in the shadows at the back of the room, ready to fill an empty glass of schnapps or replace a dropped utensil. Saint Nicholas continued his introductions.

Then I froze in place at his next:

"And now, it is my pleasure," he said in his rumbling Saint Nicholas voice, "to welcome the *Chor des Bund Deutscher Mädel Abteilung 687.*" My knees went weak and began to collapse as a toxic cocktail of emotions raced through me. Hate, fear, resentment, shame. There was applause from the tables and a few *"Ja! Ja!"s* from soldiers now more and more under the control of their *schnaps* than their superiors. I pressed myself harder against the wall, hoping to disappear into the cracks between the boards as the girls of the BDM 687 chorus, my chorus, began to file out. Led first by Blinky, then came the rest: Rosa, Trudy, Hildi all in their BDM winter uniform and touring capes, smiling, waving to the crowd. One after another they came out, until, third from the last, came Marta. I pressed myself deeper into the shadows as a sick loathing settled in the pit of my stomach. Marta, confident as ever, turned and waved to the crowd, as if she alone were on the stage, as if she alone were the one they came to see.

The chorus snapped into their positions on the risers in military precision as we were trained and practiced to do. Blinky cued the pianist and the first chords of *"Oh Tannenbaum"* Oh Christmas Tree filled the room. I watched in silence, glued to my position, thankful for the blessed shadows, trying to avert my eyes from them, hoping that no one would see me. I pulled my cap down low over my eyes. End of song, applause. Next song: *"Ihr Kinderlein, kommet"* Oh Come Little Children. And when they reached the end, more applause. I kept my eyes down, staring at the floor, studying the knotty oak boards in detail. No one must see me. Saint Nicholas came out and spoke to the crowd. *"Noch eins*?" One more? *"Ja! Ja! Ja!"* The *Schnaps* now masquerading as soldiers began to shout. I kept my eyes to the ground. I could almost hear Saint Nicholas motion to Blinky and, with a blush, Blinky motioned to the Chorus. I had seen this a dozen times or more. Then the piano began the slow, gentle opening chords of *"Stille Nacht"* Silent Night and the orchestra followed.

> *Stille Nacht, heilige Nacht,*
> *Alles schläft, einsam wacht*
> Silent Night, Holy Night
> All is calm, all is bright

It was almost over, in a moment they would all be gone. I pleaded with myself to just keep my eyes down.

Down.

Nur das traute hochheilige Paar
Round yon Virgin, Mother and Child

But I had to look.
Just one quick look.
To see Marta. As much as I hated her, loathed her, something inside of me needed to see her face. Perhaps for the very last time.

Holder Knabe im lockigen Haar
Holy Infant so tender and mild

I raised my eyes, ever so slightly. First to see the tables, then the foot of the stage. Raising my face, my sights just a little further, to now see the back row of the 687 Chorus. To see the third girl from the right. To see the face of Marta Koenigsberg.

Schlaf in himmlischer Ruh!
Sleep in heavenly Peace!

I stared into the face of Marta Koenigsberg.

Schlaf in himmlischer Ruh!
Sleep in heavenly Peace!

And, with a wicked, cunning smile, a smile of the purest satisfaction, Marta Koenigsberg was staring back at me.

FÜNFUNDZWANZIG - TWENTY FIVE

Even before the final notes of *Stille Nacht* had vanished into the woodwork, there was a great round of applause from the assembly of SS guards, officers and all of their families. Blinky led the bows and I ventured one last quick glance at Marta before the chorus departed the stage. But Marta was gone.

Single file, the chorus, led as always by Blinky, paraded down from the stage and crossed the floor of the Canteen to the stained glass exit doors. One by one, as each one passed, they turned and looked at me. The word had been passed, the traitor's daughter, the Jew of 687, was standing in the shadows against the back wall, and each took their turn to gawk. But in the faces that passed, there was not one that gave the slightest hint of joy or pleasure at my condition. Some even pressed the sleeve of their traveling cape against their mouth to keep from crying. As they left, a guard stood at the door apparently holding it open for them in a gentlemanly fashion. But his lips were moving. He was counting. Making sure the same number of girls that entered left. *Stück,* everything in *Dachau* is counted, and must always meet the count.

Guards, emboldened by their schnapps, stood, whistled and hooted as the girls walked by, and the girls rewarded their vulgar behavior with bowed heads and blushing cheeks, but there was no pleasure in their faces. From a side table, two guards moved quickly across the room to a position close to my exiting chorus. Two guards, that I had become far too familiar with: one snaggletoothed, the other a uniformed bullfrog. The bullfrog snatched a sprig of holly from a table's centerpiece and approached Hildi. Bullfrog, one side of his shirt tail escaped from his trousers, offered her the sprig of holly and Hildi accepted. Then she smiled, blushed, gave a half curtsey and continued along with the rest, drawing a round of applause from the crowd to reward the bullfrog for his "chivalry". Bullfrog responded with an unsteady drunken bow. Hildi stole one last look at me, giving a quick glance of the purest sadness, then disappeared out the door. All eyes were now focused on the romantic, alcohol fueled display. Except for mine. Something had caught my eye to my right as I continued to press against the wall. Somehow the door to the liquor closet had been unlocked and was now open just a crack. I turned away to the hooting guards, then back, just in time to see Marta slipping from the liquor closet. Hands tucked in her cape, she whisked past me to re-join the end of the parade, to make the count, giving me not so much as a glance. I shook my head, Marta could never miss a chance to pinch a bottle of *Schnaps*.

It was then our turn to return to camp. The evening *Kommando* would clean the Canteen after the guards and their families had left. But it was time for us to return to formation. *Kantinenleiter* assembled us into a line and marched us out the back door. And just like the guard, counting us, checking off our numbers as we headed single file for the gate. Just before I passed beneath the hammered *Arbeit Macht Frei*, I turned to see my fellow BDM girls marching in the opposite direction, dark shadows disappearing in a veil of falling snow, through the double gates to an awaiting bus.

#

It was Christmas night, 1938 and each of the Blocks had been given a few extra bits of wood for the stove in honor of the holiday. That snowy night in our barracks, as Mira and I lay beneath our threadbare blanket, we could no longer see our breath as we spoke. But Mira was still shivering badly. Four hours in the freezing sleet three nights prior had done their worst. Little more than a skeleton, she lay in bed staring into my eyes.

"I think it's time you knew," she began, her voice a labored whisper. " . . . about the *Bunker Hof*," she inhaled and exhaled, her pronounced rib cage hitching beneath the target on her tunic. She ran her near black tongue over cracked and bleeding lips, "I told you of the Three Good B's at *Dachau*? Yes?"

I nodded. *"Brot, Bett, Bad."* Bread, Bed, Bath.

"There are Three Bad B's as well," she labored in a breath, " *Der Bock, der Bunker und der Baum,"* the horse, the bunker, and the tree.

She stopped and turned her eyes to the ceiling, as if considering to say more, then she turned back toward me and continued, "Most are here because of who they are, what they believe and what God they pray to. But some are here because they truly belong here. Evil. Wicked men. These the *Totenköpfe*

367

search out, to administer the punishments in the *Bunker Hof*:

"*Der Bock* is a wooden horse, a child's toy but bigger. Offenders are tied across the *Bock* and whipped. Many times. Sometimes the offender, they don't survive," she ran the tip of her tongue again lightly over her split lips. "*Der Bunker* is solitary, a small space in which you cannot stand, cannot lie down, cannot even sit. Here they leave you without food for a day or two. Sometimes more. In special cases sometimes you are left and forgotten."

"You have been there, haven't you?" I whispered, my voice barely there. She looked at me but did not speak, her eyes telling me all I needed to know. She continued.

"Then there is the *Baum*. A wooden pole, stuck in the ground. Your hands are bound behind your back and they lift you, suspend you from your hands for hours. Breaks the shoulders. Sometimes they suspend three or four from the same pole, making it look like a tree. Some days the *Bunker Hof* spouts many such trees."

"It is horrible. All of it. How can people be so evil to each other?" I said.

Her eyes began to flutter closed. "It is all part of the struggle," she whispered.

Gathering her strength, she stopped. Then she closed her eyes as words, spoken at the very edge of consciousness began to slip between her lips. Words spoken from some faraway place, as if she were passing along to me the answer to some marvelous riddle she had long since unwound. "Struggle," she said, "life is a struggle. Constant. That is what life is about," she paused, "How you deal with it. That is what YOU are about." Her eyes opened, brightened a little more, then seemed to disappear, somewhere else, somewhere in the future. Her face softened into a most serene peace, and she faded off to sleep.

#

The year of 1938 died in *Dachau* as had so many prisoners before, and from the frozen moors beyond the double barbed wire fences, 1939 arrived. We had worked late at the Canteen, providing food and drinks to the *Totenköpfe* and their escorts till together they watched the old year die the quiet death so many of my fellow prisoners hoped for. But never got. We were given permission to miss evening roll call, but following the *Neujahr* celebration, we needed to report directly back to our Blocks.

It was nearing 2 am, a biting cold assaulting me, held at bay by an old blanket I had been fortunate enough to retrieved from the gas chamber. I turned the corner onto the *Block Strasse,* an icy wind catching me full in the face and watering my eyes. But through my tears, I caught sight of two figures huddled in the lee of one of the shabby barracks. One I did not know, but the other I did. It was Mira, and she was passing a meager amount of food to one of the other prisoners. The other person took the food that was offered and disappeared into the shadows. But for some reason, Mira did not do the same. In fact she had now wandered dangerously close to one of the white circles of icy light from the fixtures marching down the *Block-Strasse*, almost as if she wanted to be seen. I broke into a run to try to warn her and was within fifty meters when a guard turned the corner and saw her standing there.

"Du da drüben! Was machst du draussen?" The guard yelled, his voice like a hammer against steel in the frozen air. You there! What are you doing out?

He ran towards Mira, his heavy boots clomping down the *Block Strasse*. He grabbed her by her skeletal arm and jerked her toward him. With his other hand, he fumbled in his pocket and pulled out a tin whistle. Without a second thought I screamed out.

"NO!"

He stopped and turned toward me, stupefied that I would not only be so brazen as to call out an order to him, but to be barreling toward him down the *Block Strasse* at full tilt.

"NO! Don't do it!" I shouted again.

He fumbled his whistle to his mouth, but by that time I had reached him and pushed his arm away. He backhanded me to the frozen ground, my blanket flying open to reveal my yellow star.

"Schmutziger Jude!" Filthy Jew! Without letting go of Mira he slipped the flap on his holster open with his thumb. He pulled out his Lugar and leveled it at me.

"Do it!" I said through my teeth. "Do it and you will have Dr. Schneiderman to answer to."

He looked from my defiant face to the blue patch and back again, then reluctantly holstered his pistol. I scrabbled to my feet on the icy ground but he already had his whistle out.

Mira and I exchanged a single glance and a slight nod of her head, but it was enough. Her crystal blue eyes told me without the slightest doubt: "It's alright. My time has come."

The guard blew his whistle, and more guards appeared on the double from between the buildings and either ends of the *Block Strasse*.

I immediately turned between two barracks knowing that I could do no more for her. I pressed my blanket against my mouth and without a sound, began to cry.

#

For the next few nights, I slept alone, sick with worry for Mira, knowing the sort of fates that await anyone crossing the line in *Dachau*. Especially those that wore the "target" of someone under a "Special Surveillance." On the fourth day without her, we had just finished morning roll call and I was making my way to the Canteen to report. A light snow was falling, casting everything in shades of powder blue and gray, blanketing the camp in unnatural silence. A peaceful silence as I walked to the gate. Then, from the very edges of sound I heard it, the clatter of the metal trundle wheels on cobblestones. The rattle of metal on stone, a cold and lonely tattoo beaten for the dead on their way to the crematorium.

I forced myself not to look, to keep my eyes forward and proceed to the gate. Keep your eyes to yourself, leave the dead to the dead. But the cart was calling to me. I stopped, closed my eyes and turned in the direction of the sound. When I opened them, I saw the cart, near heaped to overflowing with skeletons held only together with parchment colored skin wrapped tight to the bone. On top of the pile, her blue eyes fixed, open, was Mira. Her arm hung down at an awkward angle, swinging slightly with the undulations of the cart, as if waving me good-bye.

I watched until the cart faded from view, its rattling silhouette disappearing behind a scrim of fine snow.

#

January at *Dachau* held its ground against the frozen winds crossing the bleak and barren moors yielding its reign only to the even colder days of February.

The empty side of the little straw mat I had shared with Mira did not remain so for long and was soon filled by a large Polish woman who spoke not a word of German.

And I was getting larger too. My belly was growing beneath my tunic and visits to Dr. Schneiderman became more regular for both I and Ladia Bungartz, the Russian woman who's due date was only two months before mine.

But it was the only source of comfort left for me in this place of abandonment. The only thing keeping me from being truly alone. From seeking my turn in the *Bunker Hof* as Mira had chosen. For within my belly, I carried something of Dannar. Something precious that he and I had created. Together. So every night I wrapped my arms around my child-to-be, pulling this magical gift inside of me even closer, if that was humanly possible. This creation of ours, this most beautiful and perfect symbol of our love together kept me alive. Gave me hope.

Work at the Canteen continued as usual through the frozen months as new SS recruits came for training, then were sent off to man the new Hydra of concentration camps being constructed across Germany. Camps with names like Auschwitz, Treblinka and Buchenwald sprouted and grew, unopposed, like a blight of fungus on a rotten log. *Kantinenleiter* tried repeatedly to push me to do more and more laborious work, but Dr. Schneiderman had eyes everywhere, and cut her off quickly. Survival and hope were now synonymous and I became adept at eating food from the trash without being seen by the guards. I am certain *Kantinenleiter* was informed of it by her own "eyes" around the camp, but nothing was or could be done about it. Dr. Schneiderman was my shield.

#

It was the first day of March and winter still held *Dachau* squarely in its jaws. But it could not hold on forever. Even the evil forces of the *Totenköpf* and the entirety of the growing Nazi war machine could not hold back the blessing of Spring on the frozen camp.

It was in the darkest hours of night as I lay in bed, my arms curled around my belly, thinking as always of Dannar and my baby when I heard a muffled gag from the farthest corner of the barrack. I slipped out of the wooden box and lowered myself to the floor. Another gag was accompanied by a low moan, clearly coming from the bunk closest to the latrine. I moved in closer until I could see what was going on, without being seen myself. In *Dachau* it is always best to stick to your own business.

But this was my business. Ladia lay stretched out in the lower bunk surrounded by four fellow female prisoners, and she was going into labor.

Two women, large by *Dachau* standards, stood on either side of Ladia holding her arms down while a third woman with intense eyes, all little more than skeletons themselves, held a gag in Ladia's mouth to keep her from screaming. Anything to avoid having the Block Seniors or, worse yet, the *Blockführer* roused from their sleep. But why weren't they in the *Revier*? Or calling Dr. Schneiderman?

Another woman in a makeshift apron, appeared to be in charge. Her face was composed and she carried herself with the precise measured movements of a midwife. Without a word, she positioned herself at the foot of the bed laying rags under Ladia's widening vagina, the baby's head already beginning to crown. Ladia continued her muffled screams, sweat pouring off of her face, her night shirt plastered to her body. The screams began to mix with moans and forced grunts, the women around her whispering words of encouragement as she expended every ounce of what little energy she had. For a full fifteen minutes this went on, pushing and grunting and muffled screams, all increasing in intensity to a crescendo until with one final push the baby was out. Ladia continued breathing rapidly, huffing and chuffing to catch her breath as the gag was removed and she could finally breathe freely. Between her knees, the midwife began wrapping the baby in some rags.

"I want to see my baby," Ladia whispered, still struggling to catch her breath, "I want to see my baby."

The midwife slowly shook her head. Ladia struggled to get off the bed but the two women at her sides continued to hold her down. Ladia fought all the harder, tears streaming down her face. "I want to see my baby," she said getting louder. The midwife held the baby in the rags and nodded to the girl with the intense eyes at the head of the bed. She returned the gag to Ladia's mouth. The composure in her eyes now darkening to resignation, the midwife turned and carried the newborn, swaddled in rags, into the latrine. Ladia fought with all of her might against her bound arms, screaming in terror and panic into the gag, her eyes bulging from their sockets trying to catch a glimpse of the infant. When she returned from the latrine, the midwife now held only the rags, bloody and soaked in afterbirth. Ladia gave one last powerful, muffled scream then collapsed back onto the bed in a state of delirium. The gag was removed from her mouth and she began to blubber uncontrollably.

"Was it a boy or a girl?" she whispered. "A son or a daughter?" The midwife knelt beside her and dabbed at Ladia's forehead with a clean rag as Ladia continued to babble, "A son or a daughter?"

"It is better this way. For the baby," the midwife said, her voice soft with compassion. "It is better this way," then she cradled Ladia's head in her arms as she continued to cry quietly, "better this way."

At the foot of the bed, the two larger women began to clean up whispering back and forth as they worked.

"Poor Ladia," she said, "she'd better save her strength. She is going to need it."

The other woman shook her head, "This is going to earn her a trip to the *Bunker Hof*."

"At the very least," the other added. "Dr. Schneiderman is going to be very upset when he finds out he has been cheated out of *Eines der beiden Kinder für seine Experimente.*

One of the two infants for his experiments.

SECHSUNDZWANZIG - TWENTY SIX

Eines der beiden Kinder für seine Experimente.

They were the first words I would hear every morning, reverberating in my head and heart. Words echoed over and over and over like demonic voices in a well. The voice of Satan ever in my ear.

One of the two infants for his experiments.

And every night I heard those words as I clutched my baby, still within my womb, trying to draw this creation of love closer, ever closer, to protect them from a place where no one was ever truly protected. I would hug the child within me, craning my neck down, my knees up, wrapping myself around them in my own fetal position. Feeling a random kick, a flutter of movement inside, like the feeling of the butterfly that first led me to Dannar. Life within me, anxiously waiting to get out, while I anxiously wanted to keep them there inside me forever. But that was not to be. My due date in the end of April was fast approaching.

The women who helped Ladia were right, of course. Mild mannered Dr. Schneiderman became volcanic when he learned Ladia had cheated him out of *Eines der beiden Kinder für seine Experimente*. Ladia spent nearly a week in the *Bunker Hof* and when she returned, she was never the same. An empty vessel of a human being, her face a broken, blank stare. Between the mercy killing of her infant and repeated stays in *dem Bunker* she had clearly lost not only her mind, but the spark of divine life as well.

Dr. Schneiderman became obsessed with making sure I would not cheat him as well and began posting an extra security guard in our barracks at night.

March came and March went, the hoar frost moors turning from white to brown, and now bearing the first hints of green as life began to return beyond the confines of the camp. April had arrived.

At the Canteen, preparations were underway for *Ostersonntag,* Easter celebrations this upcoming Sunday. The Canteen was receiving a good spring cleaning, wiping all the surfaces with soap and water and decorations were being laid out. There was to be entertainment and a celebration in two days on the Friday before, with food and drink for the SS guards and officers, so that they could spend the actual Sunday holiday at home with their families. Potted tulips were brought from the camp greenhouses and food was already being prepared. Glasses at the bar were being cleaned and *Kantinenleiter* was busy shouting orders and taking inventory on her clipboard in the liquor closet. On the center of each table were small kerosene lamps surrounded by cut flowers.

And on the stage, six men in their gray and blue striped uniforms began assembling the risers.

#

As always, I slept each night wrapping my body around my belly, trying to protect my child for as long as I was physically able, knowing that the day was fast approaching. An unstoppable certainty that made my heart sink and my soul grow dark. How many times had I seen Ladia, knowing that that may very well be me. But only if I were lucky enough to save my baby, and lose it at the same time.

We arrived that Friday morning and I moved about, setting tables and straightening table cloths.With the afternoon, guests began to arrive, happy and filled with joy knowing that they, unlike so many of my fellow prisoners, had survived another winter. Husbands and wives, children of all ages dressed in their finery found their way to tables. *Kantinenleiter* signaled us to our positions and food began to be set out. I took up my position near the bar, quick to bring a drink or fill a stein from a pitcher of beer. At the front door, the brilliant stained glass beer steins, lit by the afternoon sun, were beginning to fade as night approached. One of the other gray and blues walked around with a long taper and lit the kerosene lamps at each table.

Following the meal, the *Kommandant* again took to the stage to speak to the assembled men in their crisp black and silver uniforms as well as their wives and children. His pockmarked face split into a wide smile of perfect white teeth.

"My countrymen!" he said. "We stand on the threshold of greatness, you and I, and together under the ever watchful guidance of our *Führer* we will do great things. We have risen from the depths and now stand ready to ascend to the heights. And for this I say *Danke dir.* Thank you. So let us take a moment to enjoy our food, enjoy our drink, and enjoy a little music!" And with that the *Dachau* orchestra began to play. Mozart and Wagner, like liquid gold to the ear, wafted among the tables.

During the music I continued to pick up plates and refill steins, always returning to my position near the bar. Once again the *Kommandant* returned to the stage and motioned to the orchestra to stop and they complied. "And now, it is my pleasure," he said, "to welcome back some of our favorite ladies, the pride of *das Vaterland,* and the future of the *Reich, the Chor des Bund Deutscher Mädel Abteilung 687!"*

And my mouth dropped open.

There was applause from the tables and as always a few *"Ja! Ja!"*s from soldiers, especially a rather portly young SS guard with a bullfrog's face who had now slid his chair closer to the stage. My chorus had returned. I pressed myself harder against the wall, once again hoping to disappear into the cracks between the boards as the girls of the BDM 687 chorus began to file onto the stage. As always, led by Blinky, the girls followed: Rosa, Trudi, Hildi all in their BDM spring uniforms, long dark trousers, white blouses, touring capes, and hats, smiling, waving to the crowd. One after another until, third from the last, came Marta, now sporting a slightly different hair color, long unruly bangs covering her eyes, but still the same face, positioning herself behind Hildi. Once again I ventured a look, and Marta returned it, her smile deep and wicked. The smile of someone very much satisfied with themselves. Then Amandine spotted me and nudged Trudi and on it went until all were aware of the bald, gray and blue striped figure lurking in the shadows. I wished for all the world the wall behind me would open up and swallow me forever. But it didn't, and on the wave of her hand, Blinky signaled the pianist and the orchestra to begin. The first song up *Alle Vögel sind schon da*. All the Birds are Already There. End of song. Applause. Then came another children's favorite, *Ein Männlein steht im Walde* A Man Stands in a Forest which made me think of Dannar, and I pressed my sleeve against my mouth to keep from crying. Don't cry Kat, I told myself. Not now, not in front of the others. Not in front of Marta! For God's sake not in front of Marta! Don't give her the satisfaction! I bit the sleeve of my gray and blue tunic until the wave of tears subsided. I slid my cap forward so as not to betray to Marta the tears in my eyes.

"That was *wunderbar!*" said the *Kommandant*, applauding as he stood. "Absolutely wonderful. We are so proud of the *Bund Deutscher Mädel Abteilung 687*. You are welcome back any time to sing for us! And now that concludes our program for the . . . "

"*Noch eins!*" The bullfrog began to yell in his girlish voice. "*Noch eins!*" One more, one more! The *Kommandant* stared intently down from the stage at the disheveled plump young bullfrog, and the bullfrog fell silent. Then the pockmarked face split ear to ear in a schnapps sloppy smile and yelled to the crowd "*Warum nicht?!*" Why not?! He signaled Blinky for one more song and Blinky again signaled the entire orchestra. And on her down beat the music began: Beethoven's 9th Symphony *Ode zur Freude*, Ode to Joy.

Joyous music, joyous voices, filled the chamber built and carved and polished and served by slave labor. All wondrous, all magnificent, perfect young female voices in perfect order on the stage. The future of the Reich on display. Who could doubt they would not last a thousand years? It was there for all to see. No one could deny its perfection.

Until Hildi fell forward.

Hildi fell forward, bumping into Trudi who fell from the stage into the crowded audience. She stumbled into a table knocking over the small kerosene lantern on the centerpiece, setting the table and cloth ablaze. Women in the audience screamed and raced their children to the door as the men, tripping over themselves, eyes and minds swimming in schnapps tried to get the fire under control. Panic and mayhem battled each other for command of the room as the orchestra continued to play, never missing so much as a note.

My eyes raced across the room and back, soldiers, heads, and screaming women, crying children and shouts of *Lösche es! Lösche es!* Put it out! Put it out!, but the fire had now spread to the next table. More screams, shouts of heavy voices yelling *"Dummkopf "* and *"Schwachkopf"* Idiot and Half-wit rose above the orchestra. I had no idea what I should be doing so I remained fixed to my post.

But someone didn't want me there.

I felt a strong hand grab the back of my collar and drag me backwards into the now open door to the liquor closet. The door closed behind me and I could feel the presence of someone else in the absolute darkness.

Then that someone pulled the light cord and I was staring face to face.

With Marta.

"Surprise," she said in a voice completely devoid of surprise. Her face still held her evil smile, her eyes boring into me, the look on her face one of pure satisfaction. I bit my lip.

"So . . . we meet again," she said matter-of-factly, going on as if nothing between us had ever happened. "How's things? Looks like you are being well taken care of here. Hair cut, something to eat, nice clothes," she said feeling the material of my gray and blue striped uniform. I could feel tears beginning to well in my eyes.

"Nice material," she said and smiled, continuing to stroke my sleeve. "A little scratchy though," she wrinkled her face in disgust. "Maybe some bugs in there too," she rubbed her hand along her cape, "Not like our chorus uniforms. You remember these? Right? How soft they were?" she took the corner of the cape and stroked my cheek with it. A tear began to dribble from my eye.

"Ohhh," she said in a voice of mock pity, "don't cry," then she made a face like she had just thought of the most wonderful idea. "Say!" she said. "Why don't you try it on?" My face had now contorted into a twisted knot of emotional pain, tears beginning to leak from both eyes. "Yes!" she continued, "lets see it on you!" In one smooth motion, she slipped her hands under my tunic and pulled it up over my head, dropping it to the floor.

She froze. The callous act of heartlessness suddenly beyond all the hate she had hoped to inflict on me. She stared at my protruding belly and I began to weep softly. She bit the corner of her lip, the spell momentarily broken, then fell back squarely into her mockery. She dropped her cape and white blouse and put them on me, the feel of the soft, warm, clean clothes as if I had been dressed in heaven's wardrobe.

She looked me over, "No, that won't do at all. It must be all or nothing for the full effect!" she slipped off my striped trousers and wooden shoes and replaced them with her own pulling her boots on me as well. I could barely see, my eyes were so filled with tears as Marta sought to humiliate me one last time.

"And one last special touch," she said and traced my lips in her bright red lipstick, the smell of cosmetics savored in my nostrils, "I always thought this shade looked much better on you!" she said with just the hint of a laugh in her voice. I buried my eyes in the folds of the cape, wishing, hoping that when I opened them again she would be gone, that as miserable and wretched as my life had become, I still had one small shred of dignity. But Marta was trying to remove even that, humiliate me, steal whatever was left of my soul. I pulled the cape down from my eyes hoping against hope.

But Marta was still there, only now she was dressed in my gray and blue striped uniform. She slipped into my wooden shoes then wiped her own lipstick off with the back of her sleeve.

Marta's eyes locked on mine. The smile on her face had vanished, the mockery completely evaporated from her voice, leaving only the low, quiet tones of deadly seriousness. She reached up and buried the fingers of her right hand into her hair and gave them a slight twist. Then slowly, ever so slowly, still clenching her hair, she raised her hand . . . and her hair rose with it, revealing beneath, her completely shaved head. She raised her hair, one of her mother's wigs, clear of her naked scalp and lowered it onto my head. Then placed her hat on top of my head.

I had become her and she had become me.

She pulled my face close to hers and she spoke quickly, her eyes never breaking contact with mine. I tried to speak, but no words came out, my head completely spinning with the thought of what had just happened, what Marta had just done. Outside Beethoven was reaching his crescendo.

"Hildi is right outside this door. When I open it, you get right behind her, keep your head down tight to her back, then right out the door. Don't turn around, don't look back, straight to the bus. *Ich habs?"* she said.

I nodded, my eyes still flushed with tears and confusion. *"Ich habs,"* I croaked.

She pulled my cap on, low on her eyes, placed her hand on the handle of the door and sucked in a great breath. "Don't screw this up Kat!" she smiled, "This will be my best Houdini ever!" she turned to the door, then back to me, pressed her lips against mine for what seemed a full lifetime, pulled the light cord and disappeared out the door.

#

True to Marta's plan, Hildi was waiting right outside the door. I slipped behind her as she pretended to fluff out her cape. I took one quick look to my right. The table fires were out but smoke now filled the room. Soldiers were still scrambling around in their drunken stupor trying to make sense of what had happened. *Kantinenleiter* was assembling her staff against the kitchen wall in the smoky atmosphere trying to keep them separate from the melee.

Blinky was already outside and the rest of the girls were slowly filing out through the stained glass doors. I stayed behind Hildi and another girl got in behind me as we headed out the front door. It was dark now, circles of light lit the path from the Canteen to the double gate. Fifty meters. We stayed in single file. I could hear Blinky at the head of the line complaining about the smell of smoke now in her clothes. Don't turn around, don't look back, straight to the bus. I kept my eyes on the ground as we walked. But I had to look. Just one last time.

I turned my head slightly to see *Kantinenleiter* marching her *Kommando* of gray and blues across the quad and through the gate, *Arbeit Macht Frei* visible in the naked glare of the search lights. They formed a single file line as they moved, all the same, all uniform toward the gate. All except one. In the middle of the line, one capped gray and blue held their arm out at a slight angle from the rest, their first two fingers wrapped around each other as they passed through the gate.

"Quickly please to the bus!" Blinky said and waved us through the double gates, tapping each one of us on the heads as we went through to make sure her count was right. We passed through the second gate and the bus started up with a cough and a cloud of blue-black smoke. We boarded the bus, I being the third from the last, and found a seat near the back. Hildi took the window, I took the aisle. The bus ground its gears and began moving forward with a lurch, the headlights bathing the road before us and the edges of the moors. The driver hit second gear and again the bus gave a little lurch as we passed one watch tower after the next, falling away behind us, a bulldozer working outside the fence line beneath the lights from the guard towers. We passed the last guard tower and the bus hit third gear, leaving *Dachau* behind. For the first time, I took a clear breath. Without looking at me Hildi clasped my hand and gave it a squeeze. I could feel her smiling alongside of me. I felt a bittersweet smile beginning to cross my lips and tears began to trace down my cheeks.

"*Gottverdammt.*" Amandine whispered. Then I heard it too. A siren. And it was coming our way.

I tried to keep my head down and search for the hope that Mira had always told me about but I could find none. My stomach collapsed in a sickened heap. I stole a quick look through the rear door window, a single headlight fast approaching the back of the bus. I put my head back down and bit into the material of the cape, trying to keep from crying. The single light approached and then passed us on the driver's side, the siren from the motorcycle and side car blaring. Two *Totenköpfe* were in the motorcycle, the one in the side car making angry gestures to the bus driver to pull over. The bus driver did, grinding the gears to a halt, the air brakes coming on with a wheezing hiss. The *Totenkopf* pulled the motorcycle in front of the bus, jumped out and began beating on the door of the bus with his baton.

"*Aufmachen!*" The lead *Totenköpf* yelled. "*AUFMACHEN!*" Open up! Spittle flying in every direction with the "*Auf!*" Nervously the driver complied and the two men stormed on. Blinky stood to protest but the lead *Totenkopf* shut her down. "*Setz dich!*" Sit down! More spittle, and she slumped back into her seat. The two stormed past her, the stale, rotten egg smell of cabbage invading the bus. I lowered my head, staring at the floorboards as they moved down the aisle. With a scuff they stopped at my seat, their shiny jackboots filling my field of vision, the toe on one bearing a heavy patch. I held my breath. Then I heard the words I dreaded most:

"*Du musst zurückkommen,*" he said in his girlish voice. You must come back. I kept my head down, biting the inside of my mouth so hard I could taste blood. Then he said it again, the smell of alcohol from his breath briefly overlaying the cabbage stench of his uniform. "*Du musst zurückkommen,*" then added, "*Bitte?*" Please? I held my breath again and froze as the young SS guard leaned his bullfrog belly across me and took hold of Hildi's hand, *"Bitte, du musst zurückkommen. Ja?"* Hildi looked up at him, smiled and gave him a little nod.

The bullfrog turned and faced the rest of the bus, his ropey lips a capital "U" of delight. *"Ja! Ja! Ja!"* He made a whooping noise to the snaggletooth and together they both departed the bus, arm in arm, singing a drunken German love song:

"Hia, Hia, Hia, Ho, . . . Hia, Hia, Hia, Ho, . . . Hia, Hia, Ho . . !"

#

Once clear of the moors, the bus settled into a steady pace riding through the Bavarian countryside, patches of stars now following us beyond the clouds. My eyes feasted on the houses and farms slipping by the windows in the darkness, sights I had come to believe I would never see again. But here they were, and I was free. But I could not help thinking about Marta, how she had arranged all of this and the sacrifice she was now making for me. Then I realized she had one last Houdini left in her box of surprises.

The bus had settled onto a narrow section of road, bounded by great trees on either side.

"Halt den Bus an!!" Amandine yelled from the front of the bus. "Trudi's getting sick!"

"Ooo! Oooo!" Blinky yelled and began yelling to the bus driver to pull over. Trudi ran to the front of the bus with her hand pressed to her mouth as the bus skidded to a halt on the side of the road. Trudi burst past Blinky, and Blinky followed her out in front of the bus. Trudi began to wretch and cough and sputter as Blinky continued to "Oooo! Oooo!!"

Hildi grabbed me by the arm, pulled me to the back of the bus and opened the rear door. She pressed a rucksack and canteen into my hands and gave me a big hug. *"Viel Glück!"* she whispered. Good Luck! I looked into the rucksack and it was filled with the most wonderful things! Bread and sausages and chocolate. I looked up and all of the girls had turned around and were blowing me kisses and giving me hand signs to wish me luck. Then Hildi motioned me out of the back door of the bus and pulled the door closed behind her. I stood there on the gravel shoulder of the road and Hildi waved to me from the back window. Trudi made a miraculous recovery and was back on the bus with Blinky as I stood there. The bus' brake lights came on, the gears ground and the bus coughed a cloud of gray smoke from the tail pipe. It continued down the road until the tail lights had disappeared around a far turn and I was alone in the darkness.

I stood on the gravel shoulder of the empty road, absolutely silent, allowing my eyes to become one with the night. All around me the great black dragon's teeth of tree tops bit into a perfect hemisphere of stars overhead. And I was alone. Truly and utterly alone. I felt the baby kick within me as if asking the same questions I had no answers for. Where are we supposed to go now? What are we supposed to do? But as always, Marta had a plan.

From a hill above me a lantern moved down a trail, flickering in and out as it passed behind the tree trunks like a summer's firefly, growing in intensity as it approached. The lantern swung gently side to side to the clip-clop of hooves and the jingle of a horse's harness. A man approached in the darkness, covered by a traveler's hood and leading a horse burdened down with packs. Instinctively I took a step backwards as he approached, but there was nowhere for me to go.

He was within five meters of me when he pulled back his hood, revealing in the buttery glow of the lantern the perfect gray eyes that had so often comforted me in my dreams. I took two unsteady steps toward him and he covered the rest in three, catching me in his cabled arms. Dannar pulled me into him, to a spot I never thought I would see again and now never hoped to leave. I stared into his steel gray eyes as he held my face in his hands, tenderly wiping my tears away with his thumbs. My knees began to buckle, but he held me firm in his arms. I began to quietly laugh and cry at the same time until he slowly lowered his face to mine and placed the softest of kisses on my lips. For what seemed the endless expanse of eternity, we held that kiss, that perfect kiss, witnessed only by the heavens above. But that was enough. There could be no greater audience for the love between us. He rubbed his hand against my belly, smiled and kissed me yet again.

Then Vixen stomped his hoof as if to remind us that time was now our enemy. Dannar swept me up in his arms and steadied me in the saddle on Vixen's back. Then he climbed aboard behind me, holding tight with one arm and turning Vixen on his heel, headed back up the trail.

#

In the first half light of dawn, the stars bid us farewell from east to west until only the strongest and brightest remained. Then they too succumbed to the perfect blue now spreading across the heavens. The first rays of a new day's sun caught the very tips of the alps, cresting them in gold like the grandest clock-towers and church steeples of Munich. But what lay before us was no longer Germany. And Germany was no longer our home. It had been stolen by those who live to hate.

Up the trail we climbed, into the alps, passing through sun blessed fields of Primrose, Bellflowers, and Edelweiss. Up the trail, cresting the mountain pass between two snow draped ogres, steadfast and solid, guarding our escape into Switzerland.

My hands became cold as we climbed higher into the mountains. I stuck my hand into the pocket of the traveling cape that Marta had given to me and pulled out a small white envelope. On the front it bore a name:

"*Küken*".

I opened the note and read it.

EPILOG - EPILOGUE

The method is not listed in the *Totenbücher*, only a single line in black ink noting that prisoner number D33416, a Jewish Political Prisoner named Katerina Van Posen, died in the *Bunker Hof* on the 10th of April, 1939.

Did Marta ever try to tell anyone who she really was, or who her father was? I don't know. Even if she had, would they have believed her? Once you are in the *Bunker Hof*, people are not looking for ways for you to live, but to die. And even if her father did know, would he have saved his daughter? The one who had helped the Jew escape? Such was the depth of darkness of those times that a father could lose sight of his child. But I don't think that was ever part of her plan. Marta had lasted six days under what torture I could only imagine. For me. For my survival.

Nor do I know where she was buried. The bulldozers beyond the fence line had been busy in the first week of April, digging ditches and burying the dead in the soft, windswept moors surrounding the camp. That is my assumption. But Marta Koenigsberg is here still at *Dachau*, somewhere, sleeping beneath the snow, her heart finally at peace.

Seventy five years have passed since that date, and six million more joined Marta in the *Sturmwind* that was to follow. But I am here, and we are here, you and I. To remember. To never forget.

Not a day has passed that I have not thought of Marta and laughed and cried in turn. My Dannar stayed by my side and I to his until his passing not so many years ago. Still the strong man I had married, even, if in his last days, only in heart. But ever the galant man he hoped and lived to be.

And soon, some day, it will be my turn. I shall pass from this world, a world still rife with hatred and fear. And still, always, there will be those noble enough to stand against the tyrants. And because of them, there is hope.

And when my time does finally arrive, I too will be at peace. For on that day, I will get to see Marta again. My heart goes giddy at the thought of it, and it makes me smile! What mayhem has she created in the beyond? I am anxious to sit with her, knee to knee, and hear of her latest Houdini.

I stand alone now. A corner of sharp wind again carries the voices of children to my failing ears as my eyes sweep the white isolation of the moors, perhaps for the last time. The sun has set behind the trees, casting the world about me in long, blue, silent ghosts. The older woman, her shoulders now mantled in snow, approaches me from behind. An older man escorts her, both bundled in heavy coats against the barren cold I knew so well. Near the parking lot are more people: adults, young adults, children. They are all waiting for me.

"They're closing mama. It's time to go," my daughter says quietly. In her mature face, I can still see the young woman, the girl, the infant I once held in my arms.

I nod, "Thank you, Marta. I'll be along in a minute."

She looks at me, nods slightly, hooks her arm through the crook of her husband's and heads for the car.

From the pocket of my coat I gently remove a small clear plastic case. I open it and remove an envelope, yellow and frail with age, the flap long since separated from a lifetime of openings and re-opening. Tear stains dot the outside bearing the faded name: "Küken".

I remove the simple card as I have done so many times before. I don't need to read it, the words are forever inscribed in my memory, but there is something in feeling the texture of the card, seeing the words again in her careless, devil-may-care scrawl. Reading them, as if for the very first time:

Mein lieber Freund,
Für alles, Kat es tut mir leid. Wirklich leid . . .

My Dear Friend,

For everything, Kat, I am sorry. Truly sorry. I guess we all do stupid things sometimes. Make stupid mistakes. Your only hope is to try to find a way to make it right again. At least a little. To make it up to the ones you hurt. The ones you love. I hope you can find it in your heart to forgive your stupid friend.

And Dannar, yeah, he loves you, more than you can ever know. He never once gave up on you.

Never abandoned you. Not for an instant. Dannar loves you. And only you.

And so do I.

You were right, *Küken*, about so many things. It just took me a while to figure it all out. But I did, finally. You taught me. You can never truly be happy yourself if the ones you love are not happy. It's as simple as that.

And don't worry about me, I'm OK with things. With everything. Really. It's funny, once I realized what I had to do, and how I was going to do it, the most amazing peace settled over me. Something I had never felt before. And it never left.

And I will never leave you either.

Your friend.

Forever.

Marta

I turn my face back into the biting wind, and ease back my scarf, my hair now as white as the surrounding snow. A ray of sunshine fights its way through the trunks of trees in the distant forest, splaying the ice blue moors around me in one final moment of pure golden brilliance. One final moment of defiance against the darkness.

I pull off my glove and raise my right hand into the icy wind, then tightly wrap my two fingers together, one over the other.

As close as two things could ever be.

DAS ENDE

THANK YOU!

Thank you, dear reader, for taking the time to read my book! While Kat and Marta are fictional characters, the details of the world surrounding them were horrifically real. If this book has struck some emotional chord with you, please recommend it to a friend. For it is only in knowing the past that we do not condemn ourselves or the generations to come to repeat it. Let this dark time never be forgotten, and let it never return.

PLEASE LEAVE A REVIEW!

It has been my great honor to tell this story, and if you have been touched by it, there is no greater way to thank an author than to leave a review! It would mean the world to me if you do!

If you are unfamiliar with how to leave a review it's easy! Here's how:

- Search for "More Deeply Than Love" on Amazon (Whether you bought it there or not).

- Scroll down the left side until you see the "Customer reviews" section.

- At the bottom of this section click on "Write a customer review"

- Write your review! Let me know what you thought of my book! Let me know what you liked best and if you would recommend it to a friend.

- Click "Submit"

That's it! And for that I thank you in advance for all your support!

John Hohmann

MERLON WOLFE PRESS

We'd love to hear from you! Please sign up to be included on our mailing list to hear what we are up to!

info@merlonwolfe.com

And follow us on

X

Instagram

Facebook

ACKNOWLEDGEMENTS

A special thanks to all the people who helped me make this book what it is, readers, editors, and that all important emotional support!

For my dear Carole who fell in love with this book from the very first read and never gave up on it (or me!) until it was over the finish line!

For Kate who told me my German was *grauenhaft* (atrocious) and I needed to get it fixed. It was and I did.

For Wilfried and his wife Herma who read my manuscript and fixed my German. Any mistakes that may still remain (as for everything else in the book) are totally mine. Wilfried was raised in Bavaria and has visited *Dachau* multiple times. His input helped me get the details as close to right as I could.

For Danny who brought me to church one Christmas Eve to listen to a German choir sing *Weihnachtslieder* (Christmas Carols), a piece of my childhood I had forgotten that found its way into this book.

For Nikki, Margaret and Jen consummate readers all! Your words of support helped quell the voices of doubt in my head.

For my Father and his family, all long gone, who lived through this time in history and made sure I grew up vigilant to the dangers.

For Raynebow Shaw for her wonderful cover! I never told her what I wanted, she just knew!

And for the Holocaust survivors I have met who told me their stories. And for the ones I haven't met and will never have that chance. I hope this book, in some small way, lets people know....

NEVER FORGET

www.ingramcontent.com/pod-product-compliance
Lightning Source LLC
Chambersburg PA
CBHW071222250626
47163CB00001B/69